ZEST FOR LIFE

ZEST FOR LIFE

ZEST FOR LIFE poses the problem: what makes
men happy? what gives them the will to live,
the capacity to enjoy life despite its miseries?
Zola confronts opposing characters: Pauline,
robust, gay, courageous, and Lazare, the
neurotic intellectual.

Pauline, orphaned at ten years old and
heiress to a modest fortune, goes to live with
her relatives the Chanteaus in a poor seaside
village. At first all goes well; her sunny
nature endears her to all, and she becomes
engaged to her cousin, brilliant but unstable
Lazare. She generously subsidises his im-
practical schemes; on these and household
expenses, her fortune is gradually frittered
away. Madame Chanteau's sense of guilt at
this despoilment breeds resentment and
hatred of her niece, and she encourages
Lazare's flirtation with Louise, a rich and
pretty visitor. Pauline, heartbroken, plans
to leave, but unselfishly stays to nurse first
her ailing uncle, then her aunt in a sudden
fatal illness. The aunt's death brings her
closer to Lazare again, but seeing his hopeless
depression she quixotically fetches back
Louise and urges them to marry. But
Pauline's sacrifice brings no happiness to
neurotic Lazare; he is soon alienated from
his wife and turns to Pauline once more—
too late. Meanwhile Louise is pregnant;
when her confinement comes it is Pauline
who devotedly helps her and saves the child's
life. Deprived of the happiness to which
her zest for life entitled her, she will not deny
life; she finds content in helping others live.

ZEST FOR LIFE

ÉMILE ZOLA

Translated from the French by
JEAN STEWART

Preface by
ANGUS WILSON

LONDON
ELEK BOOKS

This translation © *1955 by*

ELEK BOOKS LTD.

2 All Saints Street

London, N.1

Reprinted 1968

Made and printed in Great Britain by
A. WHEATON & CO.
Exeter

PREFACE

OF all the ideas of the nineteenth century on which we strive to pin responsibilities for the catastrophes of our own day, optimism and materialism are the most derided. It is perfectly clear that in their crudest forms the beliefs in social perfectibility and the explanation of the Universe on mechanistic principles are threadbare. Not a little of the neglect of Émile Zola's genius has been due to his reputation as an optimistic materialist—a peculiarly contemptible combination of all that has now been exploded. Zola, in fact, was neither an optimist nor a materialist in the pejorative sense in which these words are now used. In his very earliest novels, written when he was in his twenties, in *Thérèse Raquin* for example, he held rather crude mechanistic views of human character. At the very end of his life, in the lamentable *Quatre Évangiles* he put forward very doctrinaire and absurd Utopian theories of social perfectibility. It would be hard, however, if a great writer had to be judged on the productions of his callow youth and his premature dotage. Zola's materialism was, in fact, not mechanistic at all; it was rather a sort of pantheism, a vitalism which sought man's soul in all the aspects of creation. His was not a profound intellect—the greatest novelists have not been intellectuals. His vitalism would not stand up to any serious philosophical or theological attack. It was, however, the expression of the deep love of life of a man whose imaginative fecundity brimmed over into everything he came upon. It was courageous, creative and humane. It was *not* in any sense a simple or naive optimism. Few of the great nineteenth century writers were as naively optimistic as it has been convenient for their twentieth century critics to imagine them. Zola—the black romantic—had his full measure of understanding of evil and pain, even though he was not willing to accept the idea of original sin. The author of *Earth* and *The Dram Shop* can hardly be charged with ignoring the darker sides of human life. But, the critics may say, it is perfectly possible for a man to see the evil and pain around him most clearly and yet remain confident, integrated, almost smug inside himself. Is not Zola's vitalism, his final assurance that the world was enough without the revelation of religion, simply the expression of a successful, energetic man who saw the flaws in life around and yet remained absurdly untroubled in his own soul? Was not Zola's constant activity, his enormous productivity as a writer, simply the expression of a man who was too busy to reflect deeply about the meaning of his own life?

In fact, this was not so. In the very middle of his career, at the very height of his success, Zola was a deeply troubled, unhappy man, nervously upset, obsessed with fears of death. The great triumph of his life, it may well be said, was not the wonderful novels he wrote or his courageous defence of Dreyfus, but his conquest of his own neurotic self, his victory over the dark fears that threatened the foundations of his belief in life. It is a victory the more remarkable that it was won without relinquishing his humanistic agnosticism, without capitulating to the forces of pessimism, decadence and neo-Catholicism which engulfed so many of the intellectuals at the end of the nineteenth century. It is a victory that does much to vindicate the despised 'liberal materialism' of the nineteenth century. That victory is expressed in the novel *Zest for Life*.

Zest for Life is not one of the four great novels of the Rougon Macquart series, but it is one of his most interesting novels. It is the most directly autobiographical and the most completely concerned with ideas. Already by 1880, after the success of *The Dram Shop* and *Nana*, Zola had become deeply depressed. He had overworked. The penury and near starvation of his early years had left marks that even his stern discipline of hard work could not deny. His marriage, though full of love, had proved fruitless. He felt most deeply the lack of an heir. He was obsessed with the thought of death. Some of his disciples had already begun to leave the broad plains of naturalism for more tortuous artistic paths. The idea of a school of young men following in his footsteps which might have been a substitute for children had failed. About this time he told Goncourt that he and his wife used to lie in bed at night, not speaking, yet each knowing that the other had but one thought— Death. It was a poisonous centre to the life of riches and success which were symbolized in his extravagantly furnished, over opulent new house at Médan. It was in these circumstances that he conceived the idea of *Zest for Life*.

The events of the year 1880, however, were so disastrous for Zola's personal life that he was unable to go on with the idea. In that year Flaubert died, and, for all the underlying disagreements between the two men, Flaubert was Zola's father in the world of letters. In that year, too, Zola's mother, returning from a visit to relatives in Eastern France, was taken ill in Paris and brought to her son's house at Médan to die. Her last illness was a painful and difficult one. Her underlying antagonism to Alexandrine, Zola's wife, was

6

released. She refused to have her daughter-in-law to nurse her, accusing her of poisoning the food. When, at last, the old lady died, her coffin had to be lowered from the window, for the stairs of the house were too narrow. Zola declared that for some time after this he could only think of how in a short while he and his wife would leave the house by the same route. The whole concept of *Zest for Life* was too painful for him. He did not take up the theme again until 1883 and the work was first published in the following year.

Zest for Life, with its curious flat, stagnating milieu of a little, broken-down fishing village is the story of two personalities— Lazare, the brilliant, neurotic pessimistic young man of promise which comes to nothing and Pauline Quenu, the young, healthy girl, sensible, full of animal pleasure, content with life, finding meaning in a simple life of service and good works. Lazare is the embodiment of the decadent end of nineteenth century prosperity, Wagneresque, Tchekhovian. Zola, in his notes, describes him as '*une sorte de René ou de Werther naturaliste.*' Naturalism, he says, the very school of literature he had created, had produced the sceptic who believes in nothing in the world, who denies progress. In the character of Lazare, then, he fought the neurotic side of himself and won. For it is Pauline's life in joy which triumphs. She is the daughter of the healthy, plump, sensual pork butcher Lisa Macquart of *Le Ventre de Paris* and her good works, her self-sacrifice have nothing anaemic in them. She is one of the most complete women of nineteenth century fiction. But Zola's acceptance of life goes further than pure good health or selfless living. The final scene of *Zest for Life* is one of the most curious that Zola ever wrote. I will not anticipate the reader's interest by describing it. One thing is clear, however; it is not only those who have 'every reason to love life' who, in Zola's opinion, worship it.

Apart from Lazare and Pauline, the novel contains at least two other memorable characters. Madame Chanteau is a brilliant study of a good, sensible woman twisted and destroyed by maternal love. Louise is a realistic study of a typical nineteenth century heroine— the child-wife, David Copperfield's Dora.

The style of the book is purposefully flat, rising to its expected heights in the great set scenes which Zola so delighted in writing. Jean Stewart's translation meets both demands most admirably, conveying the day to day calm of Pauline's life as well as the day to day despairing ennui of Lazare's.

ANGUS WILSON

7

CHAPTER I

WHEN the cuckoo-clock in the dining-room struck six, Chanteau gave up all hope. He dragged himself painfully out of the arm-chair where he was warming his heavy, gout-swollen legs in front of a coke fire. For the last two hours he had been expecting Madame Chanteau, who was due back that day after a five weeks' absence, bringing with her from Paris their little cousin Pauline Quenu, to whom the Chanteaus were going to act as guardians.

'It's extraordinary, Véronique,' he said, pushing open the kitchen door. 'They must have met with an accident.'

The maid, a big harsh-featured woman of thirty-five, with hands like a man's, was busy removing from the fire a leg of mutton which was undoubtedly going to be overdone. She did not grumble, but her leathery cheeks were pale with anger.

'Madame must have stayed in Paris,' she said tartly. 'This endless fuss and bother, upsetting the whole house!'

'No, no,' Chanteau explained, 'that telegram yesterday said the little girl's affairs were definitely settled . . . Madame must have reached Caen this morning; she was to stop there to see Davoine. At one o'clock she was to take the train again; at two she was to get off at Bayeux; at three, old Malivoire's coach was to drop her at Arromanches, and even allowing for some delay in putting the horses to that old berline, Madame could have been here by four o'clock, half-past four at latest . . . It's not more than ten kilometres from Arromanches to Bonneville.'

The cook, her eyes fixed on her joint, listened to all these calculations with an occasional nod of her head. After a moment's hesitation he added: 'You might go to the corner of the road and look, Véronique.'

She stared at him, paler than ever with repressed wrath. 'Indeed? why should I? . . . Since Monsieur Lazare's gone paddling about outside to meet them already, it's not worth me getting myself all muddied up.'

'You see,' murmured Chanteau gently, 'I'm beginning to feel a bit anxious about my son too. No signs of him either. What can he have been doing out on the road for a whole hour?'

Then, without another word, Véronique took down an old black woollen shawl from a peg and wrapped it round her head and shoulders. As her master was following her into the passage, she

9

said to him sharply: 'You get back in front of your fire, if you don't want to be howling all to-morrow with your aches and pains.'

She slammed the door behind her. On the porch, she put on her sabots and faced the gale, shouting: 'God almighty! that brat'll be able to boast of having made fools of us!'

Chanteau sat on, quietly. He was used to the maid's outbursts; she had entered his service the year of his marriage, when she was fifteen. When the sound of sabots had died away he escaped like a schoolboy on holiday, and went along the passage to take up his stand in front of a glass door that looked out on to the sea. There he stood for a moment in self-oblivion, a short, paunchy figure, florid-faced, and under the snowy cap of his close-cropped hair his big, prominent blue eyes stared up at the sky. He was barely fifty-six, but the attacks of gout from which he suffered had aged him prematurely. His anxiety forgotten, a faraway look in his eyes, he told himself that little Pauline would surely end by winning Véronique's heart.

And anyhow, was he to blame? When that solicitor in Paris had written to tell him that his cousin Quenu had just died, six months after his wife, he had felt unable to refuse. It was true that they had not seen much of one another, for the family was widely scattered; Chanteau's father, after leaving the South of France and wandering all over the country as a plain journeyman carpenter, had started a timber business in Caen, dealing in wood from the North of France; whereas little Quenu, on his father's death, had landed in Paris, where another uncle had, later, made over to him a big *charcuterie* in the very middle of the Halles district. And they had met on two or three occasions only, when Chanteau's painful afflic- tion had obliged him to leave his business and travel to Paris to consult famous doctors. The two men, however, had a great respect for one another; and perhaps the dying Quenu had longed for his daughter to enjoy the healthful air of the seaside. In any case the girl would be no financial burden to them; quite the reverse, since she inherited the *charcuterie*. Finally, Madame Chanteau had accepted, so enthusiastically indeed that she had insisted on sparing her husband the dangerous fatigue of a journey and, with her constant craving for activity, she had gone off alone to tramp the streets and settle the business. And, for Chanteau, his wife's satisfaction was enough.

But what could be keeping them both? His fears revived as he watched the livid sky, where the west wind was driving great black clouds like sooty rags, wisps of which trailed afar off in the sea. It

10

was one of those storms that occur in March, when the equinoctial tides batter the coasts with fury. The sea was just beginning to come in, and was as yet visible only as a white band on the horizon, a thin, distant streak of foam; the beach, to-day, lay fully exposed, a league-long expanse of dark seaweed and rocks, a bare plain smirched with puddles and mournful black patches, and wore an air of appalling melancholy under the gathering gloom of the clouds in their panic-stricken flight.

'Perhaps the wind's overturned them into a ditch,' Chanteau muttered to himself.

He felt impelled by an urge to investigate. He opened the glass door and ventured in his list slippers on to the gravel of the terrace, which overlooked the village. A few drops of rain, blown by the hurricane, lashed his face, and a terrible gust tore at his jacket of coarse blue wool. But he went on stubbornly, bare-headed, his back bent, and stood leaning his elbows on the parapet to gaze out along the road below. The road ran steeply down between two cliffs, as though the rock had been split with an axe; and the twenty-five or thirty hovels of Bonneville stood on the few yards of soil that had trickled through the crack. Every tide threatened to crush them against the hillside, on their narrow bed of cobbles. To the left there was a small beaching-ground, a bank of sand on which some men, with rhythmical shouts, were hauling up a dozen boats. There were barely two hundred inhabitants, and they got their meagre livelihood from the sea, clinging to the rocks with stupid obstinacy, like limpets. And above the wretched roofs, battered in by the waves every winter, there was nothing to be seen but the church on the right and the Chanteaus' house on the left, half-way up the cliffs, with the road running between them like a ravine. That was all there was of Bonneville.

'Filthy weather, eh?' a voice called out.

Chanteau looked up and recognized the *curé*, Abbé Horteur, a thickset man, built like a peasant, whose red hair was untouched by grey at fifty. In front of the church, in the precinct of the graveyard, the priest had set aside a patch for a kitchen-garden; and he stood there, looking at his early lettuces, hugging his cassock between his legs lest the hurricane should blow it over his head. Chanteau, unable to speak or make himself heard against the wind, had to be content with waving to him.

'I think they're well advised to bring in the boats,' bawled the *curé*. 'By ten o'clock they'd be waltzing.'

And as a sudden gust whipped up his cassock, he disappeared behind the church.

Chanteau had turned round, his shoulders hunched up, in dogged endurance. His eyes brimming with water, he threw a glance at his garden, shrivelled by the sea air, and at the brick house with its double row of five windows whose shutters seemed likely to be wrenched off their fastenings. When the squall had passed he leaned out over the road once more; but Véronique was coming back, waving her arms.

'What's this? You've gone out?... Will you please go in at once, monsieur?'

She caught him up in the passage and scolded him like a naughty child. If he was in pain to-morrow, she'd be the one who'd have to look after him, wouldn't she?

'Didn't you see anything?' he asked in a submissive tone.

'Of course I didn't see anything ... Madame's certainly taken shelter somewhere.'

He dared not tell her that she should have ventured further. Now it was his son's absence that worried him most.

'What I did see,' the maid went on, 'was that the whole place is in a hullabaloo. They're afraid they're done for this time ... Already last September the Cuches' house was split from top to bottom, and Prouane told me, when he came to ring the Angelus, that it'd certainly be down by to-morrow.'

But just at that moment a tall lad of nineteen ran up the three steps of the porch at one stride. He had a wide forehead, very clear eyes, and a wisp of downy brown beard framing his long face.

'Oh, good, here's Lazare,' said Chanteau with relief. 'How wet you are, my poor boy!'

The young man was hanging his dripping cloak in the hall.

'Well?' asked the father once more.

'Well, there was nobody!' answered Lazare. 'I went as far as Verchemont, and there I waited at the inn, under the shed, with my eyes fixed on the road, which is an absolute stream of mud. Nobody! And then I was afraid you'd be worried, so I came back.'

He had left the *lycée* at Caen the previous August, after passing his *baccalauréat*, and had spent the past eight months wandering about the cliffs, unable to decide on any occupation, absorbed in nothing but music, to the despair of his mother. She had been angry with him when she went off, for he had refused to accompany her to Paris, where she had hopes of finding a job for him. The

12

whole household was at sixes and sevens, in an atmosphere of bitterness that the closeness of family life only exacerbated.

'Now that I've told you, I'd like to go on as far as Arromanches,' added the young man.

'No, no, it's growing dark,' cried Chanteau. 'Your mother surely won't leave us without news. There's sure to be a telegram . . . Listen! that sounds like a carriage.'

Véronique had opened the door. 'It's Doctor Cazenove's gig,' she announced. 'Was he expected, monsieur? Why, good heavens, it's Madame!'

They all hurried down the steps. A great dog, a cross between a mountain sheep-dog and a Newfoundland, who was asleep in a corner of the hall, rushed forward, barking wildly. The noise brought a small white cat, with a delicate air, on to the threshold; but when she saw the muddy courtyard her tail quivered lightly with disgust, and she sat down primly at the top of the steps, to watch.

Meanwhile a lady of about fifty had jumped out of the gig, with the agility of a young girl. She was small and thin, with hair still jet-black and a pleasant face, spoilt only by a big nose betokening an ambitious nature. The dog had leapt up and laid its paws on her shoulders, trying to kiss her; she grew annoyed with him.

'Now then, Mathieu, let go! Down, you bad dog!'

Lazare came across the courtyard after the dog. He shouted out: 'No accidents, *maman*?'

'No, no,' replied Madame Chanteau.

'Good heavens, we were so worried!' said the father, following his son in spite of the wind. 'Whatever happened?'

'Oh, everything seemed to go wrong,' she explained. 'To begin with the roads are so bad that it took nearly two hours to come from Bayeux. And then at Arromanches one of Malivoire's horses went and hurt its leg, and he couldn't give us another. I thought he'd have to put us up for the night . . . And in the end the doctor was kind enough to lend us his gig. Good Martin brought us . . .'

The coachman, an old man with a wooden leg, a former sailor on whom Cazenove had performed an operation when he was a naval surgeon and who had subsequently remained in the doctor's service, was busy tying up the horse. Madame Chanteau broke off to say to him, 'Martin, help the little girl to get out.'

Nobody had thought of the child. As the hood of the gig hung down very low, nothing could be seen of her but her black skirt and her little black-gloved hands. In any case, without waiting for the coachman's help, she jumped lightly out in her turn. A squall was blowing, her garments were flapping, wisps of dark hair flew out under the black crape of her hat. She was a big girl for ten, with thick lips and a full pale face, pale as any child would be who had been brought up in a Paris back-shop. Everybody looked at her. Véronique, who had come up to greet her mistress, stopped short and stood aside, with a frozen, jealous face. Mathieu was by no means so reserved; he leapt into the child's arms and licked her face profusely.

'Don't be frightened!' cried Madame Chanteau, 'he's not fierce.'

'Oh, I'm not frightened,' Pauline answered gently, 'I'm very fond of dogs.'

And indeed she remained perfectly calm amidst Mathieu's rude embraces. Her little solemn face lit up with a smile, despite her deep mourning; then she laid a big kiss on the dog's muzzle.

'And what about the people, aren't you going to kiss them too?' went on Madame Chanteau. 'This is your uncle, since you call me your auntie; and this is your cousin, a big rascal who's not as good as you are.'

The child was not in the least shy. She kissed each of them, she found a word for each, with the gracious manners of a little Parisienne already trained in courtesy.

'Thank you very much, uncle, for having me to live with you . . . I'm sure we shall get on well together, cousin . . .'

'But isn't she sweet?' cried Chanteau, delighted.

Lazare was staring at her in surprise, for he had expected her to be much smaller, a silly scared little thing.

'Oh, yes, she's very sweet,' echoed the old lady. 'And brave, you've no idea! The wind was blowing straight at us in that carriage, and blinding us with spray. The hood was flapping like a sail and I made sure a score of times that it was going to be split. Well, she thought it was all great fun, she enjoyed it . . . But what are we doing here? We've no need to get any wetter—here's the rain beginning again.'

She turned round, looking for Véronique. When she saw her standing aloof, with a crabbed face, she said ironically:'Good day, my lass, how are you? If you are not going to ask me how I am, you might fetch up a bottle for Martin . . . We weren't able to bring our trunks. Malivoire will bring them early to-morrow.'

She broke off, and turned round towards the carriage in sudden alarm. 'And my bag! . . . I was so scared! I was afraid it had fallen out on the way.'

It was a big black leather bag, already worn white at the corners, and she refused pointblank to entrust it to her son. At last every-

14

one was moving up towards the house, when a fresh squall made them halt breathless before the door. The cat sat there, watching them with interest as they struggled against the wind; and Madame Chanteau had to be told whether Minouche had been good during her absence. At the name Minouche, Pauline gave another solemn little smile. She bent down to stroke the cat, which promptly came to rub against her skirt with its tail held high. Mathieu had begun to bark violently again to celebrate the homecoming, when he saw the family climb up the steps and reach the shelter of the hall at last.

'Oh, it's good to be home,' said the mother. 'I was beginning to think we should never get back . . . Yes, Mathieu, you're a good dog, but leave us in peace. Oh, please Lazare, make him keep quiet;he's deafening me!'

The dog persisted, and the Chanteaus' return into their dining-room took place to the accompaniment of his joyful clamour. They pushed Pauline, the new child of the house, in front of them; behind them came Mathieu, still barking, followed in his turn by Minouche, whose sensitive fur was bristling amidst all this din. Martin, in the kitchen, had already drunk two glasses of wine in quick succession, and now he went off, his wooden leg tapping on the tiled floor, shouting goodnight to everyone. Véronique had been warming up the joint at the fire. She looked in and asked: 'Are you going to eat?'

'I should say so, it's seven o'clock,' said Chanteau. 'Only, my lass, we'd better wait till Madame and the little girl have changed their clothes.'

'But I haven't got Pauline's trunk,' pointed out Madame Chanteau. 'Luckily we're not wet underneath . . . Take off your coat and hat, darling. Help her, won't you, Véronique . . . And take her shoes off too . . . I've got things here . . .'

The maid had to kneel in front of the child, who was sitting down. Meanwhile the old lady pulled out of her bag a pair of small felt slippers, which she herself put on the child's feet. Then she held out her own feet to be unshod, and dipped once more into her bag, emerging with a pair of old shoes for herself.

'Well, shall I dish up?' asked Véronique once more.

'Presently . . . Pauline, come into the kitchen to wash your hands and sponge your face . . .We're dying of hunger, we'll have a good clean-up later on.'

Pauline reappeared first, leaving her aunt with her face over a basin. Chanteau had resumed his place in front of the fire, sunk deep in his big yellow velvet armchair; and he was rubbing his legs

15

with an automatic gesture, in dread of an imminent attack, while Lazare cut slices of bread, standing at the table, where, for over an hour, four places had been laid. The two men, feeling slightly embarrassed, smiled at the child but could find nothing to say. She was calmly examining the dining-room with its walnut furniture, her eyes wandering from the sideboard and the half-dozen chairs to the hanging lamp of polished brass, her attention arrested particularly by five framed lithographs, the Four Seasons and a View of Vesuvius, which stood out against the brown wall-paper. No doubt the sham panelling of painted oak with its chalky scratches, the floor stained with old grease-spots, the general air of neglect of this communal living-room, made her homesick for the handsome marble shop that she had left the day before, for her eyes grew sad and she seemed for a moment to guess at the secret antagonisms latent under the apparent good-humour of this unfamiliar environment. Finally her gaze, after lingering over a very ancient barometer in a gilt wooden case, fastened on a strange construction that took up the whole mantelpiece, standing under a glass cover and fastened at the angles with thin strips of blue paper. It looked like a toy, a miniature wooden bridge, but one of extraordinary complicated construction.

'That was made by your great-uncle,' explained Chanteau, glad to have found a topic of conversation. 'Yes, my father began by being a carpenter. I've always kept his masterpiece.'

He was not ashamed of his origins, and Madame Chanteau had to put up with the bridge on the mantelpiece, despite the annoyance which this cumbrous curio caused her by reminding her that she had married the son of a workman. But the little girl had already stopped listening to her uncle; she had just caught sight of the immense horizon outside, and she crossed the room swiftly and took up her stand in front of the window, the muslin curtains of which were held back by cotton loops. Since leaving Paris, she had been obsessed by the thought of the sea. She dreamed of it, she kept on questioning her aunt in the train, wanting to know, at every hillside that they passed, whether the sea lay behind those mountains. At last, on the beach at Arromanches, she had fallen silent, her bosom heaving with a great sigh; then, from Arromanches to Bonneville, she had constantly thrust her head out of the carriage window, in spite of the wind, to watch the sea as it followed them. And now there was the sea still; it would be there always, like something that belonged to her. Slowly, with her eyes, she seemed to be making it her own.

16

Night was falling from the livid sky, where gusts of wind lashed the wildly rushing clouds. Nothing could be made out now, in the depths of the increasingly chaotic gloom, but the pallor of the incoming sea. It was a constantly widening expanse of white foam, a succession of sheets of water flooding the seaweed beds, covering the slabs of rock, gliding along with a gentle, lulling motion, soft as a caress. But, in the distance, the noise of the waves had grown louder, enormous white crests were gathering at the foot of the cliffs, and a deathlike twilight hung over the village, which lay deserted as all the inhabitants sheltered behind tightly-stopped doors; while the boats, abandoned on the ridge of pebbles, lay like great dead fish cast up on the beach. The rain drowned the village in a smoky mist, and only the church could still be seen clearly, in a wan corner between storm-clouds.

Pauline said nothing. Once more her small bosom heaved, as though she were about to suffocate, and she gave a sigh so prolonged that all her breath seemed to issue from her lips

'It's wider than the Seine, eh?' said Lazare, who had come to stand behind her.

He was still puzzled by this child. Since she had come, the tall lad felt shy and awkward.

'Oh yes,' she said in a low voice, without turning round. He was about to call her *tu*, but forbore. 'Aren't you afraid?' Then she looked at him in surprise. 'No, why should I be? Of course the water won't come up as far as here.'

'Well, you never know,' he said, yielding to an urge to tease her, 'sometimes the water comes over the top of the church.'

But then she broke into a hearty laugh. It was a gust of noisy, wholesome merriment, shaking her whole serious little person, the merriment of a rational creature delighted by a piece of nonsense. And she caught hold of his hands as though in play, using the familiar *tu* herself as she cried:'Oh, cousin, you must think I'm very silly! You wouldn't stay here if the water rose over the top of the church!'

Lazare was laughing too, holding the child's hands; they were allies henceforward. In the middle of their noisy merriment Madame Chanteau came back; she seemed delighted, and said, as she wiped her hands: 'Well, so you've made friends... I knew you'd get on together.'

'Shall I dish up, Madame?' interrupted Véronique, standing at the kitchen door.

'Yes, yes, my lass. Only you'd better light the lamp first. We can't see a thing."

17

Indeed, night had fallen so rapidly that the dining-room was now in complete darkness, save for the red glow of the coke fire. More delay ensued. At last the maid pulled down the lamp, and the dinner-table appeared under the bright ring of light. And everybody was sitting down, Pauline between her uncle and her cousin, opposite her aunt, when the latter got up once more, being one of those lean, lively elderly women who can never keep still.

'Where's my bag? Wait a minute, darling, I'll get you your beaker. Take the glass away, Véronique, the child's used to her beaker.'

She had pulled out a silver mug, already somewhat battered, and, wiping it with her napkin, set it before Pauline. Then she laid her bag behind her on her chair. The maid brought in soup with vermicelli, warning everyone by her sulky expression that it was badly overcooked. Nobody dared complain, for they were all very hungry, and they sucked up the soup eagerly. Boiled beef came next. Chanteau, who was very greedy, barely touched it, saving his appetite for the roast mutton. But when this appeared on the table there was a general outcry. It was like dried-up leather, it was quite inedible!

'Of course it is,' said Véronique calmly. 'You didn't ought to have kept it waiting.'

However, Pauline was cheerfully cutting up her meat into small pieces and eating it. As for Lazare, he never knew what was on his plate, and would have swallowed hunks of bread thinking they were breast of chicken. Meanwhile Chanteau looked gloomily at the joint.

'What's to go with it, Véronique?'

'Fried potatoes, monsieur.'

He made a despairing gesture, and dropped back into his armchair. Might as well eat bread as boiled beef! Oh, good Lord, what a dinner! Even the weather was against him, and prevented him from having fish. Madame Chanteau, who was a very small eater, looked at him with pity.

'Poor dear,' she said suddenly, 'I'm sorry for you . . . I'd got a present for to-morrow; but since we're on short commons to-night . . .' She had opened her bag again and was pulling out a terrine of foie gras. Chanteau's eyes lit up. Foie gras! forbidden fruit! His favourite delicacy, strictly prohibited by the doctor!

'But, you know,' his wife went on, 'I'm only allowing you one slice . . . Be sensible, or you'll never get any more.'

He had seized hold of the terrine and was helping himself with trembling hands. Terrible struggles often took place between his

18

dread of another attack and his violent greed; and almost always greed proved the stronger. Well, it couldn't be helped; it was too nice, and he'd have to put up with the pain.

Véronique, who had watched him cut himself a large slice, went back to the kitchen, muttering: 'Well! Monsieur won't half bawl!'

This was her instinctive phrase, and her employers had accepted it, so simply did she utter it. Monsieur bawled when he had one of his attacks; and the description was so apt that nobody thought of telling her to mind her manners.

The meal ended merrily. Lazare jokingly snatched the terrine from his father's hands; then, when dessert appeared—a Pont l'Évêque cheese and biscuits—to everybody's delight, Mathieu emerged. He had been asleep up till then somewhere under the table. The arrival of the biscuits had woken him up—he seemed to smell them in his sleep; and every evening, exactly at this moment, he would shake himself and go prowling round the table, trying to read people's feelings on their faces. Lazare was usually the first to be moved to pity; only, this evening, Mathieu, on his second round, fixed his gentle, human eyes on Pauline; then, instinctively recognizing a lover of animals and human beings, he laid his huge head on the child's small knee, without taking his affectionate, suppliant gaze from her.

'Oh, the greedy thing!' said Madame Chanteau. 'Gently, Mathieu, don't snatch at your food so wildly!'

The dog had swallowed at one gulp the piece of biscuit Pauline held out to him; and once more he laid his head on the child's knee, asking for another piece, still gazing up at his new friend. She was laughing and kissing him; she thought him very funny, with his dangling ears and the black patch on the left eye—the only mark on his long, curly white coat. Then came an interruption: Minouche, jealous, leapt lightly on to the table and purring, curving her back, she started butting the child's chin with her head, as daintily as a young kid. This was her way of caressing you, letting you feel her cold nose and the touch of her pointed teeth, while she pranced about on her hind legs like a baker's boy kneading dough. Pauline was delighted at this; she sat between the two animals, the cat on the left and the dog on the right, overrun by them and so shockingly exploited that she ended by sharing out all her dessert between them.

'Send them away,' said her aunt. 'They'll leave you nothing!'

'What does that matter?' she replied quite simply, happy in her self-despoilment.

Dinner ended and Véronique cleared the table. The two animals, seeing everything gone, went off without a thank you, giving themselves a final lick.

Pauline had risen and, standing in front of the window, was trying to see out. Since the first course she had been watching the window grow darker, gradually becoming inky black. Now it was an impenetrable wall, a mass of gloom that swallowed up everything, sky and sea, the village and even the church. Although she had not been alarmed by her cousin's teasing, she was looking for the sea, tormented by longing to know how high the water would rise; and she could hear nothing but its growing clamour, its high, monstrous, threatening voice, swelling louder every minute, amidst the howling of the wind and the lashing of the rain. Now the chaotic darkness showed not a gleam of light, not even the pallor of the foam; in the depths of this nothingness there was only the gallop of the waves, under the whip of the storm.

'My word!' said Chanteau, 'it's coming up strong . . . And there's still two hours before high tide.'

'If the wind was from the north,' Lazare explained, 'I think Bonneville would be finished. Luckily it's blowing sideways.'

The little girl had turned round to listen to them, her great eyes full of anxious pity.

'Bah,' said Madame Chanteau, 'we're safe here, we must let others look after themselves, everybody's got their own troubles . . . Look, darling, would you like a nice hot cup of tea? And then we'll go to bed.'

Véronique, having cleared the table, covered it with an old red tablecloth patterned with large flowers, round which the family usually sat in the evenings. They all resumed their places. Lazare, who had gone out for a minute, came back with an inkpot, a pen, and a whole bundle of papers; he settled down under the lamp and began to copy out music. Madame Chanteau, whose affectionate gaze had been fixed on her son ever since her return, suddenly became acrimonious.

'Your music again! Can't you spare us a single evening, even the day I come home?'

'But, mother, I've not gone away, I'm stopping here beside you . . . You know it doesn't prevent me from talking to you. Go on, say something to me and I'll answer you.'

And he persisted, spreading his papers over half the table. Chanteau had stretched out comfortably in his armchair, his hands dangling loosely. Mathieu was asleep in front of the fire, while

Minouche, who had leapt on to the tablecloth at one bound, was performing an elaborate toilette, with one leg in the air, carefully licking the fur on her belly. The brass lamp seemed to shed a pleasantly intimate glow, and soon Pauline, who sat there smiling through half-closed eyes at her new family, felt herself overcome by fatigue and dazed by the warmth of the room, and she yielded to sleep. Her head drooped forward till it lay in the crook of her folded arm, and she dozed off thus right under the tranquil light of the lamp. Her delicate eyelids were like a silken veil drawn over her eyes, and a light, regular breathing issued from her innocent lips.

'She must be worn out,' said Madame Chanteau, dropping her voice. 'We'll just wake her up to take her tea and then we'll put her to bed.'

Silence reigned then. Against the background of the storm only the scratching of Lazare's pen could be heard. They sat at peace, lulled by the familiarity of old habits, ruminating over life as they did every evening in the same place. For a long while the father and mother looked at one another without speaking. At last Chanteau asked hesitatingly: 'And at Caen, did you get a satisfactory statement from Davoine?'

She shrugged her shoulders furiously. 'Satisfactory statement indeed! Didn't I tell you you were letting yourself be fooled?'

Now that the child was asleep they could talk. They spoke in whispers, only intending, at first, to tell each other their news briefly. But their feelings soon carried them away and gradually all the family troubles were poured forth.

At the death of his father, the journeyman carpenter, who had carried on his timber business with the reckless boldness of an adventurous spirit, Chanteau had found the firm in a precarious position. He was little inclined to activity himself, being of a prudent, routinist disposition, and he had been content merely to save the situation by setting affairs in order, and to live in a respectable and unassuming way on his reliable returns. The only romance in his life was his marriage with a governess whom he met at a friend's home. Eugénie de la Vignière, an orphan from a family of ruined gentlefolk of Le Cotentin, hoped to inspire him with her own ambition. But Chanteau, who had never been fully educated, having been sent late to a private boarding-school, shrank from any large scale enterprise, and frustrated his wife's will to power by the inertia of his own nature. When a son was born, the mother transferred all her hopes of making a great fortune to

21

this child; she sent him to a *lycée* and, every evening, supervised his studies herself. However, a final misfortune came to upset her plans. Chanteau, who from the age of forty had been subject to gout, ended by suffering attacks so violent that he had to consider selling the business. This would mean lowering their standard of living, using up their petty savings, and, later on, casting their child on the world unprovided with the basic income of twenty thousand francs that she had dreamed of for him.

Madame Chanteau determined to look after the sale herself. The business brought in an income of some ten thousand francs, on which they lived on an ample scale, for she was fond of entertaining. It was she who discovered a certain Davoine and thought up the following transaction: Davoine would buy the timber business for a hundred thousand francs, but he would pay only fifty thousand; by allowing him the other fifty thousand the Chanteaus remained his associates and shared his profits. This fellow Davoine seemed to be a man of some intelligence and enterprise; even if he did not make the business yield more, they would be sure of their fifty thousand francs which, added to the three thousand brought in by the fifty thousand invested in mortgages, would give them a total income of eight thousand francs. They could make do with this while waiting for their son's successes to raise them out of their humble way of life.

And things had been settled thus. Chanteau had happened, two years previously, to buy a house at the seaside, at Bonneville, a bargain picked up from an insolvent customer. Instead of selling it again, as she had at one time proposed to do, Madame Chanteau had decided that they should retire there, at all events until Lazare's first triumphs. It was a sort of suicide for her to give up entertaining and bury herself in so remote a place; but as she was giving up the house with the business to Davoine she would have had to rent one somewhere else, and she bravely began to save money with the firm intention of making her triumphant re-entry into Caen later on, when her son held some important position there. Chanteau acquiesced in everything. As for his gout, it would have to put up with the seaside air; moreover, two out of three doctors whom he consulted were obliging enough to declare that the bracing sea winds would have a powerfully tonic effect on his general health. So, one morning in May, the Chanteaus, leaving fourteen-year-old Lazare at the *lycée*, had gone off to settle at Bonneville for good.

Since that heroic uprooting five years had passed, and the family's affairs were going from bad to worse. As Davoine went in for large-scale speculations he was for ever demanding fresh loans, and re-investing the profits in risky concerns, so that the accounts practically showed a deficit. At Bonneville they were reduced to living on their three thousand francs income, so frugally that they had been obliged to sell the horse and that Véronique worked the kitchen garden.

'Look here, Eugénie,' ventured Chanteau, 'if I got involved in this it was partly your fault.'

But she no longer accepted the responsibility; she readily forgot that the association with Davoine was of her making.

'What d'you mean by that—my fault?' she answered tartly. 'Is it I who am ill? If you hadn't been ill, we might be millionaires . . .'

Every time that his wife's bitterness overflowed like this he would hang his head, embarrassed and ashamed that his own body should thus harbour the enemy of his family.

'We must wait,' he muttered. 'Davoine seems confident about this deal he's planning. If the price of firwood goes up, we'll make our fortunes.'

'Well, and what then?' interrupted Lazare, still intent on copying his music, 'we've still got enough to eat . . . You really oughtn't to worry like that. Personally I don't care a rap about money.'

Madame Chanteau shrugged her shoulders once more.

'You'd do better to care a little more, and not waste your time on such rubbish.'

To think that it was she who had taught him to play the piano! The mere sight of a score exasperated her now. Her last hopes were crumbling; this son, whom she had dreamed of seeing Prefect or Judge, was talking of writing operas; and she had visions of him, some day, walking the muddy streets to give private lessons, as she had done herself.

'Well,' she went on, 'here's a rough statement of the last three months, which Davoine gave me . . . If things go on like this, we shall be owing him money by July.'

She had laid her bag on the table and took out a paper, which she handed to Chanteau. He had to take it, turned it round, and finally laid it in front of him without opening it. At that moment Véronique brought in tea. A long silence fell; the cups stood empty. Beside the sugar-basin, Minouche lay smugly with her paws folded and her eyes closed, while Mathieu, in front of the fireplace, was snoring like a man. And the sea's voice rose ever louder outside, like a formidable bass accompanying the low, peaceful sounds of this drowsy indoor scene.

23

'Suppose you wake her up, Mother?' said Lazare. 'She can't be comfortable, sleeping there.'

'Yes, yes,' muttered Madame Chanteau, absently, gazing at Pauline.

All three looked at the sleeping child. Her breathing was still quieter, her pale cheeks and her rosy lips had the still sweetness of a bunch of flowers, in the lamplight. Only her long brown hair, dishevelled by the wind, cast a shade on her delicate forehead.

And amidst all her present troubles, Madame Chanteau mentally retraced her visit to Paris, surprised by her own enthusiasm for accepting this guardianship and yet moved by an instinctive regard for a wealthy ward; so strictly honest, moreover, that she had no ulterior motive regarding the fortune which was being entrusted to her.

'When I went into the shop,' she began to relate slowly, 'there she was in her little black frock, and she kissed me, sobbing and weeping. Oh, it was a very fine shop, a pork-butcher's shop full of mirrors and marble, just opposite the Halles . . . And there was a maid there, a sturdy little thing with a fresh rosy face, who had informed the lawyer, and had seals laid, and was calmly going on selling sausages and black-pudding . . . It was this girl Adèle who told me about our poor cousin Quenu's death. Since he'd lost his wife Lisa six months before his blood seemed to be choking him, he kept putting his hand up to his throat as if to take off his tie; and finally one evening they found him lying face downwards in a bowl of lard—he'd turned quite purple . . . His uncle Gradelle died in just the same way.'

She stopped, and silence fell once more. Pauline's sleeping face lit up with a brief smile, the reflection of a passing dream.

'And what about the deed of trust,' asked Chanteau, 'did that go off all right?'

'Very well . . . But your lawyer was quite right to leave the name of the mandatory blank, for it seems that I couldn't act for you. Women don't count, in that sort of business . . . As I told you in my letter, I went straight off to talk things over with the solicitor who had sent you that extract from the will where you were appointed guardian. He promptly made out the deed in the name of his managing clerk, a thing that's often done, so they tell me. So we were able to get on with things . . . At the magistrate's I got them to appoint, for the family council, three of Lisa's relations, two young cousins, Octave Mouret and Claude Lantier, and one cousin by marriage, Monsieur Rambaud, who lives in Marseilles; and on

24

our own side, on Quenu's side, I chose three nephews, Naudet, Liardin and Delorme. It's quite a proper sort of family council, you see, and they'll let us do whatever we want for the good of the child . . . So, at the first meeting, they appointed the deputy guardian, whom I'd had to choose from among Lisa's relatives— Monsieur Saccard . . .'

'Hush, she's waking up,' broke in Lazare.

And indeed Pauline had just opened her eyes wide. She sat quite still, gazing at them with wonder as they talked; then, overwhelmed with weariness, gave a faint sleepy smile and let her eyelids close again; and her face was motionless once more, with the milky transparent look of a camellia flower.

'Isn't that Saccard the stockbroker?' asked Chanteau.

'Yes,' his wife replied. 'I saw him, we had a chat . . . A very nice man. He's involved in so many things that he warned me not to count on his help . . . You understand, we don't need anybody else. Since we're taking on the child, we're taking her on, aren't we? Personally, I don't like people interfering . . . And after that, everything was fixed up quickly. Luckily, your deed specified all the necessary powers. The seals were lifted, the fortune was assessed, the shop sold by auction. Oh, wasn't it lucky? there were two keen competitors, we got ninety thousand francs down. The solicitor had already found sixty thousand in securities, put away in a drawer. I asked him to buy some more stock, and here are a hundred and fifty thousand francs' worth of gilt-edged which I was glad to be able to bring along with me, after having given the managing clerk the acquittance and the receipt for the money, which I'd asked you to send by return of post. Look here! look at this.'

She had dipped her hand into her bag again and brought out a voluminous parcel, the parcel of securities, pressed between the cardboard covers of an old register from the pork-butcher's shop, of which the inside pages had been torn out. The cover, mottled with large green blotches, was spattered with spots of grease. Father and son both stared at the fortune thus laid out on the worn table-cloth before them.

'The tea's getting cold, mother,' said Lazare, dropping his pen at last. 'Shan't I pour it out?'

He had risen and was filling the cups. The mother sat without replying, her eyes fixed on the securities.

'Of course,' she went on slowly, 'at a final meeting of the family council, called at my request, I asked to have my travelling expenses refunded, and they agreed on an allowance of eight hundred francs for the child's keep. We're not so well off as she is, we can't afford to do it for nothing. Nobody here wants to make money out of this child, but it'd be hard for us to dip into our own pockets. We'll reinvest the interest on her bonds, and by the time she's of age we'll almost have doubled her capital . . . Good Lord, we're only doing our duty. One's got to obey the wishes of the dead. If we contribute something ourselves, well, it may bring us luck, and we certainly need that . . . The poor darling was so upset, and she wept so hard when she said goodbye to her nurse! I do want her to be happy here.'

The two men were stirred by compassion. 'Well, I'd never do anything to hurt her,' said Chanteau.

'She's sweet,' added Lazare. 'I'm very fond of her already.'

Meanwhile Mathieu, having smelt the tea in his sleep, began to shake himself and once more laid his great head on the edge of the table. Minouche, too, stretched herself, rounded her back and yawned. There was a general waking-up, and the cat ended by thrusting forward her neck to sniff at the parcel of bonds in their greasy cover. And as the Chanteaus turned to look at Pauline again, they saw her staring wide-eyed as she recognized the papers and the tattered old cash-book.

'Oh, she knows what's in there,' went on Madame Chanteau. 'I showed you in Paris, didn't I, darling? That's what your poor father and mother left you.''

Tears ran down the little girl's cheeks as her grief revived sharply, like a spring shower. And then she smiled again amidst her tears, delighted at watching Minouche who, after sniffing at the bonds for a long time, attracted no doubt by their smell, had begun to prance about again, purring loudly and butting the corners of the cashbook with her head.

'Leave it alone, Minouche!' cried Madame Chanteau. 'You can't play with money!'

Chanteau was laughing and so was Lazare. Mathieu was standing by the table, wild with excitement, with his greedy glowing eyes fixed on the papers as though they were good to eat, and barking at the cat. And the whole family relaxed in noisy delight. Pauline, delighted with the fun, had caught up Minouche in her arms and was rocking and dandling her as though she were a doll.

For fear the child might fall asleep again Madame Chanteau made her drink her tea at once. Then she called Véronique.

'Bring in the candles . . . We stop here talking, we shall never get to bed. To think it's ten o'clock! And I was half asleep at supper-time.'

But a man's voice could be heard in the kitchen, and when Véronique brought in the four lighted candles, Madame Chanteau asked her: 'Who was that you were talking to?'

'It's Prouane, madame . . . He's come to tell monsieur things are going badly down below. The tide's smashing everything, so it seems.'

Chanteau had had to consent to become Mayor of Bonneville, and Prouane, a toper who served as beadle to Abbé Horteur, ful-filled the further functions of clerk. He had reached a certain rank in the navy and could write like any schoolmaster. When they called him in, he appeared, holding his woollen cap in his hand, his jacket and boots streaming with water.

'Well, what's happened, Prouane?'

'Well, sir, it's the Cuches' house that's done for this time . . . Now if it goes on like this it'll be the Gonins' turn . . . We were all there, Tourmal, Houtelard and me and the rest . . . But what's the use? We're helpless against that devil, she's bound to carry off a piece of our land every year.'

Silence fell. The four candles were burning with tall flames, and that devil, the sea, could be heard battering at the cliffs. The tide was now at its height, and each wave as it broke shook the house, like the boom of some titanic cannon, while the shingle rattled over the rocks with a rending sound like the continuous crackle of rifle fire. And the wind's wild howl mingled with the din, and the rain intermittently redoubled its violence and lashed the walls as though with a hail of bullets.

'It's the end of the world,' murmured Madame Chanteau. 'And where are the Cuches going to take shelter?'

'Someone'll have to put them up,' answered Prouane. 'For the time being they're at the Gonins' . . . What a sight it was! the baby, who's three, soaked to the skin, and the mother in her petticoat, showing all that she's got, saving your presence! and the father with his head half bashed in by a fallen beam trying desperately to save their few bits of rags!'

Pauline had left the table. She was standing by the window once more, listening as solemnly as an adult; her face expressed distress and compassion and her full lips were quivering with passionate sympathy.

'Oh, auntie,' she said, 'poor people!'

And she gazed out into that abyss of ever denser gloom. You could tell that the sea had reached the road now, and lay below there heaving and roaring; but you could still see no sign of it, for everything—the little village, the rocks along the coast, the entire horizon—seemed to be swallowed up in inky blackness. It was a painful surprise to the child; the water that had seemed to her so beautiful was now assaulting people!

'I'll go down with you, Prouane,' cried Lazare. 'Perhaps there's something I can do.'

But the man shook his head. 'There's no point in your bothering, Monsieur Lazare, you couldn't do any more than us chaps! We're all there watching it smash us up as long as it pleases; and when it's had enough of it, well, we'll still have to be thankful . . . I just wanted to tell Monsieur le Maire.'

Then Chanteau lost his temper, vexed at the thought that these dramatic happenings were going to spoil his night and give him a lot of trouble next day.

'After all,' he cried, 'what an idiotic place to build a village! I declare you've shoved yourselves right under the waves! It's no wonder if the sea swallows your houses one by one . . . And anyhow why d'you stay in that hole? You ought to get out!'

'But where to?' asked Prouane, who was listening with an air of stupefaction. 'We're there, sir, and we have to stay there. One's got to be somewhere!'

'That's quite true,' concluded Madame Chanteau. 'And, you know, wherever you are, there's always trouble . . . We were just going up to bed. Goodnight. We'll be able to see better to-morrow.'

The man bowed and went off, and Véronique could be heard bolting the door behind him. Then they each took up a candlestick, and Mathieu and Minouche, who slept together in the kitchen, were given a last pat. Lazare had collected his music, while Madame Chanteau clutched the old cash-book containing the bonds under her arm. She also picked up off the table Davoine's statement, which her husband had forgotten there. It broke her heart to look at that paper; there was no point in leaving it lying around.

'We're going up, Véronique,' she called out. 'Don't hang about much longer, will you?'

And as no sound but a grunt answered her from the kitchen she went on, lowering her voice: 'What's the matter with her? It's not as if I were bringing her a babe in arms.'

'Let her alone,' said Chanteau. 'You know what funny moods she gets. Well, are we all here? Goodnight then.'

His bed was on the ground floor, on the other side of the passage, in the old drawing-room which had been converted into a bedroom for him. Thus, when an attack seized him, his armchair could easily be wheeled up to the table or on to the terrace. He opened his door and stopped for a moment again, his legs numb with the creeping imminence of an attack, of which the stiffness of his joints had given him warning the day before. He'd certainly been very unwise to eat that foie gras. The knowledge distressed him dreadfully.

'Goodnight,' he repeated in a doleful voice. 'You people always sleep sound . . . Goodnight, my pretty one. Have a good rest, that's right at your age.'

'Goodnight, uncle,' Pauline replied, kissing him.

The door closed. Madame Chanteau showed the child the way up; Lazare followed them.

'Well, one thing's certain, I shan't need any lullabies to put me to sleep to-night,' declared the old lady. 'And personally, I find this noise quite soothing. I don't dislike it at all . . . In Paris I quite missed being shaken about in bed.'

They had all three reached the first floor. Pauline, carrying her candle very straight, thought it great fun to walk upstairs in procession, each holding a lighted taper that cast flickering shadows. As she paused uncertainly on the landing, not knowing where her aunt was taking her, the latter gave her a gentle push.

'Go straight ahead . . . This is a spare room, and here's my room opposite . . . Come in a moment, I want to show you.'

It was a room hung with a yellow chintz patterned with green flowers and simply furnished in mahogany; there was a bed, a wardrobe and a writing-desk. In the middle a small table stood on a red rug. When she had shone her candle into every corner Madame Chanteau went up to the desk and opened the lid.

'Come and look,' she said.

She opened one of the little drawers and in it laid, with a sigh, Davoine's disastrous statement. Then she emptied another drawer above it, pulled it out and shook out the dust, and as she prepared to shut up the bonds, she said to the watching child: 'You see, I'm putting them there, they'll be all by themselves . . . D'you want to put them away yourself?'

Pauline felt unaccountably embarrassed. She flushed.

'Oh, auntie, it doesn't matter.'

But already the old cash register was in her hands, and she had to lay it in the drawer, while Lazare held up his candle to light the inside of the desk.

'There,' went on Madame Chanteau, 'you can feel quite safe now, and you needn't fear, we'd sooner die of hunger . . . Remember, the first drawer on the left. And they'll stay there till you're big enough to take them out yourself. I don't expect Minouche will come and eat them in there!'

The notion of Minouche opening the desk and eating the papers sent the child into fits of laughter. Her momentary embarrassment had disappeared and she was playing with Lazare, who, to amuse her, had begun purring like a cat and pretending to attack the drawer. He was laughing merrily too. But his mother had solemnly closed the desk and double-locked it with an emphatic gesture.

'There we are,' she said. 'Come now, Lazare, don't play the fool. Now I'm going up to see if she's got everything she needs.'

And all three filed out on the stairs again. At the second floor Pauline, hesitating once more, had opened the left hand door, when her aunt called out:'No, no, not that side! that's your cousin's room. Yours is opposite.'

Pauline had stopped short, motionless, fascinated by the size of the room, a great loft cluttered up with jumble—a piano, a divan, a huge table, books and pictures. At last she pushed open the other door and was enchanted, although her room seemed tiny after the other. The paper was a light biscuit-colour, sprinkled with blue roses. There was an iron bed hung with muslin curtains, a dressing-table, a chest of drawers and three chairs.

'Everything's there,' murmured Madame Chanteau, 'water, sugar, towels, a piece of soap . . . And sleep in peace; Véronique's in a little room next door, so if you're frightened, knock on the wall.'

'And then I'm there too,' declared Lazare. 'When a ghost appears I come in with my big sword.'

The doors of the two rooms, facing one another, stood open. Pauline stood looking from one to the other.

'There isn't any ghost,' she said merrily. 'Swords are against burglars . . . Goodnight, auntie; goodnight, cousin.'

'Goodnight, darling . . . Can you get undressed by yourself?'

'Oh, yes, of course . . . I'm not a little girl now. In Paris I used to do everything.'

They kissed her. Madame Chanteau, as she went away, told her she might lock the door. But the child was already standing by the window, eager to discover whether it looked out on to the sea. The rain was streaming so violently down the panes that she dared not open it. Everything was black outside, and yet she felt happy at hearing the sea beating away below. Then, though almost asleep on her feet with weariness, she went round the room looking at all the furniture. The thought that she had a room of her own, a room apart from other people, where she could shut herself up like a grown-up person, made her heart swell with pride. And yet, when she had pulled off her frock and was standing in her petticoat, and was about to turn the key, she suddenly felt uneasy. How could she escape if she saw somebody? With a shudder, she threw open the door again.

There was Lazare, still standing in the middle of the room opposite; he stared at her.

'What's the matter?' he asked. 'D'you need anything?'

She blushed scarlet, tried to lie and then yielded to her compelling honesty. 'No, no . . . You see, I'm frightened when the doors are locked. So I'm not going to lock it, you understand, and if I knock, it's for you to come . . . You, mind you, and not the maid!'

He came forward, captivated by her childish candour and warmth. 'Goodnight,' he said, holding out his arms.

She flung her thin little arms eagerly round his neck, innocently oblivious of her partial nakedness.

'Goodnight, cousin!'

Five minutes later she had bravely blown out her candle and was huddling in the depths of her bed under the muslin draperies. For a long time, too weary to sleep sound, she lay in a half-dream. She heard Véronique clatter carelessly upstairs and pull the furniture about as if she wanted to wake up the whole house. Then there was nothing but the storm: the rumble of thunder, the obstinate rain lashing the slates, the wind shaking the window-panes and moaning under the doors; and for a whole hour the bombardment went on, and every wave that broke seemed to shake her with a deep, muffled shock. She felt as though the house were crushed and annihilated by its own silence and were being carried away by the water like a boat. And then a cosy warmth stole over her, her wavering thoughts reverted with willing compassion to the poor people down below, driven from their beds by the sea. Then everything sank into oblivion, and she slept in utter stillness.

CHAPTER II

WITHIN the first week, Pauline's presence brought joy into the house. Her radiant health, her good sense, her calm smile allayed the secret bitterness in which the Chanteaus had been living. The father had found a nurse, the mother was happy to see that her son stayed at home more. Véronique alone still grumbled. The 150,000 francs shut up in the desk, although they remained untouched, seemed to give the family a sense of greater wealth. A new tie had been formed, a new hope had been born in the midst of their misfortunes, although its precise nature remained unknown.

The next day but one, during the night, the attack of gout that Chanteau had anticipated broke out. For a whole week he had been aware of a tingling in his joints, a shudder running through all his limbs, an invincible aversion to take exercise. He had gone to bed feeling somewhat easier, however, when, at three in the morning, the pain started in the big toe of his left foot. It leapt to his heel and then invaded his ankle. Until daybreak he lay moaning gently, sweating under his covers, anxious not to disturb anybody. The whole family lived in dread of his attacks, and he waited till the last minute before calling for help, ashamed of falling sick again and distressed about the furious reception that his illness would get. However, as Véronique was passing by his door at about eight o'clock, he was unable to repress a cry, torn from him by a particularly violent shooting pain.

'Oh Lord, there we go,' grumbled the maid. 'He's started bawling.' She went in and watched him swaying his head about and moaning, and her only comment, by way of consolation, was: 'Well, if you think Madame's going to be pleased!"

And indeed when Madame heard about it and came in herself, she let her arms drop in a gesture of exasperated despair. 'Again!' she said. 'No sooner do I get back than it starts again!'

She harboured a fifteen-year-old resentment against his gout. She hated it as the treacherous enemy that had spoilt her life, ruined her son, killed her ambitions. But for the gout, would they have exiled themselves in this remote village? and for all her kind nature, she reacted to her husband's attacks with shuddering hostility, declaring herself too clumsy, too inefficient to look after him.

'Oh Lord, what pain!' stammered the poor man. 'This attack's going to be worse than the last, I feel it . . . Don't stop there if it upsets you, but do send for Doctor Cazenove at once.'

Then the whole house was in a state of confusion. Lazare went off to Arromanches, although the family no longer had much faith in doctors. During the past fifteen years Chanteau had tried every sort of drug; and with every new experiment, the disease grew worse. His attacks, slight and indifferent at first, had soon grown more numerous and more violent; by now both feet were affected, and indeed one knee was threatened. The sufferer had already seen the fashion in cures change three times, and his wretched body had become an experimental ground on which various advertised remedies fought it out. He had first been bled copiously, then purged ruthlessly, then stuffed with colchicum and lithia-water, and the exhaustion resulting from impoverished blood and debilitated organs had transformed his acute gout into chronic gout. Local treatment had no better results; leeches left him with stiffness of the joints, opium made his attacks last longer, blisters produced ulceration. Wiesbaden and Carlsbad had no effect at all, and a season at Vichy nearly killed him.

'Oh Lord, what pain!' Chanteau kept repeating. 'It's as if dogs were tearing at my foot."

And, anxiously restless, trying to find relief by altering his position, he moved his leg about ceaselessly. But the attack grew more violent still, and each movement made him utter a groan. Soon he broke out into a continuous scream, as his pain reached its paroxysm. He was shaking with fever and consumed by a burning thirst.

Pauline, meanwhile, had slipped into the room. She was standing before the bed, watching her uncle gravely, without tears. Madame Chanteau, exasperated by his cries, was losing her head. Véronique tried to arrange the blanket, which weighed painfully on the sufferer's limbs; he shrieked louder, forbidding her to touch him. He was terrified of her; he declared that she handled him as roughly as a bundle of dirty linen.

'Then don't send for me, monsieur,' she said furiously, walking off. 'If you're going to rebuff people you'll have to look after yourself.'

Slowly, Pauline had come up to him, and her childish fingers, with nimble skill, had lifted up the blanket; he felt a momentary relief, and accepted her help. 'Thank you, dear ... There, look, that fold. It weighs five hundred pounds! Oh, not so quick, you frightened me.'

Moreover, the pain had flared up even more fiercely. As his wife wandered about the room trying to find something to do, going to the window to draw the curtain, coming back to lay a cup on the bedside table, he burst out angrily again. 'Please stop walking about, you make everything shake. At every step you take I feel as if I were being hit with a hammer.'

She did not even attempt to apologise or fulfil his wish. It always ended like this; he was left to suffer alone.

She merely said: 'Come, Pauline, you see your uncle can't stand having us around him.'

But Pauline stayed. She moved so gently that her little feet seemed to skim over the floor. And thenceforward she took up her post by the invalid, who would have nobody else in the room. As he said, he would have liked to be nursed by a breath of air. She was quick to guess at and relieve his pain, she forestalled his wishes, she shaded the light for him or fetched him the cups of gruel-water that Véronique brought to the door. What chiefly soothed the poor man was to see her constantly before him, sitting quiet and still on the edge of her chair, never taking her great compassionate eyes from him. He tried to find a little distraction by talking about his pain.

'You see, just now, it's as though a broken knife were dislocating the bones in my foot; and at the same time I could swear I was having warm water poured over my skin.'

Then the pain changed: his ankle was being bound with wire, or his muscles were being stretched to breaking-point, like violin strings. Pauline listened sympathetically, seeming to understand it all; she stayed there quite unperturbed by his plaintive cries, intent solely on making him well. She was even merry, she managed to make him laugh between two groans.

When Dr. Cazenove arrived at last he was astonished, and kissed the top of the little nurse's head. He was a man of fifty-four, lean and vigorous, who, after thirty years' service in the Navy, had recently retired to Arromanches, where an uncle had left him a house. He had been friendly with the Chanteaus ever since curing Madame Chanteau of a troublesome sprain.

'Well, so here we are again,' he said. 'I've hurried along to say hullo to you. But you know that I can't do any more about it than this child. My dear chap, when you've inherited gout and are over fifty, you've got to put up with it. Added to which you've finished yourself off with a lot of drugs . . . You know the only remedy: patience and flannel!'

He professed to be a thorough sceptic. For thirty years he had seen so many wretches die, in all sorts of climate and in the foulest conditions, that he had become basically humble; he preferred, as a rule, to let nature take its course. However, he examined the swollen toe, with its glistening, dark red skin, went on to the knee, to which the inflammation was spreading, and observed the presence of a small, hard white bead on the rim of the right ear.

'But, doctor,' groaned the sick man, 'you can't let me suffer like this!'

34

Cazenove had grown serious again. This bead of tophaceous matter intrigued him, and in face of this fresh symptom his faith revived.

'Well,' he muttered, 'I'm willing to try out alkalines and salts. It's evidently becoming chronic.' Then he lost his temper: 'Besides, it's your own fault, you don't follow my advice . . . You never take any exercise, you're always sprawling in your chair . . . And you've had wine, I'm willing to bet, and meat, haven't you? Admit that you've been eating something rich.'

'Oh, just a little foie gras,' confessed Chanteau feebly.

The doctor threw up his hands, calling the elements to witness. However, he pulled some bottles out of his overcoat pocket and began to prepare a draught. For local treatment, he merely wrapped the foot and the knee in cotton wool, binding this down with oilcloth. And when he left, it was to Pauline that he repeated his instructions: a spoonful of the medicine every two hours, as much gruel-water as the patient wanted to drink, and above all a strict starvation diet.

'If you think we'll be able to stop him eating!' said Madame Chanteau as she showed the doctor out.

'No. no, auntie, he'll be good, you'll see," Pauline ventured to assert. 'I'll see that he obeys.'

Cazenove looked at her, amused by her thoughtful air. He kissed her again, on both cheeks.

'That little girl's born to help other people,' he declared, with the penetrating look with which he used to make his diagnoses.

For a whole week, Chanteau went on screaming. The right foot had been affected, just as the attack seemed to be finished, and the pain had flared up twice as violently. The whole household was in distress. Véronique shut herself up in her kitchen so as not to hear. Even Madame Chanteau and Lazare, in their nervous anguish, sometimes took refuge outside. Only Pauline never left the sick-room, where she had to contend with the invalid's whims when he clamoured for a chop, shouting out that he was hungry, that Dr. Cazenove was an ass since he couldn't even cure him. At night, particularly, the pain grew fiercer. She barely got two or three hours' sleep. However, she was robust, as healthy a growing child as could be wished. Madame Chanteau, greatly relieved, had ended by welcoming the child's help and the peace she restored to the house. At last convalescence came, and Pauline regained her freedom; and a close friendship sprang up between herself and Lazare.

They foregathered, at first, in Lazare's big room He had had a wall knocked down and thus taken possession of half the top floor. A small iron bed stood hidden in a far corner behind an ancient battered screen. Against a wall, on unpainted wood shelves, were ranged innumerable books, sets of the classics and odd volumes which he had discovered in a loft at Caen and brought to Bonneville. By the window stood an enormous old Norman cupboard, brimful of a jumble of extraordinary objects, mineralogical samples, old-fashioned tools, broken toys. And then there was the piano, on which lay a pair of foils and a fencing mask, not to mention the huge table in the middle of the room, an old drawing-table, very high and so cluttered up with papers, pictures, jars of tobacco and pipes, that it was difficult to find the tiniest space to write on.

Pauline, let loose in this chaos, was entranced. She spent a whole month exploring the room; and every day she made some fresh discovery—an illustrated *Robinson Crusoe* on the bookshelf, a Punchinello rescued from under the cupboard. As soon as she got up in the morning she would run to her cousin's room and settle down there; she was back there in the afternoon, she practically lived there. Lazare, from the very first day, had accepted her as though she were a boy, a small brother, nine years younger than himself but so lively and amusing, with her great intelligent eyes, that he felt completely at home with her, and would smoke his pipe, sprawl in his chair reading with his feet in the air, or write lengthy letters in which he enclosed flowers. Only this playmate of his sometimes became terribly turbulent. She would suddenly climb on to the table, or jump through the hole in his old screen. One morning, surprised at her silence, he turned round and saw her standing with the fencing mask on her face and a foil in her hand, bowing to empty space. And although at first he would shout at her to keep quiet and threaten to turn her out, the pair of them usually ended with a riotous romp, leaping about like young goats with the room in wild confusion. She would fling herself at his neck and he, like a schoolboy himself, would whirl her round like a top, with her skirts flying, while they both burst into hearty childish laughter.

Then they took up music. Lazare's piano was an old Érard, dating from 1810, on which, long ago, Mlle. Eugénie de la Vignière had for some fifteen years given lessons. Its mahogany framework had lost its polish; and within, the strings yielded a faint, plaintive sound, of muffled sweetness. Lazare, who could not persuade his mother to give him a new piano, hammered at it with all his might but could not extract from it the rich romantic sounds with which his brain was overflowing. So he used to reinforce it vocally, to try and achieve the desired effect. His enthusiasm led him to take advantage of Pauline's willingness; now that he had an audience he would spend whole afternoons going through his repertoire, which consisted of the most complicated sort of music, chiefly the as yet unrecognized work of Berlioz and Wagner. And he would bellow, making as much noise with his throat as with his fingers. On these occasions Pauline was sadly bored, but she would sit quietly listening for fear of hurting her cousin's feelings.

Sometimes dusk surprised them thus. Then Lazare, dazed with rhythmical sounds, would tell her of his great dreams. He too was going to be a musician of genius, in spite of his mother, in spite of everybody. At the *lycée* at Caen he had had a violin teacher who, struck by his musical gifts, had foretold a brilliant future for him. He had taken secret lessons in composition, and now he was working on his own, and already he had a half-formulated idea, the idea of a symphony on the Earthly Paradise; he had even composed one section, Adam and Eve driven out by the Angel, a solemn, poignant march which he consented to play to Pauline one evening. The little girl approved and praised it; then she argued with him. Of course, it must be delightful to compose fine music; but perhaps he would have been wiser to obey his parents, who wanted him to become a prefect or a judge. The whole family was distressed by this quarrel between mother and son—the latter declaring his intention of going to Paris to try for the Conservatoire, the former insisting that, by October, he must settle on some respectable career. And Pauline supported her aunt's plan and had announced, with an air of calm conviction, that she would undertake to convert her cousin. The thing became a joke, and Lazare, in a rage, slammed the piano violently, calling her a 'disgusting little bourgeoise.'

For three days they were not on speaking terms, and then they made friends again. To convert her to music, Lazare conceived the notion of teaching her to play the piano. He would set her fingers on the notes and keep her for hours playing scales up and down. But he was really shocked by her lack of fervour. She would make fun of the whole thing, and thought it a great joke to set Minouche walking along the keyboard, producing barbaric symphonies with her paws; and would vow that the cat was performing the famous Exodus from the Earthly Paradise, at which the composer himself laughed. Then the wild romps would begin again;

37

she flew at his neck and he whirled her round, while Minouche, entering into the fun, leapt from the table to the cupboard. As for Mathieu, he was not admitted, for he took his pleasures too rowdily.

'Leave me alone, you disgusting little bourgeoise,' repeated Lazare one day in exasperation. 'Mother can teach you to play the piano if she likes.'

'There's no use in your music,' declared Pauline bluntly. "If I were you I'd become a doctor.

He stared at her, profoundly shocked. A doctor indeed? Where did she get that idea? He grew wildly excited, pursuing his obsession with irresistible impetuosity.

'Listen,' he cried, 'if they stop me being a musician I shall kill myself.'

Summer had completed Chanteau's convalescence, and Pauline was free to follow Lazare outside. The big room was deserted and the two friends rushed off on wild rambles. For a few days they were content with playing about on the terrace, where grew clumps of tamarisk shrivelled by the sea winds; then they invaded the courtyard, broke the chain of the well, scared the twelve skinny hens that lived on grasshoppers, hid in the empty stable and coach-house, where the plaster was flaking off the walls; then they reached the kitchen garden, an arid plot where Véronique toiled like any peasant, four beds sown with stringy vegetables and planted with pear-trees whose branches looked like the stumps of a cripple's limbs, all bowed in the same direction as though flying before the wild north-wester; and it was from here that, pushing open a small door, they found themselves on a cliff, under the free sky, facing the open sea. Pauline had never lost her passionate curiosity about the vast expanse of water, so pure and gentle now in the bright July sunshine. She had always seen the sea from every window in the house. But she had not yet been near it, and a new life began for her when she found herself free to roam with Lazare about the beaches, so lonely and yet so full of life.

How they enjoyed those rambles! Madame Chanteau grumbled, trying to keep them at home, despite her faith in the little girl's good sense. So they never went out by the courtyard, where Véronique would have seen them; they escaped through the kitchen garden and disappeared till nightfall. They quickly tired of walks around the church, the yew-sheltered graveyard, the *curé's* four lettuce-beds; and in a week, too, they exhausted the resources of Bonneville, the thirty houses clinging to the rock, the shingle bank where the fishermen beached their boats. It was more amusing to wander far off, at low tide, beneath the cliffs, walking over fine sand, where crabs went scuttling off, jumping from rock to rock amongst the seaweed to dodge the streams of limpid water full of wriggling shrimps; and there was fishing too—mussels to be eaten raw, without bread, strange creatures to be carried home, wrapped in a corner of one's handkerchief, or such unexpected finds as a stray flounder, or a small lobster lying at the bottom of a hole. Sometimes the sea would come in and catch them unawares, and then they would play at shipwreck, taking refuge on some reef until the water deigned to retreat. They revelled in it; they would come home drenched right up to the shoulders, their hair tousled by the wind, so used to the fresh salt air that they complained of feeling stifled in the evenings when they sat round under the lamp.

But their greatest joy was bathing. The beach was too rocky to attract families from Caen and Bayeux. Whereas every year fresh huts clustered on the cliffs of Arromanches, not a single bather was ever seen at Bonneville. The pair of them had discovered a heavenly spot a mile away from the village, towards Port-en-Bessin, a tiny bay, all compact of fine golden sand, sunk deep between two rocky walls. They called it Treasure Bay, fancying that gold coins came drifting in on its lonely waves. There, they were at home; they could undress in freedom. He would turn aside, still talking, to fasten his bathing-suit; she, for a moment, would catch the neck-edge of her chemise between her teeth and then appear in a woollen garment like a boy's, clinging to her hips. In a week, he had taught her to swim: she took to it better than to piano-playing, and her daring often caused her to swallow great draughts of sea-water. Sometimes a more than usually powerful wave sent them tumbling against one another, and then they would laugh with all the ecstasy of youth, rejoicing in the tingling freshness. They would come out glistening with salt, and dry their bare arms in the wind without interrupting their wild, daring play. It was even greater fun than fishing.

The days sped by; they had come to the beginning of August, and Lazare had reached no decision. In October, Pauline was to be sent to a boarding-school at Bayeux. When, dazed with happy weariness by the sea, they lay stretched out on the sand, they would talk quite seriously about their affairs. She had ended by arousing his interest in medicine, explaining that if she were a man, she could think of nothing more exciting than to cure people. It so happened that, during the past week, the Earthly Paradise had

39

been going badly, and he had begun to doubt his own genius. After all, there had been famous doctors—the great names recurred to him, Hippocrates, Ambroise Paré and so many more. But one afternoon, he uttered shouts of joy; he'd got his masterpiece; the Paradise idea was silly, he would drop all that and write the Symphony of Sorrow, in which he would set down with sublime harmonies the lamentation of mankind, sobbing desperately under the heavens; and he brought in his March of Adam and Eve, boldly turning it into a March of Death. For a week or so his enthusiasm grew hourly; he summed up the universe in his plan. Another week passed, and then one evening, to her great surprise, Pauline heard him remark that he would like to go to Paris after all to study medicine. He had realised that this would bring him nearer to the Conservatoire; the thing was to get there first, and then he'd see. Madame Chanteau was overjoyed. She would rather have seen her son become an administrator or a magistrate, but doctors were, at any rate, respectable people and earned plenty of money.

'You must be a good fairy,' she said, kissing Pauline. 'Oh, darling, how you've rewarded us for bringing you to live with us!'

Everything was settled. Lazare was to leave on the first of October. So, in September, the two friends resumed their rambles with even greater zest, anxious to bring their splendid life of freedom to a fitting close. Till nightfall they loitered, carefree, on the sands of Treasure Bay.

One evening, they were lying side by side, watching the stars appear like beads of fire in the fading sky. Pauline gazed gravely, with the tranquil wonder of a healthy child. Lazare was over-excited now that his departure was near; his eyelids fluttered nervously, as the fitful impulses of his will carried his mind cease-lessly towards fresh goals.

'The stars are lovely,' she said solemnly, after a long silence.

He let the silence fall again. His joy had lost its brightness, an inward anxiety clouded his wide-open eyes. In the sky, the stars swarmed thicker every minute, like glowing embers cast in spadefuls across infinite space.

'You haven't learnt about it yet," he murmured at last. 'Every star is a sun, around which things like our earth go spinning; and there are thousands of them, more of them behind these, still more, for ever!' He paused, and then went on, with a great shudder choking his voice: 'I don't like looking at them... They frighten me.'

From the incoming sea there rose a distant sound of lamentation, like the desperate cry of a human crowd bewailing its misery.

40

Against the vast horizon, now densely black, glittered the flying dust that was made up of worlds. And, while the earth seemed to moan under the crushing burden of those infinitely numerous stars, the child caught a sound of sobbing by her side.

'What's the matter? Aren't you well?'

He did not answer; he lay there sobbing, hiding his face behind violently clenched hands as though to stop himself seeing. When he was able to speak he stammered out: 'Oh, death! death!'

The strange scene was to haunt Pauline's memory.

Lazare at last rose wearily, and they walked back to Bonneville in the darkness, with waves washing round their feet; they could find nothing more to say to one another. She watched him walking ahead of her, and he seemed to have dwindled in height, as he bent before the wind that blew from the west.

That evening they found a newcomer awaiting them in the dining-room, chatting to the Chanteaus. For the past week the family had been expecting a visit from Louise, a child of eleven and a half, who used to spend a fortnight every year at Bonneville. There had been two fruitless journeys to Arromanches; and now she had turned up suddenly one evening when they had forgotten about her. Louise's mother had died in the arms of Madame Chanteau, commending the child to her care. The father, M. Thibaudier, a banker at Caen, had remarried six months later and by now had three children already. Preoccupied by his new family, obsessed by his calculations, he used to leave the little girl at boarding-school and was always glad to get rid of her in the holidays, when he could send her away to friends. He seldom troubled to come himself; and this time, Mademoiselle had been brought by a servant, after a week's delay. Monsieur had such a lot of worries! And the servant had gone away immediately, saying that Monsieur would try his utmost to come himself and fetch Mademoiselle.

'Hurry up, Lazare,' cried Chanteau, 'here she is!'

Louise, smiling, kissed the young man on both cheeks. They hardly knew one another, actually, for she was always immured in her boarding-school and he had barely left the *lycée* a year ago. Their acquaintance dated only from last holidays; and indeed then he had treated her with a certain formality, sensing her precocious coquetry, her contempt for rowdy childish games.

'Well, Pauline, aren't you going to kiss her?' said Madame Chanteau as she came in. 'She's a year and a half older than you are . . . I'd like you two to be friends.'

41

Pauline looked at Louise, who was slim and graceful, with irregular but very charming features and beautiful fair hair, twined and curled like a grown-up lady's. When she saw her embrace Lazare she turned pale. And when Louise gave her a cheerful kiss, she returned it with trembling lips.

'What's the matter?' asked her aunt. 'Are you cold?'

'Yes, a bit, the wind was cool,' she answered, blushing for her lie.

At supper, she ate nothing. Her eyes were fixed on the others and gleamed with a fiercer black whenever her cousin, her uncle or even Véronique paid attention to Louise. But what distressed her most was to see Mathieu, at dessert, go round the table as usual and then lay his big head on the stranger's knee. In vain she called him, he would not leave Louise, who was cramming him with lumps of sugar.

When they left the table Pauline disappeared, and Véronique, who was clearing up, presently came back from the kitchen saying with an air of triumph: 'Well, well, Madame, that precious Pauline of yours who's so kind! just go and see in the yard.'

They all went. Hidden behind the coach-house, the child was holding Mathieu with his back against the wall and, beside herself with fury, in a wild frenzy, she was hitting him on the head with all the force of her little fists. The dog, dazed, submitted without defending himself. They rushed forward, but she went on hitting, and they had to carry her off half-conscious, her limbs rigid, so ill that she was put straight to bed and her aunt had to spend half the night beside her.

'Oh, she's sweet, she's very sweet,' repeated Véronique, delighted at having at last found a flaw in this pearl of perfection.

'I remember being told in Paris about her tempers,' said Madame Chanteau. 'She's jealous; that's a horrid fault . . . During the six months she's been here I had noticed a few little incidents, but really this is the limit—to try and massacre a dog!'

Next day, when Pauline met Mathieu, she clutched him in her trembling arms, kissing him on the nose with such a flood of tears that a fresh fit of hysteria seemed imminent. And yet she could not correct her fault, it was as though some inner impulse drove all the blood in her veins up to her brain. It seemed that besides the admirable stability that she inherited from her mother and from her father, of whom she was a living image, she got from some distant ancestor on her mother's side these fits of jealous passion. As she was very sensible for a child of ten, she would explain that she tried her utmost to fight against these tempers, but that she

42

could not conquer them. They left her saddened, like an illness of which one is ashamed.

'I love you so much, why do you love somebody else?' she kept replying, hiding her head against her aunt's shoulder, when the latter lectured her in her bedroom.

And so, despite her efforts, Pauline suffered very much from the presence of Louise. Since first hearing of the expected visitor she had awaited her with anxious curiosity, and now she was counting the days, eagerly impatient for her to depart. Louise, for that matter, attracted her, with her elegance, her adult knowledgeable ways, and the winning graces of a child who has had little affection shown her at home; but when Lazare was present, it was precisely that precocious charm, that suggestion of something unknown, that disturbed and irritated Pauline. The young man, however, treated Pauline as his favourite; he made fun of the other girl, saying that she annoyed him with her airs and graces, and suggested leaving her alone to play the fine lady and going off to enjoy themselves freely. But their energetic games were set aside, and they stayed indoors looking at pictures or walked sedately on the beach. It was a fortnight absolutely wasted.

One morning, Lazare announced that he was going to leave five days earlier than he had planned. He wanted to get settled in Paris, where he was going to meet one of his old schoolfriends from Caen. And Pauline, who had been miserable for the past month at the thought of her cousin's departure, supported his decision enthusiastically and, with busy delight, helped her aunt to pack his trunk. Then, when Malivoire's old coach had carried off Lazare, she ran to shut herself up in her room and wept there for a long time. That evening she was very sweet to Louise; and the last week the latter spent at Bonneville passed pleasantly. When her father's servant came to fetch her, explaining that Monsieur had been unable to leave his bank, the two little friends threw themselves into each other's arms and swore eternal affection.

Then, slowly, a year went by. Madame Chanteau had changed her mind: instead of sending Pauline to boarding-school she kept her at home, chiefly influenced by the lamentations of Chanteau, who could not do without the child; she did not, however, admit to herself this selfish motive, but spoke of seeing to Pauline's education herself—the thought of taking up teaching again quite rejuvenated her. At school, little girls hear all sorts of horrid things; she wanted to be able to vouch for her pupil's perfect innocence. From the depths of Lazare's bookcase they retrieved a Grammar, an Arithmetic, a treatise on History and even a Summary of Mythology; and Madame Chanteau took up her ferrule once more, giving a single daily lesson, with dictations, sums and recitations. Lazare's big room was turned into a study. Pauline had to start the piano again, not to mention deportment, the principles of which were taught her very strictly by her aunt in order to correct her tomboyish ways. She was, moreover, docile and intelligent, and worked with a will even when she found the subject irksome. Only one book bored her—the Catechism. She could not understand why her aunt troubled to take her to mass on Sundays. What was the point? In Paris, she had never been taken to St. Eustache, although the church was quite near her home. She found it hard to grasp abstract ideas, so her aunt had to explain that, in the country, a well-brought-up young lady was bound to show a good example by being polite to the *curé*. Madame Chanteau herself had never been more than conventionally pious; it formed part of a good education, just like deportment.

Meanwhile, however, the sea besieged Bonneville twice a day with its endlessly rocking swell, and Pauline grew up with that immense horizon constantly before her eyes. Having lost her companion, she had given up her games. When she had galloped round the terrace with Mathieu, and walked about the kitchen garden with Minouche on her shoulder, her only form of pleasure was to watch the sea, so perpetually alive, whether livid in the dark days of December or delicately green with shimmering lights like watered silk in the early May sunshine. The year, moreover, was a fortunate one; as a further token of good luck that Pauline's presence seemed to have brought into the house, the Chanteaus received an unexpected payment of five thousand francs from Davoine, who was anxious to avoid the breaking-up of their partnership with which they had threatened him. The aunt used to go most scrupulously to Caen every quarter to collect Pauline's income; she would deduct her own expenses and the maintenance allowance fixed by the family council, and then buy fresh securities with the rest; and when she came home, she insisted on taking the child up to her bedroom and, opening the famous drawer in her desk, repeated: 'You see, I'm putting it on top of the others . . . The pile's growing bigger, eh? You needn't worry, you'll find it all there, without a centime missing.'

In August, Lazare turned up one fine morning with the news that he had passed his first year's examination with complete success. He had not been expected till a week later, but had wanted to give his mother a surprise. Everyone was overjoyed. In his fortnightly letters he had shown a growing passion for his medical studies. Now that he was home, he appeared to them to have completely altered, for he had given up talking about music and now wearied them with endless stories about his lecturers and scientific dissertations on every subject, from the dishes served at table to the winds that blew. He was possessed by a new fever, he had given himself up, wholeheartedly and fervently, to the idea of becoming a doctor of world-shaking genius.

Pauline, in particular, after flinging her arms round his neck with the unashamed demonstrativeness of a child, was puzzled by the change in him. It almost distressed her that he no longer talked about music, even a little, by way of recreation. Could one really stop loving something, when one had loved it very much? When she asked him about his symphony he began to joke about it, saying that all that nonsense was over and done with; and she felt quite sad. Then, she noticed that he seemed embarrassed in her presence and laughed unpleasantly, showing in his looks and gestures the reflection of a ten months' existence of which you couldn't talk to little girls. He had emptied his trunk himself, to hide his books— novels and illustrated scientific textbooks. He no longer whirled her about like a top with her skirts flying, and he sometimes seemed put out when she insisted on going into his room and settling down there. And yet she had not grown much bigger, and she still looked him in the eyes with her pure, innocent gaze; and after a week they were back on the old footing of boyish camaraderie. The rough sea breezes blew away the taint of the Latin Quarter, and he became childish again in the company of this child with her robust health and her ringing laughter. Everything was resumed, everything began again—the games round the big table, the races with Mathieu and Minouche down the kitchen garden, the excursions to Treasure Bay and the innocent joy of bathing in the sunshine, with shirts flapping noisily round their legs like flags. As it happened Louise, who had visited Bonneville in May, had gone to spend the summer holidays near Rouen with other friends. Two heavenly months went by, and never a cross word spoilt their friendship.

In October, the day Lazare packed his trunk, Pauline watched him piling up the books he had brought, which had stayed shut up in the cupboard without his even thinking of opening one of them.

'Are you taking them back?' she asked in great disappointment.

'Of course,' he answered. 'I need them for my work . . . Oh, by Jove, how I'm going to work! I've got to overcome all obstacles.'

45

The little house at Bonneville resumed a lifeless peace; the un-varying days went by, bringing the old daily habits, against the background of the sea's eternal rhythm. But that year there was one outstanding event in Pauline's life; in June, she made her first Communion, at the age of twelve and a half. By slow degrees, religion had taken a hold on her, a thoughtful sort of religion, superior to that contained in the answers to her catechism, which she always recited without understanding. In her rational young mind she had evolved the concept of God as a very powerful, very wise master, who controlled all things, so that everything should happen on earth in conformity with justice; and this simplified notion enabled her to get on with Abbé Horteur. The priest was of peasant stock, a dull-witted fellow who understood only the letter of religion, and who was now satisfied with a regular and seemly piety, duly observant of outward form. He looked after his own salvation; as for his parishioners, it was their own look-out if they were damned! For fifteen years he had tried to frighten them without success; he now expected nothing more from them than that they should have the good manners to go to church on impor-tant festival-days. The whole of Bonneville went, through force of habit, in spite of its habital state of sin. The priest's indifference to others' salvation took the place of tolerance. He came every Saturday to play draughts with Chanteau, although the mayor, thanks to the excuse of his gout, never set foot in the church. Madame Chanteau, for that matter, did what was necessary, by regularly attending service and taking Pauline with her. It was the *curé's* great simplicity which gradually won the child's heart. In Paris, she was used to hearing priests spoken of with contempt as hypocrites who concealed all kinds of vice under their black robes. But here, beside the sea, this priest seemed to her a genuinely good man with his heavy shoes, his sunburnt neck, and the look and speech of a poor farmer. One thing that she had noticed appealed to her particularly. Abbé Horteur was passionately addicted to a thick meerschaum pipe, yet he had scruples about it and would take refuge at the bottom of his garden to smoke in solitude among his lettuces; and the way he hid his pipe, in great embarrassment, when anybody happened to surprise him, touched the child deeply, she could not tell why. She took her communion with an air of great solemnity in company with two other small girls and a village lad. That evening, as the *curé* was dining with the Chanteaus, he declared that he had never yet had at Bonneville such a well-behaved communicant.

Things went less well this year; the rise in the price of firwood which Davoine had been expecting for so long did not take place; and bad news came from Caen—they heard that Davoine had been forced to sell at a loss and was heading for disaster. The family had to live frugally, the three thousand francs income only just sufficed for the barest household necessities, while expenses had to be cut down on all supplies. Madame Chanteau was chiefly worried about Lazare, from whom she received letters that she kept to herself. He appeared to be leading a dissipated life, and harried her with continual demands for money. In July, when she went to collect Pauline's dividends, she made a sudden descent on Davoine; two thousand francs which she had already had from him had passed into Lazare's hands; and she succeeded in extracting a further thousand, which she promptly sent to Paris. Lazare had written to her that he would not be able to come home unless his debts were paid.

They waited a whole week for him. Every morning a letter came postponing his departure till the next day. His mother and Pauline went as far as Verchemont to meet him. They embraced one another by the roadside and walked home in the dust, followed by the empty carriage carrying the trunk. But this homecoming was less cheerful than the previous year's triumphal entry. Lazare had failed in his July examination; he was full of bitter resentment against his teachers and inveighed against them the whole evening, calling them a set of asses with whom he was thoroughly fed up. Next day, in Pauline's presence, he threw his books down on a shelf in the cupboard, declaring that they could rot there. This sudden revulsion appalled her, as she listened to him jeering at medicine, defying it to cure so much as a cold in the head; and when, one day, in a burst of youthful zeal, she took up the cudgels in defence of science, his taunts at her ignorant enthusiasm made her blush scarlet. However, he was still resigned to becoming a doctor; that farce was as good as another; nothing was any good really. She grew indignant at these new ideas he had brought back. Where had he found them? In bad books, no doubt, but she dared no longer argue, embarrassed by her utter ignorance and uneasy when her cousin asserted with a sneer that there were some things he could not tell her. He baited her thus during the whole of the holidays. Now, when they went for walks, he seemed to be bored; he declared the sea was tedious and monotonous; yet he had begun writing verse to kill time, and he composed elaborate, richly-rhymed sonnets about the sea. He refused to bathe, having discovered that cold water was bad for his constitution; for, despite his denunciation of medicine, he would express dogmatic opinions, allotting life or death to people with a word. Towards the middle of September, just as Louise was expected to arrive, he suddenly spoke of returning to Paris, on the pretext that he had to prepare for his examination; these two little girls would bore him stiff, he might as well resume his Latin Quarter life a month earlier. Pauline had become gentler, the more he hurt her feelings. When he treated her brusquely, when he seemed to delight in distressing her, she would look at him with the tender, merry gaze with which she used to calm Chanteau when he was howling with anguish in one of his attacks. In her opinion, her cousin must be ill; he looked at life with an old man's eyes.

On the eve of his departure Lazare displayed such delight at leaving Bonneville that Pauline began to sob. 'You don't love me any more!'

'Silly fool! haven't I got to make my way? A big girl like you snivelling!'

Now she was brave again; she smiled at him. 'Mind you work hard this year, and come back pleased with yourself!'

'Oh, there's no point in working hard. The exam's too idiotic; if I failed, it was because I didn't bother to try . . . I'll get through it, because I'm not rich enough to be able to live with my arms folded, the only sensible thing for a man to do.'

At the beginning of October, when Louise had gone back to Caen, Pauline resumed her lessons with her aunt. The third year's course was devoted chiefly to the study of French history, in an expurgated version, and of mythology as adapted for young ladies, a branch of higher education intended to enable them to understand the paintings in museums. But the child who last year had been so studious seemed heavy-headed now; she sometimes fell asleep over her exercises, and sudden flushes reddened her face. A wild fit of temper against Véronique, who didn't love her, so she said, prostrated her for three days. And then disturbing changes were taking place in her—a slow development of her whole body, swelling curves that felt congested and painful, and a light down like a black shadow in the most secret and delicate parts of her skin. When she looked at herself furtively, in the evenings, before going to bed, she felt a kind of uneasy distress that made her quickly blow out her candle. Her voice took on a deeper tone that she disliked; she hated herself like this, and spent her days in a kind

48

of nervous expectation, hoping for she knew not what, and not daring to speak of these things to anyone.

At last, towards Christmas, Pauline's condition began to worry Madame Chanteau. She complained of sharp pains in the small of the back, she ached all over, she had bouts of feverishness. When Dr. Cazenove, who had become a great friend of hers, had questioned her, he took the aunt to one side and advised her to warn her niece. The tide of puberty was rising; and he said he had known young girls fall ill with terror at the sudden onset of that flow of blood. The aunt protested at first; the precaution seemed to her unnecessary, and she shrank from such intimate talks. Her system of education was complete ignorance, the avoidance of awkward facts so long as they did not obtrude themselves. However, as the doctor insisted, she promised to speak about it; she omitted to do so that evening, and then put it off from day to day. The child was not timid, and after all plenty of other girls had not been warned. It would be time enough to tell her when it happened, that that was the way things were, without exposing oneself beforehand to questions and explanations that might be improper.

One morning Madame Chanteau was just leaving her room when she heard cries from Pauline's, and she hurried upstairs in great anxiety. The girl was sitting up in bed, with her covers thrown back, white with terror, and screaming continuously for her aunt; her bare, parted legs were stained with blood, and she was staring at what had come out of her, all her habitual courage driven away by the shock.

'Oh, auntie, auntie!'

Madame Chanteau, at a glance, had understood. 'It's nothing, darling. Don't worry.'

But Pauline, still staring at herself, sitting as stiffly as though she had been wounded, did not even hear the words. 'Oh, auntie, I felt something wet, and look, look, it's blood! It's all up with me; the sheets are full of it.'

Her voice grew faint, she thought that all the blood in her veins was pouring out in this red stream. Her cousin's cry sprang to her lips, that desperate cry of terror at the sight of the limitless heavens which she had failed to understand. 'It's all up, I'm going to die.'

Her aunt, bewildered, was trying to find some inoffensive explanation, some lie which would calm her without telling her anything.

'Come now, dear, don't upset yourself. I should be more anxious, shouldn't I, if you were in any danger? . . . I give you my word, it happens to all women. It's just like nose-bleeding . . .'

49

'No, no, you're saying that to quieten me ... I'm going to die, I'm going to die.'

It was too late. When Dr. Cazenove came he was afraid of brain-fever. Madame Chanteau had put the girl back to bed, trying to make her feel ashamed of her terror. Some days passed, and Pauline's crisis was over, but it had left her wondering, brooding over new and puzzling things, with one question lurking at the back of her mind to which she sought the answer.

Next week Pauline started work again, and appeared to take a passionate interest in mythology. She would not leave Lazare's big room which still served her as a schoolroom; she had to be called down to meals, and appeared in a daze, numb with her long immobility. But upstairs, the book on mythology lay unread at the end of the table, and it was over the medical textbooks that Lazare had left in the cupboard that she spent whole days, wide-eyed with the urge to learn, clasping her forehead between hands that had grown ice-cold with the intensity of her concentration. Lazare, in the days of his fine fervour, had bought books which were of no immediate use to him, Longuet's *Treatise on Physiology*, Cuveilher's *Descriptive Anatomy*; and these had remained behind, while he took away his work books. She would pull them out as soon as her aunt's back was turned and then put them back at the slightest noise, deliberately, not like someone impelled by guilty curiosity but like a serious student crossed in her vocation by her family. At first she did not understand; the technical terms discouraged her, and she had to look them up in the dictionary. Afterwards, feeling the need for method, she had pored assiduously over the *Descriptive Anatomy* before going on to the *Treatise on Physiology*. Then this child of fourteen learnt, as in a schoolroom lesson, things that are hidden from virgins until their wedding night. She turned over the illustrations to the *Anatomy*, those splendid, vividly real engravings, she paused over each of the human organs, exploring the most secret of them, those which had been made to seem shameful to man and woman; and she felt no shame, she was serious, passing from the organs that give life to those that regulate life, carried away and protected from carnal thoughts by her healthy-mindedness. The gradual discovery of the human mechanism filled her with admiration. She read it all with passion; she had never felt her mind enlarged so, in the old days, by fairy tales nor by *Robinson Crusoe*. Next, the *Treatise on Physiology* served as a commentary to these illustrations; nothing remained hidden from her. She even found a manual of pathology and clinical medicine;

50

she explored the most dreadful illnesses, she studied the treatment of all sorts of disorder. Many things were beyond her, but she had the prescience of what would have to be known in order to relieve suffering. Her heart ached with pity, and the old dream revived in her of learning all things in order to cure all things.

And Pauline knew, now, why that red stream, the sign of her puberty, had poured from her as from a ripe grape crushed at the vine-harvest. Her enlightenment set her pondering gravely, in the midst of that full tide of life that she felt surging within her. She was puzzled and resentful of her aunt's silence, at the complete ignorance in which the latter tried to keep her. Why should she have been left to suffer such terror? It was unfair, for there was no harm in knowing.

Moreover, nothing happened again for two months. Madame Chanteau said one day: 'If you should notice anything again, you know, like last December, don't be alarmed, will you? There's nothing to worry about.'

'Yes, I know,' the girl replied calmly.

Her aunt stared at her in alarm.

'What d'you know?'

Then Pauline blushed at the thought of having to lie to hide the fact that she had read those books. She hated lying; she preferred to make a clean breast of it. When Madame Chanteau, opening the books on the table, caught sight of the illustrations, she was appalled. After all the trouble she'd taken to expurgate Jupiter's love affairs! Really, Lazare ought to have locked up such horrors. And she subjected the culprit to a lengthy guarded cross-examination full of indirect allusions. But Pauline's ingenuous air completed her aunt's discomfiture. Well, and what then? That's how people were made, and there was nothing wrong about it. Her excitement was purely intellectual; there was no precocious gleam of secret sensuality in her large, clear childish eyes. On the same shelf she had found some novels, which she had rejected with disgust after the first few pages, so boring did they seem to her, stuffed with incomprehensible expressions. Her aunt, increasingly disconcerted and yet somewhat relieved, merely locked the cupboard and kept the key. A week later, the key was left lying about again, and Pauline allowed herself, from time to time, by way of recreation, to read the chapter on neuroses with her cousin in mind, or the treatment of gout with a view of relieving her uncle's sufferings.

In any case, despite Madame Chanteau's strictness, nobody bothered much about propriety in Pauline's presence. She could have learnt from the few animals in the house, if she had never opened a book. Minouche in particular interested her. Four times a year, the rakish creature would go on a wild spree. She who was normally so fastidious, constantly preening herself, so scared of getting dirty that she never set a paw outside without a shudder, would vanish for two or three days at a time. She could be heard cursing and fighting, and the eyes of all the toms in Bonneville could be seen gleaming in the dark like candles. Then she would come home in a shocking state, all bedraggled, her fur so torn and dirty that she had to spend a whole week licking herself clean. After that she would resume her supercilious airs, rubbing herself against people's faces without seeming to notice that her belly was growing rounder. And one fine morning, she would be found with a litter of kittens. Véronique used to carry them all off in a corner of her apron to drown them. And Minouche, a shocking mother, did not even miss them; she was used to being rid of them in this fashion, and thought that she had fulfilled all her maternal duties. She would go on licking herself, purring, giving herself airs, until one evening she went off again shamelessly to collect a fresh bellyful, to the accompaniment of mewing and scratching. Mathieu was a far better father to these children that were not his own, for he would walk whining after Véronique's apron; he loved licking helpless little creatures clean.

'Oh, auntie, do let's leave her one this time,' Pauline would say on each occasion, shocked and delighted by the cat's amorous airs and graces. But Véronique snapped: 'No, indeed! she'd only drag it about all over the place. And besides she doesn't care about them; she has all the fun and none of the bother.'

Pauline's love of life grew and brimmed over daily, making her, as her aunt said, 'a mother to all creatures.' She responded with active affection to all living and suffering things, lavishing care and caresses on them. She had forgotten Paris; she felt as though she had always grown here, on this rugged ground, with the clean sea-breeze blowing on her. In less than a year, the child with her immature figure had become a strapping girl, sturdy-hipped and broad-chested. And the troubles that had accompanied this development vanished—the discomfort of her exuberantly-ripening body, the anxious embarrassment of her swelling bosom and that downy blackness on the dusky satin of her skin. Now, on the contrary, she rejoiced to feel herself blossoming out, growing and maturing triumphantly in the sun. She was proud of the rising tide of blood that broke in red rain. From morning to night she filled the house with song, delighting in the deeper tones of her voice. And at bed-time, when she glanced from the budding roundness of her breasts to the dark shadow like an ink-blot lying on her rosy belly, she would smile and, for a moment, happily breathe in her own unfamiliar feminine smell, as though it were a bunch of flowers. She accepted life, she loved it in all its functions, without disgust or fear, and hailed it with a paean of radiant health.

Lazare, that year, wrote no letters for six months; only a few brief notes to reassure his family. Then he overwhelmed his mother with a rapid succession of letters. He had failed again in his November examinations, he was increasingly repelled by his medical studies, which dealt with such depressing things, and he had now thrown himself into a new craze—chemistry. He had by chance made the acquaintance of the illustrious Herbelin, whose discoveries were then revolutionising science, and had entered his laboratory as an assistant, without, however, admitting that he was giving up medicine. But soon his letters were full of a new project, described at first tentatively, then with growing enthusiasm. It was a scheme for the large-scale utilization of seaweed, which was to bring in millions, thanks to the new methods and reagents discovered by the great Herbelin. Lazare enumerated the chances of success: the help promised by the great chemist, the ease with which the raw material could be procured, the low cost of equipment. Finally, he declared categorically that he did not want to become a doctor, adding as a joke that he would rather sell remedies to sick people than kill them himself. Each of his letters ended with the argument about making a rapid fortune, and he added as a further bait to his family the promise to stay at home with them and set up the factory in the neighbourhood of Bonneville.

Months passed. Lazare had not come home for the holidays. All winter, he set forth his project in close-written pages which Madame Chanteau used to read aloud in the evenings, after supper. One night in May a grand council was held, for he was asking for a definite answer. Véronique prowled around, taking off the table-cloth and laying down the red cover.

'He's the spitten image of his grandfather, an enterprising muddle-head,' declared the mother, with a glance at the sometime carpenter's masterpiece, the presence of which on the mantelpiece never ceased to annoy her.

'Certainly he doesn't get it from me, for I loathe changes,' murmured Chanteau between a couple of groans; he was lying back in his armchair, suffering from one of his attacks, which was drawing to a close. 'But you're not a very peaceful person either, my dear.'

She shrugged her shoulders, as if to say that in her case activity was maintained and directed by logic. Then she continued slowly:

'Well, there's nothing for it but to write and tell him to do as he wishes . . . I'd hoped he'd become a magistrate; I never thought medicine was very nice; and now he's going to be an apothecary . . . Well, he'd better come back and make a lot of money, that'll always be something.'

At bottom, it was the thought of the money that decided her. She embarked on a new day-dream for her beloved son; she imagined him very rich, proprietor of a firm in Caen, town councillor, deputy maybe. Chanteau had no opinions; he merely put up with things, leaving his wife the superior responsibility for the family interests. As for Pauline, in spite of her surprise and her tacit disapproval of her cousin's continual change of plans, she felt that he should be allowed to come home and try his great scheme.

'At least we'd all be living together,' she said.

'And then, for what good Monsieur Lazare's been doing himself in Paris!' Véronique made bold to add. 'He'd better come home and look after his inside a bit.'

Madame Chanteau nodded. She picked up once more the letter she had received that morning. 'Wait, now he deals with the financial side of the scheme.'

Then she read it, making comments. Some sixty thousand francs would be needed to set up the little factory. In Paris, Lazare had met one of his old schoolfellows from Caen, fat Boutigny, who had dropped Latin in the fourth form and was now a dealer in wines. Boutigny was enthusiastic about the plan and offered thirty thousand francs; he would make an excellent partner, and his practical administrative gifts would ensure material success. There remained thirty thousand francs to be borrowed, for Lazare wanted to keep control of half the property himself.

'As you've heard,' went on Madame Chanteau, 'he asks me to approach Thibaudier on his behalf. It's a good idea, Thibaudier will lend him the money right away . . . As it happens, Louise hasn't been well, and I was planning to fetch her to spend a week here, so that I shall have an opportunity to talk to her father.'

Anxiety clouded Pauline's eyes, and her lips tightened convulsively. On the opposite side of the table, Véronique stood wiping a tea-cup and watching her.

'I *had* thought of something else,' the aunt murmured, 'but as there are always risks to be run in industry I'd even vowed to myself I wouldn't mention it,' then, turning towards the girl: 'Yes, darling, it was that you should lend your cousin the thirty thousand francs yourself . . . You couldn't make a better investment, your money might perhaps bring you in twenty-five per cent, for your cousin would let you share his profits; and it would break my heart to see all that fortune going into somebody else's pocket . . . Only I don't want you to run any risk with your money. It's a sacred trust, it's up there and I shall give it back to you intact."

Pauline was listening, her face whiter, torn by inward conflict. She had inherited a streak of avarice from her parents, Quenu and Lisa, with their love for the cash piling up on the counter, and her whole early education in the *charcuterie* had taught her to respect money and to dread going short of it; and an unknown, shameful feeling, a secret meanness stirred in the depths of her kind heart. Besides, her aunt had so often showed her the drawer in the desk where her inheritance lay, that the thought of seeing it melt away in her cousin's careless hands almost irritated her. And she kept silent, tortured, furthermore, by the vision of Louise bringing the young man a great bag of silver.

'Even if you wanted to, I wouldn't let you,' went on Madame Chanteau. 'It's a matter of conscience, isn't it, dear?'

'Her money's her money,' answered Chanteau, and he let out a scream as he tried to raise his leg. 'If things turned out badly everybody'd blame us. No, no, Thibaudier will be delighted to lend it.'

But Pauline, in a sudden burst of feeling, found her voice again.

'Oh, don't distress me by doing that—let me lend Lazare the money. Isn't he my own brother? It would be too horrid if I refused him the money. Why did you ask me? Give it him, auntie, give it him all!'

The effort she had just made filled her eyes with tears; and she was smiling, ashamed of having hesitated, yet still tormented by a regret that caused her deep distress. Moreover, she had to argue with her uncle and aunt, who persisted in anticipating the disadvantages of the undertaking. On this occasion they behaved with perfect uprightness.

'Come and kiss me then,' said her aunt finally, with tears in her eyes. 'You're a good kind little girl. Lazare shall take your money, since you insist on it.'

'And aren't you going to kiss me too?' asked her uncle.

Kisses were given and tears shed all round the table. Then, while Véronique was serving tea and Pauline had gone to call Mathieu, who was barking in the courtyard, Madame Chanteau added, wiping her eyes: 'It's a great comfort, she's got a kind heart.'

'Why, to be sure,' the maid muttered, 'she'd give the shirt off her body to stop the other one giving anything.'

It was a week later, on a Saturday, that Lazare came back to Bonneville. Dr. Cazenove, who had been invited to dinner, was to bring the young man in his gig. Abbé Horteur, the other guest, had arrived first, and was playing draughts with Chanteau, who lay in his convalescent's chair. The attack had lasted three months, and he had never before suffered so acutely; now it seemed like heaven, in spite of the terrible irritation in his feet; the skin was flaking off, the oedema had almost disappeared. As Véronique was roasting pigeons, he raised his nose to sniff each time the kitchen door opened, in a fresh access of his incorrigible greed; and this called forth a sagacious remonstrance from the *curé*.

'You've not got your mind on the game, Monsieur Chanteau . . . Believe me, you ought to control yourself at supper this evening. Good fare's no good to you, in your state.'

Louise had arrived the day before. When Pauline heard the doctor's gig, they both rushed down into the courtyard. But Lazare had eyes only for his cousin, saying in amazement: 'Goodness, is that Pauline?'

'Yes, it's me.'

'Well, well, what have you been eating to grow like that? You'll be getting married next!'

She blushed, laughing joyfully, her eyes aglow with happiness at his scrutiny. He had left behind a scrap of a girl, a schoolchild in a holland overall, and now he had before him a tall young girl in a spring dress of white sprigged with pink flowers, prettily moulding her bosom and hips. And then she became grave once more, as she looked at him in turn, and thought that he had grown older, more bowed; he had lost his youthful laugh, and a slight nervous twitch ran over his face.

'Come now,' he went on, 'we shall have to take you seriously . . . Good evening, partner!'

Pauline blushed even redder; the word filled her with bliss. Her cousin, once he had kissed her, might kiss Louise; she was not jealous.

Dinner was delightful. Chanteau, scared by the doctor's threats, ate without excess. Madame Chanteau and the priest made wonderful plans for enlarging Bonneville when the seaweed scheme should have enriched the countryside. They did not go to bed till eleven o'clock.

Upstairs, as Lazare and Pauline were parting at their respective doors, the young man said light-heartedly: 'And now we're so big I suppose we aren't going to say goodnight?"

'Of course we are!' she cried, flinging her arms round his neck and kissing him full on the mouth, with her old tomboyish impetuousness.

CHAPTER III

Two days later, the tide withdrew so far that the deeper rocks were exposed. Lazare, in that burst of enthusiasm that seized him at the beginning of every new enterprise, refused to wait any longer; he set off barelegged, merely throwing on a linen jacket over his bathing-suit. Pauline went with him to investigate; she too wore a bathing-suit, and the heavy shoes that she kept for shrimping expeditions.

When they had walked out almost a mile from the cliffs, and were standing in the middle of the great expanse of seaweed, still streaming from the ebbing waters, the young man's excitement broke out as though he had only just discovered this marine harvest through which they had so often wandered together.

'Look, look!' he cried, 'what a store! And nobody makes use of it, and there's plenty more down to a depth of a hundred metres!'

Then he pointed out to her the different species, with humorous pedantry, zostera, delicately green like fine hair, stretching away to infinity in a succession of vast lawns, ulvae, with their broad, thin, lettuce-like leaves, glaucous and yet transparent, serrated fucus and bladder-wrack, both in such vast quantities that they clothed the rocks like moss. And as the pair walked on after the retreating tide they came upon larger, odder-looking species such as the laminaria— particularly the kind known as Neptune's Sword-belt, like a broad strap of greenish leather, with curled edges, seemingly cut to fit a giant's chest.

'What wasted wealth, isn't it?' he went on. 'What fools we are! In Scotland, they've at least got enough sense to eat ulvae. As for us, we make vegetable fibre out of sea-wrack and use fucus for packing fish; and we leave all the rest for the local peasants to use as poor-quality manure ... To think that science hasn't got beyond the primitive method of burning a few cartloads of it to extract soda!'

Pauline, up to her knees in water, was enjoying the salt coolness. She was, moreover, deeply interested in her cousin's explanations. 'So you're going to distil all this?' she asked.

The word 'distil' amused Lazare greatly. 'Yes, call it that if you like. But it's an awfully complicated process, as you'll see, my dear . . . Never mind, remember what I'm telling you; we've conquered the vegetation of the earth, haven't we? Plants, trees, what we use and what we eat; well, perhaps the conquest of the sea's vegetation will make us even richer, the day somebody decides to attempt it.'

Meanwhile both of them, afire with enthusiasm, were collecting samples. They gathered up armfuls, they wandered forgetfully so far afield that on the way back they got wet up to their armpits, And Lazare went on explaining things, repeating the sayings of his master Herbelin: the sea was a vast reservoir of chemical compounds, the algae helped industry by condensing, in their tissues, the salts which were greatly diluted in the water around them. And thus the problem consisted in extracting from these algae, in an economical way, all the useful compounds. He talked about taking their ashes, used commercially as impure soda, and then separating out and setting free, in a state of perfect purity, bromides and iodides of sodium and potassium, sodium sulphate, other iron and manganese salts, so as to leave no trace of the raw material. What chiefly thrilled him was the hope of letting no single useful substance escape, thanks to the low-temperature process invented by the great Herbelin. It would mean immense wealth.

'Good heavens, what a mess you're in!' cried Madame Chanteau, when they got home.

'Don't worry,' answered Lazare gaily, throwing down his bundle of seaweed in the middle of the terrace. 'Look, we're bringing you back five franc pieces!'

Next day a whole load of seaweed was fetched up in a Verchemont peasant's cart, and then, in the big room on the second floor, the research began. Pauline was appointed assistant. For a whole month they worked like madmen. The room was soon full of dried plants, bottles in which floated branchy specimens, and queer-shaped instruments: one corner of the table was occupied by a microscope, the piano was covered with cauldrons and retorts, and the cupboard itself was crammed with specialist works and files which were constantly consulted. Moreover, the experiments thus

58

made on a small scale, with meticulous care, yielded promising results. Herbelin's process was based on the discovery that certain substances crystallize at low temperatures, different for each substance; and the only thing needed was to produce and maintain the required temperatures; each substance would be deposited in turn and separated from the others. Lazare burnt the algae in a pit, then washed the ashes by the low-temperature process, using a refrigerating system based on the rapid evaporation of ammonia; but the thing would have to be carried out on a large scale, transferred from the laboratory to the factory, apparatus would have to be set up and made to work as economically as possible.

On the day when he had separated out five distinct substances from the original liquid, the room rang with shouts of triumph. There was notably a surprising proportion of potassium bromide. This popular remedy would sell like hot cakes! Pauline, who was dancing round the table with all her old childish glee, suddenly ran downstairs and bounced into the dining-room, where her uncle was reading a newspaper while her aunt was marking towels.

'Aha!' she shouted, 'you can be ill now, we've got plenty of bromide for you!'

Madame Chanteau, who had lately been suffering from nervous attacks, had been prescribed a course of bromide by Dr. Cazenove. She said with a smile: "Are you going to have enough to cure everybody, since everybody's nerves are upset these days?"

The girl, with her robust limbs and her face beaming with health and happiness, flung her arms wide as though to send her cure flying to the four corners of the earth: 'Yes, yes, we're going to stuff the whole world full of it ... There's an end to all their neuroses!'

After visiting the coast and discussing various sites, Lazare decided to set up his factory on Treasure Bay. It combined all the right conditions: a wide beach, with a floor of flat rocks, which would make it easy to collect the algae; transport would be cheap, the raw material ready to hand, and the distance sufficient without being excessive. And Pauline laughingly commented on the name they had once given the bay because of its fine golden sand; it was apter than they'd thought, for now they were going to find real treasure in the sea.

They started off splendidly, with a successful purchase of twenty thousand metres of waste ground and the prefect's authorisation, obtained after only two months' delay. At last the builders began work. Boutigny had come: he was a vulgar, redfaced little man

59

of about thirty, and the Chanteaus took a great dislike to him. He had refused to live in Bonneville, having discovered, so he said, a very comfortable house at Verchemont; and the family's hostility increased when it transpired that he had brought a woman to live there, a tart from some low haunt in Paris, no doubt. Lazare shrugged his shoulders, disgusted by such provincial ideas; the woman was a nice little thing, a blonde who must really be devoted to Boutigny since she consented to bury herself in this godforsaken place; but he did not stress the point because of Pauline. In a word, what was expected of Boutigny was the active supervision and intelligent organisation of the work; and he was wonderful, always on the go, inspired by a sort of genius for administration. Under his orders, the walls rose visibly.

Then, during the next four months, while the buildings were going up and the apparatus was being installed, the Treasure Bay factory, as they had come to call it, became the object of their daily walk. Madame Chanteau did not always go with the young people; and Lazare and Pauline went chasing off together as of old. Only Mathieu followed them; he soon tired, and would drag along wearily on his great paws and lie down there with his tongue hanging out, panting as rapidly as a blacksmith's bellows. He was the only one of the party who still went swimming; he would dash into the sea when they threw in a stick, and had the good sense to pick it up in the trough of the wave, so as not to swallow salt water. At each of his visits, Lazare urged on the contractors to greater speed; while Pauline ventured to offer practical suggestions, often very much to the point. He had been obliged to order the apparatus from Caen, after designs of his own, and workmen had come to set it up. Boutigny was beginning to display some anxiety on seeing the estimates constantly mounting up. Why couldn't they, to begin with, have been satisfied with the absolutely essential rooms, the indispensable machinery? Why all these complicated buildings, these enormous pieces of apparatus, intended for a large-scale undertaking, whereas it would have been wiser to enlarge it little by little after the conditions of manufacture and marketing were precisely understood? Lazare would fly into a passion. He saw things on a grand scale; he would have liked to build his sheds with a monumental façade overlooking the sea, to express the grandeur of his vision in front of the boundless horizon. Then the visit would end in an ecstasy of hope; what was the point of haggling over halfpence, when they had wealth in their hands? And they would walk home in great spirits; remembering Mathieu, who was always dawdling behind, Pauline would suddenly hide with Lazare behind a wall, both of them childishly delighted when the dog, surprised to find himself alone and thinking he was lost, wandered about in comical amazement.

Every evening, when they reached home, the same question greeted them. 'Well, how's it going? Are you pleased?'

And the answer, too, was always the same: 'Yes, yes . . . but they're taking such a time!'

During these months, they became the closest of friends. Lazare's feeling for Pauline was one of warm affection, mingled with gratitude for the money she had contributed to his project. He had gradually ceased to think of her as girl; once again, he lived in her company as though she were a boy, a younger brother whose qualities appealed to him more keenly every day. She had so much sense, so valiant a spirit, such cheerful kindheartedness that he had come to feel a tacit admiration for her, a secret respect, although he tried to protect himself against this by teasing her. She had quite calmly told him about the books she had read and about her aunt's horror at the sight of the anatomical drawings; and for a moment he stood surprised and embarrassed in front of this girl with her wide innocent eyes, who knew so much already. Afterwards, it only drew them together more closely; when she helped him in their joint research, he used to talk about everything quite freely, with the perfect simplicity of the scientist, using the exact word as if there were no other. And she herself tackled every question, with no other apparent motive than delight in learning and in being useful to him. But he was often amused at the number of gaps in her education, at the extraordinary jumble of incompatible notions that it comprised: her aunt's school-marm ideas, the facts of life whittled down to suit the modesty of a girls' boarding-school: then the exact knowledge acquired by her from medical text-books, the physiological truths about man and woman, shedding light on life. When she uttered a naive remark, he would laugh so loud that she lost her temper—instead of laughing at her, wouldn't he do better to correct her mistake? And usually the quarrel ended in a lesson; he completed her instruction, with a young chemist's indifference to convention. She knew so much already, she might as well know the rest. Moreover a slow process was at work within her; she kept up her reading and, little by little, co-ordinated what she heard and what she saw, although she still maintained her air of deference towards Madame Chanteau and listened to her prudish untruths with a perfectly serious air. It was only with her cousin, in their big

61

study, that she became a boy, a lab assistant, to whom he would call: 'I say, have you looked at this Floridaea? It's only got one sex.'

'Yes, yes,' she would reply, 'male organs in big clusters.'

And yet a vague uneasiness was stirring within her. When Lazare sometimes jostled her in fraternal fashion, she would stand breathless for a few seconds, her heart throbbing wildly. They had both been oblivious of her sex; and now she was becoming physically conscious of it—in her flesh, in the very pulse of her blood. One day as he was turning round he knocked her with his elbow. She uttered a cry and put her hands to her bosom. What had happened? Had he hurt her? But he had barely touched her! and instinctively he attempted to lift her fichu to see. She started back, and they both stood looking at one another in confusion and smiling awkwardly. Another day, during an experiment, she refused to put her hands in cold water. This surprised and irritated him: why ever not? What a ridiculous whim! If she wasn't going to help him, she'd better go downstairs. Then, seeing her blush, he understood, and stared at her gaping. So this tomboy, this younger brother, was unmistakably a woman! You couldn't give her the slightest touch without making her whimper, and you couldn't depend on her all the month round. Each new fact came as a surprise, an unforeseen discovery that embarrassed and disturbed them both, upsetting their comradely relations. Lazare seemed merely to find it tiresome, it was going to prove impossible to work together, since she wasn't a man and the least trifle upset her. As for Pauline, she was left with a sense of unease, an anxiety which included a growing element of delight.

Thenceforward, the girl began to experience sensations of which she spoke to nobody. She did not lie about them, she simply kept silent, out of anxious pride and also out of shame. Several times she thought she must be sickening for some serious illness, for she went to bed feeling feverish, tortured with insomnia and quite overpowered by the secret, tumultuous force of the unfamiliar sensations that assailed her; then, by day, she simply felt an exhaustion of which she never complained to her aunt. And there were sudden hot flushes, a state of nervous excitement, and unexpected thoughts that shocked her afterwards; and especially, dreams from which she would awake full of self-reproach. Despite all the books of physiology and anatomy she had studied so painstakingly and so passionately, she remained so virginal physically that at each fresh phenomenon she would relapse into childish bewilderment. She grew calmer as she thought things over; after all, she was not unique; she must expect to find her own body functioning like other people's. After supper one evening she held forth on the stupidity of dreams: wasn't it maddening to lie prone and powerless, a prey to absurd fancies? And what appeared to infuriate her most was the death of one's will-power in sleep, the complete surrender of one's personality. Her cousin, with his pessimistic theories, joined in the attack on dreams on the grounds that they disturbed the perfect bliss of nothingness; while her uncle drew a distinction between pleasant dreams, which he liked, and feverish nightmares, which he detested. But Pauline insisted with such vehemence that Madame Chanteau, surprised, asked her what these dreams of hers were about. 'Nothing, nothing,' she stammered: mere nonsense, things too vague to be remembered. And it was all still perfectly true; her dreams took place in a sort of twilight, and she felt the touch of shadowy figures; she was awakening to physical consciousness of sex without a single clear image appearing to make the sensation explicit. She saw nobody in her dreams; it was as though she had been caressed by the sea-breeze blowing in through the open window on summer nights.

Meanwhile, however, Pauline's great affection for Lazare seemed to grow more ardent every day; it was not only the awakening of her woman's instincts after seven years of brother-and-sister camaraderie; she felt, too, the need to devote herself to someone, and she had the illusion that he was stronger and more intelligent than she. Slowly, her sisterly affection was turning into love, expressing itself with the delicious hesitant accents of dawning passion—laughter that had a tremulous resonance, furtive contacts lingeringly prolonged, all the rapture of that first discovery of fine and passionate feeling, under the urgent impulsion of primitive instinct. He, protected by his Latin Quarter dissipations, having no unsatisfied curiosity, looked on her merely as a sister, unmoved by any stirring of desire. She, on the contrary, still virginal, with no other companion in her solitude but Lazare, came gradually to adore him, and surrendered her whole being to him. When they were together, she seemed to depend on his presence for her whole existence, from morning to night, her eyes ever seeking his, in her eager wish to be of service to him.

About this time, Madame Chanteau was surprised to see that Pauline showed signs of piety. Twice the young girl went to confession. Then, quite suddenly, she seemed to have quarrelled with Abbé Horteur; she even refused to go to Mass for three weeks, and only resumed the habit so as not to distress her aunt. In any case, she gave no reasons for her behaviour; she must have been offended by the Abbé's questions and comments, for he was a clumsy-tongued fellow. And it was then that Madame Chanteau, with a devoted mother's instinctive acuteness, guessed at Pauline's growing passion. She kept silence about it however, and did not mention it even to her husband. This momentous happening had taken her by surprise, for hitherto the possibility of love—even, maybe, of marriage—between the two had never entered into her calculations. Like Lazare, she had gone on treating her ward as a child; and she wanted to think things over, she vowed to herself that she would keep an eye on them, but did nothing of the sort, since at bottom she cared only for what gave her son pleasure.

The hot August days had come and the young man decided one evening that they might go and bathe next day, on their way to the factory. Obsessed by her notion of propriety, the mother went along with them, in spite of the fierce afternoon sunshine. She sat down beside Mathieu on the scorching pebbles and sheltered under her parasol, while the dog tried to stretch his head under its shade.

'Why, wherever's she off to?' asked Lazare, when he saw Pauline slip off behind a rock.

'She's gone to undress, of course,' said Madame Chanteau. 'Turn away, you're embarrassing her, it isn't proper.'

He stood there amazed, cast one more look towards the rock, where the corner of a white chemise was fluttering, then glanced at his mother again, as he resigned himself to turning his back. But he undressed hurriedly himself, without saying a word.

'Are you ready?' he called out at last. 'What a palaver! Are you dressing up to the nines?'

Pauline came nimbly running up, laughing too brightly and thus betraying a touch of embarrassment. Since her cousin's return they had not yet been bathing together. She was dressed for swimming in a one-piece costume, barely covering her hips, with a belt tightly clasping her waist; it enhanced her slenderness, and made her look, with her supple back and high bosom, like some Florentine statue. Her naked arms and legs, her little bare feet in their sandals, were as white as a child's.

'I say,' said Lazare, 'shall we go as far as the Picochets?'

'Oh yes, let's, to the Picochets,' she replied.

Madame Chanteau called out: 'Don't go too far . . . you always give me such frights!'

64

But they had already plunged into the water. The Picochets, a group of rocks some of which were exposed at high tide, lay about a mile out to sea. And the pair swam off side by side, quite leisurely, like two friends setting off for a walk along a fine straight road. To begin with Mathieu followed them, but when he saw that they kept on swimming, he came back to shake himself and splash Madame Chanteau. He was too lazy to enjoy needless adventures.

'You're the only one with sense,' the old lady remarked to him. 'How in Heaven's name can they risk their lives like that?'

She could hardly make out the swimmers' heads, which looked like tufts of seaweed bobbing about on the surface of the waves. The sea had a fairly strong swell, and its rise and fall rocked them gently as they swam forward, talking quietly to one another about the algae that were drifting beneath them in the clear water. Pauline grew tired, and turned over to float on her back, staring up into the sky and feeling infinitely small under the expanse of boundless blue. The sea that cradled her was still her greatest friend. She loved its tangy breath, its pure ice-cold waters, she surrendered to it, rejoicing to feel it streaming endlessly over her flesh and delighting in the violent exercise that made her heart beat more steadily.

Then she gave a little cry.

'What's up?' asked her cousin anxiously.

'I think my strap's broken . . . I stretched out my left arm too sharply.'

They both joked about it. She had begun to swim again gently, laughing in an embarrassed way as she realised the extent of the damage: the stitching of the shoulder-strap had given way and the whole of her left shoulder and breast were exposed. The young man, much amused, told her to search in her pockets to see if she hadn't any pins on her. When they reached the Picochets he climbed on to a rock, as they always used to do, to get his breath again before the homeward journey. She stayed in the water, swimming round the reef.

'Aren't you coming up?'

'No, I'm all right.'

He thought she was merely being tiresome, and lost his temper. What was the sense in it? Her strength might fail her on the way back if she didn't take a few minutes' rest. But she persisted obstinately, swimming about quietly without even answering him, up to her chin in water so as to hide the naked whiteness of her shoulder, which gleamed dimly like the milky mother-of-pearl of a shell. There was a sort of grotto hollowed out in the rock, towards the open sea, where they used to play at desert islands, looking out at the empty horizon. On the other side, on the beach, Madame Chanteau could be seen as a small black spot like an insect.

'Oh, you pig-headed creature!' Lazare finally exclaimed, plunging into the water once more. 'I declare, if you want to drown, I shall let you!'

Slowly they set off again. They were in no mood for talking to one another. Hearing her pant for breath, he told her to float on her back. She seemed not to have heard him. The rent was growing bigger; had she made the slightest movement to turn over, her breast would have appeared on the surface of the water, like some deep-sea flower. Then he must have understood; and noticing her exhaustion, realising that she would never reach the shore, he went resolutely up to help her. She tried to struggle and go on alone; then she was forced to give in. He clasped her tightly against him, and they reached land together thus.

Madame Chanteau had run up in terror, while Mathieu, up to his belly in the waves, set up a howl.

'Good heavens, how rash you were! I knew you were going too far!'

Pauline had fainted. Lazare carried her like a child on to the sand; and as she lay thus against his breast, half naked now, both streaming with salt water. Then she gave a sigh and opened her eyes. When she recognized the young man, she burst into great sobs and clutched him in a nervous embrace, covering his face with wild kisses. It was an unconscious reaction—the unrestrained impulse of love, springing from her mortal danger.

'Oh, how good you are, Lazare, oh, how I love you!'

He was profoundly startled by the violence of her embrace. When Madame Chanteau dressed her again, he stood aside of his own accord. They walked home to Bonneville gently and wearily; both of them seemed utterly exhausted. The mother walked between them, saying to herself that it was high time to make some decision.

Other worries, meanwhile, afflicted the family. The Treasure Bay factory had been built, and for the past week the apparatus had been tried out, with deplorable results. Lazare was forced to admit that he had set up certain pieces wrong; he went to Paris to consult his master Herbelin, and came back deeply depressed; it would all have to be set up afresh, the great chemist had already perfected his method, which involved a complete alteration of the apparatus. Meanwhile the sixty thousand francs had been used up, and Boutigny flatly refused to contribute another penny; from morning till night he talked bitterly about the way they had squandered their money, with the unbearable persistence of a practical man who knows he's right. Lazare sometimes felt like beating him. He would have thrown it all up, but for the anguish he felt at the thought of losing Pauline's thirty thousand francs in that abyss. It shocked both his honour and his pride: it was out of the question, he had to find money somewhere, you couldn't just drop a concern which would bring in millions later on.

'Don't worry,' his mother kept saying when she saw him sick with anxiety. 'We've not reached the point of not knowing where to turn for a few thousand franc notes.'

Madame Chanteau was hatching a scheme. The idea of a marriage between Lazare and Pauline, which had surprised her to begin with, now seemed quite suitable. After all, there was only nine years' difference in their ages, and there was nothing unusual in that. And surely it would settle everything! Lazare would then be working for his wife; he would stop tormenting himself about his debt, he could even borrow from Pauline the sum he needed. In the depths of her heart Madame Chanteau was obscurely worried by one scruple, the dread of eventual disaster and the ruin of her ward. Only she set this aside as an inconceivable dénouement; wasn't Lazare a genius? He would bring Pauline wealth, in fact it was she who would profit by the arrangement. Her son might be poor, but he was worth a fortune if Pauline would give it to him.

The marriage was decided on quite simply. One morning, the mother questioned the girl in her bedroom; Pauline immediately poured forth her heart with cheerful tranquillity. Then Madame Chanteau made her stay at home, on the pretext of being a little tired, and she accompanied her son to the factory. When, on the way back, she spoke to him at great length about her plan, his little cousin's love for him, the suitability of such a marriage, the advantages to be reaped from it by everybody, he appeared amazed at first. He'd never dreamt of such a thing; why, how old could the child be? Then he remained deeply moved; of course, he was very fond of her too, he'd do whatever they wanted him to.

When they reached home, Pauline had been laying the table, for the sake of something to do, while her uncle, with his newspaper lying on his knees, was watching Minouche licking her belly with a fastidious air.

' Well, well, so we're going to get married!" said Lazare, hiding his emotion under a show of noisy gaiety.

She was standing still with a plate in her hand, scarlet and speechless.

'Who's going to get married?' asked the uncle as though he had suddenly woken up.

His wife had warned him about it that morning; but the greedy way in which the cat drew its tongue over its fur had been absorbing all his attention. But he remembered immediately.

'Oh, yes,' he cried. And he cast a knowing look at the young pair, while a sudden shooting pain in his right foot distorted his lips. Pauline had quietly laid down the plate. At last she replied to Lazare: 'I'd like to, if you would.'

'Well, that's settled then, kiss one another,' concluded Madame Chanteau as she hung up her straw hat.

The girl stepped forward first, holding out her hands. He, still laughing, took them in his own and began to tease her.

'So you've stopped playing with dolls? That's why you were always hiding away, and one couldn't get even a glimpse of you when you washed the tips of your fingers? And you've chosen poor old Lazare as your victim?'

'O auntie, make him shut up, or I shall run away!' she murmured in confusion, trying to free herself.

Gradually he drew her to him, still playfully, as in the days of their schoolroom friendship; and suddenly she laid a smacking kiss on his cheek, and he gave it back haphazard on one ear. Then a secret thought seemed to sadden him, for he added in a mournful tone: 'You're making a queer sort of bargain, poor kid! If you only knew how old I am at heart! Still, since you're willing to put up with me . . .'

Dinner was a tumultuous meal; they were all talking at once, making plans for the future as though they were gathered together for the first time. Véronique, who had come in right in the middle of the betrothal, went out tight lipped, slamming the kitchen door. When dessert came, they broached the serious side of things. The mother explained that the marriage could not take place for another two years; she wanted to wait for the legal age of emancipation, for she did not want to be accused of bringing pressure to bear on a minor, with her son's help. This two years' delay appalled Pauline, but she was much touched at her aunt's honesty, and went over to kiss her. A date was settled, the young people could wait patiently, and meanwhile they would be gaining the first instalment of their future millions. The money question was thus dealt with in a burst of enthusiasm.

'Take it out of the drawer, auntie,' the girl kept on saying. 'Take whatever he needs, of course! It's his as much as mine now.'

Madame Chanteau protested. 'No, no, we shan't take out one penny more than we need . . . You know you needn't worry, I'd sooner lose my right hand . . . You need ten thousand francs over there; I'll take out ten thousand for you, and lock up the rest again safely. It's sacred.'

'With ten thousand francs,' Lazare said, 'I'm certain of success. The biggest expenses are over, and it would be a crime to lose heart. You'll see, you'll see . . . And you, darling, I want to dress you in cloth of gold, like a queen, on our wedding day.'

Their joy was increased by the unexpected arrival of Dr. Cazenove. He had just been attending to a fisherman who had crushed his hand under a boat; and they had made him stop, they forced him to drink a cup of tea. He did not seem surprised at the great news. Only, when he heard the Chanteaus growing enthusiastic about their seaweed project, he cast an anxious look at Pauline and murmured: 'It's certainly a clever idea, and worth trying out . . . But you're on firmer ground with investments. If I were you I'd want to be happy right away in my own little corner.'

He broke off, seeing a shadow flit across the girl's face. The warm affection he felt for her made him go on, against his better judgment: 'Oh, money has its points! you'd better make plenty of it. And you know, I shall dance at your wedding. Yes, I shall dance the *zambuco* of the Caribbean islanders, which I'll wager you don't know. Look, you whirl your arms about like a windmill, slap your thighs, and prance round the prisoner when he's ready cooked and the women are cutting him up.'

The months began to flow by again. Now, Pauline had regained her sunny serenity, for her frank nature hated uncertainty above all. The fact that she had confessed her love and that a date was fixed for her marriage seemed to have allayed her physical uneasiness; and she accepted, in perfect calm, the flowering of life within her, the slow unfolding of her whole body, the surge of her blood, which at one time had tormented her by day and overwhelmed her by night. Wasn't it the common law? You had to grow in order to love. In any case, her relations with Lazare were practically unchanged; they kept on working together as before—he was constantly occupied, and forearmed against any sudden impulse of desire by his transient adventures in Paris; while she was so innocent and frank, serenely protected by her learning and her virginity as by a twofold armour. Sometimes, however, they would stand in the middle of the great untidy study holding hands and laughing tenderly at one another; together, they would turn over the pages of some treatise on phytology, their heads touching, or they would lean against each other for a moment to examine a flask of purplish bromine or some violet-tinted specimen of iodine; or, again, she would bend towards him, over the instruments that littered the table and the piano, calling him to lift her up to reach the topmost shelf of the cupboard. But in these hourly contacts they never went beyond such authorised caresses as might be exchanged under the eyes of grandparents; there was nothing but the friendly affection of betrothed cousins, enlivened with the merest hint of sensual delight. As Madame Chanteau said, they behaved very sensibly.

When Louise came, and was there between them with her pretty coquettish ways, Pauline even seemed to have stopped being jealous.

A whole year went by thus. The factory was working now, and possibly the worries it caused them proved their chief protection. After the apparatus had been set up with considerable difficulty, the first results seemed excellent; to be sure, the output was mediocre, but by perfecting their method and intensifying their care and energy, they were bound eventually to produce vast quantities. Boutigny had already found ample trade openings, almost too ample indeed. The prospect of wealth seemed infallible. And thenceforward, led on by that hope, they persisted obstinately, reacting against all warnings of disaster; the factory became a yawning chasm into which they threw money by handfuls, convinced that they would find it again at the bottom in the form of gold bullion. Each fresh sacrifice increased their fanatical obstinacy.

In the early days Madame Chanteau never took any money out of the drawer in her writing desk without informing Pauline. 'Dearie, there are some bills to be paid on Saturday, you need three thousand francs. Will you come upstairs with me and choose which security we're to sell?'

'But you can choose it by yourself,' the girl replied.

'No, you know I do nothing without you. It's your money.'

Then Madame Chanteau became less punctilious. One evening Lazare confessed a debt that he had hidden from Pauline, five thousand francs' worth of copper tubing that had never even been used. His mother happened to have just been to her desk with Pauline, and, confronted with her son's despair, she went back again by herself and took out the five thousand francs, promising herself to restore them as soon as the first profits came in. But from that day on the breach had been opened. She acquired the habit, and helped herself without counting. Moreover she had come to feel aggrieved at being, at her age, continually subjected to the goodwill of a schoolgirl; and she bore Pauline a grudge for it. They'd give her back her money; and even if it was hers, that was no reason why they couldn't do a single thing without asking her permission. Once she had broken into the hoard she no longer insisted on Pauline's accompanying her to the desk. The girl was relieved, for, in spite of her generous nature, those expeditions distressed her; her good sense warned her of impending disaster, and her prudent thriftiness, inherited from her mother, protested inwardly. At first she was surprised at Madame Chanteau's silence, she realised that the money was running away none the less, and that they were simply doing without her consent. Afterwards she came to prefer things this way. At least she was spared the trying experience of seeing the pile of papers dwindling every time. Henceforward nothing took place between them but a rapid exchange of looks at certain times: the intent and anxious look of the niece, when she guessed that more money was about to be borrowed, the unsteady glance of the aunt, resentful at having to turn away her head. A ferment of hatred began to work imperceptibly.

Unfortunately that year Davoine was declared bankrupt. This catastrophe had been foreseen, but was none the less a terrible blow for the Chanteaus. They were left with their three thousand francs income. All that they could salvage from the wreck—some twelve thousand francs—was promptly invested, and brought their total up to three hundred francs a month. So, before a fortnight was out, Madame Chanteau had to borrow fifty francs from Pauline's money; the butcher from Verchemont was waiting with his bill, he couldn't be put off. And there were a hundred francs towards a laundry boiler, and so on, down to ten francs for potatoes and fifty sous for fish. She had reached the point when she was supporting Lazare and the factory from day to day with wretched, petty sums; and she now descended to borrowing coppers for household expenses in a pitiful attempt to fill the yawning gaps in her debt. Towards the end of the month particularly she could constantly be seen disappearing discreetly and coming back almost at once with her hand in her pocket, from which she would finally bring herself to pull out, one by one, the sous required to pay a bill. She had come to depend on the writing-desk drawer; she had acquired the habit, and now she was its unresisting prey. And yet, while her obsession drew her constantly to the desk, she never failed to be irritated by the slight squeak it gave when she lowered the lid. What an awful old desk! To think that she had never been able to afford a proper bureau for herself! The venerable writing-desk which once, when stuffed with wealth, had given the house a cheerful prosperous air, tortured her now; it was like that box that held all the ills of mankind, and misfortune seemed to seep through all its cracks.

One evening Pauline came in from the yard, calling out: 'It's the baker; we owe him for three days, two francs eighty-five.'

Madame Chanteau searched her pockets. 'I'll have to go up-stairs,'she muttered.

'Don't you go,' put in the girl thoughtlessly. 'I'll run up myself . . . Where's your purse?'

'No, no, you wouldn't find it . . . it's somewhere or other . . .'

The aunt was stammering, and the pair exchanged that silent look that always made them turn pale. There was a moment's painful hesitation, then Madame Chanteau went upstairs, cold with repressed rage, convinced that her ward knew where she was going to find the two francs eighty-five. After all, why had she so often shown her the money lying in that drawer? Her own former voluble honesty exasperated her; the child must be following her mentally, watching her open the drawer, rummage in it, shut it again. When she had come downstairs and paid the baker, her anger blazed forth against the girl:

'Well, your frock's in a nice mess; what have you been doing? Drawing water for the kitchen garden, eh? Why can't you let Véronique do her own jobs? My goodness, you get dirty on purpose, you don't seem to realise what it costs . . . Your allowance isn't all that big, I can't make both ends meet . . .'

And so she went on; Pauline, who had been trying to defend herself, now listened in silence, heavy-hearted. Lately, her aunt's love for her had been growing less and less, and she was well aware of it. Alone with Véronique again, she wept, and the maid began to clatter her saucepans as though to avoid taking sides. She still grumbled at the girl, but now, despite her rough ways, a sense of justice seemed to be stirring in her.

When winter came, Lazare lost heart. Once again his enthusiasm had veered round; he felt nothing but loathing and dread for the factory. In November, he was seized with terror in the face of a fresh financial crisis. He had dealt with the others successfully, but this one left him aghast, despairing of everything and denouncing science.

72

His processing scheme was stupid; however much one perfected one's methods one could never wrest from Nature what she was unwilling to yield; and he even fulminated against his master, the great Herbelin, who, having obligingly gone out of his way on a journey to visit the factory, had been upset and embarrassed at the sight of the apparatus, which, he said, had perhaps been built on too large a scale to function with the precision of his small laboratory apparatus. In short, it seemed as if the experiment were finished and the truth was that no method had as yet been found to maintain at the requisite degree of cold the low temperature necessary for the crystallization of the different substances. Lazare had indeed succeeded in extracting from his algae a certain amount of potassium bromide; but as he never managed to isolate sufficiently the four or five other substances, which had to be thrown away, the process was proving a fiasco. He was sick with disgust, and declared himself beaten. One evening when Madame Chanteau and Pauline begged him to keep calm and try one last effort, there was a painful scene; cruel words were spoken, tears were shed, doors banged so violently that Chanteau started up in terror from his armchair.

'You'll be the death of me!' the young man cried, locking himself in his room, overcome with childish despair.

Next day at lunch he brought along a sheet of paper covered with figures. Out of Pauline's hundred and eighty thousand francs, nearly a hundred thousand had already been squandered. What was the sense of going on? It would all vanish in the same way; and the panic that had seized him yesterday made him turn pale once more. Besides, his mother took his side now; she had never gone against him yet, she loved him to the point of abetting his faults. Only Pauline tried to go on arguing. The figure of a hundred thousand francs had appalled her. What! had it come to this? He had taken more than half her fortune? A hundred thousand francs were going to be wasted if he gave up the struggle now? But she spoke in vain, while Véronique cleared the table. Then, for fear of breaking out into recriminations, she ran to shut herself up in her room, heartbroken.

When she had gone out, the others sat on round the table in embarrassed silence.

'Decidedly, the girl's miserly, and that's a horrid fault,' the mother said at last. 'I don't want Lazare to have to kill himself with work and worry.'

'I hadn't been told it was such a huge sum,' the father ventured timidly. 'A hundred thousand francs! Good heavens, it's terrible.'

73

'Well, what of it? She'll get back her hundred thousand,' interrupted the mother in her curt tones. 'If our son marries her, he's quite capable of earning a hundred thousand francs.'

They set about winding up the business without delay. It was Boutigny who had frightened Lazare by presenting him with a disastrous statement of the situation. The debt amounted to nearly twenty thousand francs. When he saw that his partner had decided to withdraw he began by announcing that he was going off himself to settle in Algeria, where a wonderful position awaited him. Then he consented to take over the factory; but he seemed so unwilling to do so, he produced such complicated accounts, that in the end he got the ground, the buildings and the apparatus for the twenty thousand francs that were owed; and, at the last moment, Lazare had to consider it a triumph to extract from him a promissory note for five thousand francs, payable in quarterly instalments. Immediately afterwards, Boutigny sold the copper from the apparatus and rearranged the buildings for the large-scale production of commercial soda, following the beaten track of familiar methods, without the slightest attempt at scientific research.

Pauline, ashamed of her first reaction of cautious thrift, had recovered all her gaiety and good nature, as though to make amends for some fault. And when Lazare brought along the note for five thousand francs, Mandame Chanteau was triumphant. She made the girl take it upstairs and put it away in the drawer herself.

'Well, that's five thousand we've got back, my dear . . . They're yours, take them. My son wouldn't even keep one of them for all his trouble.'

For some time now Chanteau, confined to his invalid chair, had been tortured with anxiety. Although he dared not refuse to sign the documents she gave him, he was greatly concerned about the way his wife was administering their ward's fortune. He couldn't get that hundred thousand francs out of his head. How were they to make up such a deficit when the time came to submit their accounts? And the worst of it was that the deputy-guardian, that Saccard whose wild speculations were at that time the talk of Paris, had just remembered Pauline after apparently forgetting her for nearly eight years. He had written asking for news of her, and even proposed to drop in at Bonneville one day during a business trip to Cherbourg. What could they say if he demanded a statement of the situation, as he was entitled to do? His sudden awakening after so long a period of indifference was alarming.

When Chanteau finally broached this subject with his wife, he found her intrigued rather than anxious. For one moment she nearly hit on the truth, when she guessed that Saccard might have run through his millions and, being penniless, wanted to get his hands on Pauline's money in the hope of making it multiply tenfold. Then she began to guess wildly, wondering whether the girl herself had perhaps sought revenge by writing to her deputy-guardian. And as this suggestion horrified her husband, she evolved a complicated story about anonymous letters sent by Boutigny's woman, that hussy whom they had refused to receive in their house and who had since been making their name dirt in the shops of Verchemont and Arromanches.

'I don't care a rap for them, after all!' she said. 'The child's not eighteen, it's true, but I've only got to marry her to Lazare at once; a married woman's legally emancipated.'

'Are you sure of that?' asked Chanteau.

'Of course! I read it in the Code only this morning."

For Madame Chanteau was studying the Code now. She sought excuses there, in a struggle with her last remaining scruples; moreover she had become fascinated by the whole furtive process of legal chicanery, as the temptation of that huge sum of money lying dormant within her reach gradually wore away her honesty.

In any case, Madame Chanteau could not make up her mind to conclude the marriage. After the financial crisis Pauline would have liked to hurry things on; why wait six months, till she should be eighteen? Better get settled without insisting on Lazare securing himself a job first. She ventured to speak of it to her aunt, who, in her embarrassment, thought up a lie; she confided to Pauline, in lowered tones and behind closed doors, that Lazare had a secret worry: he was very sensitive, he hated the thought of marrying her without bringing her a fortune, now that he had jeopardized her own. The girl listened in amazement, unable to understand such romantic delicacy of feeling; however rich she had been she'd have married him all the same, because she loved him; and besides, how long would they have to wait? For ever, maybe. But Madame Chanteau protested loudly; she would undertake to overcome this exaggerated sense of honour, provided nothing was done precipitately. She made Pauline swear to say nothing, lest the young man should take it into his head to run away on finding his secret guessed at, exposed and discussed. Pauline, seized with anxiety, had to resign herself to waiting in patient silence.

Meanwhile, whenever Chanteau was tormented by his fear of Saccard, he would say to his wife: 'Why don't you let the children get married, if it's going to settle everything?'

'There's no hurry,' she would reply. 'The danger's not imminent!'

'But since you're letting them get married some day . . . You've not changed your mind, I hope? That would be the death of them.'

'Oh, the death of them! . . . As long as a thing hasn't been done, it can be left undone, if you think better of it. And then after all, they're free agents, we shall see if they're still just as keen on it.'

Pauline and Lazare had taken up their old communal life again when a particularly harsh winter kept them housebound. During the first week he seemed so sad, so full of self-reproach and of bitterness against everything, that she looked after him like an invalid, with untiring kindness; she even felt a certain pity for the big lad whose failures could be explained by his lack of persistence and the purely nervous character of his courage; and little by little she assumed over him a kind of scolding maternal authority. At first he declared excitedly that he would become a peasant, suggesting innumerable crazy schemes for getting rich quickly, vowing that he was ashamed of the bread he ate and that he would not live an hour longer at the expense of his family. Days passed, and he kept postponing the execution of his schemes, merely altering every morning the plan that was to carry him in a few strides to the peak of wealth and honour. Then Pauline, alarmed by her aunt's false disclosures, would speak sharply to him; nobody wanted him to worry like that, he'd find a job in the spring, he'd get one immediately; but till then he was to have a rest. By the end of the first month she seemed to have subdued him; he had lapsed into aimless idleness, into a mocking acceptance of what he called 'the tiresomeness of living.'

Day by day Pauline grew increasingly conscious of some unknown, disturbing element in Lazare that shocked her deeply. When she heard him sneering at everything and uttering his professions of nihilism in a harsh, toneless voice she longed for his former fits of anger that flared up like a straw fire. It was as though, buried here in remote Bonneville, in the stillness of winter, he had suddenly remembered his old Paris contacts, the books he used to read, the arguments with his fellow-students. He was clearly influenced by pessimism, but it was an ill-digested pessimism of which little remained but the inspired sallies and sombre poetry of Schopenhauer. The girl was well aware that her cousin's denuncia-

76

tion of humanity sprang chiefly from his fury at being defeated, as though the disastrous failure of his factory had shattered his whole world. But she was unable to probe deeper into its causes; she protested violently when he resumed his old thesis, the negation of progress, the ultimate futility of science. Wasn't that brute Boutigny making his fortune out of commercial soda? So what was the point of having ruined oneself trying to find something better, to discover new laws, since empiricism had won the day? This was his starting-point every time, and his conclusion—uttered with a tight-lipped, sardonic smile—was that science would only prove really useful if some day it provided the means for blowing up the whole world with some gigantic cartridge. Then he would proceed to describe, with cold sarcasm, the cunning tricks of the Will that governs the world, and the blind stupidity of mankind's wish to go on living. Life was nothing but pain; and he ended by subscribing to the teaching of the Indian fakirs that only annihilation could bring deliverance. Pauline heard him profess his loathing for action, and foretell the ultimate suicide of all nations, which would go hurtling down into outer darkness together, when they refused to beget new generations once their intelligence had evolved sufficiently to realise what a cruel, idiotic farce some unknown power was imposing on them. Then she would flare up, searching for arguments which he promptly demolished, for she was ignorant in such matters and had, as he pointed out, no head for metaphysics. But she refused to admit defeat, and bluntly consigned his Schopenhauer to the devil when he tried to read her certain passages—a man who wrote such horrible things about women! and whom she'd gladly have strangled if he hadn't had a redeeming fondness for animals. With her physical health, her straightforward enjoyment of to-day's habits and to-morrow's hopes, she silenced Lazare in her turn with her ringing laughter; she triumphed, with all the vigorous energy of youth.

'Look here,' she cried, 'you're talking nonsense. We'll think about dying when we're old.'

At the idea of death, which she dismissed so light-heartedly, he invariably grew grave and averted his eyes. Usually, he changed the subject, after muttering that people died at all ages.

Pauline realised at last that Lazare was horribly afraid of death. She remembered his long-ago cry of terror at the sight of the stars; nowadays she saw him turn pale at certain words, and fall silent as though he had some shameful illness to conceal; and she was greatly surprised at finding such a dread of annihilation in the pessimist who talked about stars being blown out like candles amidst the universal holocaust of life. His disease was of long standing and she did not even suspect how serious it was. As he grew older, Lazare was haunted by the thought of death. Until his twentieth year he had merely experienced a slight chilly shudder at nights, when he went to bed. Nowadays he could not lay his head on the pillow without feeling his whole face frozen by the idea of 'nevermore.' He became a prey to insomnia; he could not resign himself to the fatal necessity that unfolded before his imagination in gloomy symbols. Then, when weariness had overcome him, he would sometimes wake with a start, and leap upright, his eyes wide with horror and his hands clasped, stammering in the darkness: 'My God, my God!' His breast seemed to be bursting, he felt himself at the point of death; and not until he had lit his candle and become fully awake did he regain a certain degree of calm. Afterwards he felt ashamed of his terrors; what pitiful folly, to appeal to a God he denied—it was the inherited weakness of humanity, crying for help while the world crashed! But the crisis recurred none the less each evening, like some evil passion that wore him out, in spite of reason. During the daytime, too, everything seemed to remind him of it—a casual sentence, a sudden thought, springing from something read or seen. As Pauline, one evening, was reading the paper to her uncle, Lazare had to leave the room overcome with emotion, on hearing some story-teller's fanciful vision of the twentieth-century sky full of balloons in flight, carrying travellers from one continent to another. He would not be there; and these balloons, which he would not see, seemed to float away into the void of those future centuries which would elapse outside his own existence; and the thought filled him with anguish. In vain did his philosophers remind him that not a single spark of life would be lost; his ego revolted against the prospect of coming to an end. Already he had lost his gaiety in the conflict. When Pauline gazed at him, puzzled by the vagaries of his character, while he was trying, with anxious shame, to conceal his suffering, she felt moved to compassion, she wanted to be very kind to him and to make him happy.

They whiled away their days in the great room upstairs, surrounded by the seaweed, flasks and instruments which Lazare had not even the strength of mind to get rid of; and the algae were dropping to bits, the flasks growing discoloured and the instruments, under their load of dust, became unusable. Amidst the chaos, they were snugly lost to the world. Often, from morning till night, the December rain-storms beat on the roof slates, and the west wind moaned like the notes of an organ through the cracks in the wood-work. Whole weeks passed without a single ray of sunshine; they saw nothing but the grey sea, a limitless expanse of grey into which the earth seemed to dissolve. Pauline, to occupy the long vacant hours, amused herself by classifying a collection of Floridaeae which they had made in the spring. At first Lazare roamed listlessly about, content to watch her sticking down the delicate branching specimens with their water-colour tints of red and soft blue; then, sick of doing nothing and forgetting his theoretical dislike of action, he had unearthed the piano from under the battered pieces of apparatus and the dirty flasks that encumbered it. A week later, his passion for music possessed him once more. Therein lay the original source of his disorder; the frustration of the artist in him was responsible for his failure as scientist and industrialist. One morning as he was playing his March of Death, the thought of the great Symphony of Suffering that he had once planned to write stirred him once more. The rest of it was no good, he'd only kept the March; but what a subject! What a work could be made of it! He would sum up his whole philosophy in it. To begin with, Life born of the selfish whim of some power; then happiness shown as an illusion, the whole of existence as a hoax, in a few striking scenes— lovers mating, soldiers being slaughtered, a god dying on a cross; and the cry of Evil would be heard rising through it all, the wailing of creatures would fill the heavens, until the final song of delivery, a song whose celestial beauty would express the joy of universal annihilation. The very next day he set to work, thumping the piano, covering his paper with black strokes. As the instrument, increas-ingly decrepit, gasped feebly, he sang the notes himself, booming like a great bell. No task had ever before obsessed him to this point; he sat there forgetful of his mealtimes, and he deafened Pauline with the noise; she, goodnaturedly, gave her approval and copied out passages for him neatly. This time, he was convinced of it, he'd got his masterpiece.

At last, however, Lazare grew calmer. He had finished everyting but the opening, the inspiration for which escaped him. He'd have to let it lie for a while. And he sat smoking cigarettes in front of his score, spread out on the big table. Pauline meanwhile played phrases of it to him, with a beginner's clumsiness. It was at this juncture that their intimacy began to grow dangerous. He no longer had the cares of the factory to occupy his mind and tire his body; and now that he was shut up with her, at a loose end, his nerves on edge with idleness, his feeling for her grew warmer.

She was so merry, so goodhearted, so cheerfully unselfish! At first he had merely been conscious of an impulse of gratitude, an intensifying of that brotherly affection that he had felt for her since she was a child; but gradually desire, hitherto dormant, was aroused; he realised that this sturdy young brother, with whom he had so constantly rubbed shoulders quite unmoved, was a woman. Then he started blushing, just as she did, at their slightest contact. He dared no longer go near her, lean over behind her to look at the music she was copying. If their hands happened to meet they would both stand stammering, breathless, with cheeks aflame. Thenceforward all their afternoons were spent in a state of uneasiness that left them exhausted, tormented by an ill-defined longing for some missing happiness.

Sometimes, in order to escape from one of these embarrassing moments that caused them such delicious anguish, Pauline, emboldened by her chastity and her learning, would tease him. 'Didn't I tell you? I dreamed your Schopenhauer heard about our marriage from the other world, and came back at nights to pull us by the feet.'

Lazare laughed awkwardly. He realised that she was making fun of his perpetual inconsistencies, but he felt a boundless affection pervading him and casting out his hatred of the will to live.

'Be kind,' he murmured, 'you know I love you.'

She looked stern. 'Take care! you're putting off the day of deliverance, you're relapsing into egotism and self-deception.'

'Will you shut up, you wretch?'

And he chased her round the table, while she went on reciting fragments of pessimistic philosophy in a mock professorial voice. Then, when he had caught her, he dared not hold her in his arms as he used to, pinching her by way of punishment.

One day, however, he had been pursuing her so hotly that he seized her violently by the waist. She was shaking with laughter; he held her pressed back against the cupboard, wild with excitement as he felt her struggling to escape.

'Aha, I've got you this time . . . What shall I do to you, eh?'

Their faces were touching. She was still laughing, but the laughter died away on her lips.

'No, no, let me go, I won't do it any more.'

He kissed her roughly on the lips. The room seemed to swim, they felt as though a fiery wind was whirling them into the void. She was about to sink backwards, when she freed herself with a sudden effort. They stood for an instant breathless, flushing scarlet and averting their eyes from one another. Then she sat down to get her breath, and said gravely and sadly, 'You hurt me, Lazare.'

From that day on he shunned so much as the warmth of her breath, the touch of her dress. His sense of decency revolted against the thought of senseless misconduct, of hole-and-corner possession. In spite of the girl's instinctive resistance he saw that she would yield to him, dizzy with passion at their first embrace, and loving him to the point of giving herself entirely if he insisted; and he resolved to have wisdom enough for both of them, realising that he would be the chief culprit if they embarked on an adventure whose danger he alone, with his greater experience, could foretell. But this struggle with himself only increased his love for her. Everything concurred to stimulate it—the inaction of these first weeks, his pose of renunciation, his disgust with life in the midst of which had sprung up a wild yearning to live and love and fill the weary vacant hours with fresh sufferings. His state of nervous excitement was brought to a head by music—music which carried them together into a world of dreams on the ever-spreading wings of rhythm. Then he felt convinced that he had found his ruling passion, and vowed to devote his genius to it. There was no doubt about it; he'd be a famous musician, for he needed only to dip into his heart. Everything seemed to be purified; and he took to worshipping her on bended knees as his good angel, without ever thinking of hurrying on the date of their marriage.

'Look here, read this letter I've just received,' said Chanteau to his wife in great alarm one day, when she had just got back from Bonneville.

It was another letter from Saccard, a threatening one this time. He had been writing to them since November to ask for a statement of the account, and as the Chanteaus always gave evasive answers, he now announced his intention of notifying the family council of their refusal. Although she did not admit it, Madame Chanteau began to share her husband's anxiety.

'The scoundrel!' she murmured after reading the letter.

They gazed at one another in silence, white to the lips. The close air of the little dining-room seemed to resound already with the noisy scandal of a lawsuit.

'You needn't hesitate any longer,' Chanteau went on, 'Marry them, since that would set her legally free.'

But the mother seemed to find this solution more distasteful every day. She expressed fears: who could tell whether the two children would get on well together? A good pair of friends might make a shocking married couple. Lately, she'd noticed a number of things she didn't like.

'No, you see, it would be wrong to sacrifice them for our own peace of mind . . . Let's wait a little longer . . . And besides, why should we marry them now, since she was eighteen last month and we can claim legal emancipation.'

Her self-confidence was returning; she went up to fetch her Code and they studied it together. They read article 478 with relief; but they were bothered by article 480, which stated that the guardians must render their account in the presence of a trustee nominated by the family council. It was true that she held all the members of the council in the hollow of her hand, and could make them nominate whoever she chose; but whom should she choose, where could she find somebody suitable? The problem was to replace the dreaded deputy-guardian by an obliging trustee.

Suddenly she had an inspiration. 'What about Doctor Cazenove? He knows something about our problems, he won't refuse.'

Chanteau nodded his approval. But he gazed intently at his wife, as one thought obsessed him. At last he asked her: 'Then you'll give back the money, I mean all that's left of it?'

She did not answer immediately. She was looking down and turning the pages of the Code with nervous fingers. Then she said with an effort: 'Of course I'll give it back, and indeed it'll be a good riddance for us. You see what they're accusing us of already . . . I declare it's enough to make lose faith in oneself. I'd give five francs to get rid of it out of my desk to-night. And in any case we'd have had to give it back.'

The very next day, as Dr. Cazenove had come to Bonneville on his Saturday rounds, Madame Chanteau told him about the great favour they hoped he would do them. She confessed the whole situation, the way the money had been swallowed up in Lazare's disastrous experiment without the family council ever having been consulted; then she dwelt on the marriage project, the bonds of affection that united them all and that the scandal of a lawsuit threatened to break.

Before promising his help, the doctor insisted on speaking to Pauline. For a long time now, he had been aware that she was being exploited and robbed by slow degrees; if he had kept silence up till then, for fear of distressing her, it was his duty to warn her now that he was being invited to become an accomplice. The matter was discussed in the girl's bedroom. Madame Chanteau went up with the doctor and was present at the beginning of the interview; she declared that the marriage depended on Pauline's being legally free, for Lazare would never consent to marry his cousin so long as he was liable to be accused of trying to dodge submitting his accounts. After this she withdrew, protesting that she did not wish to influence the girl, whom she had already described as 'her beloved daughter'. Immediately Pauline, deeply moved, begged the doctor to render them the difficult service the necessity for which had just been explained to her. In vain did he try to enlighten her as to her position; she insisted on giving up everything, renouncing any claim; he even hinted at his fears for the future—fears of total ruin, ingratitude, great suffering in store; the darker he painted the picture, the more she protested, refusing to listen and showing a feverish anxiety to sacrifice herself.

'No, don't encourage me to regret it. I've got a hidden streak of meanness in me that I find hard enough to conquer as it is . . . Let them take it all. They can have all that's left if only they'll love me more.'

'Look here,' asked the doctor, 'it's for your cousin's sake that you're giving up everything?'

She blushed without replying.

' And what if, later on, your cousin didn't love you any more?'

She gazed at him in terror. Her eyes filled with great tears and her whole soul broke out in a cry of indignant love: 'Oh no, no . . . Why do you distress me so?'

Then Dr. Cazenove gave in. He had not the heart to wound the generous girl by destroying her affectionate illusions. Life would be cruel to her all too soon.

Madame Chanteau conducted the campaign with an astonishing capacity for intrigue. The struggle quite rejuvenated her. She had gone off to Paris again, armed with the requisite powers. She promptly won over the members of the family council to her point of view; for that matter they had never given much thought to their responsibility, treating it with characteristic indifference. Those on the Quenu side of the family, the cousins Naudet, Liardin and Delorme, supported her; and out of the three on Lisa's side, she only had to convince Octave Mouret, for the other two, Claude Lantier and Rambaud, who were then in Marseilles, had been content to send her their written approval. She had told them all an involved and touching story about the affection of the old doctor of Arromanches for Pauline, and his evident intention of leaving his fortune to the girl if he was allowed to look after her interests. As for Saccard, he yielded too, after three visits from Madame

Chanteau, who brought him a splendid idea—that of cornering all the butter of Le Cotentin, thanks to a new system of transport. So Pauline's emancipation was decided by the family council, and the former naval surgeon Cazenove was nominated as trustee, the magistrate having received the highest recommendation of him.

A fortnight after Madame Chanteau's return to Bonneville, the inspection of the tutelage accounts took place in the simplest of fashions. The doctor had come to lunch, they had lingered a little round the table chatting about the latest news from Caen, where Lazare had just spent a couple of days on account of a law-suit with which that wretch Boutigny was threatening him.

'By the way,' said the young man, 'Louise is going to pay us a surprise visit next week . . . I hardly recognised her. She's living at home now, and she's become so elegant . . . Oh, we did have fun!'

Pauline was looking at him, surprised by the warmth of feeling his voice betrayed.

'Talking of Louise,' cried Madame Chanteau, 'I travelled with a lady from Caen who knows the Thibaudiers. You could have knocked me down with a feather! It seems Thibaudier's giving his daughter a dowry of a hundred thousand francs! With her mother's hundred thousand, the child will have two hundred thousand . . . What d'you think of that? Two hundred thousand, she's a rich girl now!'

'Pooh,' said Lazare, 'she doesn't need that, she's as pretty as a picture . . . And such a tease!'

A cloud darkened Pauline's eyes and her lips twitched nervously. Then the doctor, who had not taken his gaze off her, raised the small glass of rum that he had been drinking.

'Look here, we haven't drunk your health . . . Here's to your happiness, my friends. Get married quickly and have a lot of children!'

Madame Chanteau, unsmiling, held out her glass slowly, while Chanteau, who was forbidden to touch spirits, merely nodded his approval. But Lazare had grasped Pauline's hand in a charmingly spontaneous gesture that sent all the blood rushing to the girl's cheeks again. Wasn't she his good angel, as he called her, the ever-abundant source of feeling which would supply the life-blood for his genius? She returned the pressure of his hand. They all clinked glasses.

'May you live to be a hundred!' went on the doctor, who had a theory that a hundred was the finest time of a man's life.

84

It was Lazare's turn to grow pale. That figure, casually uttered, sent a shiver running through him; it made him think of the time when he would have ceased to be, the dread of which forever haunted his innermost being. In a hundred years, what would be left of him? What stranger would be drinking where he now stood, in front of this table? He tossed off the little glass with a trembling hand, while Pauline who had seized the other hand again, was once more pressing it with almost motherly protectiveness, as though the icy breath of ' nevermore' had left its trace on that wan face.

There was a silence. Then Madame Chanteau said in a solemn tone: 'Now, shall we conclude our business?'

She had decided that the signing should take place in her room; this would give it greater formality. Since he had begun to take salicylate, Chanteau had found walking easier. He followed her up the stairs, leaning on the banister; and as Lazare was talking of going to smoke a cigar on the terrace, she called him back, insisting that he must be present, if only for form's sake. The doctor and Pauline had gone in front. Mathieu, puzzled by this procession, brought up the rear.

'What a nuisance that dog is, always trailing round after one!' cried Madame Chanteau, as she tried to close the door. 'Well, come on in then, I don't want to have you scratching . . . There now, nobody'll come and disturb us . . . You see everything is ready.'

As she implied, pens and an inkpot were set out on the table. The place had that close atmosphere, that lifeless silence of rooms into which people seldom go. Only Minouche used to spend lazy days there, when she managed to slip in there in the mornings. As it happened she had been asleep in the depths of the eiderdown, and she raised her head in surprise at this invasion, staring with her green eyes.

'Sit down, sit down,' Chanteau kept saying.

Then things were quickly despatched. Madame Chanteau affected to withdraw, leaving her husband to play the part which she had been rehearsing with him since the day before. In order to comply with the law, he had, ten days previously, handed over to Pauline, in the doctor's presence, the tutelage accounts set out in a thick notebook, receipts on one side and expenditure on the other; everything had been deducted, not merely the ward's maintenance allowance but even the expenses of drawing up deeds and of journeys to Caen and Paris. It only remained therefore to get the accounts accepted by private agreement. But Cazenove, who took his trusteeship seriously, raised certain objections with regard to the finances of the factory; and he obliged Chanteau to go into details. Pauline gazed beseechingly at the doctor: what was the good? She herself had helped to draw up the accounts, which her aunt had copied out in her best handwriting.

Minouche, meanwhile, had sat up in the middle of the eiderdown, the better to watch the curious proceedings. Mathieu, after meekly laying his big head on the edge of the rug, had now rolled over on to his back, yielding to the pleasure of being on the warm, cosy wool; and he was rubbing himself and wriggling about, uttering grunts of delight.

'Lazare, make him keep quiet!' Madame Chanteau said at last, impatiently. 'We can't hear ourselves speak.'

The young man was standing in front of the window, watching a white sail passing in the distance, in an attempt to conceal his embarrassment. He felt a sense of shame on hearing his father give precise details of the sums of money swallowed up by his ill-fated factory.

'Shut up, Mathieu,' he said, stretching out his foot.

The dog thought he was having his belly patted, which he adored, and he only grunted louder. Luckily there was nothing more to do but to append the signatures. Pauline assented to everything, hurriedly, with one stroke of the pen. Then the doctor, as though reluctantly, scrawled his name with an enormous flourish across the document. A painful silence fell.

'The credit account,' Madame Chanteau went on at last, 'thus stands at seventy-thousand, two hundred and ten francs, thirty centimes . . . I will hand this over to Pauline.'

She went up to her dressing-desk; the lid gave the muffled creak which had so often distressed her. But now she was in solemn mood; she opened the drawer, disclosing the old cash-book cover; it was still the same, with its green mottlings and its grease-spots; only it had grown slimmer, the dwindled heap of securities no longer threatened to burst open the parchment back. •

'No, no,' Pauline cried. 'Keep it, auntie!'

Madame Chanteau was on her dignity. 'We've rendered our account, and we must hand back the money . . . It's your property. You remember what I told you eight years ago, when I put it there? We don't want to keep a penny of it.'

She pulled out the securities, she forced the girl to count them. There were seventy-five thousand francs' worth, with a little parcel of gold wrapped in a piece of newspaper making up the balance.

'But where am I to put this?' asked Pauline, flushed with the thought of handling such a great sum of money.

'Shut it up in your cupboard,' replied her aunt. 'You're big enough to look after your own money. I don't want even to see it again . . . Look, if you don't want it, give it to Minouche who's watching you.'

The Chanteaus had paid up, and their spirits rose again. Lazare, feeling relieved, played with the dog, made him chase his own tail, twisting his back and spinning round endlessly like a top; while Dr. Cazenove, in his new rôle as trustee, was promising Pauline to cash her securities and find new investments for her.

And meanwhile, down below, Véronique roughly clattered her pots and pans. She had gone upstairs and, with her ear glued to the key-hole, had overheard certain figures. During the past few weeks, the secret growth of her affection for the girl had routed her last remaining prejudices.

'They've run through half of what's hers, I declare!' she grumbled angrily. 'No, it's not decent . . . Of course she hadn't needed to come amongst us, but was that a reason to fleece her stark naked? . . . No, I know what's fair, and I shall end by getting fond of the child!'

CHAPTER IV

THAT Saturday, when Louise, who was coming to spend a couple of months with the Chanteaus, stepped on to the terrace, she found the whole family assembled there. The day was drawing to a close; it had been a very hot August day, with a refreshing sea-breeze. Abbé Horteur was already there, playing draughts with Chanteau, while Madame Chanteau sat beside them embroidering a hand-kerchief. And a few yards away, Pauline was standing in front of a stone bench on which she had installed four small urchins from the village, two girls and two boys.

'Why, you're here already!' cried Madame Chanteau. 'I was just folding up my work to go and meet you at the cross-roads.'

Louise gaily explained that old Malivoire had brought her like the wind. She was all right, she didn't even want to change her dress, and while her godmother went in to see that her room was ready, she merely hung up her hat on the hook of a shutter. She kissed everybody and then came back to put her arm round Pauline's waist, with a merry, affectionate air.

'Come on, look at me! . . . Hey, haven't we both grown up now? You know, I'm over nineteen, I'm quite an old maid . . .' She broke off, and added quickly, 'By the way, congratulations . . . Oh, don't pretend, I'm told it's to be next month.'

Pauline had returned her embrace, with the fond and serious air of an elder sister, although she was the younger by eighteen months. A slight flush rose to her cheeks at the allusion to her marriage with Lazare.

'No, really, you've been misinformed,' she answered. 'Nothing's settled, we're only thinking of this autumn.'

And indeed Madame Chanteau, in answer to a direct appeal, had mentioned the autumn, despite her reluctance, which the young couple had already begun to notice. She had reverted to her original pretext, saying that she'd rather her son found a job first.

'Oh, all right,' went on Louise, 'you're a close one, aren't you? Anyhow, you'll invite me, won't you? And where's Lazare: isn't he here?'

Chanteau, who had just been beaten by the *abbé*, answered for her. 'You didn't meet him then, Louisette? We were just saying you'd be coming along together. Yes, he's at Bayeux, he's had business with the sub-prefect. But he'll be back to-night, latish maybe.' And, returning to his game: 'My turn to begin, Abbé . . . You know, we're going to get our famous jetties, for the department can't refuse us a grant in this case.'

This was a new enterprise into which Lazare had thrown himself. At the last spring tides, in March, the sea had carried away two more of Bonneville's houses. The village, on its narrow shingle beach, was gradually being eaten away, and seemed likely to be utterly crushed against the cliff unless measures were taken to protect it with proper defences. But it was so unimportant, with its thirty hovels, that Chanteau, in his capacity as mayor, had been trying in vain for the last ten years to call the sub-prefect's attention to the desperate plight of the inhabitants. At last Lazare, urged on by Pauline, whose great aim was to spur him into activity, and evolved a scheme for restraining the sea by a system of jetties and breakwaters. Only funds were needed—twelve thousand francs at least.

'I'm going to huff this one of yours, my friend,' said the priest, taking a pawn. Then he held forth complacently about Bonneville as it used to be. 'The old people say there was once a farm lower down than the church, about a mile out from where the beach is now. The sea's been encroaching on them for five hundred years. It's unbelievable; they must be paying for their horrible sins, from one generation to another.'

Pauline, meanwhile, had gone back to the bench where the four dirty, ragged urchins were waiting for her with mouths agape.

'Whatever are those?' asked Louise, not daring to draw nearer.

'Those,' Pauline replied, 'are my little friends.'

Nowadays her active charity extended to the whole countryside. She had an instinctive love for the wretched, was not repelled by their misfortunes, and even carried this taste so far as to make little splints for hens that had broken their legs and put out saucers of soup for stray cats at night. She was constantly concerned about suffering creatures, and it was a necessity and a delight to her to relieve their pain. And the poor used to flock to her outstretched hands as thieving sparrows flock to the open windows of a granary. The whole of Bonneville, that handful of fishermen racked by misfortunes and battered by the high tide, would go up to see the young lady, as they called her. But she chiefly loved the children, the small boys with tattered trousers that showed their pink flesh, the pallid little girls who never got enough to eat and stared ravenously at the pieces of bread and butter that she distributed. And the shrewd parents took advantage of her soft-heartedness and sent along the puniest and most ragged of their brats to arouse her compassion even more.

'You see,' she said laughingly, 'I have my At Home day, like a lady, on a Saturday . . . Hey, you, little Gonin, stop pinching that silly great Houtelard boy! I shall get angry if you don't behave . . . Let's try and do things methodically.'

Then the distribution began. She ordered them and hustled them about in a motherly fashion. The first she called up was the Houtelard boy, a lad of ten, sallow-skinned, with a dull sickly look. He showed her his leg; he had a long scratch on his knee and his father had sent him to the young lady to have something put on it. It was she who provided the whole countryside with arnica and soothing lotion. Her passion for healing had made her little by little acquire a well-stocked medicine chest, of which she was proud. When she had dressed the child's leg she lowered her voice to tell Louise the details of the case.

'My dear, they're rich people, these Houtelards, the biggest and richest fishers in Bonneville. You know, they own that big boat . . . Only they're appallingly miserly, they live in absolute squalor and wretchedness. And the worst of it is that the father, after having beaten his wife to death, married his servant, a horrible creature, even harder-hearted than he is. Now, between the two of them, they're killing this poor thing.'

And without noticing her friend's look of uneasy disgust, she raised her voice. 'Your turn next, little one . . . Did you drink your bottle of tonic?'

This was the daughter of Prouane, the beadle. She looked like a childish Saint Teresa, covered with scrofula, lean and intense-looking, with great prominent eyes already ablaze with hysteria. She was eleven, and looked barely seven.

'Yes, miss,' she stuttered, 'I drunk it.'

'Liar!' cried the priest, without taking his eyes from the draughts board, 'your father smelt of wine again last night.'

At this Pauline grew angry. The Prouanes, who had no boat, made their living by picking up crabs and mussels and catching shrimps. But thanks to the father's position as beadle, they could still have had their daily bread, had it not been for their drunkenness. The father and mother could be seen sprawling across the doorway, knocked out by *calvados*, the terrible Normandy brandy; while the little girl clambered over their bodies to drain their glasses. When he was short of *calvados* Prouane used to drink his daughter's quinine wine.

'After all the trouble I took to make it!' said Pauline. 'Listen, I shall keep the bottle, you can come and drink it here every evening at five o'clock . . . And I shall give you a little raw mince; the doctor ordered it.'

Then came the turn of a big lad of twelve, Cuche's son, a lean, skinny urchin, already depraved. To him she handed a loaf, a bowl of soup and a five-franc piece. His was another shocking story; after the destruction of his house, Cuche had left his wife and gone to live at a cousin's; and the wife, having taken refuge in a ruined customs-house post, now slept with the whole neighbourhood, in spite of her repulsive ugliness. Her clients paid her in kind, and sometimes gave her a few coppers. The boy, who watched it all, was starving. But he would bound away like a wild goat if anyone talked of rescuing him from such a sink of iniquity.

Louise averted her head uneasily while Pauline, without a trace of embarrassment, told her this story. The freedom of the younger girl's upbringing enabled her to face the sordid aspects of human life with the calm courage of charity; she knew everything and talked about everything with innocent frankness. The other, on the contrary, had her own store of knowledge, acquired through ten years at a boarding-school; her schoolgirl fantasies had perverted her imagination, and she blushed at the ideas that the words suggested; you might think about such things but you mustn't speak of them.

'For instance,' Pauline went on, 'this last little girl, this nice little rosy, fair thing—nine years old—is the daughter of the Gonins, the couple with whom that rascal Cuche has gone to live. These Gonins were comfortably off and had their own boat; but the father became paralysed in the legs, which is not uncommon in our villages; and Cuche, who was just an ordinary sailor, soon got possession of the boat and the woman as well. Now the house belongs to him, and he beats the cripple, a tall old man who has to spend his days and nights lying in an old coal-bunker, while the sailor and his cousin have kept the bed for themselves, in the same room . . . So I'm looking after the child. The pity of it is that when blows are flying she comes in for a few, and besides, she's too intelligent and sees certain things . . .' She broke off to question the child. 'How are things at home?'

The little girl had been watching attentively as Pauline told her story in a low voice; her pretty, depraved little face was alight with sly merriment as she guessed the details.

'They beat him again,' she answered, still sniggering. 'Last night ma got up and took a log . . . Oh, miss, it'd be very kind of you to give him a little wine, for they've put a jug in front of the bunker and told him they're going to let him die.'

Louise gave a disgusted gesture. What revolting people! And her friend took an interest in such horrors! Was it possible that so near a big town like Caen there existed remote corners where the inhabitants lived thus like absolute savages? For surely only savages would be capable of offending the laws of God and man in this way.

'No, my dear,' she murmured, sitting down near Chanteau, 'I've had quite enough of your little friends! Let the sea roll over them, I shan't be sorry for them!'

The *abbé* had just crowned one of his men. He called out: 'Sodom and Gomorrah! I've been warning them for the past twenty years. Now it's their own look-out!'

'I've asked for a school,' said Chanteau, distressed to see his game in danger, 'but there aren't enough of them, their children have to be sent to Verchemont; and they don't go to lessons, or else they play truant along the roadside.'

Pauline looked at them in astonishment. If the wretched were clean there would be no need to wash them. Evil and poverty were interconnected, and she was never repelled by suffering, even when it appeared to be the result of vice. She merely made an expansive gesture that implied the vast tolerance of her charity. She was just promising the Gonin child to visit her father when Véronique appeared, pushing another small girl in front of her.

'Here you are, miss, here's another of them.'

The newcomer was very young, five at the most, completely in rags, with a filthy face and tangled hair. Immediately, with the amazing self-possession of an infant prodigy already inured to highway beggary, she began to moan: 'Have pity on us . . . My poor father has broken his leg . . .'

'This is the Tournals' daughter, isn't she?' Pauline asked the maid.

But the priest burst out furiously: 'Oh, the little slut! Don't listen to her, it's twenty-five years since her father sprained his ankle . . . They're a family of thieves, who live on nothing but robbery! The father helps smugglers, the mother pillages the fields of Verchemont, the grandfather goes poaching at night in the state oyster-bed at Roqueboise . . . And you see what they've turned their daughter into: a beggar, a thief whom they send into people's houses to pick up anything that's lying about . . . See how she's ogling my tobacco-box.'

And indeed the child's sharp eyes, after raking every corner of the terrace, had lit up eagerly at the sight of the priest's old tobacco-box. But she retained all her self-possession and repeated, as though the *curé* had not told the family history: 'Broken his leg . . . Give us something, kind lady.'

This time, Louise had to laugh, highly amused at the sight of this little runt of five, already as rascally as her parents. Pauline, un-smiling, drew out her purse and took from it another five-franc piece.

'Listen,' she said, 'I'll give you another every Saturday, if I'm sure you haven't been roaming the roads during the week.'

'Hide the silver,' called out Abbé Horteur again, 'she'll rob you.'

But Pauline, without replying, was sending the children away. They slouched off uttering cries of 'Thank you' and 'God bless you for it.' Meanwhile Madame Chanteau, who had come back after seeing to Louise's room, was scolding Véronique in an undertone. This was unbearable—the maid herself had now taken to letting in beggars! As if Mademoiselle didn't bring enough of them into the house! A lot of scum that wasted her substance and then made fun of her! Of course her money was her own, she could waste it if she liked; but really it was getting rather immoral, the way she

encouraged vice. Madame Chanteau had heard the girl's promise
to give the Tourmal child five francs every Saturday. Another
twenty francs a month! A satrap's fortune wouldn't stand it.

'You know I don't want to see that thief here again,' she told
Pauline. 'You may be mistress of your own fortune now, but I can't
allow you to ruin yourself so stupidly. I'm morally responsible . . .
Yes, ruin yourself, my dear, and faster than you think!'

Véronique, who had gone back into her kitchen, raging against
Madame's reproof, reappeared shouting rudely: 'Here's the butcher;
he wants his bill, forty-six francs ten.'

Madame Chanteau stopped short, in great confusion. She hunted
in her pockets and then, with a gesture of surprise, murmured:
'I say, Pauline, have you enough on you? I've got no change,
I should have to run upstairs. We'll settle afterwards.'

Pauline went out after the maid to pay the butcher. Since she
had been keeping her money in her cupboard the same farce was
repeated every time a bill had to be paid. She was being regularly
robbed of continual small sums in a way that seemed perfectly
natural. The aunt no longer even needed to take money from the
hoard; she asked for it and allowed the girl to despoil herself with
her own hands. In the beginning she kept an account, she had paid
back ten francs here and fifteen francs there; then the accounts
grew so muddled that now she merely talked of settling up later,
when the marriage took place; notwithstanding which, on the first
of each month, Pauline punctually paid her *pension*, which had now
been raised to ninety francs.

'There's your money gone flying again!' grumbled Véronique in
the passage. 'I'd have sent her to fetch her own change, you bet!
Surely to God it's not right they should fleece you like this!'

When Pauline came back with the receipted bill and handed it
to her aunt, the *curé* was triumphing noisily. Chanteau was being
beaten; decidedly, he wouldn't be able to take one. The sun was
setting; its slanting rays shed a crimson glow over the sea, which
was rolling in lazily. And Louise smiled as she gazed, dreamy-
eyed, at the jubilance of the immense horizon.

'There's Louisette gone off into the clouds,' said Madame
Chanteau. 'Hey, Louisette, I've had your trunk taken up . . .
We're next door to each other again.'

Lazare did not get back till the following day. After his visit
to the sub-prefect, he had decided to go on to Caen and see the
prefect himself. And, if he hadn't actually bought the subsidy back
in his pocket, he was convinced, so he said, that the General Council

would vote them at least the sum of twelve thousand francs. The prefect, on seeing him to the door, had made categorical promises to that effect; they would not leave Bonneville in the lurch, the administration was ready to second the zealous effort of the inhabitants of the commune. Only Lazare was in despair because he foresaw all kinds of delays, and the slightest check to the realisation of any one of his desires was real torture to him nowadays.

'On my word,' he cried, 'if I had the twelve thousand francs I'd rather lend them . . . And we wouldn't even need such a sum to make the first experiment . . . And you'll see what worries we shall have once they've voted their subsidy! We shall be pestered by all the engineers in the department. Whereas if we were to begin without them, they'd be obliged to accept our results . . . I'm confident in my plan. The prefect, to whom I explained it briefly, was amazed at its cheapness and simplicity.'

He was wildly excited at the thought of defeating the sea. He had borne it a grudge ever since secretly holding it responsible for his ruin, over the algae experiment. Though he dared not abuse it openly he harboured the hope of revenging himself one day. And what vengeance could be finer than to check it in its career of destruction, calling out authoritatively: 'Thou shalt go no further!' There was, moreover, quite apart from the grandeur of the struggle, an element of philanthropy in the scheme that crowned his excitement. When his mother watched him spending his days carving pieces of wood and poring over mechanical text-books, she thought with a shudder of his grandfather, the enterprising, muddle-headed carpenter whose masterpiece lay, useless and unheeded, under a glass case. Was the old man's spirit to be born again, to complete the ruin of the family? Then she allowed herself to be won over by her adored son. If he succeeded—and of course he would succeed—it would, at any rate, be a first step: a noble deed, a disinterested achievement which would call attention to him, and from which he could easily go on to whatever he liked, as high as his ambition led him. Thenceforward the whole household thought of nothing but of humbling the sea, of chaining it up at the foot of the terrace as meek as a beaten dog.

Lazare's plan, moreover, was an extremely simple one, as he had said. It consisted of thick stakes sunk into the sand, covered with planks, behind which the shingle that had been rolled in by the tide would form an impregnable wall against which the waves would break in vain. Thus the sea would itself have built the redoubt that would repel it. Jetties consisting of long beams resting on struts and acting as breakwaters, projecting in front of the shingle walls, would complete the system. Eventually, if the necessary funds were to hand, two or three large piers could be built, huge structures of planks laid on a framework of serried posts which would check the force of the highest tides. Lazare had found the original idea in the *Manual of the Complete Carpenter*, a quaintly-illustrated volume that had probably been bought long ago by his grandfather; but he had improved on the idea, he was doing a great deal of research, studying the theory of forces and the strength of different materials; he was particularly proud of a new way of grouping and inclining the jetties which, in his view, made success an absolute certainty.

Pauline had once again taken an interest in his studies. Like him, she was always intrigued by experiments that brought her to grips with the unknown. Only, being more level-headed, she had no illusions this time about the possibility of disappointment. When she watched the sea flowing in and sweeping the shore with its great swell, she cast a doubtful glance at the toys Lazare had built, the rows of stakes, jetties and breakwaters in miniature that now cluttered up the big study.

One night the girl sat very late at her window. For the past ten days her cousin had been talking of throwing it all up; one evening at supper he had exclaimed that he'd go off to Australia, since there was no place for him in France. And she thought over these things, while the tide, now at the full, battered Bonneville in the heart of the darkness. Every shock seemed to go right through her; she thought she could hear, at regular intervals, the wailing of the wretches whom the sea was devouring. Then the still unresolved conflict between her love of money and her goodness of heart became intolerable. She closed the window to shut out the sounds. But the distant reverberations shook her where she lay. Why not attempt the impossible? What did it matter if her money was cast into the sea, provided there was a single chance of saving the village? And she fell asleep at dawn, imagining the delight of her cousin, set free from his black depressions, with his true vocation, maybe, found at last; she would have made him happy, and for her, he came first of all.

Next day she called out to him before going downstairs. She was laughing. 'D'you know, I dreamt I lent you the twelve thousand francs.'

He grew angry, violently rejecting her offer. 'Do you want me to go away and never come back? No, the factory was quite bad enough. It makes me die of shame, though I don't talk about it.'

Two hours later he had accepted; he clasped her hands with passionate enthusiasm. It would simply be a loan; her money would run no risks, for there could be no doubt that the General Council would vote the subsidy, particularly once the work had been begun. And that very evening the carpenter from Arromanches was sent for. There were interminable conferences, walks along the coast, eager discussions about costs. The whole house went crazy about it.

Madame Chanteau, however, was furious when she heard about the twelve thousand francs loan. Lazare was astonished and puzzled. His mother overwhelmed him with the oddest arguments; it was true that Pauline lent them small sums from time to time, but she'd end by thinking herself indispensable. They might quite well have asked Louise's father to advance the money. Louise herself, with her dowry of two hundred thousand frances, didn't make so much fuss about her fortune. Madame Chanteau was constantly referring to those two hundred thousand francs, and she seemed to feel contempt and irritation for that other fortune, which after melting away in her writing desk was still melting away in Pauline's cupboard.

Chanteau, egged on by his wife, displayed annoyance too. It made Pauline very sad; even when she gave them her money, she felt that they loved her less than they used to; an atmosphere of resentment which she could not explain had grown up around her and was increasing daily. As for Dr. Cazenove, he grumbled too, when she consulted him for form's sake; but he had been obliged to agree to all the sums she lent, both small and large. His trustee-ship was purely illusory; he could not fight these people, who welcomed him as an old friend. On the day of the twelve thousand francs loan, he gave up all responsibility.

'My dear child,' he said, drawing Pauline aside, 'I don't want to be your accomplice any more. Stop consulting me; ruin yourself as your heart tells you . . . You're well aware that I shall never resist your pleas; and really it makes me suffer afterwards. My conscience feels horribly guilty . . . I'd rather not know about things I can't approve of.'

She looked at him deeply touched. Then, after a pause: 'Thank you, dear doctor . . . But isn't it the best way? What does anything matter, as long as I'm happy?'

He had taken her hands and he clasped them with sad, fatherly affection. 'Yes, as long as you're happy . . . Oh, one can pay dearly enough for unhappiness too, sometimes.'

Naturally, in the excitement of his battle against the sea, Lazare had deserted his music. The piano was covered with a layer of fine dust, and the score of his great symphony had gone back into a drawer, thanks to Pauline, who had collected the pages of it, picking up some of them from under the furniture. In any case, certain movements had failed to satisfy him; for instance, the heavenly sweetness of ultimate annihilation, which had been rendered in a rather commonplace fashion by a rhythm of a waltz, would perhaps be better expressed by a very slow march. One evening he had declared his intention of beginning it all over again when he had time. And his flare-up of desire, the uneasiness aroused by continual contact with this girl, seemed to have fled with the fever of his inspiration. His masterpiece had been postponed to a more favourable time; so, it seemed, had his grand passion, which he could apparently put off or hurry on at will. Once more he treated his cousin as an old friend or a legitimate spouse who would fall into his arms whenever he chose to open them. Since April, they no longer lived so closely shut up together; the wind cooled their hot faces. The great study was deserted and the pair of them roamed over the rocky beach in front of Bonneville, studying the spots where the palisades and jetties were to be erected. Often they waded home through the cool water, weary and pure-hearted as in the long-ago days of childhood. When Pauline, to tease him, played the famous March of Death, Lazare would cry: 'Oh, shut up! That's all nonsense.'

The very evening of the carpenter's visit, Chanteau was taken ill with an attack of gout. Now his crises recurred almost every month; salicylate, which had relieved them at first, seemed rather to increase their violence. And Pauline had to spend a whole fortnight chained to her uncle's bedside. Lazare, who was continuing his investigations on the beach, started taking Louise along with him, so that she should be out of ear-shot of the invalid, whose cries terrified her. As she occupied the spare room just over Chanteau's, she could not get to sleep unless she blocked her ears and buried her head in the pillow. Once outside, she was all smiles again, enjoying her walk and quite forgetting the poor man and his howls of pain.

They spent a delightful fortnight. At first the young man was puzzled by his new companion; she was very different from the other, apt to shriek when a crab brushed against her boot, and so scared of water that she thought she was drowning if she had to jump over a puddle. The shingle hurt her tiny feet; she clung to her parasol and wore long gloves to her elbows, in constant fear of exposing a corner of her delicate skin to the sun. Then, after his first surprise, he was gradually seduced by the pretty, timid ways of this helpless creature, always ready to appeal to him for protection. This girl brought with her no mere open-air freshness, but a warm scent of heliotrope that went to his head; now he no longer had a boy scampering by his side but a real woman, and his heart beat faster when a gust of wind gave him a sudden glimpse of her stockinged ankles. And yet she was less beautiful than the other; she was older and had lost her rosy bloom; but her gentle winning ways, the soft suppleness of her slight limbs, her whole dainty person seemed brimming with promises of bliss. It was as though he had suddenly discovered her; he could not recognize in her the thin little girl he had once known. Was it possible that the long years at her boarding-school had turned her into this disturbing creature, so conscious of sex for all her virginity, in the depths of whose limpid eyes there lurked all the lies she had been taught? And little by little he began to feel curiously attracted by her, with a sort of perverted passion, in which their old childish friendship was transformed into a subtle sensuality.

When Pauline was able to leave her uncle's room and go out with Lazare once more, she was instantly conscious of a new atmosphere between him and Louise. There were looks and laughs from which she was excluded; she tried to make them explain what was amusing them, and found she could not laugh at it. At first she assumed an attitude of motherly superiority, treating them as crazy youngsters amused at trifles. But soon she grew distressed, and every walk seemed to wear her out. She never complained, however; she merely referred to constant headaches; then, when her cousin advised her not to go out, she would get angry, and refuse to leave his side, even in the house. One night, about two o'clock, as he had stayed up late to finish a plan, he heard footsteps and opened his door in surprise; and his amazement increased when he saw her standing in the darkness, dressed only in her petticoat, leaning over the banisters and listening for sounds from the room below. She thought she'd heard someone crying, she said; but the lie brought a blush to her cheeks, and he coloured too, as a sudden suspicion struck him. No further words were spoken, but thereafter an estrangement grew up between them. He would turn away, thinking her absurd to sulk about trifles; while she, as her misery deepened, refused to leave him alone with Louise for one minute; she watched their slightest gestures, and suffered tortures in her room at night if she had seen them whispering together on the way back from the beach.

Meanwhile, the work had gone on; a gang of carpenters had nailed stout planks on to a row of stakes and were now completing the first jetty. It was a purely experimental one, built hurriedly in view of an imminent spring tide; if the timbers held, they were to finish building the defences. Unfortunately the weather was terrible. The rain poured down without respite, and the whole of Bonneville got soaked watching the stakes being sunk with the aid of an earth-rammer. When the day finally came that the spring tide was expected, the sea was dark with an inky sky; and by eight o'clock the rain had begun again, drowning the horizon in an icy mist. This was a bitter disappointment, for the whole family had planned to go together to watch the planks and beams triumphantly resisting the assault of the great waters.

Madame Chanteau decided to stay behind with her husband, who was still very unwell. And great efforts were made to persuade Pauline to stay too, for she had been suffering from a sore throat all week; she was rather hoarse and her temperature rose slightly every night. But she rejected all good advice and insisted on going to the beach, since Lazare and Louise were going. Louise, though she always looked so frail, as though she were on the point of swooning, had amazing reserves of nervous strength, when any sort of pleasure kept her going.

And so the three of them set forth after lunch. A squall had just swept away the clouds, and this unexpected respite was greeted with cries of triumph and delight. The sky showed such wide patches of blue, across which a few ragged clouds still drifted, that the girls insisted on merely taking their parasols. Lazare alone carried an umbrella. However, he made himself responsible for their well-being; he would find somewhere to shelter them if the rain began again.

The two girls were walking in front. But, going down the steep slope into Bonneville, Louise appeared to stumble on the sodden earth, and Lazare ran up to her and offered to support her. Pauline was obliged to follow them. The high spirits with which she had set off had vanished, and her suspicious eyes noticed that her cousin's elbow kept touching Louise's waist as though in a continual caress. Soon she lost sight of everything but this contact; all else vanished, the beach where the local fishermen were cynically waiting, and the incoming sea, and the jetty, already white with foam. On the horizon a dark band was spreading visibly; it was a swift-moving storm-cloud.

'Oh, damn it,' murmured the young man, turning his head, 'we're in for another soaking . . . But the rain'll surely allow us time to see things, and then we can take refuge with the Houtelards over the way.'

The tide, which had the wind against it, was coming in with maddening slowness. No doubt the wind would prevent it from being as strong as they had expected. However, nobody left the beach. The jetty, by now half submerged, was acting very well, cleaving the waves, which broke and swirled in seething foam up to the spectators' feet. But the greatest triumph was the victorious resistance of the stakes. Every time a wave swept over them, the shingle that it washed up could be heard dropping and piling up behind the planks, like the sudden discharge of a cartload of pebbles; the wall was building itself, and this meant success, the promised rampart was materialising.

'I told you so!' Lazare shouted. 'Now you can tell the sea to go to blazes!'

By his side Prouane, who had been drunk for three days, was shaking his head and stuttering: 'Wait and see what happens when the wind blows the other way.'

The rest of the fishermen kept silence. But from the sour smile on the lips of Cuche and Houtelard it was obvious that they had little faith in all these contraptions. Besides, the sea might crush them, but they did not want to see it beaten by this bourgeois whippersnapper. They'd have a good laugh, the day when it carried away his beams like chaff! It'd maybe smash up the country-side, but it'd be a joke all the same.

Suddenly the storm burst. Great drops fell from the livid cloud which had invaded three-quarters of the sky.

'It's nothing, let's wait a little longer,' Lazare repeated, beside himself with excitement. 'Look, look, not a single stake has moved!'

He had opened his umbrella over Louise's head. She was pressing close to him, like a shivering turtle-dove. They had forgotten Pauline, who was still looking at them, seized with gloomy rage, feeling the warmth of their embrace like a slap in the face. The rain had become torrential, and he suddenly turned round.

'What's this?' he cried. 'Are you crazy? Open your parasol, at least!'

She stood stiffly under the deluge, as though she did not feel it. She answered hoarsely: 'Leave me alone, I'm all right.'

'Oh, please, Lazare,' said Louise, distressed, 'make her come! There's room for three of us.'

But Pauline did not even deign to answer now, in her fierce stubbornness. She was all right; why couldn't they leave her alone? And as, worn out with pleading, he went on: 'It's too silly, let's dash along to the Houtelards',' she snapped back roughly: 'Dash along where you like . . . As we've come here to watch, I'm going to watch.'

The fishermen had run away. She stayed there under the downpour, motionless, facing the timbers, which were now completely covered by the waves. The sight seemed to absorb her, in spite of the spray that blurred everything now, a grey spray rising from the rain-pitted sea. Her streaming dress had great black patches of wetness on the arms and shoulders. And she only consented to stir from the spot when the west wind had driven away the cloud.

The three of them walked home in silence. Not a word was said about the incident to either of the elder Chanteaus. Pauline had gone quickly to change her clothes, while Lazare described the complete success of the experiment. That evening, at supper, a fresh attack of fever seized her; but she pretended there was nothing wrong, in spite of the evident difficulty with which she swallowed each mouthful. She even snubbed Louise curtly when the latter, with tender solicitude, persisted in enquiring how she felt.

'Really, her bad temper's getting unbearable,' muttered Madame Chanteau behind her back. 'It's useless trying to speak to her.'

That night, about one o'clock, Lazare was woken by the sound of a guttural cough, so painfully dry that he sat up to listen to it. His first thought was for his mother; then, as he still listened closely, the sudden thud of a body falling made the floor shake, and he leapt out of bed and dressed hurriedly. It could only be Pauline, for the noise came from the other side of the wall. With frantic fingers, he kept breaking matches; at last he managed to go out with his candlestick, and saw, to his surprise, that the door opposite was wide open. The girl was lying on her side across the threshold, in her nightgown, her arms and legs bare.

'What's happened?' he cried, 'did you slip?'

The thought that she might have been prowling about to spy on him again flashed across his mind. But she did not answer, she did not move, and he saw that she was lying with closed eyes as if she had been knocked out. It looked as though she had been on her way to seek help when, overcome by a fit of dizziness, she had collapsed on the floor.

'Pauline, answer me, do . . . Where does it hurt you?'

101

He bent down and shone the light in her face. She was very flushed and seemed to be burning with a high fever. The instinctive shyness that had made him hesitate at the sight of the half-naked girl and shrink from picking her up bodily to lay her on the bed promptly gave way to his anxious brotherly affection. He lost sight of her nudity and grasped her round the waist and thighs, unconscious of the contact of her woman's skin against his chest. And when he had laid her back on her bed he asked her again, before even thinking of covering her: 'Good heavens, speak to me . . . Have you hurt yourself?'

The motion had made her open her eyes. But she still lay silent, staring up at him; and as he persisted in questioning her, she finally put her hand to her throat.

'Is it your throat that hurts you?'

Then she answered with difficulty, in a strange wheezing whisper: 'Don't make me speak, please . . . it hurts so.'

And immediately a fit of coughing seized her, the same guttural cough that he had heard from his room. Her face turned almost blue, and the pain was so intense that her eyes filled with great tears. She put both hands to her poor racked head, that throbbed with the hammer-blows of a savage headache.

'You caught that this afternoon,' he faltered, panic-stricken. 'What a crazy thing to do when you weren't well!'

But he broke off as his eyes met her beseeching gaze. Her hand fumbled for the blankets, and he drew them up to her chin.

'Will you open your mouth and let me look?'

She could hardly unclench her jaws. Holding the candle close, he was just able to catch a glimpse of the back of her throat; it was dry and shiny, and bright red. It was obviously a quinsy. Only her raging fever and her appalling headache terrified him as to the possible nature of this quinsy. The sick girl's face expressed such an anguished feeling of suffocation that he was seized with a wild fear lest she should choke to death in front of him. She could no longer swallow; every effort to gulp shook her whole body. A fresh bout of coughing made her lose consciousness once more. Wild with fear, he ran to batter at the maid's door with his fists.

'Véronique, Véronique, get up! Pauline's dying!'

When Véronique, half-dressed and in great alarm, came into the girl's room she found him cursing and gesticulating in the middle of it.

'What a godforsaken place this is! You could die like a dog here; over seven miles to fetch a doctor.' He came up to her. 'Try and send somebody; get the doctor to come immediately!'

She went up to the bed and gazed at the sick girl, startled to see how flushed she was, and terrified, for she had begun to love this child whom at first she had hated.

'I'll go myself,' she said simply. 'It'll be quicker. Madame can light the fire downstairs if you need it.'

And, half awake, she pulled on her heavy boots and wrapped herself in a shawl; then, after warning Madame Chanteau on her way down, she set off with great strides along the muddy road. The church clock was striking two, and the night was so black that she kept stumbling over the heaps of stones.

'What has happened?' asked Madame Chanteau when she came upstairs.

Lazare barely answered her. He had just been searching frantically in the cupboard for his old medical textbooks; and he was bending over the chest-of-drawers, turning the pages with trembling fingers and trying to remember what he had once learnt. But it was all a confused jumble in his mind; he kept referring to the table of contents, unable to find anything.

Madame Chanteau had sat down. 'It's probably only a bad headache,' she remarked repeatedly, 'the best thing is to let her sleep.'

Then he burst forth. 'A headache! A headache! Listen, mother, you drive me wild, sitting there doing nothing. Go downstairs and heat some water.'

'There's no need to disturb Louise, I suppose?'

'No, no, no need at all. I don't need anybody. I'll call you.'

When he was by himself, he went back to Pauline and took her hand to count her pulse. He counted a hundred and fifteen. And he felt that burning hand clasping his own with a lingering pressure. The girl's heavy eyelids lay closed, but she expressed her thanks and her forgiveness through this hand-clasp. Although she could not smile, she wanted to make him understand that she had heard, and was deeply touched to know that he was there alone with her, thinking of nobody but her. Usually he had a horror of seeing people suffer, and would run away if any of the family were at all unwell; he made a poor nurse, so he said, his nerves were so unreliable that he was always afraid of bursting into tears. And so she felt surprise mingled with gratitude at the sight of his unselfish devotion. He himself could not have explained the warmth of feeling that sustained him, the compulsion to rely on himself alone in looking after her. The ardent pressure of her little hand overwhelmed him; he wanted to inspire her with courage.

'It's nothing, darling. I'm expecting Cazenove ... Above all don't be frightened.'

She kept her eyes closed, and murmured plaintively: 'Oh, I'm not frightened ... It's a bother for you, that's what upsets me most.' Then in an even lower whisper, no louder than a breath: 'Say you forgive me ... I was horrid to-day.'

He had bent down to kiss her on the forehead as though she were his wife. And then he turned away, for the tears were choking him. He thought of preparing a sedative draught, at least, until the doctor should come. The girl's little medicine chest was there, in a narrow cupboard. Only he was afraid of making a mistake; he kept asking her about the bottles, and finally poured a few drops of morphia into a glass of sweetened water. When she swallowed a spoonful of it, the pain was so intense that he hesitated each time whether to give her another. He did nothing more; he felt powerless to attempt anything else. Waiting became a torture. When he could no longer bear to watch her suffering, when his legs ached from standing in front of the bed, he would reopen his books, thinking that he would at last find out the sickness and the remedy. Could it be diphtheria? although he hadn't noticed any false membranes in front of the soft palate; and he stubbornly went on reading the description and treatment of diphtheria, losing himself in the middle of long sentences whose meaning escaped him and diligently studying useless details, like a child learning by heart a lesson it does not understand. Then a sigh would bring him back to the bedside, shaking with fear, his head buzzing with scientific words whose uncouth syllables increased his anxiety.

'Well?' asked Madame Chanteau, who had come in softly.

'Still the same,' he answered. And then, in a frenzy: 'It's awful, the time it takes that doctor ... you could die twenty times over.' As the doors were standing open Mathieu, who slept under the kitchen table, had come upstairs; it was a mania of his to follow people into every room of the house. His big paws padded on the floor like old felt slippers. He was enjoying this midnight escapade; he tried to jump up beside Pauline and started chasing his tail, with an animal's unawareness of his master's grief. And Lazare, infuriated by this untimely delight, gave him a kick.

'Get out or I'll strangle you! Can't you see, idiot?'

The dog, startled at being hit, began to sniff the air as if he had suddenly understood, and went to lie down humbly under the bed. But Lazare's savagery had shocked Madame Chanteau. Without

104

waiting, she went down to the kitchen again, saying in a curt voice: 'Whenever you're ready . . . the water's getting hot.'

Lazare heard her, in the stairway, grumbling that it was disgusting to hit an animal like that, and that he'd end by beating her too if she stayed there. He, who was usually so devoted to his mother, gave way to a gesture of maddened irritation behind her back. He kept going to look at Pauline. Now, crushed by the fever, she seemed to have quite lost consciousness; there was nothing left of her, amid the shuddering silence of the room, but the harsh grating of her breath, that seemed on the point of becoming a death-rattle. Terror seized him again, an unreasoning and absurd terror; she was certainly going to suffocate if help did not come. He strode up and down the room, casting ceaseless glances at the clock. It was barely three; Véronique couldn't have reached the doctor's yet. He traced her journey in the darkness, along the road to Arromanches: now she had passed the oak wood, she had reached the little bridge, she would save five minutes if she ran down the hill. Then a violent urge to know made him open the window, although he could make out nothing in that gulf of darkness. A single light was burning down in Bonneville, probably a fisherman's lantern as he put out to sea. It was appallingly dismal, a boundless chaos in which he seemed to feel all life go tumbling to extinction. He closed the window, then opened it, only to close it again soon after. He had come to lose all sense of time, and he was astonished to hear three strike. By now the doctor must have got his horses harnessed and the gig would be chasing along the road, piercing the darkness with its yellow eye. And Lazare was so numb with impatience, as the sick girl's breathing grew ever more laboured, that he came to with a start when, towards four o'clock, rapid footsteps were heard on the stairs.

'It's you at last!' he cried.

Dr. Cazenove immediately asked for a second candle to be lit, so as to examine Pauline. Lazare held one of them, while Véronique, dishevelled by the wind and plastered with mud to the waist, brought up the other to the foot of the bed. Madame Chanteau looked on. The patient, who was very drowsy, could not open her lips without a moan. The doctor laid her down again gently; he had been deeply worried when he first arrived, but now came back into the middle of the room with a calmer look.

'What a fright your Véronique gave me!' he whispered. 'From the fantastic things she told me I imagined it was a case of poison; you see I've stuffed my pockets with drugs.'

'It's a quinsy, isn't it?' asked Lazare.

'Yes, a straightforward quinsy . . . there's no immediate danger.'

Madame Chanteau made a triumphant gesture, as though to say 'I told you so.'

'No immediate danger,' repeated Lazare, his fears reviving, 'are you afraid of complications?'

'No,' replied the doctor after a slight hesitation, 'but with these damned sore throats you never can tell.'

And he admitted that there was nothing to be done. He wanted to wait until next day before bleeding the patient. Then, as the young man besought him to make some attempt to relieve her at least, he consented to try mustard poultices. Véronique brought up a basin of hot water, and the doctor himself laid on the wet plasters, sliding them along the girl's legs from the knee to the ankle. They only added to her suffering, for the fever persisted and the headache was growing intolerable. Soothing gargles were also suggested, and Madame Chanteau prepared an infusion of blackberry leaves, which had to be given up after the first attempt, since the pain made the movement of her throat quite impossible. It was nearly six and day was breaking when the doctor finally left.

'I shall come back about noon,' he told Lazare in the passage. 'Don't worry; she's suffering pain, but that's all.'

'Is suffering nothing, then?' cried the young man, whom the thought of pain shocked deeply, 'People ought not to have to suffer pain.'

Cazenove stared at him, then raised his arms to heaven, in face of such an extraordinary claim.

When Lazare went back into the room, he sent his mother and Véronique to lie down for a little; he himself could not have slept. And he saw the day break in the untidy room, the mournful dawn that follows nights of agony. His head pressed against the window pane, he was gazing despairingly at the livid sky when a sound made him turn his head. He thought Pauline must be trying to get up. But it was Mathieu, whom everybody had forgotten; he had at last emerged from under the bed and gone up beside the girl, one of whose hands was hanging loosely over the side of the bed. The dog began licking it so gently that Lazare, deeply touched, laid his hand on his neck and said: 'You see, poor old fellow, your mistress is sick... but it'll be all right, you know! We'll all three be able to go for runs together . . .'

Pauline had opened her eyes and, though her face was twisted with pain, she smiled.

Then began that anguished existence, that nightmare life that one leads in a sick person's room. Lazare, impelled by a feeling of fierce affection, drove everybody else away from it; he barely allowed his mother and Louise to look in and ask for news in the morning; only Véronique, whose fondness for the sick girl he felt to be genuine, was admitted. To begin with Madame Chanteau tried to impress on him that it was improper for a man to look after a young girl in this way; but he protested—wasn't he her husband? and in any case, of course doctors could look after women. Indeed, there was no sort of self-conscious modesty in their relationship. Suffering and the threat of death drove out all sensual awareness. He tended her in countless ways, lifting her up and laying her down like a compassionate brother, conscious of nothing about this desirable body except the fever that shook it. It was like a continuation of their younger vigorous days, a return to the time of their first bathes together, innocent in their nakedness, when he treated her as a mere child. The world vanished, nothing else existed any more, but the medicine to be drunk, the hours spent in vain expectation of an improvement, the meanest details of physical life suddenly assuming a supreme importance. And nights followed days, and Lazare's whole existence seemed suspended over the void, in constant terror of being hurled down into darkness.

Every morning Dr. Cazenove visited Pauline; he even, sometimes came back in the evenings after his dinner. At his second visit, he had decided to try copious bleeding. But the fever, after a temporary check, had revived. Two days went by, and he was obviously perturbed, unable to explain the stubbornness of the attack. As the girl was finding it increasingly hard to open her mouth he could not examine the back of her throat, which appeared to be swollen and lividly red. At last, as Pauline complained of a growing pressure as though her neck was about to burst open, the doctor told Lazare one morning: 'I suspect a tumour.'

The young man took him into his own room. The day before, he had been looking at his old *Manual of Pathology*, and had read the section on retro-pharyngal abscesses, which protrude into the oesophagus and, by compressing the trachea, are liable to cause death by suffocation. He turned very pale, and asked: 'Is it all up with her?'

'I hope not,' answered the doctor. 'We shall have to see.'

But he himself could no longer conceal his anxiety. He had to admit his almost total powerlessness in the present case. How could one look for an abscess inside that contracted mouth? And besides, to lance it prematurely would involve serious drawbacks. The best thing to do was to let it take its course, which would be very long and very painful.

'I'm not God Almighty!' he cried, when Lazare charged him with the futility of his learning.

Dr. Cazenove's fondness for Pauline found expression in an exaggeratedly brusque, blustering manner. The tall old man, lean as a briar, had had his emotions deeply stirred. During more than thirty years he had roamed the world over, moving from ship to ship, working in hospitals in every corner of the colonies; he had coped with epidemics on board ship, gruesome tropical diseases, elephantiasis in Cayenne and snake-bite in India; he had killed men of every colour, tried out poisons on Chinamen, risked the lives of negroes in tricky experiments in vivisection. And now a little girl with a sore place in her throat upset him so much that he could not sleep; his hands, strong as steel, trembled, and his old familiarity with death lost its power, at the thought that things might end badly. And he strove to conceal so unworthy an emotion by a show of contempt for suffering. Men were born to suffer, what was the use of distressing oneself about it?

Every morning Lazare would say to him: 'Try something, doctor, I implore you . . . It's frightful, she can't even doze off for a moment. She was screaming all night.'

'But, great heavens, it's not my fault,' he would end by saying, exasperated. 'I surely can't cut her throat to try and save her.'

Then the young man, too, grew angry. 'So medicine's no use!'

'No use at all when the machine breaks down. Quinine can stop a fever, purgatives move the bowels, and you must bleed a case of apoplexy. But everything else is just luck. You've got to trust to nature.'

This outburst was called forth by his rage at not knowing what to do. Usually he dared not repudiate medicine so boldly, although he had practised for too long not to be both humble and sceptical. He would spend whole hours sitting beside the bed, studying the patient, and then, often, go away without even leaving a prescription; his hands were tied, and he could do nothing but watch the full development of this abscess, in which the little less or the little more might mean life or death.

Lazare dragged out a whole week in an agony of fear. He, too, expected nature to come to a stop at any minute. Each time he heard the sick girl draw a painful breath he thought it was her last. The tumour took vivid shape in his mind, he visualised it as

108

something enormous, blocking the trachea; if it should swell any more, the air could not pass in. His two years of ill-digested medical studies increased his terror. And it was above all the sight of pain that maddened him, made all his nerves revolt in wild protest against existence. Why should such a horrible thing as pain exist? Wasn't it all monstrously useless, this torturing of the flesh, this searing and racking of the muscles, when the victim was a poor girl's body, so delicate in its whiteness? Obsessed by the thought of suffering, he turned constantly to her bedside. He questioned her, at the risk of wearying her; was the pain worse? Where was it now? Sometimes she took hold of his hand and laid it on her neck; it was there, like a lump of molten lead, choking her with its throbbing. Her headache gave her no respite, she didn't know which way to lay her head, tormented by insomnia; since the fever had first seized her, ten days ago, she had not had two hours' sleep. One evening, to crown her misery, acute earache developed; and when these attacks came on she fainted with pain, feeling as though her jaws were being crushed. But, with splendid courage, she did not let Lazare know what agony she was enduring; she felt that he was almost as sick as she, that her fever was raging in his blood and her abscess constricting his throat. Often, indeed, she lied to him, forcing a smile at the very moment of her fiercest sufferings; the pain was growing dull, she would say, and urged him to rest a little. The worst of it was that the back of her throat was now so inflamed that she could no longer swallow without uttering a scream. Lazare would wake up with a start; was it beginning again? Once more he questioned her, he wanted to know where it hurt; while, with aching face and closed eyes, she still struggled to deceive him, muttering that it was nothing, just something that had tickled her.

'Go to sleep, don't bother about me . . . I'm going to sleep too.'

At night, again, she would pretend to go to sleep so that he should lie down. But he insisted on sitting up beside her, in an armchair. The nights were so bad that he never watched the close of day without a superstitious terror. Would the sun ever rise again?

One night Lazare was sitting close go the bed and holding Pauline's hand in his own, as he often did, to let her know that he would stay there and would never desert her. Dr. Cazenove had gone off at ten o'clock, declaring in a frenzy that he could no longer be answerable for anything. Until that moment the young man had had the comfort of thinking Pauline unaware of her own danger. In her presence they all spoke of a mere inflammation of the throat, very painful no doubt, but which would pass as easily as a cold in the head. She herself seemed quite calm, with a brave face and unfailing gaiety despite her suffering. When she heard them talk about her convalescence and make plans, she would smile. And that very night she had just been listening to Lazare planning a walk along the shore for her first outing. Then silence fell, and she seemed to be sleeping, when after a long quarter of an hour she murmured quite distinctly: 'My poor dear, I don't think I shall ever be your wife.'

He felt a shock, and a slight icy shiver ran down his spine.

'What do you mean?' he asked.

She had opened her eyes and was looking at him with her expression of courageous resignation. 'Oh yes, I know what's the matter with me . . . And I'd rather know, so that I can at least kiss you all . . . '

Then Lazare protested vehemently that such ideas were crazy; in less than a week she'd be on her feet again. He let go of her hand and rushed into his own room on some pretext, for his sobs were choking him. There in the darkness, he broke down completely, sprawling across his bed, in which he nowadays no longer slept. A frightful conviction had suddenly gripped his heart: Pauline was going to die, perhaps she would not live out the night. And the thought that she knew this, that her silence up till now had been that of a brave woman considerate of others' feelings even at the point of death, completed his despair. She knew; she would watch her death agony approaching; and he would be there, impotent. Already he seemed to be taking his last farewell of her; he could see it all happening, with harrowing details, in the darkness of his room. It was the end of everything; and grasping the pillow with shaking arms, he buried his head in it to smother his convulsive sobs.

However, the night ended without a catastrophe. Two more days passed. But now there was between them a new bond, the ever present thought of death. She made no further allusion to the gravity of her condition, she even found strength to smile; while he succeeded in pretending to be perfectly calm and looking forward to her immediate recovery; and yet, in her case as in his, an endless farewell seemed to be taking place, as their eyes met with a lingering gaze like a caress. At night, particularly, when he kept watch beside her, they could almost hear each other's thoughts, as the threat of eternal separation filled the very silence with tender emotion. It was an experience of incomparably painful sweetness; they had never felt so much at one before.

110

One morning at dawn Lazare realised with surprise how little the thought of his own death disturbed him now. He tried to remember dates: since the day when Pauline had fallen ill he had not once felt down his spine the chill shudder of dread of ceasing to be. If he trembled at the thought of losing his mate, that was another sort of fear, in which the destruction of his ego had no place. His heart bled within him, but it seemed as if the battle he was waging against death made him death's equal, gave him the courage to look it in the face. Moreover his dread was numbed by a kind of drowsiness which was perhaps merely due to his dazed exhaustion. He shut his eyes so as not to see the sun rising, he tried to revive his shudder of anguish by provoking himself to fear, by repeatedly telling himself that he too must die some day; nothing in him responded, it had become indifferent to him, everything seemed to have assumed an extraordinary lightness. Even his pessimism lost its force in the presence of this bed of pain; instead of intensifying his hatred of the world, his revolt against suffering took the shape of a burning desire for health, an exasperated love of life. He no longer talked of blowing up the earth like an old uninhabitable dwelling; the only image that haunted him was that of Pauline grown well again, walking off arm in arm with him in the bright sunshine; and he felt only one need, to take her again, firm-footed and laughing, along the paths they had once followed.

It was that very day that Lazare thought the end had come. By eight o'clock the sick girl was seized with nausea, and every retching effort brought on a most alarming fit of choking. Soon she started shivering; she shook with rigors of such violence that her teeth could be heard chattering. Lazare, terrified, shouted out of the window that a child must be sent to Arromanches for the doctor, although the latter was expected at about eleven as usual. The house had been plunged into gloomy silence since Pauline no longer filled it with the lively hum of her activity. Chanteau spent his days downstairs in silence, staring at his legs, in terror of an attack now that there was nobody to look after him; Madame Chanteau forced Louise to go out, and the two of them spent all their time out of the house, in ever closer intimacy; and only Véronique's heavy tread, ceaselessly going up and down, disturbed the quiet of the staircase and the empty rooms. Three times Lazare had gone to lean over the banisters, impatient to know whether the maid had persuaded anyone to take his message. He had just come back into the room and was watching the patient, who seemed a little calmer, when the door, which had been left ajar, gave a slight creak.

'Well, Véronique?'

But it was his mother. That morning she had planned to take Louise to visit friends in the neighbourhood of Verchemont.

'Little Cuche went off immediately,' she said. 'He's got good legs.'

Then after a silence she asked: 'No improvement?'

With a mute, despairing gesture Lazare pointed to Pauline lying motionless, as though dead, her face bathed in a cold sweat.

'Well then, we won't go to Verchemont,' his mother went on. 'Really, these mysterious illnesses are incredibly tenacious! The poor child's certainly having a dreadful time.'

She had sat down, and kept reeling off remarks in the same low, monotonous voice. 'To think we'd planned to set off at seven o'clock! It was lucky Louise didn't wake up early enough. And all the callers I've had this morning! You'd think they did it on purpose. The grocer from Arromanches called with his bill, I had to pay it ... and now the baker's downstairs; another monthly account, forty francs' worth of bread—I really can't think where it all goes to.'

Lazare was not listening to her, completely absorbed as he was by his dread of seeing the rigors recur. But the muffled murmur of this torrent of words irritated him. He tried to get rid of her.

'Give Véronique a couple of towels and ask her to bring them up to me.'

'Of course I shall have to pay that baker,' she went on, as if she had not heard him. 'He's spoken to me, so he can't be told I'm not at home ... Oh! I'm fed up with this house! It's getting too much for me; I shall end by throwing it all up ... If only Pauline wasn't so ill she'd advance us the ninety francs of her *pension*. It's the 20th to-day, it only makes ten days' difference ... The poor child looks very weak.'

Lazare turned on her sharply. 'What's that? What do you want?'

'You don't know where she keeps her money?'

'No.'

'It must be in her cupboard. Suppose you looked?'

He refused with a gesture of exasperation. His hands were shaking.

'Please, mother! For heaven's sake leave me alone.'

These few sentences had been whispered softly, at the far end of the room. A painful silence had fallen. Then a faint voice sounded from the bed: 'Lazare, take the key from under my pillow and give auntie whatever she wants.'

They were both struck with amazement. Lazare protested, unwilling to search the cupboard; but he had to give way, so as not to distress Pauline. When he had handed a hundred franc note to his mother and went back to slip the key under the pillow, he found the sick girl in the grip of a fresh tremor that shook her like a sapling about to break. And, from her poor closed eyes, two great tears rolled down her cheeks.

Dr. Cazenove did not appear till his usual time. He had not even seen young Cuche, who was no doubt larking about by the roadside. As soon as he had listened to Lazare and taken one look at Pauline, he exclaimed: 'She's saved!'

Those fits of nausea, those terrible tremors had simply been signs that the abscess was breaking at last. Now there was no more danger of choking; henceforward the trouble would clear up of itself. There was great rejoicing. Lazare went down with the doctor, and as Martin, the old sailor who had remained in the latter's service, was drinking a glass of wine in the kitchen, they all wanted to drink a toast. Madame Chanteau and Louise had some walnut cordial.

'I was never really anxious,' the former was saying. 'I felt sure it would be nothing.'

'All the same, the poor child's had a rough time,' retorted Véronique. 'My word, I couldn't be happier, not if you were to give me five francs.'

At that moment Abbé Horteur appeared. He had come to ask for news, and he accepted a drop of cordial, since all the rest were drinking it. He had been every day to enquire, just out of good neighbourliness; for, at his first visit, when Lazare had made clear to him that he would not let him see the sick girl for fear of alarming her, the priest had calmly replied that he quite understood. He would just go on saying masses for the poor young lady. Chanteau, clinking glasses with him, praised him for his tolerance.

'You see, she recovered without my prayers!'

'Everyone saves himself as best he can,' declared the *curé* sententiously, draining his glass.

When the doctor had gone, Louise insisted on going up to kiss Pauline. The latter was still in fearful pain, but pain now seemed not to matter. Lazare gaily called out to her to take heart; he had stopped pretending now, he even exaggerated the danger that was past by saying that he had thrice held her for dead in his arms. She, however, did not so openly display her joy at being saved. But she was deeply moved by the sweetness of being alive, after having had the courage to grow used to death. An expression of tender feeling passed over her pain-racked face, and she clasped his hand, murmuring with a smile: 'Lazare, dear, there's no escape for you, I shall be your wife.'

At last her convalescence began, with long periods of sleep. She slept for whole days, very peacefully, breathing sweetly, in healing oblivion. Minouche, who had been driven from the room during the tense hours of her illness, took advantage of this calm to slip in again; she would jump lightly on to the bed and roll up quickly into a ball by her mistress' side, and pass whole days there enjoying the warmth of the sheets; sometimes she spent long hours preening herself, interminably licking her fur, but her movements were so smooth that the sick girl was not even conscious of them. Meanwhile Mathieu, who had also been admitted to the room, lay snoring in almost human fashion on the bedside rug.

One of Pauline's first whims, the very next Saturday, was to send for her little village friends. After being on a strict starvation diet for three weeks, she had at last been allowed an occasional boiled egg. She was able to receive the children sitting up; she was still extremely weak. Lazare had had to hunt in the cupboard again to find five-franc pieces for her. But after she had talked to her poor children, and insisted on settling what she called her arrears, she felt so utterly exhausted that she had to be put back to bed in a state of unconsciousness. She also took a great interest in the jetty and palisades, asking each day whether they were standing firm. Some of the beams had already given way, but her cousin lied to her, implying that only a couple of planks had come adrift. One morning, when she was alone, she got out of bed, anxious to watch the spring tide battering the timbers in the distance; and this time again her newfound strength had let her down, and she would have collapsed but for Véronique, who came in just in time to catch her in her arms.

'Take care, I shall tie you up if you're not good,' Lazare said jokingly.

He still persisted in sitting up beside her at nights; but, dropping with fatigue, he would fall asleep in his armchair. At first he had taken a keen delight in watching her drink her first cups of broth. The return of health to that young body was an enchanting sight, a renewal of life in which he himself seemed to share. Then he gradually grew accustomed to health again and ceased to rejoice at it as an unhoped-for blessing. And he was left in a sort of daze, a sort of nervous reaction after his struggle, with the confused sense that everything was once more meaningless.

One night Lazare was in a deep sleep when Pauline heard him wake with a sigh of anguish. She could see him in the dim glow of the night-light looking panic-stricken, wide-eyed with horror, his hands clasped in an imploring gesture. He was muttering brokenly: 'Oh God, oh God!'

She leaned towards him with anxious swiftness. 'What's the matter, Lazare? Are you ill?'

Her voice made him start. Had he been watched? He felt embarrassed and was driven to reply with a clumsy lie. 'Oh, I'm all right . . . but I heard you cry out just now.'

The fear of death had reappeared in his sleep, a causeless fear, as though it had emerged from nothingness itself, a fear whose icy breath had woken him with a great shudder. Oh God! he would have to die some day! The thought surged up within him, while Pauline, who had laid back her head on her pillow, gazed at him with a mother's compassionate look.

CHAPTER V

EVERY evening in the dining-room, after Véronique had cleared the table, the same conversation took place between Madame Chanteau and Louise, while Chanteau, absorbed in his newspaper, merely replied with a single word to his wife's infrequent questions. During the fortnight when Lazare had felt Pauline to be in danger he had not even come down to meals; now he dined downstairs, but as soon as dessert was served he would go back to sit with the convalescent. And no sooner had he set foot on the stair than Madame Chanteau would start grumbling again, as she had done the night before.

At first she displayed her tender-heartedness. 'Poor boy, he's wearing himself out . . . Really, it's unreasonable to endanger one's health so. He hasn't slept for three weeks now . . . And he's even paler than he was yesterday.'

And she was full of compassion for Pauline too; the dear child was in dreadful pain, you couldn't spend a single moment up there without being horribly upset. But little by little she came to dwell on the disturbance that the invalid was creating in the whole house; everything was at sixes and sevens, you couldn't get a hot meal, really life was becoming not worth living. At this point she broke off to ask her husband: 'I don't suppose Véronique even thought of bringing you your marshmallow infusion, did she?'

'Yes, yes,' he replied over the top of his paper.

Then she dropped her voice, speaking to Louise. 'It's funny, that wretched Pauline has never brought us luck. And to think that some people consider her a good angel! Oh yes, I know the gossip that's going round... At Caen they're saying—aren't they, Louisette?—that she's brought us wealth. Wealth indeed! You can tell me the truth. I'm not afraid of scandalmongers.'

'Well,' murmured the girl, 'they gossip about you as they do about everybody else. Last month I had to tell off a solicitor's wife who was discussing it without knowing the first thing about it . . . You can't stop people talking.'

After that Madame Chanteau let herself go. Yes, they were having to suffer for their own good nature. Hadn't they managed to live without anybody's help, before Pauline arrived? Where would she be now—on what Paris street-corner—if they hadn't consented to take her in? And really, fancy gossiping about her money! That money from which they themselves had never got anything but misery, that money which seemed to have brought ruin into their home. For surely, the facts spoke loud enough: her son would never have launched into that stupid seaweed business nor wasted his time trying to stop the sea from crushing Bonneville, if it hadn't been for that wretched Pauline putting crazy notions into his head. It was her own lookout if she'd lost some cash in it; as for the poor boy, he'd lost his health and his future there! Madame Chanteau poured forth her bitter resentment against the 150,000 francs, the feverish memory of which seemed to hang about her writing-desk. It was the thought of the large sums that had been squandered and the small sums that were still being taken every day, increasing the debt, that infuriated her thus, as though she realised that therein lay the poison that had corrupted her honesty. To-day the corruption was complete; she loathed Pauline for all the money she owed her.

'What can you say to a stubborn creature like that?' she went on. 'She's horribly mean fundamentally, and yet she's the most shocking spendthrift. She's ready to throw twelve thousand francs into the sea for those Bonneville fishermen who just laugh at us, and to feed all the lousy brats in the neighbourhood, but I give you my word I'm scared stiff if I have to ask her for forty sous. Explain that if you can! She's got a heart of stone, for all her air of giving everything away to other people.'

116

Often Véronique would come in, carrying crockery or bringing tea; and she would linger and listen, and sometimes even venture to intervene.

'A heart of stone! Mademoiselle Pauline? Oh, how can you say that, Madame?'

Madame Chanteau would silence her with a stern glare. Then, elbows on the table, she would embark on complicated calculations, as though talking to herself.

'Thank the Lord I don't have to look after it now, that money of hers, but I'd like to know how much there's left of it. Not seventy thousand, I'll wager ... Well now! let's count it up: three thousand francs already for testing those timbers, and at least two hundred in charity each month, and the ninety francs of her pension here. It goes quickly ... Would you like to bet, Louisette, that she'll ruin herself? Yes, you'll see her reduced to beggary ... And if she ruins herself, who'll want her, how will she manage to live?'

At this Véronique could not contain herself. 'I should hope Madame wouldn't turn her out?'

'Eh, what's that?' went on her mistress, furiously, 'What rubbish is that you're talking? Of course there's no question of turning anybody out. I've never turned anybody out ... I'm only saying that when anyone's inherited a fortune there's nothing looks sillier than to throw it away and become a burden on other people ... Get along to your kitchen and look for me there, my lass!'

The maid went off, mumbling protests under her breath. And a silence fell while Louise poured out the tea. Nothing was heard save the light rustle of the newspaper, which Chanteau read right through, even to the advertisements. Sometimes he exchanged a few words with the girl.

'Go on, put in another lump of sugar ... Have you heard from your father yet?'

'Not a word!' she answered, laughing. 'But you know, if I'm a nuisance I can go. You've got quite enough to cope with now Pauline's ill ... I wanted to leave, but you insisted on my staying.'

He tried to interrupt her. 'There's no question of that. It's very sweet of you to keep us company, while the poor child's upstairs.'

'I can take refuge at Arromanches till my father comes, if you've had enough of me,' she went on as though she had not heard him, just to tease him. 'My aunt Léonie has hired a chalet there; and there are plenty of people about and a beach where one can at least bathe ... Only my aunt Léonie's a dreadful bore!'

117

Chanteau always ended by laughing at the girl's affectionate mischievous ways. And yet, though he dared not admit it in front of his wife, his whole heart was for Pauline, who nursed him with such gentleness. And he would bury himself in his paper again, as soon as Madame Chanteau emerged abruptly from her brown study as though from a dream.

'You see, there's one thing I can't forgive her, and that's having taken my son from me . . . He hardly stays at table for a quarter of an hour; he's always dashing off when you want to talk to him!'

'It'll soon be over,' Louise pointed out. 'Somebody has to sit up with her.'

The mother shook her head, with pursed lips. The words that she seemed anxious to hold back burst forth in spite of her.

'That may be! but still it's queer, for a young man to be always with a sick girl . . . Oh, I haven't minced my words, I've said what I thought about it, if there's trouble in store I can't help it!'

And as Louise gazed at her uneasily she added: 'Besides, it's not healthy to breathe, the air in that room. She might well quite give him her sore throat . . . Those girls that look so plump sometimes have all sorts of infection in their blood. Shall I tell you something? Well, I don't think she's healthy.'

Louise went on gently defending her friend. She thought Pauline was so sweet, and that was her sole argument in answer to the accusations of hard-heartedness and unhealthiness. She liked an atmosphere of pleasantness, of comfortable stability, and therefore she challenged the excessive harshness of Madame Chanteau's resentment, although, each day, she would sit listening with a smile to vituperations even bitterer than the previous day's. She would protest, stimulated by the violence of the other woman's words, flushed with secret pleasure at feeling that she was a favourite, the mistress of the household now. She was like Minouche, getting her pleasure from rubbing against others, and harmless so long as no one interfered with her enjoyment.

And every evening after covering the same ground, the conversation would lead to the following phrase, uttered with deliberation:

'No, Louisette, the sort of wife my son needs . . .' And from that Madame Chanteau would launch out again, expatiating on the qualities she expected in a perfect daughter-in-law; keeping her eyes fixed on the girl's meanwhile, in an effort to impress her with the things she left unsaid. She described Louise to the life: a well-brought-up young person, with some experience of the world,

118

capable of entertaining guests, charming rather than beautiful, above all very feminine, for, as she declared, she loathed the boyish type of girl, who made candour an excuse for coarseness. Then there was the question of money, the only decisive one, to which she made the briefest allusion: of course, a dowry didn't matter, but her son had great plans and could not contemplate a match that might ruin him.

'See, dear, if Pauline hadn't a penny, if she'd landed here without a shirt to her back, well, the marriage would have been made years ago. Only do you wonder that I'm anxious, when I see how the money melts away in her hands. She'll do a lot, won't she, after this, with her sixty thousand francs? No, Lazare deserves something better than that—I'll never give him to a madwoman who'll stint him in food and fritter away her money on crackbrained schemes.'

'Oh, money doesn't mean anything,' Louise would answer, lowering her eyes. 'And yet one has to have it.'

Without any further allusion being made to her dowry, the two hundred thousand francs seemed to be there on the table, gleaming in the still light of the hanging lamp. It was the sight of them and the feel of them that roused Madame Chanteau to fever-pitch, made her brush aside the other girl's miserable sixty thousand francs and yearn to win the newcomer with her intact fortune. She had noticed that her son had been attracted to Louise before the unfortunate happenings that now kept him upstairs. Suppose the girl loved him too, why should they not get married? The father would give his consent, particularly in a case of mutual passion. And she encouraged this passion, she spent the rest of the evening murmuring provocative phrases.

'My Lazare is so good! Nobody knows him. Even you, Louisette, you can't imagine how tender he can be . . . Oh, I shan't be sorry for his wife! Whoever gets him can be sure of being loved! . . . And he's always so healthy. His skin's so soft and white! My grandfather, the Chevalier de la Vignière, had such white skin that he used to go to fancy-dress balls as a woman, in a low-necked dress.'

Louise would blush and laugh, highly amused at these details. She would willingly have stayed all night listening to the mother courting her on her son's behalf, like a respectable procuress, whispering intimate secrets that might go very far between two women. But Chanteau was growing sleepy behind his newspaper.

'Isn't it time to go to bed?' he asked with a yawn.

Then, as he had long since lost track of the conversation: 'In spite of what you say, she's a good soul . . . I shall be glad when

119

the day comes that she can come down and eat a meal beside me.'

'We shall all be glad,' cried Madame Chanteau tartly. 'One can talk and say what one thinks, but that doesn't prevent one from being fond of people.'

'The poor darling,' declared Louise in her turn, 'I'd gladly take over half the pain if it were possible . . . She's so sweet!'

Véronique, who was bringing in the candlesticks, intervened once more. 'You're quite right to be her friend, Mademoiselle Louise, for you'd have to have a paving-stone instead of a heart to plot anything harmful against her.'

'All right, nobody asked for your opinion,' retorted Madame Chanteau. 'You'd do better to clean your candlesticks. Just look how filthy this one is!'

They all got up. Chanteau, escaping from this stormy altercation, shut himself up in his ground-floor room. But when the two women had reached the first floor, where their bedrooms faced one another, they did not go to bed immediately. Almost invariably Madame Chanteau drew Louise into her room for a minute, and there she went on talking about Lazare, displayed pictures of him, and actually brought out mementoes of his childhood—one of his first teeth, a faded lock of baby hair, even old garments, his first communion bow, his first pair of trousers.

'Look, here's a lock of his hair,' she said one evening. 'I can spare it, for I've got some of all ages.'

And when Louise had at last gone to bed she could not sleep, obsessed as she was by the thought of the young man who was thus thrust upon her by his mother. She tossed about, racked by insomnia, and his image, white-skinned, stood out against the darkness. Often she listened intently to see whether he was walking about on the floor above; and the thought that he was doubtless still keeping watch by Pauline's bedside increased her feverish agitation, so that she had to throw back the sheet and sleep with her bosom bared.

Upstairs, convalescence was progressing slowly. Although the patient was out of danger, she was still very weak, exhausted by attacks of fever that astonished the doctor. As Lazare remarked, doctors were always being astonished. He himself grew hourly more irritable. The sudden lassitude that had come over him as soon as the crisis was over seemed to increase, becoming a kind of anxious uneasiness. Now that he no longer had to battle with death he could not bear the stuffy room, the doses of medicine that he had to give her at stated hours, all the petty miseries of illness,

120

which at first he had tackled with such ardour. Now that she no longer had need of him, he relapsed into the boredom of his empty existence; he would sit with arms dangling idly; move from one chair to another, pace the room with despairing looks at its four walls, or stand in unseeing oblivion in front of the window. As soon as he opened a book to read beside her, he had to stifle his yawns behind its pages.

'Lazare,' Pauline said one day, 'you should go out. Véronique could manage.'

He refused, violently. Had she had enough of him, that she wanted to send him away? It would be a fine thing if he deserted her thus before setting her properly on her feet! At last he calmed down, while she gently explained her point.

'You wouldn't be deserting me, just by taking a breath of air. Go out in the afternoons . . . We shan't be any better off if you fall ill too!'

But she was tactless enough to add: 'I can see you yawning all day long.'

'Yawning?' he cried. 'Why not say at once that I've got no heart? Really, if that's all the thanks I get . . .'

Next day Pauline played her cards better. She affected a keen desire to see the building of the jetties and stockades continued; the winter high tides were imminent, and the experimental defences would be carried away unless the whole system was completed. But Lazare's enthusiasm had waned; he was dissatisfied with the way certain vital joints had been constructed, new designs would have to be made; and then they were liable to exceed the estimates, and the General Council hadn't voted them a penny. For two days she had to work on his inventor's pride; was he going to submit to being beaten by the sea, in front of all the local people, who were already laughing at him? As for the money, it would certainly be refunded, if she lent it him as they'd agreed. Gradually his zeal revived. He drew up fresh plans, he sent for the carpenter from Arromanches, with whom he had discussions in his room, leaving the door open so that he could dash in whenever she called.

'Now,' he declared one morning, as he kissed her, ' the sea won't break so much as a matchstick; we shall be all right this time . . . As soon as you can walk we'll go and look at the state of the timbers.'

As it happened Louise had come up to inquire after the invalid, and, as she bent over to kiss Pauline too, the latter whispered in her ear: 'Take him out!'

At first Lazare refused; he was expecting the doctor. But Louise laughingly insisted that he was too much of a gentleman to let her go alone to the Gonins', where she went to choose for herself the shrimps that she sent to Caen. On the way, he could have a look at the jetty.

'Go off, I'd like you to,' Pauline said. 'Take him by the arm, Louise. That's right, don't let go of him!'

She seemed in high spirits as the other two scuffled playfully; but when they went out she grew serious again and leaned out of bed to listen to their footsteps and laughter dying away down the stairs.

A quarter of an hour later, Véronique appeared with the doctor. Then she took up her post by Pauline's beside, without neglecting her pots and pans; she would come up constantly and spend an hour or so between two sauces. It did not happen all at once; Lazare came in again that evening, but he went off once more next day, and every day, growing keener on his outdoor life, he cut short his visits, only staying long enough to ask how she was. Moreover it was Pauline herself who drove him out if he even suggested sitting down. When he came back with Louise she would make them tell her all about their walk, delighting in their high spirits and the breath of fresh air they brought back in their windswept hair. Their relations seemed to be so comradely that she lost her suspicions about them. And as soon as she saw Véronique bringing her medicine she would call out gaily: 'Off you go now, you're in my way!'

Sometimes she would call back Louise, entrusting her with Lazare as if he were a child. 'Try and see that he doesn't get bored. He needs to be amused . . . And have a good walk, I don't want to see you back all day.'

When she was by herself her fixed gaze seemed to follow them into the distance. She spent the days reading, waiting for her strength to be restored, so weak still that two or three hours sitting in her armchair exhausted her. Often she would let the book slip on to her knees, wandering off in a daydream after her cousin and her friend. If they had gone along the shore they must have reached the caves, where it was so pleasant on the sand when the high tide cooled the air. And she thought that the persistence of these visions sprang from her regret at not being able to go with them. Moreover, she was bored with reading; the novels that lay about the house were love-stories that showed faithlessness in a romantic light, and these had always revolted her straightforward nature, her instinctive need to give herself once and for all. Was it possible

122

that one could deceive one's own heart, that, having once loved, one should cease to love? She pushed aside the book. And now her dreaming gaze could see them in the distance, beyond the walls—her cousin bringing home her friend, helping her weary steps, pressed close to one another, laughing and whispering.

'Your medicine, mademoiselle,'—the sudden sound of Véronique's gruff voice behind her would wake her with a start.

By the end of the first week Lazare no longer came in without knocking. One morning as he pushed open the door he caught sight of Pauline, bare-armed, sitting up in bed combing her hair.

'Oh, I'm sorry!' he muttered, starting back.

'Why ever?' she cried, 'are you frightened of me?'

Then he made up his mind to go in, but he was afraid of embarrassing her, and turned his head away while she finished doing up her hair.

'I say, will you pass me a camisole?' she said calmly. 'There, in the first drawer . . . I must be getting better, I'm growing vain!'

He was flustered, and could find nothing but chemises. At last when he had thrown her a camisole he waited in front of the window until she had buttoned it right up to her chin. A fortnight earlier, when he thought her on the point of death, he had lifted her up in his arms like a little girl, without even noticing her nakedness. And now, he was upset by the mere untidiness of the room. And she too, affected by his embarrassment, soon stopped asking him to attend to her personal needs, as he had done for a brief while.

'Please shut the door, Véronique,' she called out one day, as she heard the young man's footstep in the passage. 'Hide all this, and hand me that fichu.'

Pauline's health, meanwhile, was improving steadily. Her great delight, when she was able to stand alone and look out of the window, was to watch the building of the jetties going on in the distance. The noise of hammering could be heard quite clearly, and the gang of seven or eight men could be seen moving like great ants against the yellow shingle of the sea-shore. Between two tides, they hustled; then, as the waves came in, they had to retreat. But Pauline was chiefly interested in watching Lazare's white jacket and Louise's pink dress, which shone bright in the sunshine. Her gaze pursued them, kept lighting upon them, so that she could have told how they had spent their day, down to the slightest gesture. Now that the work was being intensified the pair of them could not go far afield to the caves behind the cliff. She had them constantly in view, less than a mile away, on a quaint miniature scale, like

123

dolls, under the immense sky. And the jealous joy that she took in being with them thus helped, though she did not know it, to restore her strength and spirits.

'Well, it keeps you amused, doesn't it, watching those men,' Véronique would say each day as she swept the room. 'Of course it's better for you than reading. I always find books give me a splitting headache. And when you need building up, you see, you ought to gape at the sun like turkeys do, and drink great mouthfuls of it.'

She was not naturally conversational, in fact she was considered secretive. But with Pauline she would chatter out of friendliness, thinking it did her good.

'Funny business, all the same! Oh well, provided it satisfies Monsieur Lazare . . . When I say satisfies him, he doesn't look all that keen! But he's proud, and he'd stick to it, even though it bored him stiff . . . Besides if he takes his eyes off those boozers for one minute they drive the nails in crooked.' She ran her broom under the bed and went on: 'As for the Duchess . . .'

Pauline, who was listening with half an ear, was startled by this word.

'What's that? The duchess?'

'Why, Mademoiselle Louise of course! Wouldn't anyone think she'd come out of Jupiter's thigh? . . . If you could see all the little pots she's got in her room, her creams and lotions! As soon as you go in it hits you in the throat, it smells so good . . . And yet she's not so pretty as you.'

'Oh, I'm just a country bumpkin,' the girl replied with a smile. 'Louise is very graceful.'

'Maybe so, but she's got no flesh on her all the same. I've often seen her washing herself . . . If I was a man, I'd certainly have no hesitation!'

Carried away by the fire of her conviction, she came up to lean at the window beside Pauline.

'Just see her there on the sand, she looks like a regular shrimp! Of course it's far away, you can't expect her to look as big as a house. But surely one didn't ought to look like nothing at all . . . Ah, there's Monsieur Lazare lifting her up so she shan't wet her boots. He's not got much of an armful, believe me! Of course there are some men who like skin and bone . . ."

Véronique stopped short, as she felt Pauline quiver at her side. She kept returning to the subject, possessed of an itch to speak further of it. Nowadays, everything she heard and saw seemed to stick in her throat and choke her; the conversations in the evening when the young girl was torn to pieces, the furtive laughter of Lazare and Louise, the ingratitude of the whole house, verging on treachery. If she had rushed upstairs as soon as an excessive injustice revolted her good sense, she would have told the convalescent everything; but the fear of making Pauline ill again kept her in the kitchen, stamping about furiously and savaging her saucepans, swearing that it couldn't last, that she'd break out once and for all. Then, upstairs, as soon as she had let fall a disturbing word, she tried to take it back, she explained it away with touching clumsiness.

'Thank the Lord, Monsieur Lazare doesn't care for skin and bone! He's been in Paris, he's got too much taste . . . You see, he's just set her down again, as if he were throwing away a match-stick.'

And Véronique, fearing lest she should let slip further unnecessary remarks, brandished her feather-duster and went on with her cleaning; while Pauline, sunk in thought, gazed out until darkness fell at the horizon where Louise's blue dress and Lazare's white jacket showed among the dark forms of the workmen.

When her convalescence was almost complete, Chanteau was seized with a violent attack of gout, which determined the girl to go downstairs in spite of her weakness. The first time she came out of her room it was to go and sit by a sickbed. As Madame Chanteau said bitterly, the house was a regular hospital. Of late her husband had been confined to his invalid chair. After a series of attacks, his whole body was now affected; the disease had spread from the feet to the knees, then to the elbows and hands. The small white bead on the ear had gone, but other, larger ones had appeared; and all his joints were swollen, the chalky deposit was forming everywhere under the skin in whitish protuberances like shrimps' eyes. His gout was chronic and incurable, the sort that rigidifies and deforms the limbs.

'My God, what pain!' repeated Chanteau. 'My left leg is as stiff as wood; I can't move my foot nor my knee . . . And now my elbow's aching too. Just look at it!'

Pauline observed a badly inflamed tumour on the left elbow. It was this joint that troubled him most; the pain soon grew intolerable. He sighed, with his arm outstretched and his eyes fixed on his hand, a pitiable hand with knotty, swollen finger-joints and a crooked thumb, that seemed to have been smashed with a hammer.

'I can't bear it like this, you'll have to help me . . . I'd found such a good position, and it began again right away. I feel as if my bones were being scraped with a saw . . . Try and lift me up a little.'

Twenty times an hour he had to be moved round. He was in a state of continual agitation, always in hope of finding relief. But she still felt so weak that she dared not move him alone. She whispered: 'Véronique, help me lift him gently.'

'No, no,' he cried, 'not Véronique! She jolts me.'

Then Pauline had to make an effort that nearly broke her back. And however lightly she turned him over, he uttered a howl that sent the maid rushing off, swearing that you'd have to be a saint like Mademoiselle not to get fed up with a job like that, for Monsieur's howls would make God Almighty take to his heels.

Although the attacks grew less acute, they did not leave off, but persisted night and day; the maddening discomfort, enhanced by the anguish of immobility, amounted to indescribable torment. No longer did his feet alone seem to be gnawed at by some animal; now his whole body was being crushed, as though by a relentless millstone. And no relief was possible; Pauline could only stay there, obedient to his whims, always ready to help him change his position, without ever affording him one hour's peace thereby. The worst of it was that suffering made him unjust and savage; he spoke furiously to her, as though to a clumsy servant.

'Oh, you're as stupid as Véronique! Stop poking your fingers into me like that! You're as rough as a sergeant-major! Get out, I won't have you touching me.'

Unshakable in her patience, she never answered back, but behaved towards him with even greater gentleness. When she felt that he was growing too irritated she would hide for a moment behind the curtains, hoping that, not seeing her, he might calm down. Often she wept there silently, not at the old man's brutality but at the dreadful torments that made him so unkind. And she would hear him mutter in the midst of his groans: 'She's gone, the heartless creature . . . I'm quite likely to kick the bucket and I'll have no one but the cat to close my eyes . . . It's surely to God not right to forsake a Christian creature like this. I bet she's in the kitchen having a drink of broth.'

Then, after struggling for a moment, he would groan still louder and finally bring himself to say: 'Pauline, are you there? Come and help me up a bit, I can't bear it like this any longer . . . Couldn't we try on the left side?'

He would become gentle and penitent, asking her to forgive him for being unkind. Sometimes he made her bring in Mathieu to keep him company, fancying that the dog's presence helped him. But Minouche, above all, was his faithful companion, for she loved the close atmosphere of sickrooms, and she spent whole days in an armchair facing the bed. She seemed startled, however, when he cried out too sharply; she would sit up, watching his sufferings, with indignant amazement in her round eyes, like a righteous man whose peace had been disturbed. Each time Pauline went to the door with Dr. Cazenove she implored: 'Can't you give him an injection of morphia? It breaks my heart to hear him.'

The doctor refused. What was the use? The attack would only recur the more violently. Since salicylate appeared to have aggravated the disease, he preferred not to try any new drug. However, he suggested trying a milk diet once the acute phase of the attacks was over. Until then, absolute starvation, diuretic drinks and nothing else.

' The fact is,' he repeated, 'he's a glutton, and he's paying a high price for his treats. He's been eating game, I know, I saw the feathers. Well, it's his own lookout. I've warned him often enough, let him suffer since he chooses to guzzle and risk the consequences! But it would be much more unfair, my dear, if you had to go back to bed. Be sensible, won't you? You've still got to look after your own health.'

She never spared herself, all her hours were given up to him, and all sense of time, of life itself, escaped her during the long days that she spent beside her uncle, her ears ringing with the sound of his wails, with which the whole room quivered. This obsession was so powerful that it made her forget Lazare and Louise, merely exchanging a few words with them as they hurried past and only seeing them on the rare occasions when she went through the dining-room. As it happened, the work on the jetties was finished, and for the past week a period of violent rainstorms had kept the two young people at home; and whenever the thought that they were together suddenly occurred to her, she was glad to know that they were close at hand.

Madame Chanteau had never seemed so busy. She was taking advantage, so she said, of the confusion into which her husband's attacks threw the household to look through her papers, do her accounts and bring her correspondence up to date. And so, every afternoon, she would shut herself up in her room, deserting Louise, who promptly went up to see Lazare, for she detested being alone. They had formed the habit of staying together till dinner-time in the big second-floor room, which had for so long been both school-room and playroom to Pauline. The young man's narrow iron bed was still there, hidden behind the screen; while the piano accumulated dust, and the enormous table disappeared under an untidy pile of papers, books and pamphlets. In the middle of the table, between two heaps of dried seaweed, stood a jetty the size of a toy, carved out of deal with a penknife, which reminded one of the grandfather's masterpiece, that bridge in its glass case that adorned the dining-room.

Lazare's nerves had been on edge lately. The end of the building operations had brought him the relief of getting rid of an oppressive and irksome task, without any of the joy of seeing his idea materialise. Other plans preoccupied him now, confused schemes for the future; he would take a post at Caen, he would produce a work that would carry him to the heights. But he still took no serious steps, relapsing into an idleness that left him embittered and detracted hourly from his strength and courage. This feeling of discontent was aggravated by the deep shock that Pauline's illness had given to his system, by a continual craving for the open air, and by a strange state of physical excitement, as though he were obeying an imperious compulsion to be revenged on pain. Louise's presence further provoked his nervous agitation; she could not speak to him without leaning on his shoulder, breathing and laughing prettily in his face; and her kittenish graces, her seductive feminine perfume, all the disturbing affectionate abandon of her ways went to his head. He became possessed of a morbid, scruple-racked desire for her. With a childhood friend, in his mother's own house, the thing was impossible, and his sense of decency made his arms suddenly drop powerless when he caught hold of her in play and felt the swift hot surge of blood to his skin. In this conflict it was never the thought of Pauline that stopped him; she would have known nothing about it—husbands often deceive their wives with servant girls. And at night he would make up stories; he would pretend that Véronique, grown unbearable, had been dismissed and that Louise was just a little maid, whom he went to visit bare-foot. How tiresomely things had turned out! And from morning till night he inveighed with enhanced bitterness against love and women, uttering ferocious sallies. Women were the source of all evil, they were stupid and frivolous, and by provoking desire made suffering permanent; and love was nothing but an illusion, the selfish urge of future generations to be born. He brought in the whole of Schopenhauer, with outbursts of coarseness that shocked

128

and amused the girl. And by degrees his love for her increased; a genuine passion grew out of his savage scorn, and he threw himself into this new love with all his original fervour, in ceaseless search for a happiness that was always frustrated.

On Louise's side, there was for a long time nothing but natural coquetry; she loved delicate attentions, whispered compliments, and superficial contacts with agreeable men; she promptly felt lost and depressed if people ceased to take an interest in her. Her senses were still virginal and unawakened, and she wanted nothing more than the trivial chatter and harmless familiarities of an assiduously attentive courtship. When Lazare forgot her for a moment, to write a letter or to become absorbed in one of his sudden, apparently causeless fits of melancholy, she became so unhappy that she began to tease and provoke him, preferring danger to neglect. Then there came a day when, feeling the young man's burning breath on the nape of her delicate neck, she was seized with apprehension. She knew enough, from her long years at boarding-school, to be aware of all that threatened her; and thenceforward she lived in a state of delicious and terrified anticipation of possible disaster; not that she wished for this in the least, or even thought clearly about it, for she was quite confident of being able to avoid it, although she would not stop exposing herself to it—so essential to her feminine satisfaction was this superficial conflict between the instinct to yield and its repression.

Upstairs in the big room, Lazare and Louise were drawn even more closely to one another, while the whole family seemed to be conspiring to bring about their fall. He was sick with idleness and solitude, while she had been stirred by the intimate details, the excited descriptions Madame Chanteau had given of her son. They had taken refuge up there, on the pretext of escaping from the cries of the gout-racked father downstairs; and they lived there without touching a book, without opening the piano, solely concerned with themselves, dazing themselves with endless talk.

On the day when Chanteau's attack reached its paroxysm, the whole house shook with his cries. They were long-drawn-out, broken lamentations, like the howls of a beast being slaughtered. After lunch, which she had swallowed rapidly in nervous exasperation, Madame Chanteau made her escape, saying: 'I can't face it, I should start howling too. If anybody wants me, I'm going to my own room to write. And you, Lazare, take Louise up to your room, quickly. Shut yourselves in, try to amuse her, for she's not having much fun, poor Louisette!'

Her door, on the floor above, could be heard slamming violently, while her son and the girl went up a flight higher.

Pauline had gone back beside her uncle. She alone remained calm, full of pity for such pain. If she could do no more than stay there, she wanted at least to give the poor man the comfort of not suffering in solitude; she felt that he could bear his pain more bravely when she was looking at him, even if she did not speak to him. For hours she would sit thus beside the bed, and she succeeded in calming him a little with her great compassionate eyes. But to-day, he lay with his head thrown back on the bolster, his arm outstretched, racked with the pain in his elbow, and he did not even see her, he only shrieked louder when she appeared.

About four o'clock Pauline, in despair, went to find Véronique in the kitchen, leaving the door open. She expected to be back immediately.

'We really must do something,' she murmured. 'I'd like to try cold water compresses. The doctor says it's dangerous but that it sometimes works . . . I'll need some linen.'

Véronique was in an atrocious temper.

'Linen! I've just been up to get dishcloths, and I got a fine welcome. Mustn't disturb them, so it seems. A pretty state of things!'

'Suppose you ask Lazare?' went on Pauline, who still did not understand.

But the maid, in a fury, with her arms akimbo, let fall her remark without thinking. 'Yes, indeed, they're far too busy licking each other's faces up there!'

'What do you mean?' faltered the girl, turning very pale.

Véronique, taken aback by the sound of her voice, tried to retrieve the secret that she had withheld for so long; she sought an explanation, a lie, without finding anything convincing. She had grasped Pauline by the wrists as a precaution; but the girl suddenly shook herself free, and dashed madly up the stairs, choking and convulsed with anger; and the maid, terrified by her unrecognizable white mask of a face, dared not follow her. The house seemed to be asleep, silence hung over the upper floors, and only Chanteau's wail rang out in the still air. The girl reached the first floor in one precipitate rush, and there ran against her aunt, who was standing there, guarding the landing like a sentry; she might have been keeping watch there for a long time.

'Where are you going?' she asked.

Pauline, speechless with rage and irritated by this obstruction, could not reply.

'Let me pass,' she finally stammered.

And she made a terrible gesture, which sent Madame Chanteau shrinking back. Then she rushed off once more, up to the second floor, while her aunt, petrified, raised her arms without uttering a cry. It was one of those fits of furious rebellion that were liable, like sudden storms, to shatter the sunny peace of her nature, and that, in her early youth, used to leave her in a state of collapse. She had long since considered herself cured; but the wild wind of jealousy had swept her away so roughly that she could not have stopped without injury to herself.

Upstairs, when Pauline reached Lazare's door, she hurled herself against it. The key was twisted and the door burst open, banging the wall. And what she saw within drove her even more frantic. Lazare was holding Louise pressed back against the cupboard and devouring her chin and throat with kisses, while she, almost swooning in sudden sexual panic, offered no resistance. They had begun in fun, no doubt, but the game was ending badly.

There was a moment's stupor. All three stared at one another. At last Pauline cried: 'Oh, you slut, you slut!'

It was the woman's treachery that maddened her most. With a gesture of contempt she had dismissed Lazare, as a child whose weakness she knew of old. But this woman, who spoke to her with intimate affection, this woman who was stealing her husband from her while she was downstairs nursing a sick man! She seized her by the shoulders, she shook her, she felt an urge to strike her.

'Tell me, why did you do that? . . . It was a vile thing to do, d'you hear?'

Louise, desperate and wild-eyed, stammered: 'He got hold of me, he nearly broke my bones.'

'He? Nonsense! He'd have burst into tears if you'd so much as pushed him away.'

The sight of the room whipped up her resentment still further; Lazare's room, where they had loved one another, where she too had felt the young man's passionate breath, turned her blood to fire. How could she be revenged on this woman? Lazare, dazed with shame, was about to intervene at last when she let go of Louise so abruptly that the girl's shoulders were flung back against the cupboard.

'I tell you I don't trust myself! . . . Go away.'

And from that moment she could think of nothing else. She pursued Louise through the room and drove her into the passage and down the stairs, lashing her with the same cry :

131

'Go away! go away! . . . Get your things and go away!'

Meanwhile Madame Chanteau was still on the first floor landing. The swiftness of events had not allowed her to break in. But now she found her voice again; with a wave of her hand she ordered her son to shut himself in his room; then with affected astonishment she endeavoured to calm Pauline. The latter, having chased Louise into her bedroom, was still clamouring: 'Go away, go away!'

'What d'you mean? How can she go away? Are you crazy?'

Then the girl stammered out the story. She was shocked to the core; to her straightforward nature, it was the most shameful action, inexcusable and unpardonable; it offended her passionate honesty and the loyalty of her love; the more she thought about it the wilder she grew. When you'd once given your heart, you couldn't take it back!

'Go away! Pack your trunk at once! Go away!'

Louise, quite overwhelmed and unable to find a word in self-defence, had already opened a drawer and was taking out her underclothes. But Madame Chanteau flared up.

'Stop, Louisette! . . . Really, am I mistress in my own house? Who dares give orders here and presumes to send people away? It's disgusting, we're not in a street market!'

'Didn't you hear?' cried Pauline. 'I've just caught her up there with Lazare . . . He was kissing her.'

The mother shrugged her shoulders. All her accumulated animosity burst forth in one expression of shameful suspicion.

'They were only in fun, where's the harm? . . . And when you were in bed and he was looking after you, did we poke our noses into whatever you might be doing?'

The girl's excitement dropped abruptly. She stood motionless and white, taken aback at this reversal of the indictment against herself. So now she was the guilty one, and her aunt appeared to believe the most appalling things!

'What do you mean?' she murmured. 'If you believed that, you would surely not have allowed it in your own house?'

'Why, you're big enough! But my son's not going to fall into evil ways; other women are still respectable, and you'll please leave them alone.'

Pauline stood speechless for a moment, her great innocent eyes fixed on Madame Chanteau, who averted her own. Then she went up to her own room, saying curtly: 'All right, I'll go away myself.'

Silence fell once more, a heavy silence that seemed to swamp the entire house. And amidst this sudden calm her uncle's howl rang out once more, the cry of a dying and forsaken animal. Without respite. it swelled ever louder, rising above and finally drowning all other sounds.

And now Madame Chanteau regretted having rashly voiced her suspicion. She felt that she had done irreparable damage, and was alarmed at the thought that Pauline might carry out her threat of immediate departure.

With such a stubborn creature, anything might happen; and what would people say about herself and her husband if their ward went trapesing about the countryside, telling the story of their quarrel? She might take refuge with Dr. Cazenove, and that would create a horrible scandal in the neighbourhood. At the back of Madame Chanteau's anxiety lay her terror of the past, her haunting dread that the lost money might be brought up against them.

'Don't cry, Louisette,' she repeated, her anger reviving. 'You see we're in a fine mess through her fault. And she's always so violent, it's impossible to live in peace! . . . I'll try and fix things up.'

'Please, please,' broke in Louise, 'let me go. I'd be too unhappy if I stayed. She's quite right, I want to go.'

'Not to-night, in any case. I must hand you over to your father. Wait a minute, I'll go up and see if she's really packing her trunk.'

Madame Chanteau crept gently to listen at Pauline's door. She heard her walking hurriedly to and fro, opening and shutting drawers. For one moment she thought of going in and having things out, so that all differences would be drowned in a flood of tears. But she was afraid to do so, feeling that she would blush and stammer in front of that child, and this increased her animosity. And instead of knocking she went down to the kitchen, treading softly. An idea had struck her.

'Did you hear the scene Mademoiselle has just been making?' she asked Véronique, who had begun to polish her brass with sullen fury.

The maid, her head bent over her polishing-powder, made no reply.

'She's becoming unbearable. I can't get anything out of her myself. Just fancy, she wants to leave us now; yes, she's getting her things ready. Suppose you went up and tried to argue with her?'

And as she still got no reply:

'Are you deaf?'

'If I don't answer, it's because I won't do it!' cried Véronique abruptly, wild with fury, rubbing a candlestick hard enough to take the skin off her fingers. 'She's quite right to go off, if I'd been her I'd have removed myself long ago.'

Madame Chanteau listened to her open-mouthed, stupefied by this brimming torrent of words.

'I'm no chatterbox, Madame; but it doesn't do to drive me, because then I say everything . . . It's this way, I'd have chucked that child in the sea the day you brought her, only I can't stand seeing people done harm to, and you all treat her so cruelly that one of these days I shall hit out at the first person that touches her . . . Oh, I don't care what you do, you can give me my notice, I'll let her know the whole story! Yes, yes, all that you've been doing to her, for all you pretend to be such good people!'

'Will you shut up, you lunatic?' muttered the old lady, disturbed by this fresh scene.

'No, I won't shut up . . . It's too nasty, d'you hear? For years now it's been making me choke with rage. Wasn't it enough for you to have her money? Did you have to go and cut her heart in quarters? Oh, I know what I know, I've seen you plotting it all . . . And mark my words, Monsieur Lazare may not be such a schemer, but he's just as bad, he'd deal her a death-blow through sheer selfishness, for fear of getting bored . . . Mercy me, some people are born for others to prey on them!'

She brandished her candlestick, then seized a saucepan and rubbed it so violently that it reverberated like a drum. Madame Chanteau had considered throwing her out; but, managing to control herself, she asked coldly:

'So you won't go and speak to her? It's for her own sake, to save her from making a fool of herself.'

Véronique stood silent again. At last she grumbled: 'I'll go up, then . . . After all, reason's reason, nobody ever did any good by acting in a temper.'

Deliberately, she went and washed her hands; then she took off her dirty apron. When she finally brought herself to open the door into the passage, a lamentable sound was heard; it was the incessant, maddening wail of the invalid. Madame Chanteau, who was following her, was struck with an idea, and went on in an urgent whisper: 'Tell her that she can't leave Monsieur in the state he's in . . . D'you hear him?'

'Oh, as to that,' admitted Véronique, 'he's bawling good and plenty, that's quite true.'

She went up, while Madame, who had turned her head in the direction of her husband's room, was careful not to close the door of it. The plaintive sound rose up the stairway, augmented by the resonance of the landings. Upstairs, the maid found Mademoiselle on the point of departure, having made a small bundle of her essential clothing, and determined to have the rest collected next day by old Malivoire. She was calm again, still very pale, heart-broken but coldly reasonable, with no trace of anger.

To everything that Véronique said she merely replied: 'Either she goes or I do,' avoiding any mention of Louise's name.

When Véronique reported this answer to Madame Chanteau, the latter was in Louise's bedroom; the girl, who was in a state of terror and started at the sound of a door, had insisted on dressing and preparing to leave immediately. Then Madame Chanteau had to resign herself; she sent to Verchemont for the baker's cart, and decided to accompany the girl to her aunt Léonie's at Arromanches; they would make up some story to tell her, using as pretext the increased violence of Chanteau's attacks and the unbearableness of his cries.

After the two women had gone off, seen into the carriage by Lazare, Véronique shouted from the hall, at the top of her voice: 'You can come down now, miss; there's nobody here now.'

The house seemed to be empty, the heavy silence had fallen once more, and the invalid's continual lamentation rang out more shrilly. As Pauline was going down the last step Lazare, coming back from the yard, stood face to face with her. Her whole body was seized with a nervous tremor. He stopped for a second, wanting no doubt to blame himself and ask her forgiveness. But his tears choked him, and he rushed up to his room without being able to utter a word. Pauline, dry-eyed and grave-faced, had gone into her uncle's room.

Chanteau was still sprawling across the bed, his arm outstretched, his head thrown back on the bolster. He dared no longer move, he must even have been unaware of the girl's absence, as he lay with eyes tight shut and mouth open to howl more freely. None of the sounds in the house reached him, his only concern was to yell with all the breath in his lungs. And his wails gradually grew longer and more despairing, until they disturbed Minouche, who had had four more kittens taken from her that morning, and who, having already forgotten them, was purring complacently on an armchair.

When Pauline returned to her post, her uncle was yelling so loud that the cat rose, pricking up her ears anxiously. She began to stare at him with her indignant look, like a virtuous person whose quiet has been disturbed. Really, things were becoming impossible if you couldn't even purr in peace! And she withdrew, with her tail lifted high.

CHAPTER VI

WHEN Madame Chanteau came back that evening, a few minutes before supper, she made no allusion to Louise. She simply called Véronique to help her off with her boots. Her left foot was painful.

'My goodness, it's no wonder,' muttered the maid. 'It's swollen.'

And indeed the seams of the leather had left red marks on the flabby white flesh. Lazare, who had just come down, looked at it.

'You must have walked too much,' he said.

But she had merely walked a short distance through Arromanches. Moreover, that day, she was breathing with difficulty, afflicted with a choking sensation that had been increasingly troublesome during the past few months. So she blamed her boots.

'Shoemakers don't seem able to bring themselves to make the insteps high enough . . . It's torture for me to be laced up tightly.'

As the foot stopped aching once she had her slippers on, no more notice was taken of it. Next day, the swelling had reached the ankle. But the following night it vanished completely.

A week went by. From the very first evening meal that brought Pauline face to face with mother and son, on the night of the catastrophe, each of them had striven to behave in an everyday fashion. No allusions were made, and it was just as if nothing new had occurred among them. Family life went on mechanically, with the old sequence of affectionate habits, the customary good-mornings and goodnights, the absent-minded kisses given at regular times. It was a relief, however, when Chanteau was able to be wheeled up to the table. This time his ankles were wholly rigid, and he was unable to stand up. But he nevertheless enjoyed the calm of a respite from pain, to such a point that, selfishly absorbed in his own well-being, he remained unmoved by the happiness or grief of his family. When Madame Chanteau ventured to speak to him about Louise's hurried departure, he begged her not to talk about such sad things. Pauline, since she was no longer confined to her uncle's room, tried to find occupation for herself, but could not conceal her misery. Evenings were particularly painful, when uneasiness pierced through the veneer of customary peace. Their way of life was the same as of old, with the daily round of trivial occurrences; but every now and then a nervous gesture, or even a silence, would make them all conscious of the inner rent, the wound of which they never spoke but which grew greater all the time.

Lazare, at first, had been full of self-contempt. The thought of Pauline's moral superiority, her integrity, her uprightness, had filled him with shame and anger. Why had he not the courage to confess everything to her frankly and ask her forgiveness? He could have told her the whole adventure—how his senses had been surprised, how the other girl's seductive femininity had gone to his head; and she was broad-minded enough to have understood. But an insurmountable embarrassment prevented him, he was afraid of lowering himself still further in her eyes by an explanation which, maybe, would set him stammering like a child. And then, at the back of his reluctance, there lay the fear of fresh deceitfulness, for Louise still haunted him; he kept on imagining her, at night particularly, with a fierce regret at not having possessed her when he held her swooning under his kisses. In spite of himself, his long walks led him constantly in the direction of Arromanches. One evening he went as far as her aunt Léonie's little house; he prowled round the walls, and then fled abruptly when he heard a shutter banging, deeply distressed at the wrong action he had been on the point of committing. And this sense of his own unworthiness increased his embarrassment; he condemned himself, without being able to kill his desire; he had just enough strength and honour left to avoid Pauline so as to save himself from the ultimate baseness of perjury. Perhaps he still loved her, but the other girl's enticing image was continually before him, blotting out the past and obstructing the future.

Pauline, for her part, was waiting for him to beg her pardon. In her first indignant reaction she had vowed to be unforgiving. Subsequently she had suffered in secret at not being asked to forgive. Why did he never speak to her, why did he seem so agitated, why did he always stay out of doors as though he dreaded being alone with her? She was ready to listen to him and to forget everything, if only he would show a little remorse. The hoped-for explanation never came, and she worried secretly, forming one hypothesis after another, while pride kept her silent; and as the painful days dragged slowly by, she was able to master herself enough to resume her old active ways; but this heroic calm concealed an unremitting anguish, and she sobbed at night in her bedroom, stifling her cries in her pillow. Not a word was said about their marriage, although it was evidently in everybody's mind. Autumn was drawing near, what was going to be done? They all avoided expressing an opinion on the question, and the decision seemed to have been postponed till some later date, when they would have the courage to discuss it again.

This was the period of her life when Madame Chanteau finally lost all calm. She had always been apt to wear herself out; but the secret process of disintegration of her better nature seemed to have reached its destructive climax; she had never appeared so unbalanced, so consumed with nervous agitation. And the necessity for self-restraint only exacerbated her disorder. Money was the root of her sufferings; her obsession with money had grown gradually till it swept away her good sense and her good feelings. Her thoughts reverted constantly to Pauline, whom she now blamed for Louise's departure as though for an act of robbery that had despoiled her son. It was like a bleeding wound within her that would not heal; the slightest facts were magnified, she could not forget a single gesture, the girl's cry of: 'Go away!' still haunted her, and she imagined she was being driven out too, and with her all the happiness and wealth of her family. At night, as she tossed in an uneasy sleep, she actually regretted that death had not rid them of that accursed Pauline. Her mind was full of conflicting plans and complicated calculations, yet she could not find a reasonable method of getting rid of the girl. At the same time, by a sort of reaction, her fondness for her son increased; she adored him more, perhaps, than she had ever done when he was an infant, all her own, rocked in her arms. From morning till night she followed him with anxious eyes. Then, as soon as they were alone, she would embrace him and implore him not to distress himself. He wasn't hiding anything from her, was he? He didn't indulge in weeping when nobody was there? And she would swear to him that everything would be all right, that she'd willingly strangle anybody else provided he might be happy. After a fortnight of such ceaseless conflicts, her face assumed a waxen pallor, although she had not lost weight. Twice the swelling in her legs had come up again and then disappeared.

One morning she rang for Véronique and showed her her legs, which had swollen up to the thighs during the night.

'Look what's happening to me! Isn't it tiresome? And I wanted to go out to-day! . . . Now I shall have to stay in bed. Don't say anything for fear of worrying Lazare.'

She herself did not seem to be alarmed by it. She merely said she was a little tired, and everyone assumed it was just a sort of stiffness. As Lazare had gone out wandering along the coast, and Pauline avoided going downstairs because she felt her presence unwelcome, the sick woman poured out to the maid a torrent of furious accusations against the girl. The immobility to which she was condemned, the palpitations that choked her at the slightest movement, seemed to goad her into ever-increasing fury.

'What's she doing downstairs, eh? Up to no good, for sure . . . You'll see, she won't even bring me up a glass of water.'

'But, madame,' answered Véronique, 'why, it's you yourself that rebuff her.'

'Nonsense! you know her. There's no worse hypocrite than she is. In front of people she acts ever so good-natured, but she preys on you behind your back . . . Oh yes, my lass, you were the only clear-sighted one, the day I brought her here. If she'd never come into the house we shouldn't have come to the pass we have . . . And she'll be the end of us: Monsieur suffers the tortures of the damned since she's been looking after him; I'm all upset because she frets me so, and as for my son, it's driving him out of his wits . . .'

'Oh, madame, how can you say so? She's so good to you all!'

Until nightfall, Madame Chanteau poured forth her feelings. It all came out, including the savage dismissal of Louise, and, above all, the business of the money. And so when Véronique was able to go downstairs after dinner, and found Pauline in the kitchen putting away the dishes, she gave vent herself to all her pent-up feelings. For a long time now she had repressed her secret knowledge and her indignation; but this time the words came out of themselves.

'Oh, miss, it's too good of you to be careful of their dishes. If I was you I'd smash the lot!'

'Why ever?' asked the girl in surprise.

'Because you could never be as bad as they make out.' And starting from there, she went back to the beginning of it all.

'Isn't it a thing to put God Almighty in a rage? She's sucked your money from you a penny at a time, in the dirtiest way you can imagine. I declare, anyone would think it was she who paid for your keep . . . When it was in her desk, that money of yours, she used to make no end of a fuss about it, as if she was guarding a girl's maidenhead; but that didn't prevent her from getting her claws into it, and making big holes in it . . . Oh, my goodness, what an act she put on to saddle you with the business of the factory, and then use the rest of the hoard to keep the pot boiling. Shall I tell you something? Well, without you, they'd all have died of hunger . . . And so she was in a fine taking when the other lot, in Paris, nearly had a row over the accounts! Why, you could have had her sent straight to the assize-court . . . And that didn't stop her nasty ways, she's still devouring you, she'll swallow up your last farthing . . . You think I'm telling a lie, maybe? Look here, I'll take my Bible oath I saw it and heard it with my own ears, and I'm not telling you the worst, out of respect for you, miss, like when you were ill, and she was in a rage at not being able to rummage in your cupboard.'

Pauline was listening, unable to find a single word with which to cut her short. Often the thought that her relations were living at her expense and spitefully despoiling her had clouded her happiest days. But she had always refused to think about such things, preferring to shut her eyes to them and accusing herself of meanness. And this time she was being obliged to learn it all, and the brutal way in which the disclosure was made seemed to make the offence more heinous. Every sentence awakened some echo in her memory; she could reconstruct former incidents the meaning of which had escaped her, and retrace day by day Madame Chanteau's machinations about her fortune. Slowly, she had dropped into a chair, as though oppressed with a great weariness. Her lips were twisted as if in pain.

'You're exaggerating,' she murmured.

'Exaggerating? Not likely,'' went on Véronique with violence. 'It's not so much the question of the cash that drives me mad. See here, what I shall never forgive her for is taking away Monsieur Lazare from you after having given him to you . . . Yes, I know what I'm saying! You weren't rich enough any longer, he had to have an heiress. What d'you think of that, eh? They rob you, then they despise you because you've got nothing left . . . No, I won't stop, miss! It isn't right to fleece a person and then break her heart into the bargain! Since you loved your cousin, and he could only repay you for everything with kindness, it was downright abominable to have robbed you of that too. And she did it all, I saw her. Yes, yes, every evening she'd lead the girl on, she'd get her all worked up about the young man, with a lot of filthy tricks. As true as this lamp's shining, it was she that threw them at one another. Yes indeed! She'd have held the candle for them, she'd have played the go-between if she could have made that marriage inevitable. It's no fault of hers if they didn't go quite far enough . . .

Take her part then, now that she's crushed you under her feet, and it's on account of her that you cry your heart out at nights; for I can hear you from my room; the whole thing makes me ill, all this misery and injustice . . .'

'Oh, please, hush,' stammered Pauline, her courage breaking down, 'you make me too unhappy.'

Great tears rolled down her cheeks. She felt that the woman was not lying, and her lacerated feelings bled within her. Every incident alluded to assumed vivid reality; she could see Louise swooning in Lazare's embrace, while Madame Chanteau kept watch at the door. Oh God, what had she done that everybody should betray her, when she was so loyal to them all?

'I implore you, don't say any more, I can't bear it.'

Then Véronique, seeing her so distressed, merely added in a muffled tone: 'It's for your sake and not for hers if I don't say any more . . . Why, she's up there now, and has been since morning, spewing out a lot of filth about you! I just break out in the end, for it makes my blood boil when I hear her putting an evil meaning on all the good you've done her . . . On my word of honour, she pretends you've ruined them and that you're killing her son. Go and listen at the door if you don't believe me.'

Then, as Pauline burst into sobs, Véronique in a panic took her head between her hands and kissed her hair, repeating: 'No. no, miss, I won't say any more . . . And yet you've got to know. It's too silly to let yourself be preyed on like that . . . Now calm down, I won't say any more.'

There was silence; the maid extinguished the embers that still glowed in the stove. But she could not prevent herself from adding in a low voice: 'I know why she's swelling up; her wickedness is going down into her knees.'

Pauline, who had been staring at one of the tiles in the kitchen floor, her mind full of confused thoughts and heavy with grief, raised her eyes. Why did Véronique say that? Had the swelling re-appeared? The maid, embarrassed, had to break her promise of secrecy. It was all right to criticise Madame, but one had to obey her. Well, then, both legs had been affected, since last night, but Monsieur Lazare mustn't be told about it. While the maid was giving these details Pauline's expression changed from sad despondency to anxiety. In spite of all she had just learnt she was alarmed about a symptom whose gravity she recognized.

'But she can't be left like that,' she said, getting up. 'She's in danger.'

'Danger indeed!' cried Véronique brutally. 'She doesn't look like it, and she doesn't think of it in any case, she's far too busy slandering other people and throning it in her bed like a sultan . . . Besides, she's asleep now, we'll have to wait till to-morrow. That's the day the doctor comes to Bonneville, in any case.'

Next day, Lazare could no longer be left in ignorance of his mother's condition. All night Pauline had been listening, wakening every hour and constantly thinking that she heard cries from the floor below. Then at dawn she had fallen asleep so deeply that nine o'clock was striking when the sound of a door made her start from her bed. As she was going down to get news, having dressed hastily, she ran into Lazare on the first-floor landing; he was coming out of his mother's room. The swelling had reached the abdomen and Véronique had at last decided to tell the young man.

'Well?' asked Pauline.

Lazare, his face distraught, did not answer for a moment. With a gesture that was habitual with him he pressed his shaking fingers to his chin. And when he spoke at last, it was to whisper brokenly: 'She's done for.'

He went upstairs with an air of bewilderment. Pauline followed him. When they were in the big second-floor room, into which she had not set foot since she had caught him there with Louise, she closed the door and tried to reassure him.

'Look, you don't even know what's the matter with her. Do at least wait till the doctor's been . . . She's very strong, there's always hope.'

But he persisted, struck by a sudden heartrending conviction: 'She's done for, she's done for.'

The blow had fallen on him unexpectedly. When he rose that morning he had looked out at the sea as usual, yawning with boredom and grumbling at the futile emptiness of life. Then, when his mother had shewn him her legs up to the knee, the sight of those poor dropsy-swollen limbs, enormous and pallid like logs of dead wood, had filled him with pity and terror. What! So misfortune could fall on you at any minute! And even now, sitting on a corner of his great table, his whole body shaking, he dared not name aloud the disease which he had just recognized. He had always been haunted by a dread of heart disease, whether for himself or for those dear to him, and his two years' medical studies had failed to impress on him the equality of all illnesses before death. To be smitten at the heart, the very source of life, still seemed to him the cruellest, most pitiless form of death. And it was from such a death that his

142

mother was going to die and that he himself would certainly die eventually!

'Why do you distress yourself so?' went on Pauline. 'Some cases of dropsy live a very long time. Don't you remember Madame Simonnot? She ended by dying of pneumonia.'

But he shook his head; he was not a child, to be taken in like that. His dangling feet trampled the air, his body never stopped shaking, while he kept his eyes obstinately on the window. Then, for the first time since their estrangement she kissed him on the forehead, as she used to do. They stood side by side in the room where they had grown up and all their bitterness was swallowed up by the great grief that had threatened them. She dried her eyes. Lazare, unable to weep, went on repeating mechanically: 'She's done for, she's done for.'

At about eleven o'clock, when Dr. Cazenove called, as he generally did on Saturdays on his way back from Bonneville, he displayed great astonishment at finding Madame Chanteau in bed. What was the matter with the good lady? And he even made a joke of it— they were all becoming molly-coddles, the house would definitely have to be turned into an infirmary. But when he had examined the patient, felt her limbs and sounded her heart, he grew graver; indeed he needed all the self-possession born of long experience not to betray a certain alarm.

In any case, Madame Chanteau was quite unaware of the gravity of her condition.

'I hope you're going to pull me out of this, doctor,' she said in a cheerful tone. 'You see I've only one dread, and that is that the swelling may choke me if it rises any higher.'

'Don't worry, it won't rise like that,' he said, laughing himself. 'Besides, we'll soon stop it.'

Lazare, who had come in after the examination, was listening to him with a shudder, longing to take him on one side and question him, to get the truth at last.

'There, dear madame,' the doctor went on, 'don't worry, I'll come back and have a chat with you to-morrow . . . Good-bye, I'm going down to write my prescriptions.'

Downstairs, Pauline prevented him from going into the dining-room, for Chanteau was still under the impression that it was nothing but an attack of stiffness. She had already set out paper and ink on the kitchen table. Faced with their anxious impatience, Dr. Cazenove admitted that it was serious; but he used long complicated phrases and avoided drawing any conclusions.

'There's no hope, is there?' cried Lazare, with a sort of irritation. 'It's her heart, isn't it?'

Pauline cast an imploring look, which the doctor understood.

'Her heart?' he said, 'I shouldn't think so. In any case, even if she doesn't recover from it, she can still last quite a long time, with care.'

The young man gave his characteristic shrug of the shoulders, like an angry child who is not taken in by the stories he is told. He went on: 'And you never warned me, doctor, although you've been looking after her lately! . . . These horrors never come on suddenly. Hadn't you noticed anything?'

'Oh yes,' muttered Cazenove, 'I had noticed one or two little things.' Then, as Lazare began to laugh contemptuously, 'Listen, my lad, I think I'm less of a fool than most people, and yet it's not the first time an illness has taken me by surprise and left me puzzled . . . You're maddening, you expect one to know everything, when it's quite an achievement to understand the elements of such a complicated machine as the human carcase.'

His temper rose, and he scribbled his prescription with an angry hand, scoring the thin paper with his pen. The tall old fellow's gestures were as brusque as in the days of his service at sea; but when he stood up again his old face, tanned by the sea-winds, grew gentler as he saw before him Lazare and Pauline in despair, their heads bowed.

'My poor children,' he went on, 'we'll do our best to pull her through . . . You know that I'm not going to play the learned man with you. Well, frankly, I can't say anything. It doesn't seem to me, though, that there's any immediate danger.'

And he went off, after making sure that Lazare had some tincture of digitalis. He had simply prescribed massage of the legs with this tincture, and a few drops of it in a glass of sweetened water. That was enough for the moment, and he would bring some pills next day. Perhaps he would decide to try bleeding. Pauline, meanwhile went out with him as far as his gig, to try and discover the real truth; but the real truth, actually, was that he dared not give an opinion. When she came back into the kitchen she found Lazare reading over the prescription. The one word *digitalis* had made him blanch again.

'Don't worry so much!' said Véronique, who had started peeling potatoes so that she could stay there and listen. 'Doctors are all killers. If this one doesn't know what to say, that means there can't be much wrong.'

They lingered, arguing, round the dish where the cook was cutting up her potatoes. Pauline, too, seemed easier in her mind. That morning she had gone in to greet her aunt with a kiss and found her looking well; with such a colour, you couldn't be dying. But Lazare kept turning the prescription round and round between feverish fingers. The word *digitalis* seemed written in letters of fire; his mother was done for.

'I'm going up,' he said at last.

At the door he hesitated, then asked his cousin: 'Will you come in for a minute?'

She, too, had a moment's hesitation. 'I'm afraid of upsetting her,' she murmured.

An awkward silence fell, and he went up alone, without adding a word.

At lunch, Lazare came down again, so as not to worry his father; he was very pale. From time to time the bell would ring for Véronique, who walked about with platefuls of soup, which the sick woman would rarely touch; and when she came down again she would tell Pauline that the poor young man was going crazy up there. It was pitiful to see him shaking as though with a fever by his mother's side, so awkward with his hands, and looking as miserable as if he expected her to pass away in his arms at any moment. Towards three o'clock the maid had just gone up again when she leaned over the banisters and called the girl. Then, when the latter had reached the first floor landing:

'You ought to go in, miss, and give him a hand. Never mind if it annoys her! She wants him to turn her over, and if you could see how he shudders and daren't even touch her! . . . And she won't let me go near her.'

Pauline went in. Madame Chanteau, sitting up squarely against three pillows, might have been staying in bed out of sheer laziness, but for the painful gasping breath that shook her shoulders. In front of her, Lazare was stammering: 'Do you want me to turn you on to the right side?'

'Yes, push me over a bit . . . Oh, my poor boy, you don't seem able to understand!'

Already, the girl had gently taken hold of her and was turning her over. 'Let me do it, I'm used to it with uncle . . . Is that all right?'

Madame Chanteau, irritated, grumbled that she was being jostled. She could not make a single movement without immediately choking; and she would lie there panting for a moment, her

145

face ashen. Lazare had withdrawn behind the curtains of the bed
to hide his despair. He stayed there, however, while Pauline rubbed
the sick woman's legs with tincture of digitalis. He turned his head
away, but a compulsion to look brought his gaze back to those
monstrous limbs, those inert bundles of pallid flesh, the sight of
which wrung his heart with anguish. When his cousin saw him
so distraught, she thought it wiser to send him away. She went
close to him and whispered, since Madame Chanteau was dropping
off to sleep, exhausted merely from having her position changed:

'You'd better go away.'

He resisted for a moment, his eyes blinded with tears. But he
was obliged to give in, and went downstairs muttering in his shame:
'Oh God, I can't, I can't!'

When the sick woman awoke she did not at first notice her son's
absence. She seemed overcome with stupor, withdrawn, entirely
obsessed by the selfish need to feel herself alive. Only Pauline's
presence seemed to disturb her, although the latter tried to hide
from her view, sitting silent and motionless in a corner. When her
aunt peered forward she felt bound to explain things briefly.

'It's only me, don't worry; Lazare's gone to Verchemont, where
he had to see the carpenter.'

'All right,' mumbled Madame Chanteau.

'Your illness isn't bad enough, is it, to stop him seeing to his
business?'

'Of course not.'

From that moment she seldom spoke about her son, in spite of
the adoration she had displayed for him only the day before. He
was fading out of her now diminished life, after having been the
be-all and end-all of her existence. The morbid degeneration of
the brain which was taking place in her left her with no thought
beyond physical anxiety about her own health. She accepted her
niece's attentions without appearing conscious of the substitution
that had taken place; she was merely concerned to follow her with
her eyes, as though disturbed by the growing mistrust that she felt
at seeing Pauline contantly coming and going round her bed.

And meanwhile Lazare had gone down into the kitchen, distraught, his legs weak with weariness. The whole house frightened
him; he could not bear to stay in his room, whose emptiness overpowered him, he dared not go through the sitting-room, where the
sight of his father peacefully reading his newspaper convulsed him
with grief. So he kept coming back to the kitchen, the only spot
full of warmth and life; it reassured him to find Véronique there,

battling with her saucepans as in the old untroubled days. When she saw him sitting down beside the stove again, on his favourite straw-bottomed chair, she told him frankly what she thought of his lack of courage.

'Really, Monsieur Lazare, you're not being much help. It's that poor Mademoiselle that's going to have to tackle it all again. One'd think there'd never been anybody ill before; and after all, you looked after your cousin very well when she nearly died of her sore throat . . . Eh, you can't deny it, you stayed up there a fortnight nursing her like a child.'

Lazare listened to her in great surprise. The inconsistency had never struck him; why should his emotional reactions have been so illogically different?

'It's quite true,' he kept saying, 'quite true.'

'You wouldn't let anybody go in,' went on the maid, 'and Mademoiselle was even more pitiful to look at than Madame, she was in such pain. I used to come down from there in a regular turmoil, I didn't feel I could swallow so much as a scrap of bread . . . And now to-day, you're all of a dither because you've seen your mother laid up! You wouldn't even take her up a cup of tisane . . . Your mother may be whatever she is, but she's still your mother.'

He had stopped listening, he was staring into space. At last he muttered: 'What's to be done? I can't help it . . . It's perhaps because it's mother, but I can't . . . When I see her legs like that, and tell myself she's done for, something gives way inside me and I should howl like an animal if I didn't run out of the room.'

His whole body began to quiver again, he had bent to pick up a knife that had fallen from the table and was examining it with unseeing, tear-blinded eyes. Silence fell. Véronique bent her head over her stockpot, to hide the emotion which made her, too, speechless. At last she began again:

'Look here, Monsieur Lazare, you'd better go down to the beach. You get in my way, always hanging around here . . . And take Mathieu with you. He's a perfect nuisance, he doesn't know what to do with himself either, and I've an awful struggle preventing him from going up to Madame's room.'

Next day, Dr. Cazenove still showed some uncertainty. There might be a sudden catastrophe, or else, if the dropsy diminished, the sick woman might recover for an indefinite length of time. He gave up the idea of bleeding and merely prescribed the pills which he had brought, together with the continued use of digitalis. His air of depression and secret irritation betrayed that he had little faith in these remedies, in one of those cases of organic disorder where the gradual weakening of all the organs renders medical science useless. Besides, he declared that the invalid was not suffering. And indeed Madame Chanteau complained of no acute pain; her legs were as heavy as lead, and the choking sensation was worse whenever she moved; but while she lay there on her back, motionless, her voice was still as loud and her eyes as bright, so that she was herself deceived. Seeing her so brave, none of those around her, except her son, would give way to despair. When the doctor climbed into his carriage again, he told them not to be too sorry for themselves, for it was a great mercy, for oneself and for one's family, not to watch oneself dying.

The first night had been hard for Pauline. Lying half-stretched out in an armchair, she had been unable to sleep, with the stertorous breathing of the dying woman in her ears. Whenever she grew drowsy, she would feel that the sound was shaking the whole house and making everything crack. Then, when her eyes were open, she was gripped by a feeling of oppression, and lived through all the torments that had spoilt her life during the last few months. Even by the side of this deathbed, she could find no inner peace; she could not forgive. In the nightmare hours of her gloomy vigil she remembered Véronique's disclosures with particular anguish. Her former moods of violence, her jealous resentment revived as she lay brooding wretchedly over all the details. No longer to be loved, oh God! To be betrayed by those one loves! To be left alone, seething with scorn and indignation! Her wound, reopened, bled; she had never felt so acutely conscious of the wrong done her by Lazare. Since they had killed her, let them die themselves! And her aunt's loud breathing obsessed her, like a ceaseless reminder of the theft of her money and the theft of her love, until she felt her own breast bursting with it.

The break of day found Pauline's conflict still unresolved. She felt no return of affection, only a sense of duty kept her in the sickroom. This set the crown on her misery: was she too growing hard-hearted? The whole day passed in this uneasy state; she nursed her patient with assiduous care, dissatisfied with herself and hurt by the sick woman's mistrust. The latter rewarded all her attentions with a surly grunt, and pursued her with a suspicious eye, watching everything she did. If she asked Pauline for a handkerchief, she would sniff at it before using it, and when she saw the girl bringing her a hot-water bottle, she insisted on feeling the bottle.

'What's the matter with her?' Pauline whispered to the maid. 'Does she think I'm capable of doing her harm?'

After the doctor had gone, as Véronique was offering Madame Chanteau a spoonful of medicine, the latter, not seeing her neice, who was looking for linen in the cupboard, murmured: 'Did the doctor prepare this stuff?'

'No, Madame, Miss Pauline did.'

Then she tasted it with the tip of her lips and made a face.

'It smells of copper . . . I don't know what she's making me take, but I've had the taste of copper in my stomach ever since yesterday.'

And with a sudden gesture she threw the contents of the spoon behind her bed. Véronique was left gasping.

'Well now, for goodness sake! What's the idea?'

'I don't want to go off yet,' said Madame Chanteau, lying back, her head on the pillow. 'Just listen—my lungs are still strong. And she might quite well die before me, for her flesh isn't healthy.'

Pauline had heard. She turned round, cut to the heart, and looked at Véronique. Instead of coming forward, she shrank further back, ashamed for her aunt's sake of so atrocious a suspicion. Her inner tension suddenly relaxed, and she was moved by deep pity for the wretched woman whom fear and hatred had so ravaged; and far from experiencing increased bitterness, she felt overwhelmed with compassionate distress when, bending down, she caught sight of all the medicaments that the sick woman had thrown under the bed for fear of being poisoned. Until nightfall she behaved with valiant gentleness, as though unaware of the anxious scrutiny to which her hands were subjected. Her fervent wish was, by dint of kind nursing, to conquer the dying woman's fears, so that she should not carry this appalling thought down to the grave with her.

She forbade Véronique to alarm Lazare further by telling him the story.

Only once since morning had Madame Chanteau asked for her son; and then she had appeared satisfied with the first thing they had told her, expressing no surprise at not seeing him again. Moreover she spoke of her husband even less; she did not worry as to what became of him, all alone in the dining-room. Everything seemed to have become indifferent to her, as though the icy coldness of her legs had spread gradually upwards till it froze her heart. At each meal-time Pauline had to go downstairs, so as to deceive her uncle. That evening she even lied to Lazare, assuring him that the swelling was decreasing.

But during the night the disorder made alarming progress. Next morning, when the girl and the maid saw the sick woman in broad daylight they were startled by the wild expression in her eyes. Her face had not altered, and she still had no fever; only her mind seemed affected; her brain was finally giving way under the pressure of her obsession. This was the last phase; a single passion had gradually devoured her whole being and driven her mad.

The morning, until the arrival of Dr. Cazenove, was a terrible ordeal. Madame Chanteau refused to let her niece even come near her.

'Let me look after you, please,' urged Pauline. 'I'll just lift you up for a minute, for you're lying so uncomfortably.'

Then the dying woman struggled as though she were being strangled.

'No, no, you've got scissors, you're digging them into my flesh on purpose . . . I can feel them, I'm bleeding all over.'

Deeply distressed, the girl had to move away; and she was weak with fatigue and grief, desperate at the frustration of her wish to help. To get the slightest service accepted she had to endure insults and accusations that reduced her to tears. Sometimes she gave way and collapsed on to a chair, weeping, utterly at a loss how to win back the former fondness that had turned to fury. Then she would grow resigned again and make fresh, ingenious efforts, with increased gentleness. But to-day her persistence precipitated a crisis that left her trembling for a long time.

'Now, aunt,' she said, as she got ready the spoon, 'it's time for your medicine. You know the doctor's told you to be sure and take it regularly.'

Madame Chanteau insisted on seeing and finally smelling the bottle.

'Is it the same as yesterday?'

'Yes, auntie.'

'I won't touch it.'

However, by dint of prayers and caresses, her niece persuaded her to swallow one more spoonful. The invalid's face expressed profound mistrust, and as soon as she had the medicine in her mouth she spat it out violently, shaken by a fit of coughing and mumbling amidst her hiccoughs: 'It's vitriol, it's burning me.'

Her loathing and terror of Pauline, which had grown little by little since the day when she had taken the first twenty-franc piece, now burst forth in a flood of wild words, as her mania reached its peak; while the girl listened aghast, without finding a word in self-defence.

150

'If you think I'm not aware of it! You put copper and vitriol in everything . . . That's what's choking me. There's nothing wrong with me, I could have got up this morning if you hadn't dissolved verdigris in my broth last night . . . Yes, you've had enough of me, you'd like to see me buried. But I'm tough, and it's I who'll see you buried.'

Her words were growing increasingly confused, she was choking, and her lips turned so black that a catastrophe seemed imminent.

'Oh, auntie, auntie,' whispered Pauline in terror, 'if you knew how much harm you're doing yourself!'

'Well, that's what you want, isn't it? Oh, yes, I know you, you've made your plan a long time ago, you came here with the sole object of murdering us and plundering us. You want to get the house and I'm in your way . . . Ah, you devil, I should have crushed you on the very first day . . . I hate you, I hate you!'

Pauline stood motionless, weeping silently. She could only repeat, as though in involuntary protest: 'Oh God, oh God!'

But Madame Chanteau grew exhausted, and an infantile terror succeeded the violence of her frenzy. She had sunk back on to the pillows.

'Don't come near me, don't touch me . . . I shall shout for help if you touch me. No, no, I won't drink. It's poison.'

And she clutched at the blankets, she hid her face in the pillows, rolling her head about, pressing her lips tightly together. When her niece, distracted, came up to try and calm her, she uttered wild yells.

'Be reasonable, auntie . . . I won't make you drink anything if you don't want to.'

'Yes, you've got the bottle . . . Oh, I'm afraid, I'm afraid . . .'

She was at the last gasp, her head, thrown back in terror, was hanging too low and becoming mottled with purple. The girl, convinced that she was dying, rang for the maid. The two of them, with great difficulty, raised her up and laid her on the pillows again.

Then Pauline's personal sufferings, her heart's anguish, were finally swept away in this common grief. She had forgotten the fresh wound which, only yesterday, had been bleeding; she had lost all passion and all jealousy, in the face of such sorrow. All were drowned in the depths of a boundless compassion; she would have liked to be able to love more, to sacrifice herself, to give herself, to bear injustice and insult, if thereby she could better relieve the sufferings of others. She would gallantly have shouldered the

151

major burden of life's pain. From that moment she knew no further weakness, she displayed in the presence of the dying the same resigned calm that she had shown when threatened by death herself. She was always ready; nothing discouraged her. And even her former fondness had revived; she forgave her aunt for her frenzied outbursts and pitied her for the gradual growth of her delusion, preferring to remember her as she used to be and loving her as she had loved her at ten years old, when they had arrived at Bonneville together one stormy evening.

That day, Dr. Cazenove did not come till after lunch; he had been kept at Verchemont by an accident, a farmer's broken arm which he had had to set. When he had seen Madame Chanteau and came down to the kitchen he did not conceal his unfavourable impression. As it happened, Lazare was there, sitting by the stove, a prey to restless idleness.

'There's no hope, is there?' he asked. 'Last night I was re-reading Bouillaud's work on heart disease ...'

Pauline, who had come down with the doctor, once more cast an imploring glance at the latter, which made him interrupt the young man wrathfully.

'Heart indeed! My good fellow, you can talk about nothing but the heart! ... How can we say anything definitely? I think the liver's in a worse state still. Only, when the machine breaks down, everything's affected, to be sure, the lungs, the stomach and the heart itself ... Instead of reading Bouillaud at nights, which only serves to make you ill, too, you'd do better to have a good sleep.'

As though by a secret agreement, they all told Lazare now that his mother was dying of liver trouble. He did not believe a word of it, and in his sleepless hours kept turning over his old textbooks; then he would get confused about the symptoms, and the doctor's explanation that the organs were affected one after the other ended by alarming him even more.

'But really,' he went on in distress, 'how much longer do you think that she can last out?'

Cazenove made a vague gesture. 'A fortnight or a month, maybe ... Don't ask me to say, I'd only give a wrong answer, and you'd have every right to say that we know nothing and can do nothing ... It's appalling what strides the disease has made since yesterday.'

Véronique, who was busy wiping glasses, gazed at him open-mouthed. So it was true, then, that Madame was very ill, that Madame was going to die? Until then, refusing to believe in any real danger, she had gone on grumbling in corners, repeating that it was all repressed spitefulness, just on purpose to upset everybody. She stood utterly stupefied, and as Pauline told her to go up to Madame so as not to leave her alone, she went out, wiping her hands on her apron, unable to utter a word but: 'Well, I never! Well, I never!'

'Doctor,' went on Pauline, who alone had kept her head, 'we ought to think of my uncle too . . . D'you think he ought to be warned? Do go in and see him before you leave.'

Just then, however, Abbé Horteur appeared. He had only heard that morning about what he called Madame Chanteau's indisposition. When he learned how gravely ill she was, his sunburnt face, always so cheerful out of doors, assumed an expression of genuine sorrow. The poor lady! Was it possible? she'd seemed so plucky only three days before. Then after a pause he asked: 'Can I see her?'

He had cast an anxious look at Lazare, knowing that the latter was an unbeliever and foreseeing a rebuff. But the young man, oppressed with grief, did not seem to have understood. It was Pauline who told him bluntly: 'No, not to-day, *Monsieur le curé*. She doesn't know how ill she is and your presence would give her a shock. We'll see about it to-morrow.'

'All right,' the priest said hurriedly, 'there's no urgency, I trust. But we must each do our duty, mustn't we? . . . The doctor, for instance, who doesn't believe in God . . .'

For the last few minutes the doctor had been staring at one of the table legs, deeply absorbed, lost in the doubting thoughts that assailed him when he felt baffled by Nature. He had heard, though, and he interrupted Abbé Horteur.

'Who told you I don't believe in God? God isn't impossible, one sees such funny things! . . . After all, who knows?'

He shook his head, and seemed to wake up. 'Look here,' he went on, ' you'll come in with me to shake hands with good Monsieur Chanteau. He's going to need a lot of courage.'

'If it would help to distract him,' the *curé* obligingly offered, 'I'd stay and have a game of draughts with him.'

They both went into the dining-room, while Pauline hurried back to be with her aunt. Lazare, left to himself, rose, hesitated a moment as though to follow her, then went to listen to his father's voice, but lacked the courage to go in; then he went back and collapsed on to his chair again, in despairing idleness.

The doctor and the priest had found Chanteau playing with a ball of paper, made from a prospectus that had been enclosed with his newspaper; he was rolling it about the table. Minouche, beside him, was looking on with her green eyes. Contemptuous of this primitive toy, she lay with her paws tucked under her belly, unwilling to face the exertion of baring her claws. The ball had stopped in front of her nose.

'Hullo, there you are,' said Chanteau. 'That's very kind of you, I get so bored all alone . . . Well doctor, is she better? Oh, I'm not worried, she's the toughest person in the house, she'll survive us all.'

The doctor thought this a good occasion to enlighten him.

'No doubt, her condition doesn't seem to be very critical. But she's growing very weak.'

'No, no, doctor,' cried Chanteau, 'you don't know her. She's got amazing resilience. Before three days are up you'll see her on her feet again.'

And he refused to understand, so great was his need to believe in his wife's health. The doctor, unwilling to break things to him brutally, was obliged to keep silence. In any case, it was just as well to wait. His gout was fortunately giving him a little respite; his pain was not too acute, although his legs were so badly affected that he now had to be carried from his bed to his armchair.

'If it weren't for these cursed legs,'' he kept saying, 'I could at least go up and see her.'

'Resign yourself, my friend,' said Abbé Horteur, who for his part was anxious to fulfil his consolatory mission. 'Every man must bear his own cross . . . We're all in God's hands . . .'

But he perceived that these words, far from comforting Chanteau, bored him and even seemed to worry him. So he good-naturedly broke off his ready-made exhortations and offered a more effective form of distraction.

'Would you like a game? It'll clear your head.'

And he went to fetch the draught-board himself, from the top of a cupboard. Chanteau, delighted, said goodbye to the doctor with a handclasp. Just as the two men were becoming engrossed in their game, oblivious of the whole world, Minouche, irritated no doubt by seeing the ball of paper lying before her so long, pounced on it and sent it flying with a blow of her paw, then pursued it round the room with crazy leaps and bounds.

'Tiresome creature!' cried Chanteau, disturbed in his game. 'She wouldn't play with me just now and now she's preventing us from thinking by having a game all to herself!'

'Let her be,' said the *curé*, full of benevolence. 'Cats get their pleasure in their own way.'

As Dr. Cazenove went back through the kitchen, he saw Lazare still sprawling in the same chair; carried away by a sudden wave of feeling he put his long arms round the young man and gave him a fatherly kiss, without saying a word. Véronique happened to come down just then, driving Mathieu in front of her. The dog kept on roaming about the stairs, uttering a little nasal whine like a plaintive bird's cry; and whenever he found the door of the sickroom open he would come and whimper there, piercing their ears with the persistence of that shrill, flageolet-like sound.

'Get along with you!' cried the maid. 'It's not your music that'll set her right.' Then, seeing Lazare, she added: 'Take him away somewhere, it'll get us rid of him and it'll do you good.'

This was an order from Pauline. She had commissioned Véronique to send Lazare out of the house, to force him to take long walks. But he refused, feeling too weak even to get up. However, the dog had come to stand in front of him and was beginning to whimper again.

'Poor old Mathieu, he's not as young as he was,' said the doctor, looking at him.

'Well, he's fourteen,' answered Véronique. 'That doesn't stop him chasing mice like a lunatic . . . See, his nose is all raw and his eyes are red. That's because he smelt one under the stove last night; and he didn't sleep a wink, he turned my kitchen topsy turvy with his nose, and his paws are still all of a quiver. Such a big dog after such a small beast, isn't it ridiculous! Besides, it's not only mice, but everything tiny that crawls about, whether it's one-day-old chicks or Minouche's kittens, he gets so worked up about them he won't eat or drink. Sometimes he'll spend hours sniffing under a piece of furniture where a cockroach has been . . . And just now, it's true to say he can smell queer things happening in the house . . .'

She broke off, seeing the tears brim in Lazare's eyes.

'Go for a turn, my lad,' went on the doctor. 'You're no use here, you'd be better off outside.'

At last the young man rose with a painful effort. 'Come on, poor old Mathieu,' he said, 'come on.'

When he had seen the doctor into his carriage he went off with the dog, along the cliffs. From time to time he had to wait for Mathieu, who had indeed aged very much. His hindquarters were becoming paralysed and his big paws flopped about on the ground like slippers. He had given up digging holes in the kitchen garden, and he soon dropped down dizzy when he ran after his tail. Above all he tired

155

very rapidly, he coughed if he went into the water, and would lie down and snore after a quarter of an hour's walk. On the beach, he came and walked right against his master's legs.

Lazare stood motionless for a minute, watching a fishing smack from Port-en-Bessin whose grey sail skimmed over the water like a seagull's wing. Then he set off walking again. His mother was going to die! The thought reverberated through his being in a series of powerful shocks. When he stopped thinking about it a deeper shock would agitate him; and each one came as a surprise, for he could not get used to the idea, and his bewilderment, constantly springing up afresh, left no room for any other sensation. At times even this idea lost its clarity, and he felt the painful vagueness of a nightmare, where the only definite thing that emerged was the anxious anticipation of a great disaster. For long minutes everything around him disappeared; then, when once more he saw the sand, the seaweed, the distant sea, the immense horizon, he would stand puzzled for a moment, not recognizing the scene. Was this where he had walked so often? The whole meaning of things seemed to have altered for him, he had never before had such an acute perception of shapes and colours. His mother was going to die! And he kept on walking, as though to escape from that deafening murmur.

Suddenly he heard a panting sound behind him. He turned round and recognized the dog with his tongue hanging out, quite exhausted. Then he spoke aloud. 'Poor old Mathieu, you're done in . . . All right, we're going home. However much one tries to shake oneself one can't help thinking.'

In the evening they hurried through their meal. Lazare whose constricted stomach could only tolerate a few mouthfuls of bread, hastened to go up to his own room, telling his father some story about an urgent piece of work. On the first floor he went to his mother's room, and forced himself to sit there for five minutes before giving her a goodnight kiss. She, in any case, was quite oblivious of him, and never worried as to what became of him during the day. When he bent over her she held out her cheek to him, taking this perfunctory goodnight for granted, growing more instinctively self-centred every hour, as her end drew near. And he escaped; Pauline cut short the visit, inventing some pretext to send him out.

But upstairs, in his big room on the top floor, Lazare's anguish was intensified. The night, the long-drawn-out night, was particularly oppressive to his troubled mind. He had taken up candles, so as not to be left without light; he lit them one after the other, until daylight, possessed of a horror of darkness. When he lay down, he tried in vain to read, but only his old medical textbooks had any power to interest him now; and he thrust these aside, for they had come to frighten him. Then he lay on his back, his eyes wide open, conscious only that something terrible was happening close to him, behind the wall, something that oppressed and choked him. The breathing of his dying mother sounded in his ears, that breathing that had grown so loud that for the past few days he could hear it from every step of the stairs, as he hurried nervously down. The whole house seemed to exhale the sound like a moan; he felt shaken by it in bed, and when an occasional silence fell he would run anxiously, barefooted, on to the landing and lean over the banisters. Down below, Pauline and Véronique, who were keeping watch together, had left the door open so as to air the room. And he saw the pale rectangle of light still thrown by the nightlight on to the floor, and he heard the sound of that loud breathing again, amplified and prolonged in the darkness. When he went back to bed he, too, left his door open, for he had to listen to that death-rattle, it obsessed him, pursuing him even when, towards dawn, he slipped into an uneasy doze. As at the time of his cousin's illness, his own dread of death had disappeared. His mother was going to die, everything was going to die, and he resigned himself to this wholesale collapse of life without any other feeling than exasperation at his own powerlessness to alter anything.

It was on the following day that Madame Chanteau's death-agony began, a garrulous death-agony that went on for twenty-four hours. She had grown calmer and was no longer maddened by the fear of poison; she talked to herself incessantly, in clear tones and rapid phrases, without lifting her head from the pillow. It was not a conversation, for she was speaking to nobody; it merely seemed as if, as the whole machine broke down, the brain were gathering speed like a clock being unwound, and this torrent of little hurried words was the final ticking of her mind as it came to the end of its chain. Her whole past was unfolded; she spoke not a word about the present, about her husband, her son or her niece, or that Bonneville house where for ten years she had nursed her wounded ambition. She had become once again Mlle. de la Vignière, governess to the most distinguished families in Caen; she uttered, familiarly, names which neither Pauline nor Véronique had ever heard; she told long, incoherent stories, interspersed with parentheses, much of which was new even to the maid, who had grown old in her service. She seemed to be clearing out all her youthful memories from her head before dying, just as one empties a box of old letters, yellowed with time. Pauline, for all her courage, felt a shudder run through her, disturbed at this revelation of the unknown, this involuntary confession bringing the hidden past to light during the very process of death. And the sound that filled the house now was not merely the sound of breathing but this ghastly chatter. Lazare, when he passed by the door, picked up fragments of it. He turned them over in his mind, found no sense in them, and took fright as at some unfamiliar story which his mother was already telling on the further side of life, to a host of invisible people.

When Dr. Chanteau arrived he found Chanteau and Abbé Horteur in the dining-room, playing draughts, as though they had not moved from there and were merely carrying on their last night's game. The cat, sitting beside them, appeared engrossed in studying the draught-board. The *curé* had come early in the morning to resume his consolatory function. Pauline now saw no objection to his going up, and when the doctor visited his patient, the priest left his game and accompanied him, as though he had simply come to pay a friendly call and enquire after the sick woman. Madame Chanteau could still recognize him; she insisted on being raised up on her pillows, and welcomed them like a fine lady of Caen receiving her guests, cheerful and lucid in her delirium. The good doctor must be pleased with her, surely? She was going to get up; and she made polite enquiries of the *abbé* about his own health. Horteur, who had come up with the intention of fulfilling his priestly duties, dared not open his lips, so taken aback was he by this death-bed chatter. Moreover, Pauline was present, and she would have prevented him from broaching certain subjects. She herself found courage to assume an air of confident cheerfulness. When the two men withdrew, she went with them on to the landing, where the doctor, lowering his voice, gave her instructions for the end. The words ' rapid decomposition,' 'phenol' recurred, while from the room there still poured forth the confused murmur of the dying woman's inexhaustible flow of words.

'So you think she'll see the day out?' asked the girl.

'Yes, she'll probably last till to-morrow,' answered Cazenove. 'But don't lift her any more, she might pass out in your arms . . . In any case I'll be back this evening.'

It was agreed that Abbé Horteur should stay with Chanteau and prepare his mind for the catastrophe. Véronique stood in the doorway, listening with a frightened air as these arrangements were made. Since she had accepted the possibility of Madame's death, she had not opened her lips, waiting on her mistress assiduously like a devoted beast of burden. But they all fell silent as Lazare came upstairs; he had wandered through the house, unable to face being present at the doctor's visit and thus learning the true extent of the danger. The sudden hush that greeted him told him the truth in spite of himself.

'My dear boy,' the doctor said, 'you should come back with me. You could lunch with me and I'd bring you home in the evening.'

The young man had turned paler still.

'No, thank you,' he whispered, 'I don't want to leave the house.'

From that moment Lazare waited; a horrible tension gripped his heart, as though an iron belt were bound round his sides. The day seemed unending, and yet it passed without his knowing how the hours went by. He never remembered what he had done that day; he had gone up and down the stairs, and looked out at the distant sea, whose vast surge lulled him into a deeper daze. The irresistible march of time, minute by minute, seemed now and then to materialize within him into a thursting bar of granite that swept everything into the abyss. Then in a fit of nervous exasperation he would long for it all to be over, so that he could relax at last from the appalling strain of waiting.

About four o'clock, as he was returning to his room once more, he suddenly went to his mother's; he wanted to see her, he felt that he had to kiss her once again. But when he bent over her, she went on unwinding her tangled skein of sentences, she did not even hold out her cheek to him in the weary gesture with which she had greeted him since her illness began. Perhaps she did not even see him. This was not his mother, this creature with the livid face and blackened lips.

'Go away,' said Pauline to him gently, 'go out for a bit . . . I tell you the time hasn't come yet.'

And instead of going up to his room Lazare took to his heels. He went out carrying the vision of that painful, unrecognizable face. His cousin was lying to him, the time was near; only he felt stifled, he needed space; and he began to walk like one possessed. That kiss had been the last. The thought that he would never see his mother again, never, had shaken him desperately. But, thinking he heard someone running after him, he turned round; and when he recognized Mathieu, who was pattering along on clumsy paws, trying to catch him up, he flew into a rage for no reason; he picked up stones and threw at the dog, stammering out abuse, to drive him home. Mathieu, bewildered at his reception, moved away, then turned back and gazed at him with gentle eyes in which tears seemed to glisten. Lazare could not find it in his heart to drive away the animal, who followed him from afar as though to keep watch over his despair. The immense sea, too, fretted his nerves; and he rushed into the fields, seeking the most desolate spots so that he might feel alone and unseen. Until nightfall he wandered, crossing ploughed land and leaping over hedges. He was at last making his way home, exhausted, when he saw something that struck him with superstitious terror: at the edge of a lonely road a single tall poplar loomed black, while the rising moon topped it with a yellow flame; and it seemed like a great candle burning by some gigantic death-bed that stretched across the countryside.

'Here, Mathieu,' he gasped, 'let's hurry.'

He ran home as fast as he had started out. The dog had ventured to come up to him and was licking his hands.

Although night had fallen, there was no light in the kitchen. It lay empty and dark, its ceiling reddened by the glow from the embers in the stove. The darkness frightened Lazare, and he could not bring himself to go further. He stood distraught, amid a confusion of pots and dishcloths, listening to the sounds that shuddered through the house. From the room next door came his father's little cough and the low continuous drone of the Abbé Horteur's voice. But what chiefly alarmed him was a sound of hurried footsteps and whispers on the staircase, and from the floor above an unaccountable murmur like the muffled hubbub of some job being rapidly accomplished. He dared not understand; was it finished, then? And he was sitting there motionless, without the strength to go up and find out the truth, when he saw Véronique coming down; she ran in, lit a candle and carried it away, so hurriedly that she did not give him a word or even a glance. The kitchen, which had been lit up for a moment, now lay in darkness again. Upstairs, the sound of scurrying feet died down. The maid reappeared, this time to fetch an earthenware dish—still with the same scared, silent haste. Lazare felt certain then that it was all over. And he sat at the table in a state of collapse, waiting amidst the gloom for he knew not what, his ears buzzing with the great silence that had now fallen.

Upstairs, Madame Chanteau had for the past two hours been in the throes of death, and the horror of it terrified Pauline and Véronique. As she gasped her life away, her fear of poison had revived, and she struggled to sit up, still chattering continuously but little by little agitated by furious delirium. She wanted to jump out of bed and run from the house, where someone was going to murder her. The girl and the maid had to exert their utmost force to hold her back.

'Leave me alone, you'll have me killed... I've got to go at once, at once!...'

Véronique tried to calm her down. 'Look at us, madame . . . You can't imagine us capable of doing you harm?'

The dying woman, exhausted, panted for a moment. She seemed to search the room with her glazed, unseeing eyes. Then she began again:

'Shut the desk. It's in the drawer . . . Now she's coming upstairs. Oh, I'm frightened, I tell you I can hear her! Don't give her the key, let me go, at once, at once . . .'

And she struggled on her pillows, while Pauline tried to hold her.

'Auntie, there's nobody, there's only us.'

'No, no, listen, here she is . . . Oh God, I'm going to die, the vixen made me drink it all . . . I'm going to die, I'm going to die!'

Her teeth were chattering as she crouched in her niece's arms, not recognizing her. The girl, deeply distressed, pressed her to her heart; she had given up all attempt to combat her aunt's abominable suspicion, and was resigned to letting her carry it to the grave with her.

Fortunately Véronique was watching, She stretched out her hands, muttering: 'Take care, miss!'

It was the final crisis. Madame Chanteau, with a violent effort, had succeeded in thrusting her swollen legs out of the bed; and but for the maid's assistance she would have fallen to the ground. She was completely demented, uttering nothing but inarticulate cries and holding her fists clenched as though for a hand-to-hand struggle; she seemed to be defending herself against a visionary enemy that gripped her by the throat. In this last moment she must have seen her own death, for she stared at them with conscious eyes dilated with horror. A frightful pain made her clasp her hands briefly to her chest. Then she fell back against the pillows and turned black. She was dead.

There was a great silence. Pauline, though at the end of her tether, insisted on closing the eyes; it was the limit she had set to her own endurance. She left Véronique to watch beside the body, together with Prouane's wife, whom she had sent for after the doctor's visit; and once outside the room, on the staircase, she felt faint; she had to sit down for a moment on a step, for her courage failed her to go down and break the news to Lazare and Chanteau.

The walls were spinning round her. A few minutes passed; then she grasped the stair-rail again; hearing Abbé Horteur's voice in the dining-room, she went into the kitchen instead. But there she caught sight of Lazare, whose dark form was outlined against the red glow of the stove. Without a word, she went forward, her arms open. He had understood, he collapsed against her shoulder, while she clasped him in a long embrace. Then they kissed one another's faces. She was weeping silently; he was unable to shed a tear, so choked with grief that he could scarcely breathe. At last she unclasped her arms and uttered the first words that came to her lips: 'Why are you in the dark?'

He made a gesture as if to say that, in his grief, he needed no light.

'We must light a candle,' she went on.

Lazare had sunk on to a chair, incapable of standing upright. Mathieu, greatly perturbed, prowled round the courtyard, sniffing at the damp night air. He came in again and stared fixedly at them, each in turn, then went and laid his big head on his master's knees; and he stayed there motionless, with his eyes fixed on Lazare's, in intimate questioning. Then Lazare began to tremble under the dog's gaze. Suddenly his tears gushed forth, and he burst into loud sobs, with his hands clasped round the old household pet that his mother had loved for fourteen years. He was muttering brokenly: 'Oh, poor old fellow, poor old fellow . . . We shall never see her again.'

Pauline, despite her agitation, had finally found and lighted a candle. She made no attempt to comfort him, relieved to see him weeping. A painful task still awaited her, that of breaking the news to her uncle. But while she was making up her mind to enter the dining-room, where Véronique had brought a lamp as soon as dusk fell, the Abbé Horteur had succeeded by dint of long ecclesiastical phrases in bringing Chanteau to accept the idea that his wife was doomed and that the end was only a matter of hours. And so when the old man saw his niece come in, red-eyed and overcome with emotion, he guessed at the catastrophe. His first cry was: 'Oh God, I'd only wanted one thing, to see her once more alive . . . Oh, these cursed legs, these cursed legs!'

This became his fixed refrain. He shed small tears that dried quickly, he uttered faint invalid's sighs; and then he reverted to his legs again, abused them, ended by pitying himself. There had been a brief discussion about the possibility of carrying him upstairs to kiss the dead woman; then, apart from the difficulty

162

of the undertaking, it was considered risky to expose him to the emotional strain of this last farewell, which in any case he had ceased to expect. And so he stayed in the dining-room in front of the overturned draught-board, not knowing what to do with his poor crippled hands, and too muddle-headed, so he said, even to read and understand his newspaper. When he was put to bed, far-off memories must have stirred within him, for he wept a great deal.

Then two long nights and an interminable day went by, those terrible hours when Death becomes an inmate of the home. Cazenove had only come back to certify the death, surprised, once again, at the swiftness with which the end had come. Lazare did not go to bed at all the first night, but spent it writing letters to distant relatives. The body was taken to the cemetery at Caen and buried in the family vault. The doctor had kindly undertaken to see to all formalities, and only one painful one remained: Chanteau, as Mayor of Bonneville, had to receive formal notification of the death. As Pauline had no suitable black dress she was obliged to improvise one with the aid of an old skirt and a merino shawl from which she cut herself a bodice. The first night went by, and then the day, amidst the agitation of these tasks. But the second night seemed never-ending, under the painful strain of waiting for the morrow. Nobody could sleep, all the doors were left open and candles stood scattered on the stairs and on the furniture; while the smell of phenol had spread even into the furthest rooms. They were all stiff and aching with grief, their mouths dry, their eyes blurred; and they felt nothing but a secret longing to seize hold of life again.

At last, next morning, at ten o'clock, the bell of the little church across the road began to toll. Out of regard for Abbé Horteur, who had been very good to them under these distressing circumstances, it had been decided to let the religious ceremony be performed at Bonneville before taking the body to the cemetery at Caen. As soon as he heard the bell Chanteau stirred in his armchair.

'I want to see her go off, at any rate,' he kept on saying. 'Oh, these wretched legs! why am I cursed with such wretched legs?'

In vain they tried to spare him the dreadful sight. The bell was ringing faster, and he grew angry and cried: 'Push me into the passage. I can hear quite well that she's being brought down . . . Quickly, quickly. I want to see her go off.'

And Pauline and Lazare, in their deep mourning, ready gloved, had to obey him. One on his right and one on his left, they pushed the chair to the foot of the stairs. The body was indeed being brought down, by four men, who staggered under its weight. When he saw the coffin, with its new wood, its gleaming handles, its newly-engraved brass plate, Chanteau made an instinctive effort to get up; but the leaden weight of his legs pinned him down, and he had to stay in his chair, shaking all over with such a violent tremor that his jaws chattered as loudly as though he were talking to himself. The narrow staircase made the downward progress difficult, and he watched the big yellow box come down slowly towards him; and when it brushed against his feet, he bent forward to see what had been written on the plate. Now the passage was wider and the men moved swiftly towards the stretcher that had been left standing in the porch. He watched them still; he watched forty years of his life being taken away, all the things of former days, the good and the bad, and he longed wildly for them, as one longs for one's lost youth. Behind the chair, Pauline and Lazare were in tears.

'No, no, let me be,' he said, as they prepared to push him back to his usual place in the dining-room. 'Go away. I want to watch.'

The coffin had been laid on the stretcher, and another group of men took it up. The procession was forming in the courtyard, which was crowded with the local people. Mathieu had been shut up all morning, and now his moaning sounded from under the stable door, in the midst of the great hush, while Minouche, sitting on the kitchen window-sill, stared wonderingly at the crowd of people and the box that they were taking away. As they did not move off fast enough the cat got bored and began licking her belly.

'Aren't you going?' Chanteau asked Véronique, whom he had just noticed by his side.

'No, sir,' she answered in a strangled voice. 'Mademoiselle told me to stay with you.'

The church bell went on tolling, and the body left the courtyard at last, followed by Lazare and Pauline, black-clad in the bright sunshine. And from his invalid chair, in the open doorway of the hall, Chanteau watched it go away.

CHAPTER VII

LAZARE and Pauline were detained in Caen for a couple of days by the complicated funeral ceremony and certain business matters that had to be attended to. When they started home, after a last visit to the graveyard, the weather had changed, and a gale was blowing along the coast. They left Arromanches in pouring rain, and the wind was so strong that the hood of the carriage was nearly torn off. Pauline remembered her first journey, when Madame Chanteau had brought her from Paris; a storm like this one had been raging, and her poor aunt had kept warning her not to lean out of the window and, every other minute, fastening her scarf round her neck. Lazare, in his corner, was also deep in thought; at every turn in the road he thought he saw his mother waiting eagerly to embrace him; once, in December, she had walked six miles to meet him, and he had found her sitting on this very milestone. Meanwhile the rain fell without respite; the girl and her cousin did not exchange a single word between Arromanches and Bonneville.

Just as they were nearing home, however, the rain stopped; but the wind blew more fiercely than ever, and the coachman had to get down and lead the horse by the bridle. At last the carriage drew up before the gate; and just then, Houtelard the fisherman came running past.

'Oh, Monsieur Lazare,' he cried, 'it's all up this time . . . It's been smashing up your contraption.'

From this point in the road, the sea was invisible; but the young man raised his head and caught sight of Véronique standing on the terrace, gazing out at the shore. On the other side of the road Abbé Horteur was standing in the shelter of his garden wall for fear the wind should tear his cassock in two, and he, too, was looking towards the sea. He leaned forward and shouted: 'It's sweeping away your jetties!'

Then Lazare went down to the beach, and Pauline followed him, despite the appalling weather. When they reached the bottom of the cliff they stopped short, aghast at the sight that awaited them. The tide, one of the September spring tides, was coming in with a shattering din; it had not been expected to be dangerous, but the north wind that had been blowing since the previous day had swollen it so abnormally high that mountains of water seemed to rear up on the horizon and roll forward to crash on the rocks. In the distance the sea was black under the shadow of the clouds that galloped across the livid sky.

'Go up,' the young man said to his cousin. 'I'm just going to have a look; I'll be back immediately.'

She did not answer, but followed him down to the shore. There, the jetties and a large breakwater that had recently been built were being subjected to a fearful assault. A succession of ever larger waves was beating like battering-rams; an innumerable host of waves, fresh masses constantly hurled against them. Great green-backed monsters with manes of foam swarmed as far as the eye could see and drew ever nearer, driven by some giant power; then, as they crashed in fury, they flew up in spray and collapsed in white froth, to be sucked up and carried away again by the waters. And every time a wave was shattered against them, the timbers of the jetties cracked. One of them had already had its struts broken and the long central beam, held only by one end, was swaying desperately like a dead body whose limbs have been severed by grapeshot. Two others were holding out better; but they seemed to be shaking in their fastenings, growing weary and shrinking in the embrace of the surging water that was trying to wear them down before it broke them.

'I told you so,' repeated Prouane, who stood, very drunk, leaning against the broken hulk of an old boat, 'see what happens when the wind blows off-sea ... A lot it cares about that young fellow's bits of sticks!"

Jeering laughter greeted these words. The whole of Bonneville was there, men, women and children, delighted at the tremendous blows the jetties were receiving. The sea might crush their hovels, but they loved it with awe-struck admiration, and they would have taken it as an affront to themselves if some interfering bourgeois had tamed it with four wooden beams and a score of pegs. And they felt as proud and excited as at some personal triumph when they saw it rouse itself at last and throw off its muzzle with a toss of the head.

'Look at that!' cried Houtelard. 'The sea's on the rampage! Whew! There's a couple of legs gone!'

They were yelling at one another. Cuche counted the waves. 'It'll take three, you'll see ... One, that's loosened it ... Two, that's swept it off! Oh, the devil, it did it in two! What a devil it is though!'

They spoke the words like an endearment; they uttered imprecations that were almost affectionate. The children danced with excitement when an even more terrifying mass of water crashed down and shattered the framework of a jetty at one blow. Another! another! They'd all be done for, they'd be crushed like sea-fleas under the heel of a child's sabot. But the tide was still rising, and the breakwater was still standing. That was the sight they were all waiting for, the decisive battle. At last the first waves swirled round the supporting timbers; now the fun was going to begin.

'Pity he's not there, the young fellow!' jeered the scamp Tourmal. 'He could lean up against them to strengthen them!'

A warning whistle silenced him, for some fishermen had just noticed Lazare and Pauline. They had heard his words; they stood there, very pale, silently watching the disaster. The smashing of the beams was nothing; but the tide was due to rise for another two hours, and the village would certainly suffer if the breakwater failed to hold out. Lazare had his arm round his cousin's waist and held her close to him to protect her from the blasts of wind that swept down on them like scythe-strokes. The sky was dark and gloomy, the waves howled, and the pair stood motionless in their deep mourning, amidst the flying spray and the ever-louder, ever-shriller noise of the sea. Around them now the fishermen were waiting, with a sneer still on their lips and a growing anxiety in their hearts.

'It won't be long now,' muttered Houtelard.

Yet the breakwater at first withstood the attack. Each time a wave broke foaming over it the tarred timbers emerged again, black against the white water. But once one piece of wood was broken, the adjoining pieces began to give way too, one at a time. Not for fifty years had the oldest inhabitants witnessed such a heavy sea. Soon they were forced to retreat; the beams that had been wrenched off battered the others and completed the destruction of the breakwater, the wreckage of which was tossed violently on to the shore. One solitary post stood upright, like a sea-mark erected on a reef. Bonneville had stopped laughing; women were carrying off their weeping children. The devil was after them again; and in a sort of resigned stupor they watched inevitable ruin bearing down on them, from their great neighbour the sea, that sustained and yet slew them. There was a helter-skelter flight, a clatter of heavy shoes; they all took refuge behind the shingle walls, the last line of defence for their homes. Then posts began to give way and boards to cave in, and the huge waves swept over the walls, which were too low. All resistance was overcome and a mass of water rushed on to shiver the windows of Houtelard's house and flood his kitchen. There was a wild stampede and nothing was left but the victorious sea, sweeping over the beach.

'Don't go in!' someone shouted to Houtelard. 'The roof's coming down.'

Slowly Lazare and Pauline had retreated before the flood. They could do nothing to help. As they were making their way home the girl stopped, half way up the hill, to cast a last glance at the threatened village.

167

'Poor things!' she murmured.

But Lazare could not forgive them for their idiotic laughter. Cut to the quick by the disaster, which was a personal defeat for him, he made an angry gesture, and said at last: 'Let them have the sea in their beds, since they love it so! I'm damned if I'll try to stop it!'

Véronique was coming down to meet them with an umbrella, for the rain had begun to fall again. The Abbé Horteur, still sheltering behind his wall, shouted something that they failed to hear. The dreadful weather, the destruction of the jetties, the distress of the village and the danger in which they had left it, added to the mournfulness of their homecoming. When they entered the house it seemed to them bare and ice-cold; only the wind swept through the desolate rooms with a continuous moan. Chanteau, huddled drowsily in front of the coke fire, began to weep when they appeared. Neither of them went upstairs to change their clothes, dreading the fearful memories that the stairs would recall. The table was already laid and the lamp lit, so they had supper immediately. It was a gloomy evening; their sparse words were interrupted by tremendous shocks from the sea, making the walls tremble. When Véronique brought in the tea she told them that the Houtelards' house and five others were already down; this time, half the village was likely to be destroyed. Chanteau, in despair at being unable to recover any sort of stability amidst his sufferings, silenced her by saying that his own distress was quite enough for him and that he didn't want to hear about other people's. When he had been put to bed, the others retired too, in utter exhaustion. Lazare kept his light burning till dawn; and Pauline, troubled in her mind, opened her door gently a dozen times that night to listen; but only a deathly silence rose from the first floor, deserted now.

On the following day, the young man began to live through those slow and painful hours that follow great bereavements. It was as though he had recovered from a faint, after some fall, which had left all his limbs aching; he was fully conscious now, his memories were clear, he had emerged from the state of nightmare that had possessed him, with its hectic visions. He saw the past again, in every detail; he endured his own sufferings over again. The fact of death, with which he had hitherto had no contact, was here in his own home. Death had brutally snatched away his poor mother, in a few days. The horror of ceasing to be had become tangible; there were four of you, and then a gap was made and there were only three of you, shivering with misery, pressing closer to one another, desperately, hoping to win back some of the warmth that was gone. Was this what death meant? This sense of nevermore, this clutching with trembling arms at a shadow, and being left with nothing but a terrified yearning?

He endured his mother's loss afresh every hour, each time her image recurred to his mind. He had not suffered so intensely at first, when his cousin had come back and flung herself in his arms, nor even during the long anguish of the funeral. He only realized his fearful loss now that he was back in the empty house; and his grief was aggravated by remorse at not having wept more bitterly under the stress of her last moments, when something of her was still there. He was tormented by the fear that he had not loved his mother enough ; at times, he was overcome by choking tears. He thought about her constantly, he was haunted by her image. If he went up the stairs he expected to see her come out of her room and cross the passage with her quick light step. Often he would turn round, thinking he heard her, so obsessed by her that he actually had the illusion that a fold of her dress was vanishing behind a door. She was not angry with him, she did not even look at him; it was only a familiar apparition, a shadow of the life that was past. At nights he dared not put out his light, lest in the darkness he should hear furtive steps draw near his bed and feel something breathe gently on his brow. And the wound, instead of healing, grew ever larger; the slightest reminder brought him a nervous shock and a swift, vivid vision that vanished immediately, leaving him with that anguished sense of 'nevermore.'

Everything in the house brought back his mother to him. Her room had been left untouched; the furniture had not been moved, and a thimble lay on the edge of a small table beside a piece of embroidery. On the mantelpiece the clock had finally stopped at thirty-seven minutes past seven. He shunned going in there. Then sometimes, as he was hurrying up the stairs, a sudden resolution drove him to enter. And as he stood there with wildly beating heart it seemed to him that the old familiar furniture, the writing-desk, the table and above all the bed had assumed a sort of majesty that made them different. A wan light filtered in through the perpetually closed shutters, and its dimness added to his agitation as he went to lay a kiss on the pillow where his mother's head had grown cold in death. One morning, when he went in, he stopped short in astonishment; the shutters had been flung open to let in the daylight; a bright flood of sunshine lay across the bed, right up to the pillow; and flowers had been put everywhere, on all the furniture and in every available jug. Then he remembered that it was an anniversary: the dead woman's birthday, which they had always kept every year and which his cousin had remembered. They were only poor autumn flowers, daisies and asters and the last roses, already touched with frost; but they filled the room with the fragrance of life and their joyful colours gleamed on either side of the lifeless clock-face, where time itself seemed to have stopped. He was deeply moved by this feminine tribute of remembrance, and wept for a long time.

And the dining-room, the kitchen, even the terrace were full of his mother too. The slightest objects he picked up, the sudden sense that some familiar habit was in abeyance, made him conscious of her. It had become an obsession, of which he never spoke, striving with a sort of anxious reticence to conceal his constant torment, his unceasing dialogue with death. And he went so far as to avoid uttering the name of the one that haunted him, as though he had grown forgetful and had given up all thought of her, whereas not a minute passed but he felt the sharp stab of memory in his heart. Only his cousin's eye saw through him. Then he would lie boldly, swearing that he had put out his light at midnight or that some imaginary piece of work was absorbing him, and he would fly into a rage if he was questioned further. His bedroom was his haven; he would go up there to surrender to his grief, feeling calmer in the nook where he had grown up, without the fear of betraying to others the secret of his anguish.

From the beginning he had, indeed, made an effort to go out, to resume his long walks. This would at least have enabled him to escape from the sulky silence of the maid and the painful spectacle of his father, sunk dejectedly in his armchair and at a loss what to do with his hands. But an invincible dislike for walking had come over him; he was bored outside, to the point of nausea. That sea with its perpetual rocking motion, that stubborn swell that battered the coast twice a day, exasperated him; it was a mindless force, foreign to his grief, which had worn out the same stones for hundreds of years without ever mourning a human death. It was too huge, too cold; and he would hurry home to shut himself up so as to feel less small, less crushed between the infinitude of water and the infinitude of sky. One place alone attracted him, the graveyard that surrounded the church; his mother was not there, and he was able to think about her there in tender serenity; the place had a singularly calming effect on him, despite his terror of annihilation.

The graves lay slumbering in the grass, yew-trees grew in the shadow of the nave, and no sound was heard save the cry of curlews rocked on the sea-breeze. And he would lie there for hours in forgetfulness, unable to read on the tombstones the names of the old dead, which the rains that beat down from the west had quite obliterated.

If Lazare had had faith in another life, if he had been able to believe that some day one would meet one's loved ones again, beyond the dark wall—but he lacked this consolation. He was too deeply convinced that a human being's existence as an individual comes to an end with death and is dispersed amid the everlasting-ness of life. Underlying this conviction was the secret revolt of his ego against the thought of ceasing to be. What a joy it would be to begin a new life elsewhere, among the stars, with one's parents and friends! How the thought of meeting lost loved ones would sweeten one's last moments, how eagerly would one embrace them, and what bliss to live together once more in immortality! He suffered agonies when he considered religion's charitable lie, which compassionately conceals the terrible truth from feeble creatures. No, everything finished at death, nothing that we had loved was ever reborn, our farewells were for ever. For ever! For ever! That was the dreadful thought that carried his mind hurtling down abysses of emptiness.

One morning as Lazare had stopped in the shade of the yew-trees he caught sight of Abbé Horteur in his kitchen garden, which was separated from the churchyard only by a low wall. The priest, wearing an old grey smock and sabots, was digging a cabbage patch; with his face tanned by the harsh sea air and his neck reddened by the sun, he looked like an old peasant bent over the hard soil. His stipend was negligible, and in this remote little parish he received no perquisites, so that he might have died of hunger had he not grown a few vegetables himself. What money he had went in alms; he lived alone, with no servant but a little girl, and was often reduced to cooking his own meals. To crown his misfortunes, the soil was worthless on these rocks, the wind withered his lettuces, and the wretched man had to battle with pebbles in order to produce a most meagre crop of onions. Nevertheless he still hid when he had on his smock, for fear people should make fun of religion. And Lazare was about to withdraw, when he saw the priest pull a pipe out of his pocket, stuff it full with his thumb and light it, smacking his lips loudly. But as he was ecstatically enjoying the first puffs, the *abbé* in his turn caught sight of the young man. He made a scared gesture as though to hide his pipe, and then began to laugh, shouting: 'So you're taking the air . . . Come on in, you shall see my garden.'

When Lazare had come close to him, he added joyously: 'I say, you've caught me being self-indulgent . . . But it's all I've got, my friend, and I'm sure God won't mind.'

Thenceforward, smoking noisily, he only took out his pipe to utter brief remarks. Thus, he couldn't help thinking about the *curé* of Verchemont; lucky man, he had a splendid garden, with real soil where everything grew; and didn't it seem hard lines, that the *curé* never so much as raked it. Then he grumbled about his potatoes, which for the past two years had rotted, although the ground seemed to suit them.

'Don't let me disturb you,' said Lazare. 'Carry on with your work.'

The priest immediately picked up his spade again.

'Well, I think I will . . . my young rascals'll be coming in for their catechism class, and I'd like to get this bed finished first.'

Lazare had sat down on a granite slab, some old tombstone which had been set up against the little churchyard wall to form a seat. He watched Abbé Horteur battling with the pebbles and listened to him talking in his shrill, childish old man's voice; and he felt a longing to be poor and innocent like that, with senses untroubled and head void of thought. The Bishop must think him very simple-minded, to let him grow old in this wretched parish. Besides, he was one of those who never complain and whose ambition is satisfied when they have bread to eat and water to drink.

'It can't be very cheerful living among these crosses,' said the young man, uttering his thoughts aloud.

The priest stopped digging in surprise.

'Not cheerful? What d'you mean?'

'Why, you have death constantly before your eyes, you must dream of it at night.'

The priest took his pipe out of his mouth and spat, deliberately. 'I declare I never think about it . . . We're all in God's hands.'

And he set his heel on his spade again and drove it into the earth. His faith preserved him from fear, he never ventured beyond the teachings of his catechism: you died and you went to heaven, nothing could be less complicated or more reassuring. He was smiling stubbornly; there was no room in his narrow skull for anything besides the one fixed idea of salvation.

172

Thenceforward Lazare took to going nearly every morning into the *curé's* garden. He would sit down on the old stone, forgetful of his own troubles as he watched the priest tending his vegetables; the sight of such blind innocence, living close to death without dread, gave him temporary peace. Why should he not become childlike again, as this old man was? And in the depths of his heart there lurked a secret hope of reawakening his lost faith by these conversations with one so guileless, whose tranquil ignorance delighted him. He brought along a pipe himself and they smoked together, chatting about the slugs that were eating the lettuces or the high cost of manure; for, with the tolerance and experience born of many years as confessor, the priest rarely spoke of God but kept Him for his own personal salvation. Others minded their own affairs and he would mind his. After thirty years of futile warnings he now confined himself to the strict performance of his priestly duties, with the peasant's well-regulated charity that begins at home. It was very kind of the lad to come and see him every day; and not wanting to worry him or argue about what they'd taught him in Paris, he preferred to talk endlessly about his garden; while the young man, his head ringing with this idle chat, thought himself on the point of entering into the golden age of innocence, where fear is no more.

But the days went by, and Lazare would find himself in the evenings in his room alone with the memory of his mother, lacking the courage to put out the light. Faith was dead. One day when he was smoking with Abbé Horteur, both sitting on the stone seat, the priest hurriedly put away his pipe on hearing footsteps behind the pear-trees. It was Pauline, coming to fetch her cousin.

'The doctor's at the house,' she explained, 'and I've asked him to lunch . . . Come up at once, won't you?'

She was smiling, for she had caught sight of the pipe underneath the *abbé's* smock. He pulled it out at once, laughing good-temperedly as he always did when people caught him smoking.

'It's too silly,' he said, 'anyone would think I was committing a crime . . . See, I'll light up again in front of you.'

'I tell you what, *Monsieur le curé*,' went on Pauline gaily, 'come and lunch with us and the doctor, and you can smoke your pipe with dessert.'

The priest, delighted, promptly exclaimed: 'Why, I'd love to . . . Go ahead and I'll slip on my cassock. And I'll bring my pipe, I give you my word!'

For the first time, laughter rang out again in the dining-room as they ate their meal. The *abbé* smoked when the table was cleared, to everyone's amusement; but he enjoyed his treat with such simple good nature that it immediately appeared perfectly natural. Chanteau had eaten well and was relaxing, relieved to feel life stirring in the house once more. Dr. Cazenove told yarns about savages, while Pauline beamed, delighted at this noisy merriment which would perhaps distract Lazare and rescue him from his depression.

After this, the girl endeavoured to revive the Saturday evening dinners which her aunt's death had interrupted. The *curé* and the doctor came back regularly, and the old habit was resumed. The talk was light-hearted and the widower slapped his legs, declaring that he was so cheerful by nature that he could still dance, if it weren't for his damned gout. Only the son remained distraught, talking with savage animation and breaking off with a sudden shudder in the midst of some outburst.

One Saturday evening, just as they had begun the roast meat, the priest was sent for to a death-bed. He went off without emptying his glass or listening to the doctor, who, having seen the sick man before coming to dinner, shouted after him that he would find the fellow dead. That evening, the priest had shown himself so dull-witted that even Chanteau declared, as soon as he had gone: 'He's none too bright, some days.'

'I'd gladly change places with him,' said Lazare roughly. 'He's happier than we are.'

The doctor began to laugh. 'That may be. But Mathieu and Minouche are happier than we are, too. Oh, that's typical of you modern young men; you've nibbled at science and it's made you ill, because you've not been able to satisfy that old craving for the absolute that you absorbed in your nurseries. You'd like science to give you all the answers at one go, whereas we're only just beginning to understand it, and it'll probably never be anything but an eternal quest. And so you repudiate science, you fall back on religion, and religion won't have you any more. Then you relapse into pessimism . . . Yes, it's the disease of our age, of the end of the century: you're all inverted Werthers.'

He grew excited, for this was his favourite thesis. In their discussions Lazare, on his side, exaggerated his denial of any certainty, his belief in the finality and universality of evil.

'How can you live,' he asked, 'when things are constantly giving way under your feet?'

The old man flared up like a boy. 'But why can't you just live? Isn't living enough? Joy lies in action.'

And he suddenly turned to Pauline, who was listening with a smile. 'Come now, you tell him how you manage always to keep cheerful.'

'Oh,' she replied in a joking tone, 'I try and forget myself so as not to get depressed, and I think about other people, which keeps me busy and helps me to put up with my own troubles.'

This answer seemed to irritate Lazare, who maintained, from ill-natured contradictoriness, that women ought to have religious faith. He pretended to be unable to understand why she had given up all religious observances long ago. And she gave her reasons, quite calmly.

'It's perfectly simple; I found confession painful, as I think a lot of other women do. And then I cannot believe things that seem unreasonable to me. Then what's the good of lying, by pretending to accept them? . . . Besides I don't worry about the unknown, it's bound to be logical, so the best thing is to wait as calmly as possible.'

'Hush, here's the abbé,' interrupted Chanteau, who was getting bored with this conversation.

The man had died; the abbé finished his dinner in peace, and everyone drank a small glass of chartreuse.

Pauline had now taken over the running of the home, with the cheerful efficiency of a good housekeeper. She had control of all purchases and of every household detail, and wore the bunch of keys dangling from her waist. It had happened as a matter of course, and Véronique did not seem to have taken it amiss. Nevertheless, ever since Madame Chanteau's death, the maid had been morose and apathetic, as though in a daze. A change of mood seemed to have taken place in her; her affection for the dead woman had revived, whereas towards Pauline she behaved with mistrustful sullenness. However gently the girl spoke to her she took offence at the slightest word, and she could be heard grumbling away to herself in the kitchen. And whenever she thought out loud thus, after long periods of stubborn silence, her constant theme was bewilderment at the catastrophe. Could she have known that Madame was going to die? Of course she'd never have said what she did say! Justice came before everything, one had no right to kill people even when they had their faults. Anyhow, she washed her hands of it; bad luck to the person who was the real cause of the tragedy! But this assertion did not bring her peace of mind, and she went on grumbling against her imaginary sin.

'Why do you go on worrying about it?' Pauline asked her one day. 'We did all we could, but there's nothing you can do against death.'

'No, no, people don't die just like that. . . Whatever Madame may have been, she'd had me from a youngster, and I'd cut off my tongue if I felt I'd had anything to do with her trouble . . . Don't let's talk about it, it'd only make things worse.'

No further word about marriage had been uttered by either Pauline or Lazare. Chanteau had once ventured to allude to the question, as Pauline sat beside him with her sewing, to try and amuse him; he wanted to get things settled, now that there was no obstacle. He was moved chiefly by a wish to keep her near him and a dread of falling into the hands of the maid again, should he ever lose Pauline. She had given him to understand that nothing could be decided until the period of deep mourning was over. This prudent reply was not dictated only by respect for convention; she hoped that time would bring the answer to a question that she dared not ask herself. The terrible shock of that sudden death, which had so deeply disturbed them both, had imposed a sort of truce on their painful relationship. They were gradually recovering from it, only to endure fresh sufferings as they became aware of their own personal drama underneath the irreparable bereavement; the discovery and dismissal of Louise, the destruction of their mutual love, the problem of their whole existence. What could they decide on now? Did they still love one another? Was marriage still possible, was it wise? Still bewildered by the catastrophe, they wavered, and neither seemed anxious to force a hasty decision.

Meanwhile, however, for Pauline, the memory of the offence had grown less bitter. She had long since forgiven Lazare, and was ready to hold out both hands to him as soon as he should show some remorse. And she was not moved by any jealous wish to triumph over his humiliation; she was concerned for him alone, to such an extent that she would release him from his promise if he had ceased to love her. All her anguish arose from uncertainty whether he still thought of Louise or whether, on the contrary, he had forgotten her and returned to his old childhood love. When she envisaged giving up Lazare sooner than making him unhappy, she felt overwhelmed with misery; she thought she would have the courage to do it, but she hoped to die afterwards.

Soon after her aunt's death, a generous thought had occurred to her; she planned a reconciliation with Louise. Chanteau could write the letter and she would add a line to say that all was forgotten. They were so depressed and lonely that the presence of Louise, with her childish liveliness, would cheer them up. Moreover, after so cruel a shock, the recent past seemed very far away; besides, she felt remorse at the violence of her outburst. But each time she wanted to mention it to her uncle, something held her back. Would she not be jeopardizing the future by exposing Lazare to a temptation that might be his undoing? Nevertheless, she might have found the courage and pride to subject him to such an ordeal, had not her sense of justice rebelled. Treachery was the one unpardonable thing. And besides, could not she, unaided, bring back joy into the house? Why call in a stranger, when she felt herself overflowing with unselfish love? There was a trace of unconscious pride in her self-sacrifice, of jealousy in her charity; her heart glowed at the prospect of being solely responsible for her family's happiness.

And henceforward this became the main purpose of Pauline's life. She applied all her energy and ingenuity to bringing happiness to those around her. She was, as never before, valiantly cheerful and kind. She greeted every morning with a smile, striving to conceal her own miseries so as not to increase those of others. She defied disaster by her sweet companionableness and disarmed ill-will by her equable temper. She had recovered her strength now, she was robust and sound as a young tree, and her radiant health shed joy around her. She delighted in beginning each new day, and took pleasure in doing just what she had done the day before, expecting nothing more, and hoping for an untroubled morrow. Véronique, who had become full of unaccountable whims and moods, might grumble away, standing at her kitchen range; but a sense of new life was driving sadness from the house, and laughter as of old rang out in the rooms and echoed gaily up the stairs. But the person who was most delighted was her uncle, for he had always hated melancholy, and loved to crack jokes now that he was confined to his armchair. His existence was becoming intolerable, and yet he clung to it with the frantic grasp of a cripple who wants to go on living, even though in pain. Each day he lived through seemed to him a victory, and his niece's presence warmed the house like a burst of sunlight, in whose radiance he did not fear death.

Pauline had, nevertheless, one grief; she failed to comfort Lazare. It worried her to see him relapse into his black moods. Underlying his grief at his bereavement was a recrudescence of his old terror of death. Since time had softened the first pangs, this terror had revived, intensified by the dread of hereditary disease. He, too, was doomed to die of heart trouble; and he went about convinced of the imminence of his own tragic end. And he was constantly observing the processes of life at work within himself, in such a state of nervous excitement that he could actually hear the wheels of the machine going round: he was aware of the laborious contractions of his stomach, the red secretions of his kidneys, the secret warmth of his liver; but above the sound of the other organs he was chiefly deafened by his heart, which seemed to reverberate like a peal of bells in all his limbs, even in the tips of his fingers. If he laid his elbow on a table, his heart throbbed in his elbow: if he leaned the back of his neck against an armchair, his heart throbbed in his neck; if he sat down, if he lay down, his heart throbbed in his thighs, in his sides, in his belly; and the great bell droned away without respite, measuring out his life with the grinding noise of a clock running down. Then, obsessed by his ceaseless scrutiny of his own body, he came to believe that it was going to crack up at any moment, that his organs were worn out and were falling to pieces, that the heart, grown monstrous, was breaking up the machine itself with great hammer-blows. Could this be called living, this constant awareness of the processes of life, this terrified contemplation of the machine's fragility, this anticipation of the grain of sand which was to destroy it?

And so Lazare's anguish had increased. For many years, when he lay down to sleep, the thought of death had sent a cold shiver over his flesh. Now he dared not even go to sleep, for he was haunted by the fear of never waking again. He hated sleep, he loathed feeling himself lose consciousness when he slipped from a waking state into the dizzy abyss of nothingness. Then his sudden awakenings gave him a fresh shock, dragging him up from the darkness as though a giant had grasped him by the hair and flung him back into life, still gibbering with terror from visiting the unknown region. O God, O God! He would have to die! Never yet had he clasped his hands in such a frenzy of despair. Every evening he suffered such torment that he preferred not to go to bed. He had noticed that if, by day, he lay down on a divan, he fell asleep as gently and peacefully as a child. Then he enjoyed deep, heavy, healing slumbers, which unfortunately made it quite impossible for him to sleep at night. He gradually became used to insomnia and made up for it by his long afternoon siestas; he would merely doze off in the morning, when dawn drove away darkness and its terrors.

However, he enjoyed an occasional respite. Sometimes two or three evenings would pass without the fear of death haunting him. One day Pauline found in his room a calendar dotted with red pencil marks. In surprise, she asked him about it.

'Whatever do these marks mean? . . . What a lot of dates you've ticked!'

He stammered: 'Why, I don't tick anything . . . I don't know . . .'

She went on merrily: 'I thought it was only girls that confided in calendars the things they can't tell anybody . . . How nice it would be if you ticked the days you'd thought about us! . . . Oho, you've got secrets!'

But as his embarrassment increased, she was charitable enough to desist. She had seen a shadow flit over his wan face, the familiar shadow of the secret torment of which she could not cure him.

He had astonished her, lately, by a fresh mania. Firmly convinced as he was of the imminence of his death, he could not leave a room, close a book or use any object without feeling that this would be his last action, that he would never again see that object or that book, or that room; and so he had contracted the habit of taking perpetual leave of things, impelled by a morbid desire to touch them and see them once again. The concept of symmetry was also involved; he must take three steps to the left and three to the right; each piece of furniture, on either side of a fireplace or a door, must be touched an equal number of times; with an underlying superstitious belief that by touching anything a certain number of times, five or seven for instance, in a particular order, he could prevent the farewell from being final. In spite of his keen intelligence and his denial of the supernatural he observed these foolish rites with the docility of a savage, although he concealed them like some shameful disease. It was the reaction of overwrought nerves in this professed pessimist and positivist, this believer in nothing but facts and experience. And it became infuriating to watch.

'What's the matter with you, tramping about like that?' Pauline would call out. 'That's the third time you've been up to that cupboard to touch the key. Don't worry, it won't fly away.'

In the evening he could not bring himself to leave the dining-room till he had arranged the chairs in a given order, closed the door a certain number of times, and then come back again to lay his hands right after left, on his grandfather's masterpiece. Pauline, waiting for him at the foot of the stairs, finally burst out laughing.

'What a maniac you'll be by the time you're eighty! . . . I ask you, what's the sense in fiddling about with things like that?'

Eventually she gave up joking about it, for his nervous condition worried her. One morning she surprised him laying seven kisses on the frame of the bed where his mother had died; and she took fright, guessing at the torments with which he was poisoning his existence. When he turned pale on reading in a newspaper some future date in the twentieth century, she looked at him with her compassionate air, which made him avert his head. He felt that she had read his mind, and he ran to hide in his room, ashamed and embarrassed as a woman caught naked. How often had he despised his own weakness! How often had he vowed to try and conquer his disease! He argued with himself, he succeeded in looking Death in the face; then, to brave it, instead of sitting up in his armchair he would lie down on his bed at once. Let Death come, he looked forward to it as a deliverance! But immediately the throbbing of his heart made him forget his vows and the icy breath chilled his flesh, and he held out his hands uttering his cry: O God, O God! Such terrible relapses filled him with shame and despair. And at such times he was made even more wretched by his cousin's tender pity. The days became so oppressive that he began them without ever hoping to see the end of them. In this disintegration of his being, he had first lost all his gaiety, and now his strength itself was deserting him.

Pauline, however, in the pride of her self-sacrifice, was bent on victory. She knew Lazare's trouble, and she tried to give him some of her own courage, by making him love life. But here her goodwill was constantly frustrated. She had at first attempted a frontal attack; she had begun teasing him again about 'that hateful pessimism.' Just fancy! It was she now who prayed at the the shrine of great Saint Schopenhauer, while he, like all those pessimistic humbugs, was quite willing to blow up the world with a petard but refused pointblank to be included in the show! He responded to her mockery with a forced laugh, and it seemed to cause him so much pain that she did not renew it. She then tried to sooth him as though he were a fretful child; she endeavoured to surround him with a pleasant atmosphere, full of cheerful peace. He always beheld her happy, fresh, full of the fragrance of life. The house brimmed with sunshine. He had merely to let himself live, and he could not do so; this happiness only exacerbated his terror of what lay beyond. Finally she resorted to craft; she planned to launch him into some large-scale undertaking that would take his mind off himself. Sick with idleness, interested in nothing, he found reading too arduous, and spent his days in self-torture.

For a brief moment, Pauline's hopes rose. They had gone for a short walk along the shore when Lazare, on seeing the ruins of his jetties and breakwater, of which a few beams still stood, began to explain to her a new system of defences, which he declared, must infallibly withstand any attack. The trouble had come from the weakness of the struts; their thickness would have to be doubled

180

and the central beam inclined more sharply. His voice throbbed and his eyes gleamed as of old, and she urged him to set to work. The village was in great distress, every spring tide carried away another piece of it; if he went to see the prefect he would undoubtedly get the grant. In any case, she offered to advance the money again, saying she would be proud to do such an act of charity. Her chief wish was to impel him into activity once again, even if it took all that was left of her money. But already he was shrugging his shoulders. What was the use? And he turned pale, for the thought had struck him that if he began this work he would die before he had accomplished it. And so to control his agitation he brought up his old grudge against the fishermen of Bonneville.

'The fellows who made fun of me when that damned sea was working its havoc? No, no, let it finish them off; they shan't have another chance to laugh at my bits of sticks, as they call them.'

Gently, Pauline attempted to calm him. These poor wretches were in such distress! Since the tide that had carried away Houtelard's house, the solidest of them all, and three poor hovels as well, their misery had increased still further. Houtelard, formerly the rich man of the neighbourhood, had indeed found an old barn to settle in, some twenty yards inland; but the other fishermen, not knowing where to take shelter, were now camping in some sort of huts built out of old hulks. Their destitution was pitiful; they lived in primitive promiscuity, women and children higgledy-piggledy, riddled with vermin and vice. The region's alms were squandered on spirits. As for the presents given them in kind—clothes, kitchen utensils, furniture—the wretches sold them too to buy bottles of that deadly *calvados* that laid them out across their own thresholds. Only Pauline continued to plead for them; the *curé* had given them up, and Chanteau talked of handing in his resignation, for he no longer wanted to be mayor of such a herd of swine. And Lazare, when his cousin tried to arouse his pity for that little community of boozers, victims of the cruel weather, repeated his father's unfailing argument: 'Who forces them to stay here? Let them build their homes somewhere else . . . They shouldn't be such idiots as to settle down right under the waves like that!'

Everybody made the same comment; people grew angry with them, calling them stubborn fools. Then they would assume an air of sullen suspicion. Why should they leave the place where they were born? Things had gone on like this for hundreds and hundreds of years, and there was no point in going elsewhere. As Prouane said, when he was very drunk: 'You are bound to get eaten up by something or other.'

Pauline would smile and nod her head, for happiness, to her mind, depended neither on people nor on things but on adapting oneself to people and things in a sensible way. She redoubled her kind efforts, she distributed ever more generous alms. At last, to her delight, she persuaded Lazare to participate in her charity, hoping to distract him, to bring him through pity to self-forgetfulness. Every Saturday he stayed at home with her and both, from four o'clock till six, received her small friends from the village, that queue of ragged children sent by their parents to beg from the young lady. It was a rabble of snotty, verminous urchins, boys and girls.

One Saturday, as it was raining, Pauline could not distribute her alms on the terrace as was her custom. Lazare had to fetch a bench into the kitchen.

'What, sir,' exclaimed Véronique, 'is Mademoiselle thinking of bringing all these lousy brats in here? That's a fine idea, if you want to find creatures in your soup.'

The girl had come in with her bag of silver coins and her box of remedies. 'Oh, you can give the place a quick sweep,' she laughed. 'Besides, it's pouring so, the rain'll have cleaned them up, poor little things.'

And indeed, the first that came in were pink-faced, washed clean by the downpour. But they were so wet that pools ran off their rags on to the flagged floor; and the maid's ill-temper increased, particularly when Mademoiselle ordered her to light a fire to dry them a little. The bench was carried in front of the fireplace. Soon there was a serried row of shivering ragamuffins, impudent and sly, casting greedy eyes on any food that was lying about, bottles of wine that had been opened, the remains of a piece of meat or a bunch of carrots lying on a block of wood.

'The very idea!' Véronique went on grumbling. 'Growing children who ought all to be earning their own living! You'll see, they'll let you go on treating them as babies till they're twenty-five.''

Mademoiselle had to ask her to be quiet. 'That's enough, please! Growing doesn't stop them being hungry.'

She had sat down at the table, having before her the money and the gifts in kind, and she was about to begin her roll-call, when Lazare, who was standing up, protested on catching sight of Houtelard's son in the crowd.

'I'd forbidden you to come back, you good-for-nothing lout! Aren't your parents ashamed of sending you here to beg, when they've still got something to eat and there are so many others dying of hunger?'

Young Houtelard, a thin, overgrown lad of fifteen, with a timid melancholy face, began to cry.

'They beat me when I don't come . . . The woman, she got hold of the rope, and dad pushed me out.'

And he pulled up his sleeve to show the purple bruise made by a knotted rope. The woman was his father's second wife, his former servant, who flogged him unmercifully. Since their ruin, their avarice had grown harsher and more sordid. Now they lived in utter squalor and took their revenge on the lad.

'Put an arnica compress on his elbow,' Pauline gently asked Lazare. Then she offered the boy a five-franc piece. 'See! you give them that, so that they shan't beat you. And if they beat you, if you've got bruises on your body next Saturday, tell them you won't get a farthing.'

The other urchins on the bench, cheered by the warmth of the blazing fire behind them, were sniggering and nudging one another in the ribs. Their clothes were steaming and big drops fell from their bare feet. One of them, a tiny lad, had stolen a carrot, which he was munching furtively.

'Get up, Cuche,' went on Pauline. 'Did you tell your mother that I'm hoping to get her admitted soon to the Bayeux Home for Incurables?'

Cuche's wife, that wretched creature whom her husband had deserted and who prostituted herself to any man, in any cave along the coast, for a few coppers or a scrap of bacon, had broken her leg in July; it had left her crippled, with a hideous limp, and yet her repulsive ugliness, further enhanced by this infirmity, lost her none of her usual customers.

'Yes, I told her,' replied the boy in a hoarse voice. 'She doesn't want to.'

He was going on seventeen, and had grown sturdy. He stood there with his hands dangling, swaying about awkwardly.

'What d'you mean—she doesn't want to?' cried Lazare. 'And you don't want to either, for I'd told you to come this week and lend a hand in the kitchen garden, and I'm still waiting.'

The lad went on swaying about. 'I didn't have time.'

Then Pauline, seeing that her cousin was about to lose his temper, intervened.

'Sit down again, we'll talk about that later. Try and think it over, or I shall get angry too.'

Next came the turn of the little Gonin girl. She was thirteen, and still had a pretty, rosy face under a mop of fair hair. Without waiting to be asked she launched into a torrent of chatter, telling with the crudest details how her father's paralysis had affected his arms and his tongue, so that he could only utter grunts like an animal. Cuche, their cousin, the former sailor who had deserted his wife and moved in to bed and board with them, had flung himself on the old man that very morning, intending to finish him off.

'Our ma beats him too. At nights she gets up in her shift, with our cousin, and empties pots of cold water on our dad, because he groans so loud it disturbs them . . . If you could see what a state they've put him in! He's all bare, miss, he ought to have some linen, for he rubs himself raw . . .'

'All right, shut up!' Lazare interrupted her, while Pauline, moved to pity, sent Véronique to fetch a pair of sheets.

He found the child far too knowing for her age. It struck him that, although she came in for a stray slap sometimes, she had probably begun to maltreat her father too; besides which, all that she was given, money, meat, linen, instead of going to the cripple, was used by the wife and the cousin for their own pleasure. He cross-questioned the child sharply: 'What were you doing the day before yesterday in Houteland's boat, with a man, who ran away?'

She gave a sly laugh. 'It wasn't a man it was him,' she answered, indicating young Cuche with a jerk of her chin. 'He shoved me from behind. . . .'

Lazare broke in once more. 'Oh yes, I saw you, you'd got your rags right over your head. Oh, you've begun early enough, at thirteen!'

Pauline laid her hand on his arm, for all the other children, even the youngest, were listening with wide, laughing eyes, alight with precocious depravity. How could the rot be stopped when all the breed—male, female and young—huddled together, contaminating one another? When Pauline had given the child the pair of sheets and a bottle of wine she spoke to her quietly for a moment, trying to warn her about the consequences of such horrid things, which would spoil her health and her looks before she was a grown woman. It was the only way to check her.

Lazare, to speed up the almsgiving, which had begun to disgust and irritate him, had called up Prouane's daughter.

'Your father and mother were drunk again last night . . . I heard you were the tipsiest of the three.'

'Oh no, sir, I'd got a headache.'

He set before her a plate containing little balls of raw meat.

'Eat this.'

She was consumed with scrofula again, and her nervous disorder had reappeared, at the critical age of puberty. Her trouble was aggravated by liquor, for she had begun drinking with her parents. After swallowing three meat-balls she jibbed, making a disgusted face.

'I've had enough, I can't eat any more.'

Pauline was holding a bottle. 'All right,' she said. 'If you don't eat your meat you shan't have your little glass of quinine wine.'

Then, her gleaming eyes fixed on the brimming glass, the child overcame her repugnance; after which she tossed off her wine with the flick of the wrist of an experienced drinker. But she seemed unwilling to go, and finally begged the young lady to let her take away the bottle, saying that it was too much bother coming every day, and promising to take it to bed with her and hide it so cleverly in her skirts that her father and mother wouldn't be able to get hold of it. Mademoiselle refused pointblank.

'So that you could drink it straight off before you reached the bottom of the hill,' Lazare said. 'It's you we mistrust now, you little toper!'

The bench was growing empty as the children left it one by one to collect their money, their bread and meat. Some of them, when they received their share, wanted to linger in front of the pleasant fire; but Véronique, who had just noticed that half her bunch of carrots had been eaten, threw them out mercilessly into the rain. The very idea! Carrots with the earth still on them! Soon nobody was left but Cuche's boy, waiting in sulky depression for Mademoiselle's sermon. She called him, talked to him for a long time in a low voice, and ended by giving him his usual Saturday loaf and five-franc piece; and he went off with his rolling gait, like some surly, stubborn animal, having promised to come and work but meaning to do nothing of the sort.

Véronique was just heaving a sigh of relief when she suddenly exclaimed: 'But they've not all gone! Here's another in the corner!'

It was the Tourmal child, the misshapen little highway beggar, who at ten years old was no bigger than a dwarf. The only thing about her that grew was her impudence; she whined with ever-increasing persistence, having been trained to beg from her cradle, like some child prodigy whose bones have been broken to make a circus tumbler. She was crouching between the sideboard and the

185

fireplace, as though, afraid of being caught in wrongdoing, she had
let herself slip into the nook. It did not look natural.

'What are you doing there?' asked Pauline.

'I'm getting warm.'

Véronique cast an anxious eye round the kitchen. Already on
previous Saturdays, even when the children sat on the terrace,
various small objects had disappeared. But everything seemed in
order, and the little girl, who had quickly stood up, began to
clamour shrilly: 'Pa's in hospital, grandpa's hurt himself at work,
mother's got no dress to go out in . . . Have pity on us, kind
lady . . .'

'Stop pestering us, you liar!' cried Lazare, exasperated. 'Your
father's in gaol for smuggling, and the day your grandfather twisted
his wrist, he'd been robbing the oyster-beds at Roqueboise; not to
mention that if your mother's got no dress to wear, she must go
thieving in her chemise, for the innkeeper at Verchemont has
accused her of wringing the necks of five of his hens . . . What
do you take us for, that you tell us lies about things we know
better than you do? Go and tell your stories to travellers on the
highway.!'

The child did not even seem to have heard him. She began
again, with impudent self-possession. 'Have pity on us, kind lady,
the men are ill and mother daren't go out . . . The good Lord'll
reward you for it . . .'

'Here, run off and stop telling lies,' said Pauline, giving her a
coin to silence her.

The child did not want to be told twice. She went out of the
kitchen at one bound, and she ran across the yard as fast as her
short legs could carry her. But at the same moment the maid
uttered a yell.

'Oh, good heavens, the mug that was on the sideboard . . . She's
carried off Mademoiselle's silver mug!'

Immediately she flew out after the thief. Two minutes later she
lugged her in by the arm, looking as fierce as a policeman. It was a
difficult business searching the child, for she struggled, bit and
scratched, yelling as though she was being massacred. The mug
was not in her pockets, they found it in the rag that served her as a
chemise, right against her skin. And then she stopped crying and
declared brazenly that she did not know it was there; it must have
fallen on her while she was sitting on the floor.

'Monsieur le Curé said she'd rob you,' Véronique reiterated. 'I
tell you, we ought to send for the police.'

Lazare, too, spoke of gaol, infuriated by the aggressive air of the child, who was rearing her head like a young adder whose tail has been crushed. His fingers itched to box her ears.

'Hand back what you were given,' he cried. 'Where's the co: ?'

She had raised it to her lips to swallow it when Pauline set her free, saying: 'Keep it all the same, and tell them at home it's to be the last. After this I shall go and find out for myself what you need. Off with you!'

The little scamp's bare feet could be heard splashing in the puddles; then silence fell. Véronique pulled out the bench roughly and bent down with a sponge to mop up the pools of water that had dripped from the ragged clothes. Well, her kitchen was in a fine mess, and it stank so after those wretched brats that she opened all the doors and the window. Mademoiselle, grave and silent, collected her bag and her remedies; while Monsieur, looking furious and yawning with disgust and boredom, went off to wash his hands at the fountain.

It made Pauline unhappy to see that Lazare took no interest in her small village friends. If he still consented to help her on Saturdays it was purely to oblige her, for his heart was not in the business. Whereas nothing disheartened her—neither poverty nor vice—these unpleasant things angered and saddened him. Her love of other people kept her calm and gay, while he, when he stopped thinking about himself, only found in the outside world fresh sources of depression. Little by little he came to suffer real distress at the sight of the mob of dirty brats, in whom adult sins of every sort were already in germ. This good-for-nothing breed set the crown on his wretchedness; he left them feeling exhausted and despondent, full of hatred and contempt for the human herd. After two hours of good works, he felt really vicious; he denounced almsgiving, he sneered at charity, and asserted that it would be better to crush this nest of harmful insects underfoot than to help them grow. Pauline listened to him, amazed at his vehemence, and greatly distressed that they felt so differently about things.

That Saturday, when they were alone again, the young man gave vent to all his misery in one single remark:

'I feel as if I'd come out of a sewer.'

Then he added: 'How can you be fond of those monsters?'

'You see, I love them for their own sakes and not for mine.' the girl replied. 'Why, you'd pick up a mangy dog by the roadside!'

He made a gesture of protest. 'A dog's not a human being.'

'Isn't the relief of suffering an end in itself?' she went on. 'It's a pity they don't mend their ways, for they'd perhaps be less wretched. But when they've been fed and warmed, well, that's enough for me, it makes me happy; it's that much less suffering in the world . . . Why should they have to reward us for what we do for them?' And she concluded sadly: 'My poor dear, I see that you don't care for it, you'd better not help any more . . . I don't want to upset your feelings and make you unkinder than you really are.'

Lazare seemed to elude her, and she was deeply grieved at this, feeling powerless to lift him out of his mood of anxiety and boredom. When she saw him so overwrought she could not believe that his secret torment was alone to blame, and kept imagining other motives for his melancholy; the image of Louise recurred to her mind. That must be it; he was still thinking of that girl, going about in misery because he could not see her again. Then Pauline, chilled to the heart, strove to recover her pride in self-sacrifice, vowing once more to create enough joy around her to make all her loved ones happy.

One evening Lazare said a cruel thing. 'How lonely one is here!' he remarked with a yawn.

She looked at him. Was this a hint? But her courage failed to ask him outright. Her goodness of heart was being sorely tried; her life was once again becoming a torture.

A final shock awaited Lazare. His old Mathieu was not well. The poor dog, who had been fourteen years old the previous March, was fast losing the power of his hind legs. When a fit of numbness seized him he could barely walk, and would stay in the yard, stretched out in the sunshine, watching people go by with his mournful eyes. Those old eyes were what distressed Lazare most— eyes grown dim, clouded with a bluish film, vacant as a blind man's. And yet he could still see, he would drag himself along to lay his great head on his master's knee and stare fixedly at him, sadly, as though he understood it all. And he was no longer handsome; his curly white coat had turned yellow, his jet-black nose had grown pale; he was a pitiful sight, grubby and dejected, for they dared not wash him on account of his great age. He had given up all his games, he no longer rolled on his back nor chased his tail, he was no longer stirred by fits of compassion for Minouche's kittens when the maid carried them off to drown them in the sea. Now he spent his days drowsing like an old man, and he found such difficulty in standing up, it was such a strain on his weak legs, that some

188

member of the household, moved with pity, would often hold him up for a minute so that he could start walking.

Internal haemorrhages weakened him still further every day. A vet. had been sent for, but had burst out laughing when he saw the dog. What, had he put himself out for such a creature? The best thing was to destroy it. You had to try and keep a man alive, but what was the use of letting an incurable animal linger on in pain? The vet. had been shown the door, with six francs for his trouble.

On Saturday, Mathieu was losing so much blood that he had to be shut up in the coach-house. He left a trail of great red drops behind him. As Dr. Cazenove had come early, he offered Lazare to look at the dog, who was treated as one of the family. They found him lying down, his head held high, grown very weak, but with a spark of life in his eyes still. The doctor examined him at great length, with the thoughtful air that he wore at a patient's bedside. A last he said:

'Such a copious discharge of blood must come from a cancerous degeneration of the kidneys. He's done for. But he may still last a few days, unless a sudden haemorrhage finishes him off.'

Mathieu's desperate condition cast a gloom over the meal. They recalled how Madame Chanteau had loved him, and his battles with other dogs, and his youthful pranks, the cutlets he had stolen off the grill, the new-laid eggs he had devoured. However, at dessert, when Abbé Horteur brought out his pipe, their spirits rose again, and they listened to the priest telling about his pears, which promised to be splendid that year. Chanteau, in spite of the faint tingling that foretold an attack, ended by singing a merry song of his youth. They were all enjoying themselves, and even Lazare grew gay.

Suddenly, about nine o'clock, as tea had been served, Pauline exclaimed: 'Look, here he is, poor old Mathieu!'

And there was Mathieu, bleeding and emaciated, creeping unsteadily into the dining-room. Immediately, Véronique could be heard bustling after him with a cloth. She came in saying: 'I needed something out of the coach-house, and he escaped. Right up to the end he wants to be where you are; you can't take a step without having him among your skirts . . . Come on now, you can't stop there.'

Gently and humbly, the dog dropped his old shaky head.

'Oh, let him stop,' begged Pauline.

But the maid was indignant. 'Good gracious no! . . . I'm fed up with wiping up the blood behind him. My kitchen's been full of it for the last two days. It's disgusting . . . The room'll be in a fine mess if he goes wandering about everywhere . . . Come along, gee up! Hurry up now!'

'Let him stop,' Lazare repeated. 'Go away.'

Then, while Véronique slammed the door in a fury, Mathieu, as though he had understood, came to lay his head on his master's knee. Everyone wanted to make him welcome, breaking pieces of sugar for him and trying to excite him. In the old days, the favourite game of an evening was to lay a piece of sugar on the far side of the table; he would quickly run round, but the piece had already been taken away and put at the opposite end; and he kept running round, and the sugar kept escaping him, till, bewildered and stupefied by this continual sleight of hand, he would start barking furiously. This was the game that Lazare tried to revive, in the kindly hope of enlivening the poor creature's last moments. The dog wagged his tail for an instant, and turned round, only to stumble against Pauline's chair. He could not see the sugar, and his wasted body wandered off crookedly, while red drops of blood spattered the floor all round the room. Chanteau had stopped humming, and everybody's heart ached at the sight of the poor dying Mathieu groping his way as he remembered the games played by greedy Mathieu of old.

'Don't tire him,' the doctor said gently. 'You're killing him.'

The *curé*, who was smoking in silence, commented, no doubt to explain his own emotion to himself: 'These big dogs are like human beings.'

At ten o'clock, when the priest and the doctor had gone, Lazare, before going up to his room, went to shut Mathieu up in the coach-house himself. He laid the dog on some fresh straw, made sure that his bowl of water was by him, embraced him and then prepared to leave him alone. But the dog, with a painful effort, had already staggered up and was following his master. Lazare had to lay him down again three times. At last he submitted, and lay there with his head raised, watching his master go away, with such a sad gaze that Lazare, heartbroken, went back to kiss him once more.

Upstairs, Lazare tried to read till midnight. In the end he went to bed, but he could not sleep, haunted by the image of Mathieu lying there on his straw bed, with his unsteady gaze turned towards the door. By to-morrow his dog would be dead. And despite himself he kept on sitting up and listening, thinking he heard Mathieu barking outside in the yard. His watchful ear caught all sorts of imaginary noises. About two o'clock he fancied he heard moans, and leapt out of bed. Where did that weeping come from? He went on to the landing; the house was dark and silent, and not a sound came from Pauline's room. Then he could no longer resist his urge to go downstairs. His eager wish to see the dog once more spurred him on; he quickly slipped on a pair of trousers and hurried downstairs with his candle.

In the coach-house, Mathieu had got up from the straw. He had chosen rather to drag himself a little way off on to the beaten earth. When he saw his master come in he had not even strength left to raise his head. Lazare, after standing his candlestick on a pile of old planks, had bent down, surprised at the dark colour of the earth; and he fell on his knees, heartbroken, when he saw that the dog was dying in a welter of blood. His life-blood was flowing out of him, and he wagged his tail feebly, while a faint gleam lit up his deep eyes.

'Oh, my poor old dog,' muttered Lazare, 'my poor old dog!'

He was speaking out loud, saying: 'Wait, I'll move you . . . No, that would hurt you . . . But you're so wet! And I haven't even got a sponge. Would you like a drink?'

Mathieu's eyes were still fixed on him. Slowly, a gasping sound began to rattle his sides. The pool of blood grew silently wider, as though it issued from a hidden spring. Ladders and broken barrels cast great shadows, and the candle gave a feeble light. There was a rustle of straw; it was the cat, Minouche, who was lying on the straw bed prepared for Mathieu, and who had been disturbed by the light.

'D'you want a drink, old fellow?' repeated Lazare.

He had found a rag, he dipped it into the bowl of water and pressed it against the dying animal's muzzle. This seemed to give it some relief; the fever-scorched nose grew somewhat cooler. Half an hour went by, and Lazare never stopped dipping the rag in water, with that lamentable sight always before his eyes and his heart heavy with boundless grief. As beside a sick-bed, he was seized with the wildest hopes: perhaps he was about to bring back life by means of this simple process of bathing.

'What is it then?' he said suddenly. 'D'you want to stand up?'

Shaken by a violent shudder, Mathieu was striving to raise himself. He stiffened his limbs, while his neck swelled with hiccoughs that came in great waves from his sides. But the end had come, and he collapsed across his master's knees, still keeping his eyes, under their heavy lids, fixed on him in an effort to see him once more. Overwhelmed by the intelligence in this dying gaze,

Lazare held the dog on his knees; and the great body, as long and heavy as a man's, endured a human being's death agony in his frantic arms. It lasted a few minutes. Then he saw real tears, great tears roll down the dim eyes, while the jaws opened convulsively to let the tongue give out one more caress.

'My poor old boy!' cried Lazare, bursting into tears himself. Mathieu was dead. A little bloodstained foam trickled from his jaws. When he lay stretched out on the ground he seemed to be sleeping.

Then Lazare felt that everything had come to an end once more. His dog was dead now, and he felt a disproportionate grief, a despair that swallowed up his whole existence. This death revived other deaths; the wound had not been more cruel when he had crossed the yard behind his mother's coffin. He had lost yet another part of her; his bereavement was complete. The months of concealed suffering revived, his nightmare-haunted nights, his walks in the little graveyard, his terror at the thought of eternally ceasing to be.

There was a sound; Lazare turned round and saw Minouche quietly preening herself on the straw. But the door had creaked as Pauline came in, impelled by the same preoccupation as her cousin. When he saw her his grief redoubled and he, who had mourned his mother in secret with a sort of fierce shyness, burst out: 'O God, O God! She loved him so much! Do you remember? She had him when he was a puppy and it was she that fed him, and he used to follow her about all over the house!'

Then he added: 'There's nothing left, we're dreadfully alone.' Tears rose to Pauline's eyes. She had bent over to look at poor Mathieu in the dim light of the candle. Without attempting to comfort Lazare, she made a despondent gesture, for she felt herself useless and powerless.

CHAPTER VIII

BOREDOM was at the root of Lazare's unhappiness, an oppressive, unremitting boredom, exuding from everything like the muddy water of a poisoned spring. He was bored with leisure, with work, with himself even more than with others. Meanwhile he blamed his own idleness for it, he ended by being ashamed of it. Wasn't it disgraceful for a man of his age to waste the best years of his life in this wretched Bonneville? Up till then he had had excuses; but nothing held him back now, and he despised himself for staying there uselessly, dependent on his family when they themselves had barely enough to live on. He ought to have earned a fortune for them; he had sworn to do so once, and he had proved himself an utter failure. No doubt he still had no lack of plans for the future—ambitious enterprises, visions of acquiring sudden wealth by a stroke of genius; only, when he emerged from his dream, he lacked the courage to get down to action.

'I can't go on like this,' he would often say to Pauline. 'I must do some work ... I'd like to start a newspaper at Caen.'

And each time she would answer: 'Wait till the end of your mourning. There's no hurry ... Think things over before you embark on anything like that.'

The truth was that she was alarmed at the idea of such a newspaper, in spite of her wish to see him occupied. A new failure might be the end of him; and she remembered how everything he had attempted, music, medicine, the factory, had come to nothing. Moreover, a couple of hours later he would refuse even to write a letter, as though he were overcome with exhaustion.

More weeks passed, and another spring tide carried away three houses in Bonneville. Now, when the fishermen met Lazare, they asked him whether he'd given things up. Of course there was nothing to be done, but all the same it made one mad to see all that good timber wasted. And as they uttered their complaints, beseeching him not to leave the place a prey to the waves, he could sense the aggressive mockery of seamen who are proud of their sea's death-dealing buffets. Gradually he grew so irritated by it that he avoided going through the village. The sight of the ruined breakwater and jetties in the distance became unbearable to him.

Prouane stopped him one day, when he was visiting the *curé*.

'Monsieur Lazare,' he said humbly, with a malicious twinkle in his eyes, 'you know the bits of wood that are rotting down there on the beach?'

'Yes, what about them?'

'If you're not going to do anything with them, you might give them to us ... We could at least warm ourselves with them.'

Repressed anger made the young man flare up without reflecting: 'It can't be done; I'm putting the carpenters to work again next week.'

This set all the tongues in the district wagging. They were going to see some fun again, since young Chanteau was being so pig-headed. A fortnight went by, and the fishermen never met him without asking him whether it was true that he'd failed to find any workmen. And in the end he actually took up the problem of the jetties once more, partly to satisfy his cousin, who was anxious to find him some occupation close at hand. But he set to work without enthusiasm this time, the only thing that sustained him was his resentment against the sea, which he felt confident of conquering; it would come and lick the shingle at Bonneville like a tamed beast.

Once again Lazare drew up plans. He had calculated new angles of resistance and reinforced the struts. The expense, however, was not likely to be very great, as they could use most of the old wood. The carpenter submitted an estimate for four thousand francs. And as the sum was so inconsiderable Lazare agreed to let Pauline advance it, convinced, so he said, that he would have no difficulty in getting the subsidy from the General Council; it was indeed the only way of recouping the original losses, for the Council would certainly not grant a penny as long as the jetties lay in ruins. This aspect of the question stimulated him a little, and the work went on apace. Moreover he was very busy, going every week to Caen to see the Prefect and the influential councillors. The laying of the timbers was almost completed when he at last secured a promise that an engineer should be sent to make a report, on the basis of which the Council would then vote the subsidy. The engineer spent a whole day at Bonneville; he was a charming person, who graciously accepted the Chanteaus' invitation to lunch after his walk on the beach; they avoided asking his opinion for fear of influencing him, but at lunch he behaved with such gallantry to Pauline that even she became confident of the scheme's success. And so, a fortnight later, when Lazare came back from a trip to Caen, the whole household was stupefied and appalled to hear the news he brought. He was speechless with rage; that fop of an engineer had made a shocking report! Oh, he'd remained quite civil, but he'd made fun of every piece of wood, with an extraordinary wealth of technical terms. In any case it was only to be expected; those gentlemen wouldn't give you credit for building an official rabbit hutch without their help. And the worst of it was that, on the strength of the report, the Council had turned down the request for a subsidy.

The young man experienced a fresh crisis of depression. The jetties were finished, and he swore they would resist the strongest tides, so that all the Civil Engineers put together would burst with jealous rage at it; but that would not give his cousin back her money, and he reproached himself bitterly for having involved her in this disaster. She, however, having conquered her thrifty instincts, claimed all the responsibility, reminding him that she had forced him to accept the loan from her; it was a charitable undertaking and she regretted nothing; she would have given more to save the wretched village. And yet when the carpenter sent in his bill she could not repress a gesture of pained surprise; the four thousand francs of the estimate had risen to nearly eight thousand. Altogether she had put more than twenty thousand francs into that handful of timbers, which the first storm was liable to carry away.

By this time, Pauline's fortune was reduced to some forty thousand francs. This made an income of two thousand, barely enough to live on if she were left alone and homeless. The money had gradually trickled away on household expenses, which she had continued to pay for open-handed. Henceforward, therefore, she began to keep a close watch on them, with the strict economy of a prudent house-keeper. The Chanteaus no longer even had their three hundred francs a month; for, on the death of the mother, they had discovered that a certain number of securities had been sold, without being able to find out what had become of the money realised. By adding her own income to theirs she only had some four hundred francs, and as the household expenses were heavy she had to perform miracles of thrift to save money for her charities. Since the previous winter Dr. Cazenove's guardianship had come to an end. Pauline had reached her majority and had absolute control over her property and person; to be sure, the doctor had never put any obstacle in her way, for he always refused to be consulted, and his legal responsibilities had ceased weeks before they both realised it; nevertheless she felt that she was mistress of the house, with no account to render to anybody, for her uncle begged her to deal with everything without ever consulting him. Lazare, too, detested all money matters. So she controlled the common purse, taking her aunt's place with such practical good sense that the two men sometimes marvelled at it. Véronique alone considered Made-moiselle dreadfully stingy; why, they had to put up with a pound of butter every Saturday!

The days followed one another with monotonous regularity. This order, this constant renewal of the daily round spelt happiness for Pauline, but only intensified Lazare's boredom. He had never ranged the house in such disquietude of spirit as now, when an atmosphere of cheerful peace pervaded every room. The work on the defences was finished, and this proved a great relief to him, for he became obsessed by everything he took up; but no sooner had he relapsed into idleness than he fell a prey once more to shame and uneasiness. Every morning he formed fresh plans for the future; he had thrown over the idea of a newspaper as being beneath him; he inveighed against the poverty that kept him from peacefully devoting himself to some great work of literature or history; finally he toyed with a scheme for becoming a teacher, passing examinations if needs be, to make sure of a livelihood while he pursued his literary work. There seemed to be nothing left between himself and Pauline but their old-time camaraderie, a habit of affection that made them like brother and sister. Though they lived in such close intimacy, he never mentioned their marriage, either because he had forgotten all about it or because it had been so much discussed that he took it for granted. She, for her part, avoided speaking of it, feeling certain that Lazare would consent at the first mention of it. Meanwhile, however, his desire for her had dwindled a little every day; she was aware of this without realising that her powerlessness to save him from boredom sprang from no other cause.

One evening at dusk when she went up to tell him dinner was ready, she caught him hurriedly concealing some object that she could not distinguish.

'What's that?' she asked, laughing. 'A poem for my birthday?'

'Oh no,' he stammered, in considerable confusion. 'Nothing at all!'

It was an old glove that Louise had left behind, which he had just discovered behind a pile of books. The glove, which was of Saxony leather, had retained a powerful musky odour, to which the girl's favourite heliotrope perfume added a trace of vanilla-like sweetness. And Lazare, highly sensitive to smells as he was, had been acutely disturbed by this blend of flower and flesh; he had stood distracted, with the glove to his lips, absorbed in voluptuous memories.

From that day on, in addition to the great void that his mother's death had left in his heart, he was haunted once more by desire for Louise. He had never forgotten her, but her memory had lain dormant during his grief and it had taken this thing of hers to bring her back to him vividly, with the very warmth of her breath on him. When he was alone he would take up the glove again, smell it and kiss it, fancying that he was holding her in his arms once more and burying his lips in her neck. The constant strain under which he lived, the nervous irritation brought on by his long idleness, made this sensual intoxication the more powerful; he indulged

196

himself to the point of exhaustion. And though he emerged from these debauchs dissatisfied with himself, he always relapsed, carried away by a passion he could not master. This increased his dark depression, until he even behaved brusquely to his cousin, as though he bore her a grudge for his own lapses. She made no physical appeal to him, and he would sometimes escape from a quiet cheerful chat with her to fly to his vice, locking himself in to wallow in hectic memories of the other woman. Then he would go downstairs again, sick with life.

In a month he was so utterly changed that Pauline, in despair, spent nights of anguish. By day she could keep up her courage, for the cares of the household, which she managed with gentle authority, kept her constantly occupied. But at night, when she had shut her door, she could let herself go in her grief, and her courage all fell away and she wept like a feeble child. No hope was left her, her kindness suffered an ever crueller defeat. Was it possible then? Charity was not enough, one could love people and yet make them unhappy; for she saw that her cousin was unhappy, perhaps through her fault. Then, underlying her uncertainty, there was the growing fear of some rival influence. If for a long time she had reassured herself by ascribing his depression to their recent bereavement, the image of Louise now recurred to her mind, that same image that had appeared to her immediately after the death of Madame Chanteau, that she had driven away with confident pride in the power of her own love and that now returned every evening to haunt her despairing heart.

It became an obsession with her. As soon as she had set down her candlestick she would sit wearily on the edge of the bed, lacking courage to take off her dress. The cheerfulness she had shown all day, her patience and orderliness, crushed her like an over-heavy garment; the day, like those that had gone before and those that would follow, had dragged by in that atmosphere of despondency with which Lazare's depression affected the whole house. What was the point of trying to be cheerful if she could not even bring a ray of sunlight into that beloved place? The cruel word he had once spoken echoed in her mind: they lived too much alone, and the fault lay in her jealousy, which had driven others away. She did not name Louise, she did not want to think of her, and nevertheless she kept seeing her go past with her pretty airs, amusing Lazare with her languid coquetry, teasing him with a whisk of her skirt. The minutes would run by, and she could not rid her mind of that picture. It was surely for that girl that he was longing;

nothing could be easier than to cure him by sending for her. And every evening Pauline, when she went up to her room and sank down exhausted on the edge of her bed, would relapse into the same vision, tortured by the thought that her loved one's happiness might now lie in that other woman's hands.

She experienced moments of violent revolt, however. She would leave her bed and go to open the window, gasping for breath. Then, in front of the black immensity, overlooking the sea whose melancholy sound rose to her ears, she would stay leaning for hours, unable to sleep, while the sea-wind fanned her burning bosom. No, she would never be so despicable as to tolerate that girl's return. Had she not caught them in one another's arms? Wasn't it the lowest sort of treachery, enacted close at hand, in the next room to hers, in that home that she had considered her own? The meanness of the deed remained unpardonable; she would be abetting it if she threw them together once more. Her jealous resentment flared up when she imagined these sights; she choked with sobs, hiding her face against her bare arms, her lips pressed into her own flesh. The night wore on, the wind blew over her neck and tossed her hair without calming the angry blood that throbbed in her veins. But secretly, invincibly, even while she rebelled most violently, the conflict between her goodness and her passion was going on. A gentle voice, as yet unfamiliar to her, persisted in telling her in a whisper about the joys of charity, the happiness of giving oneself up for others. She tried to silence it; self-sacrifice, carried to this point, was weakness and folly; and nevertheless she listened to it because soon she could not help doing so. Gradually she recognized her own voice, arguing with herself; what did her own sufferings matter, provided those she loved were happy? Her sobbing grew quieter as she listened to the tide rising in the heart of the darkness, exhausted and faint and not yet defeated.

One night she had gone to bed after weeping for a long time at the window. As soon as she had blown out her candle and lay there in the darkness with her eyes wide open, she came to a sudden decision: next day, the very first thing, she would make her uncle write to Louise inviting her to spend a month at Bonneville. Nothing seemed easier or more natural; and immediately she fell into a sound sleep, deeper and calmer than she had known for weeks. But next day when she had come down to breakfast and was sitting once more between her uncle and her cousin, at the family table where the places were set for the three bowls of milk, she suddenly felt stifled and her courage seemed to fail her.

'You're not eating,' said Chanteau. 'What's the matter?'

'Nothing's the matter,' she replied. 'On the contrary, I had a wonderful sleep.'

Merely to look at Lazare revived her conflict. He was eating in silence, already weary of the new day that had just begun; and she lacked strength to give him to another. The idea that another would take him, would kiss him to comfort him, was intolerable to her. When he had gone out, however, she tried to do what she had decided.

'Are your hands any worse to-day?' she asked her uncle.

He looked at his hands, on which the tophus was gradually gaining ground, and moved his joints painfully.

'No,' he said. 'The right hand even seems more flexible. If the *curé* comes we'll have a game.' Then, after a pause, 'Why d'you ask me that?'

No doubt she had been hoping he would be unable to write. She flushed, and weakly postponed the letter to the morrow, stammering: 'Oh, I just wanted to know.'

From that day on, she lost all peace of mind. In her room, after violent fits of weeping, she would succeed in conquering herself, and would vow to dictate the letter to her uncle next morning. But as soon as she was back in the daily round of the household, amongst those she loved, she lost all her strength. It was the little insignificant things that broke her heart—cutting a slice of bread for her cousin, giving his shoes to Véronique to be cleaned, all the familiar domestic routine. How happy they might have been among the old familiar ways of home! What was the point of bringing in a stranger? Why disturb such well-loved habits, which for so many years had made up their lives? And at the thought that some day she would no longer be the one who cut the bread thus, who attended to the clothes, a sense of despair overwhelmed her, and she felt all the looked-forward-to happiness of her existence crumble away. This anguish which had become part of the meanest household duties now poisoned all her busy days.

'What has gone wrong?' she sometimes asked herself out loud. 'We love one another, and yet we're not happy ... Our affection only spreads unhappiness all round us.'

She tried ceaselessly to understand. It came perhaps from some disharmony between her character and her cousin's. And yet she would have been glad to give way, to abdicate all self-will; but she could not do so, since, despite everything, her good sense prevailed, and she felt bound to try and impose the things that seemed to her reasonable. Often her patience failed her, and there would be bouts of ill-temper. She would have liked to laugh and drown all these miseries in gaiety, but she could no longer do so, for her nerves, too, were on edge.

'A fine state of things!' Véronique would repeat from morning till night. 'There's only three of you, and you'll end by tearing one another to bits ... Madame could be pretty nasty some days, but at least when she lived we hadn't reached the stage of throwing saucepans at each other's heads.'

Chanteau, too, was feeling the effect of this slow, unaccountable loss of affection. When he had an attack, he bawled louder than ever, as the maid put it. And he became a capricious, aggressive invalid, given to plaguing people perpetually. The house was once more becoming intolerable.

Then the girl, fighting down her last spasms of jealousy, asked herself whether she had the right to impose her own happiness on Lazare. Of course she wanted him to be happy above all, even at the cost of her own tears. Why, then, should she segregate him like this, forcing him to endure a solitude from which he seemed to suffer? No doubt he still loved her, he would come back to her when he judged her better by comparing her with the other woman. In any case she ought to let him choose; it was only just, and the idea of justice was paramount with her.

Every quarter Pauline used to go in to Caen to draw their income. She would go off in the morning and come back at night, after exhausting a long list of small purchases and errands which she had drawn up during the previous three months. That year, when the June quarter came round, they waited in vain till nine o'clock for her to come back to dinner. Chanteau was very worried, and sent Lazare to look along the road, for fear of an accident; while Véronique, quite calm, declared that they needn't worry; Mademoiselle must have found herself delayed and, wanting to finish her jobs, must certainly have decided to stay the night. They spent an anxious night at Bonneville; and next day, from breakfast onward, their fears revived. About noon, as his father was growing desperate, Lazare decided to set off to Arromanches, when the maid, who was posted as sentry on the road, reappeared, calling out: 'Here *is* Mademoiselle!'

Chanteau's armchair had to be pushed on to the terrace. The father and son waited there, while Véronique told her story.

'It's Malivoire's berline ... I recognized Mademoiselle from a long way off by her crepe ribbons. Only it seemed funny, I thought

I saw somebody else with her. What can that wretched horse be doing?'

At last the carriage stopped in front of the door. Lazare had gone forward and was opening his lips to question Pauline, who had jumped nimbly down, when he stopped short in amazement; behind her, another girl was jumping down, a girl in a pin-striped lilac silk dress.

They were both laughing, like the best of friends. He was so astonished that he went back to father saying: 'She's brought Louise!'

'Louise? Oh, what a good idea!' cried Chanteau. And when they both stood before him, side by side, the one still in deep mourning, the other in her pretty summer dress, he went on, delighted at having a visitor to entertain him: 'So you've made it up ... You know I never could understand that business. Wasn't it silly, eh? And it was naughty of you, poor Louisette, to be angry with us, while we've been having so much sorrow. Anyhow, it's all over, isn't it?'

The girls stood motionless, in embarrassment. They were flushing, and avoided one another's eyes. Louise kissed Chanteau to hide her confusion. But he wanted an explanation.

'Did you meet by chance?'

Then she turned towards her friend, her eyes brimming with affectionate tears. 'Pauline had come to our house. I was just coming back. And you musn't scold her for staying, for I absolutely insisted on it ... As the telegraph doesn't go beyond Arromanches, we thought we should be here as soon as a telegram ... Am I forgiven?'

She kissed Chanteau once more, with her old caressing ways. He was perfectly satisfied; when anything contributed to his pleasure, he pronounced it good.

'And what about Lazare?' he went on, 'haven't you anything to say to him?'

The young man had stayed in the background, wearing a constrained smile. His father's remark increased his embarrassment, particularly as Louise was standing there, blushing again, without attempting to go near him. Why was she there? Why had his cousin brought back this rival, whom she had so roughly driven away? He could not get over his bewilderment.

'Kiss her, Lazare, since she daren't,' said Pauline softly.

She was very white in her mourning, but her face was calm now and her eyes clear. She was gazing at them both with her air

201

of maternal solicitude, as during the critical moments of her house-hold responsibilities; and she merely smiled when he made up his mind at last to brush the young girl's proffered cheek with his lips.

On seeing this, Véronique, who was standing there with her arms dangling, went back into her kitchen, absolutely horrified. She could not understand it either. After what had happened, it showed a mean sort of spirit! Mademoiselle really was impossible when she insisted on being kind. Not satisfied with bringing lousy little brats right among her crockery she was now providing mistresses for Monsieur Lazare! A nice state of things they were coming to! When the maid had vented her rage by growling away over her stove, she came back and shouted:

'You know lunch has been waiting for an hour. The potatoes are burnt to a cinder.'

They ate with zest, but only Chanteau was unconstrainedly cheerful; his merriment prevented him from noticing the persistent uneasiness of the other three. They behaved with affectionate consideration towards each other, but betrayed an underlying anxious sadness, as after some quarrel where mutual forgiveness has not wiped out the memory of irreparable wrongs. Subsequently, the afternoon was spent in settling in the visitor; she was back in her first-floor room, and if, that evening, Madame Chanteau had come down to dinner with her light, tripping step, the past would have revived in its entirety.

For almost a week the strain persisted. Lazare, who dared not question Pauline, could still not account for what he considered an extraordinary caprice; for the thought never occurred to him that she might be sacrificing herself and, with simple greatness of soul, leaving him free to choose. He himself, while desire ravaged his idle hours, had never dreamed of marrying Louise. Thus, since they had all three come together again, a false situation had arisen which distressed them all. Their conversation would hang fire awkwardly, certain remarks would remain half-finished on their lips for fear of an involuntary allusion. Pauline, surprised at this unexpected result, was forced to exaggerate her gaiety to try and recover the happy, carefree atmosphere of old. One thing gave her great joy at first; she thought she could feel Lazare's love returning to her. Louise's presence seemed to have appeased him, and he almost shunned her, avoiding being alone with her, horrified at the thought that he might once again betray his cousin's trust. And he turned towards the latter once again in an access of feverish affection, fondly declaring that she was the best of all women, a real saint of whom he was unworthy. She felt very happy, rejoicing blissfully in her victory when she saw him so ungracious towards the other woman. By the end of the week, indeed, she even scolded him for it.

'Why d'you run away whenever she's with me? It distresses me. She hasn't come here to be scowled at.'

Lazare avoided answering, and merely made a vague gesture. Then for the first and only time, she referred to the past:

'If I brought her here, it was so that you might know I've forgiven you long ago. I wanted to obliterate that bad dream; there's nothing left of it now . . . And you see, I'm not afraid any longer, I trust you both.'

He took her in his arms and pressed her closely. Then he promised to behave kindly towards Louise.

From that moment, the days passed in delightful friendliness. Lazare no longer seemed bored. Instead of shutting himself up like a hermit and making himself ill with solitude, he invented games and suggested expeditions from which they all returned exhilarated with fresh air. And it was then that, imperceptibly, he fell once more under Louise's spell. He grew accustomed to her presence, ventured to take her arm, became obsessed once again by that disturbing perfume which rose from every flounce of her garments. At first he fought against it, and tried to break away when he felt the first stirrings of desire. But when, during their cliff-top walks, they came on a stream to be crossed, it was Pauline who urged him to help Louise over; she herself jumped boldly, like a boy, while the other girl, twittering like a wounded swallow, subsided into the young man's arms. Then on the homeward journey Louise would lean on him, and their whisperings and muffled laughter would begin again. Pauline was still quite undisturbed by it all; she went pluckily on, unaware that she was risking her happiness by not being weary and in need of help. And it was with a sort of dauntless gaiety that she forced them to walk in front of her, arm in arm, as though to prove her trust in them. Neither of them, in any case, would have betrayed it; if Lazare was slipping under the spell again, he still struggled against it, and after each lapse he tried harder to steel himself and behaved with greater affection to his cousin. His senses had been taken by surprise, and, while he yielded with rapture, he vowed that this time the thing should not go beyond the bounds of harmless fun. Why should he refuse himself this pleasure, since he had resolved to behave like an honourable man? And Louise had greater scruples still; not that she felt guilty of coquetry, for she was demonstratively affectionate by nature, offering herself unconsciously in a gesture. with a breath; but she would not have taken one step nor spoken one word if she had thought it would distress Pauline. She had been touched to the heart by the latter's forgiveness of the past, and she wanted to prove herself worthy of it; she adored Pauline now, with one of those exuberant feminine passions that take the form of vows and kisses and all sorts of ardent endearments. She watched Pauline continually, ready to run to her if she thought she saw the least cloud on her brow. She would suddenly drop Lazare's arm and take Pauline's, vexed with herself for having weakened even for a moment; and she would try to entertain her, clinging to her side, even cold-shouldering the young man. She had never seemed as charming as in this continual flutter, torn between her urge to attract and her regret at yielding to it, filling the house with the whirl of her skirts and her caressing, kittenish languors.

Gradually Pauline's anguish returned. Her brief hope, her momentary triumph only enhanced its bitterness. She suffered now not from those violent pangs, those fits of jealousy that used to drive her frantic for an hour on end, but from a slow, oppressive torment as though a heavy weight had fallen on her and was crushing her minute by minute. Henceforward no respite was possible, no hope was left; her unhappiness had surely reached its nadir. True, she had no fault to find with them, they both overwhelmed her with kindness, struggling against the attraction that drew them to one another; and it was that very kindness that distressed her most; she regained her clear-sightedness now that they seemed to be conspiring to spare her the painful knowledge of their love. Compassion, from those two lovers, became an intolerable thing. Did not everything confess their love—rapid whispering when she left them together, sudden silences when she reappeared, Louise's violent kisses, Lazare's affectionate humility? She would rather they had been guilty and betrayed her in some secret corner; whereas this deliberate honourableness, these compensatory caresses which told her everything, left her defenceless without either will or energy to win back her own rights. When she had fetched her rival home, she had intended to fight her if needs be; but what could she do against a couple who were so distressed at loving one another? She had brought about the situation herself; she merely needed to have married Lazare without worrying as to whether she was forcing his hand. But even to-day, despite her torments, the idea of overruling him thus, of demanding the fulfilment of a promise which, no doubt, he regretted, shocked her profoundly. Even if it had killed her she would have refused him, had he loved another.

Meanwhile, Pauline played a mother's role in the home; she nursed Chanteau through a bad attack, she helped out Véronique, who was growing slovenly; as for Lazare and Louise, she pretended to treat them as riotous children, so that she could smile at their escapades. And in the end her laughter rang out louder than theirs, clear as a clarion, telling of health and vital courage. The whole house was full of gaiety. From morning till night she bustled about, refusing to accompany the others on their walks under pretext of spring-cleaning or washing or jam-making. And Lazare had grown noisy; he would whistle on the stairs, bang the doors, complaining that the days were too short and too quiet. Although he did nothing in particular, the new passion that possessed him seemed to take more than all his time and strength. Once again he was about to conquer the world; each day, at dinner, he would bring forth some extraordinary new plan for the future. He had already rejected the thought of writing, and admitted that he had given up preparing for the examinations he had wanted to pass in order to become a teacher; for a long time he had used this excuse to shut himself up, in such despondency that he had not even opened a book; and to-day he made fun of his own stupidity. He'd have been a fool to tie himself down like that in order, some day, to write novels and plays! No, nothing counted but politics, and henceforward his plan was quite clear; he was slightly acquainted with the deputy for Caen, and he would go to Paris with him as his secretary; there, in a few months, he would make his way. The Empire badly needed intelligent fellows. When Pauline, disturbed at this wild flow of ideas, tried to curb his excitement by suggesting some humble, steady job, he protested against her prudence and jokingly called her 'granny.' And the din began again; the house rang with merriment whose blatancy betrayed an undercurrent of hidden misery.

One day, when Lazare and Louise had gone to Verchemont by themselves, Pauline, needing a recipe for cleaning velvet, had gone to hunt in her cousin's big cupboard, where she thought she had seen it on a scrap of paper between the pages of a book. And there, amongst his pamphlets, she found her friend's old glove, that forgotten glove which had so often excited his senses to the point of hallucination. She saw daylight suddenly, recognizing the object

205

that he had put away with such embarrassment that evening when she had come up suddenly to fetch him to dinner. Good heavens, he had wanted that girl even before she came back; he had lived with her memory, he had worn out that scrap of leather with his lips because a trace of her scent lingered on it! Great sobs shook her, and her eyes brimmed with tears as she stared at the glove in her trembling hands.

'Well, did you find it, miss?' said Véronique's loud voice from the landing, as she followed her up. 'I tell you the best way is to rub it with a bit of bacon rind.'

She came in, and at first did not understand what was happening, when she saw Pauline in tears, tensely clutching an old glove. But the scent that hung about the room finally told her the cause of this despair.

'Well!' she went on, with rough bluntness that was becoming habitual with her, 'you ought to have expected what's happened . . . I'd warned you once. You throw them together again, and they have their fun . . . And then maybe Madame was right, that pretty puss excited him more than you do.' She nodded her head and went on, talking to herself in sombre tones: 'Oh, Madame saw things clearly, in spite of her faults . . . I can't get over her being dead.'

That evening in her room, when Pauline had closed the door and laid her candlestick on the chest of drawers, she sank down on the edge of the bed, telling herself that she ought to let Lazare marry Louise. All day long a great buzzing had gone on in her head, preventing her from formulating a single clear idea; and it was only at this hour of the night, when she could give way to her grief unseen, that she reached this inevitable conclusion. She would have to let them get married; the thought echoed within her like an order, like the voice of reason and justice, which she could not silence. For one moment, despite all her courage, she turned round in terror, thinking she heard her aunt's voice calling to her to obey. Then she flung herself down, fully clothed, and buried her head in the pillow to stifle her cries. What, give him to another, and know that another held him in her arms, for ever, without hope of winning him back? No, she'd never have the courage, she'd sooner go on living her wretched life; nobody should have him, neither she nor that girl, and he himself might pine away while he waited. For a long time she struggled with herself, shaken with jealous fury, which called up before her appalling sensual images. Invariably, her natural impulses prevailed at first, with a violence unabated either by maturity or reason. Then she collapsed, exhausted, her senses utterly numbed.

Afterwards, lying prone on her back, without strength even to undress, Pauline argued with herself for a long time. She succeeded in proving to herself that Louise could do more than she for Lazare's happiness. Had not this frail child, with her tender caressing ways, already rescued him from his ennui? It must be that he needed somebody like that, whose arms were continually clinging round his neck, whose kisses drove away his black thoughts, his dread of death. And Pauline belittled herself, thinking herself too cold, devoid of feminine graces, having nothing but good-nature, which does not satisfy young men. Another consideration finally convinced her. She was ruined, and her cousin's plans for the future, those plans that made her so anxious, were going to require a great deal of money. Had she the right to force him to go on living in their present impoverishment, the humble way of life from which he obviously suffered? They would lead a terrible existence, spoilt by continual regrets and bitter recriminations springing from frustrated ambition. She would bring him poverty with all its rancour, whereas Louise, who was rich, would open up the way to the great possibilities of which he dreamed. It was said that the girl's father was keeping a place ready for his future son-in-law; no doubt this meant a position in the bank, and although Lazare affected to disdain finance, some arrangement could certainly be made. She could no longer hesitate, it now appeared to her that she would be committing a base action if she did not bring about this marriage. As she lay there sleepless she came to see it as a natural and necessary solution, which she must achieve as soon as possible under pain of losing her self-respect.

The whole night passed amid this conflict. When day broke, Pauline undressed at last. She was very calm, and she lay in bed enjoying complete rest, although she could not yet sleep. She had never felt so light, so uplifted, so detached. Everything was finished, she had severed the bonds of her egotism, she had no further hope of anything or in anybody; and in the depths of her heart she felt a subtle delight in self-sacrifice. She could not even recover her old wish to be sufficient for the happiness of those she loved, that self-assertive urge that now appeared to her as the last defence of her jealousy. All her pride in renunciation had left her, and she was willing for her loved ones to find happiness without her. This was the supreme point of unselfish love; to withdraw, giving all and yet feeling one had not given enough, loving so much that one rejoiced at a happiness that one had not caused and in which one would not share. The sun was rising when she fell into a deep sleep.

That morning Pauline came down very late. When she awoke she was glad to feel the previous night's resolution still clear and unshaken in her heart. Then she realised that she had forgotten all about herself, and that she must nevertheless take thought for the morrow, in the new situation which she was proposing to bring about. She might have the courage to unite Lazare and Louise in marriage; she would never have enough to stay with them, sharing the intimacy of their happiness; devotion has its limits, and she dreaded a return of her fits of violence, some frightful scene which she would never survive. Besides, was she not doing enough already? Who would be cruel enough to impose on her such superfluous torture? Her decision was made promptly and irrevocably; she would go off, she would leave this house with all its disturbing memories. Her whole life would be changed, and she did not flinch.

At breakfast she behaved with a quiet cheerfulness which had now become habitual. The sight of Lazare and Louise side by side, whispering and laughing, did not shake her courage, it merely struck a great chill into her heart. Then, as it was a Saturday, she encouraged them both to go off for a long walk, so that she should be alone when Dr. Cazenove came. They went off, and she took the further precaution of going to wait for the doctor on the road. As soon as he caught sight of her, he tried to make her get up into his carriage to bring her home. But she begged him to get down, and they walked slowly back together, while Martin, a hundred yards ahead of them, drove on the empty carriage.

In a few simple words, Pauline poured forth her heart. She told him everything, her plan for giving Lazare to Louise, her wish to leave the house. She felt it necessary to make this confession, for she was anxious not to act on impulse, and the old doctor was the only person who could listen to her.

Cazenove stopped abruptly in the middle of the road and clasped her in his long, lean arms. He was trembling with emotion, he laid a great kiss on her hair, and spoke to her with an affectionate '*tu*.'

'You're right, my lass ... And, you know, I'm delighted, for things might have ended even worse. It's been worrying me for months. I hated going to your house, knowing you were so unhappy. Oh, they've played some dirty tricks on you, those worthy people; first your money and then your heart ...'

The girl tried to interrupt him. 'Please, my dear friend . . . You're being too hard on them.'

'Maybe, but that doesn't prevent me from being glad for your sake. Go on, give away your Lazare, you're not making the other girl such a wonderful present . : . Oh, no doubt, he's got charm, and the best of intentions; but I'd rather the other was unhappy with him. Those young fellows who get bored with everything are too much of a burden, even for such stout shoulders as yours. I'd rather you had a butcher's boy, yes, a butcher's boy who'd laugh heartily from morning till night.'

Then, seeing the tears spring to her eyes: 'Well, you love him, let's say no more about it. And kiss me again, since you're a brave enough lass to be sensible . . . What a fool he is not to understand!'

He had taken her arm and was pressing her close to him. Then they set off again, talking seriously as they went. Undoubtedly, her wisest course was to leave Bonneville; and he undertook to find her a post. He happened to have a relative at Saint-Lô, a rich old lady who was anxious to find a companion. The girl would be very happy there, particularly as the lady, having no children, might take a fancy to her and perhaps adopt her later. Everything was decided, he promised her a definite answer within three days, and they agreed not to speak to anybody about this irrevocable decision to leave. She was afraid that it might seem like a threat; she intended to arrange the marriage and then go off quietly the next day, since her presence would thenceforward be superfluous.

On the third day Pauline received a letter from the doctor; she was expected at Saint-Lô as soon as she was free. And that same day, while Lazare was out of the way, she took Louise to the bottom of the kitchen garden, to an old seat sheltered by a clump of tamarisk. Opposite, above a little wall, there was nothing to be seen but the sea and the sky, a vast expanse of blue, divided at the horizon by a single long line.

'Darling,' said Pauline in her motherly tone, 'let's have a quiet talk, shall we? . . . You love me a little . . .'

'Oh yes,' broke in Louise, putting her arm round her.

'Well, if you love me, you're wrong not to tell me everything . . . Why d'you keep secrets from me?'

'I haven't any secrets.'

'Yes, you're not thinking clearly . . . Come on, tell me everything.'

For an instant the two girls looked at one another so closely that their breaths mingled. And then a look of constraint crept into the elder girl's eyes under the clear gaze of the other. The silence grew painful.

'Tell me all about it. Once one has talked over a thing one's practically made it all right. and it's only by concealing it that you make something nasty out of it. Isn't that so? It would be dreadful to quarrel, to repeat what made us all so very sorry.'

Then Louise burst into violent sobs. She clutched Pauline convulsively round the waist and buried her head on her friend's shoulder, stammering amidst her tears: 'Oh, it's wrong to bring that up. It ought never to be spoken of, never! Send me away at once rather than cause me such distress.'

Pauline tried in vain to calm her.

'No, I know what you mean . . . You still don't trust me. Why d'you talk about my secret? I haven't got a secret, I do my utmost for you to have nothing to blame me for. It's not my fault if there are some things that worry me; I try and control even my way of laughing, without anybody noticing . . . And if you don't believe me, well, I'll go away, I'll go immediately.'

They were all alone, with boundless space about them. The kitchen garden, shrivelled by the west wind, stretched before their feet like a waste land, while beyond it the motionless sea spread out to infinity.

'But listen!' cried Pauline, 'I'm not finding fault with you, on the contrary I'm trying to reassure you.'

And taking her by the shoulder, forcing her to lift her eyes, she said gently, like a mother questioning her daughter: 'You love Lazare? . . . And he loves you too, I know.'

The blood rushed to Louise's cheeks. She was trembling even more violently, she wanted to break loose and run away.

'Oh dear, I must be very clumsy, if you don't understand me! Would I broach a question like this just to torment you? . . . You love one another, don't you? Well, I want you to marry one another, it's quite simple.'

Louise, bewildered, had stopped struggling. Astonishment checked her tears and held her motionless, her hands dangling inert.

'What? And what about you?"

'My darling, I've been thinking things over seriously for some weeks, especially at nights, for you can see things more clearly when you're lying awake . . . And I realised that my feeling for Lazare was just friendship. Haven't you noticed it yourself? We're like good comrades, like a couple of boys, without any sort of lovers' passion between us . . .'

210

She was hunting for words to make her lie seem plausible. But her rival still stared fixedly at her, as if she had pierced the hidden meaning of her words.

'Why do you lie? she whispered at last. 'Can you stop loving, once you've loved?'

Pauline grew troubled. 'Oh, what does it matter? You love each other, it's quite natural he should marry you . . . I was brought up with him. I'll still be his sister. When people have waited so long for one another they're liable to change their minds . . . And then there are a lot of other reasons . . .'

She became aware that she was getting out of her depth, losing her way, and she went on in a burst of frankness: 'Oh, darling, let me do it! If I love him enough to want him to be your husband, it's because I believe now that you're necessary to his happiness. Do you mind that? Wouldn't you do the same in my place? Come on, let's talk about it quietly. Won't you be in my plot? Shan't we come to an understanding together to force him to be happy? Even if he grew angry, if he thought he owed me something, you'd have to help me to persuade him, for you're the one he loves, you're the one he needs . . . Please, please, be my accomplice, let's plan it all, now that we're alone.'

But Louise could feel the shuddering anguish that underlay her entreaties, and made a final protest.

'No, no, I won't accept it! It would be abominable to do such a thing. You still love him, I can feel that very well, and you're trying to invent things to torture yourself still further . . . Instead of helping you I'm going to tell him everything. Yes, as soon as he comes back . . .'

Pauline clasped her close with charitable arms, and pressed her head against her own breast to prevent her from saying any more.

'Hush, you bad child! . . . We must do it, let's think of him.'

Silence fell once more, and they lingered in this embrace. Louise, exhausted already, was weakening, was yielding in her languid, caressing way; and a flood of tears rose in her eyes once more, but this time they were gentle, slow-flowing tears. She spoke no word, but thanked her friend with an occasional gentle pressure, as if she could find no discreeter, more heartfelt way of doing so. Pauline seemed far above her, so high and so anguished that Louise dared not even look up for fear of meeting her eyes. However, after a few minutes she ventured to throw back her head in smiling confusion, then put up her lips and gave Pauline a silent kiss. In the distance, under the stainless sky, not a single wave disturbed the immense

211

blue of the sea. Their unspoken words went drifting for a long interval amidst the purity, the simplicity of it all.

When Lazare came back, Pauline went to see him in his room, that great room she loved so well, in which they had grown up together. She was anxious to complete her work that very day. With him, she went straight to the point, speaking resolutely. The room was full of memories of the past; dried algae were strewn everywhere, the model of the jetties encumbered the piano, the table was overflowing with scientific textbooks and sheets of music.

'Lazare,' she said, 'can we have a talk? I've got something serious to say to you.'

He looked surprised, and came to stand in front of her.

'What is it?' he asked. 'Is father worse?'

'No, listen ... We must tackle the question, for it won't do us any good avoiding it. You remember that my aunt had planned our marriage; we talked about it a lot, and now for months it hasn't been mentioned. Well, I think we should be wise to give up the plan now.'

The young man had turned pale; he would not allow her to finish, but interrupted violently: 'Why, whatever are you talking about? ... Aren't you my wife? To-morrow, if you like, we'll go and tell the Abbé to finish the business ... And that's what you call a serious matter!'

She replied, quite quietly: 'It's very serious, since it makes you angry ... I tell you we've got to talk about it. True, we're old friends, but I'm rather afraid we're not cut out to be lovers. What's the good of persisting in a plan that might not make for happiness for either of us?'

Then Lazare burst forth into a flood of broken words. Was she trying to pick a quarrel with him? He really couldn't be hanging round her neck the whole time! If the marriage had been put off from month to month she surely realised that it wasn't his fault. And it was unfair to say that he didn't love her any more. He had loved her so much, in this very room, that he dared not touch her with his finger-tips for fear of being carried away and behaving wrongly. At that reminder of the past a blush rose to Pauline's cheeks; he was right, she remembered that flare-up of desire, that burning breath upon her. But how far away were those hours of shuddering delight, and what a cold brotherly affection he showed for her now! And so she answered sadly: 'My poor dear, if you really loved me, instead of arguing like this you'd be in my arms already, weeping, and you'd find other ways of convincing me.'

He grew still paler and made a vague gesture of protest as he sank on to a chair.

'No,' she went on, 'it's obvious you've stopped loving me . . . It can't be helped, we were probably not made for one another. When we were shut up together you couldn't avoid thinking of me. And later on you changed your mind, it didn't last, because there was nothing about me that made you want to cling to me.'

He writhed in his chair, stammering in a final spasm of exasperation: 'But what are you getting at? I ask you, what does it all mean? I come home quite quietly. I go upstairs to put on my slippers, and you suddenly appear and without warning start this crazy story . . . I don't love you any more, we're not made for one another, we must break off our marriage . . . Once again, what does it all mean?'

Pauline had gone up close to him and said, slowly: 'What it means is that you love someone else, and I advise you to marry her.'

For an instant Lazare stood dumb. Then he resorted to sarcasm; well, so they were going to have scenes again, her jealousy was going to upset everything once more! She couldn't see him enjoying himself for one single day, she had to create a vacuum around him. Pauline listened to him with an air of profound distress; and suddenly she laid her shaking hands on his shoulders, and uttered an involuntary, heartfelt cry.

'Oh my dear, how can you think I'm trying to torture you! . . . Don't you understand that I want nothing but your happiness, that I'd put up with anything to give you an hour's pleasure? You love Louise, don't you? Well, I'm telling you to marry her . . . Understand me? I don't count any more, I'm giving her to you.'

He stared at her in alarm. With his nervous, unstable nature, he flew from one extreme of feeling to the other at the least shock. His eyelids fluttered, and he burst into tears.

'Oh, hush, I'm a wretch! Yes, I despise myself for all that's been happening in this house for years . . . I'm in your debt, don't deny it! We took your money, I squandered it like a fool and now I've sunk low enough for you to give me back my word, like alms, to release me from it out of pity, as if I were a man devoid of courage and honour.'

'Lazare, Lazare,' she murmured, terrified.

He had jumped up in wild fury, and was striding about, beating his breast with his fist.

'Leave me alone! I ought to kill myself right away, that's what I deserve. Aren't you the one I should love? Isn't it disgusting to want that other girl, probably because she wasn't meant for me, because she isn't as good as you are, or as healthy, how do I know? When a man sinks as low as that it's because he's rotten at the core ... You see I'm hiding nothing, I'm not trying to make excuses ... Listen, sooner than accept your sacrifice, I'd turn Louise out of the house myself and go off to America, and never see either of you again.'

She endeavoured, at great length, to calm him and argue with him. Could he not, for once, take life as it came, without exaggerating things? Didn't he see that she was talking sensibly to him, after a great deal of reflection? Such a marriage would be a good thing for all concerned. If she could talk about it so calmly it was because, far from suffering from it now, she was anxious to bring it about. But, carried away by her wish to convince him, she was tactless enough to allude to Louise's fortune and to drop a hint that Thibaudier, if the marriage took place, would find a position for his son-in-law.

'That's right,' he cried in a fresh access of violence, 'sell me now! Why don't you say straight away that I've no right to want you any more because I ruined you, and there only remains for me to debase myself still further by looking elsewhere for a rich girl to marry? ... Oh no, I tell you, it's all too horrible. Never, d'you hear? Never!'

Pauline, at the end of her tether, gave up pleading with him. There was silence. Lazare had sunk back on to his chair, exhausted, while she in turn paced the room, slowly, lingering in front of each piece of furniture; and from these old familiar things, from the table which she had worn with leaning on it, from the cupboard in which her childhood's toys were still buried, from all the scattered objects that brought back the past to her, there rose into her heart a hope to which she tried not to listen, the sweetness of which nevertheless gradually overwhelmed her. Suppose he really loved her enough to refuse to belong to another! But she knew of old how his fine impulsive fervours were followed, on the morrow, by a sudden collapse of will-power. Besides, she must not yield to hope, she was afraid of being tricked by her own weakness.

'Think it over,' she ended, pausing in front of him. 'I don't want to torture us any more ... To-morrow I'm sure you'll be more reasonable.'

The next day, however, passed in a state of great tension. Once more an atmosphere of secret sadness and resentment hung over the house. Louise was red-eyed, Lazare avoided her and spent the time shut up in his room. Then, during the following days the strain was gradually lifted; once more there was laughter and whispering, and sly affectionate contacts. Pauline waited, a prey to the wildest hopes, in spite of reason. She felt as if she had never known suffering before this dreadful uncertainty. At last one evening, at dusk, when she went down into the kitchen to fetch a candle, she came on Lazare and Louise kissing one another in the passage. The girl ran off laughing, and he, emboldened by the shadows, seized hold of Pauline next and kissed her on both cheeks in a hearty, brotherly way.

'I've thought it over,' he whispered. 'You're the best and the wisest . . . But I still love you, I love you as I loved my mother.'

She found strength to reply: 'That's settled then. I'm very glad.'

For fear of fainting, she dared not go into the kitchen, for the coldness of her face told her how white she was. She went upstairs to her room without a light, saying she had forgotten something. And there in the darkness she thought she was going to die, gasping for breath, unable even to shed tears. What had she done to him, O God! that he should carry cruelty so far as to enlarge her wound? Why could he not have accepted immediately, on the day when she had all her strength, without undermining her by a vain hope? Now the sacrifice was twice as hard, she was losing him a second time, all the more painfully that she had thought he was hers once more. Good Heavens! she did not lack courage, but it was not right to make her task so terrible.

Everything was quickly settled. Véronique was stupefied; she could not make head or tail of it, she thought things were all topsy turvy since Madame's death. But the one whom this new solution shocked most deeply was Chanteau. He, who usually bothered about nothing and just nodded his approval of what others did, as though absorbed in egoistic enjoyment of the few minutes of respite he stole from pain, began to cry when Pauline herself told him of the new arrangement. He stared at her and stammered out an incoherent confession: it wasn't his fault, he would have liked to do things otherwise, both about the money and about the marriage; but she knew he hadn't been well enough. Then she kissed him, swearing to him that it was she who, deliberately, was making Lazare marry Louise. At first he dared not believe her; he blinked his eyes, in which the tears still lingered, repeating: 'You mean that? You really mean it?'

Then, as he saw her laughing, he was quickly comforted and even became quite joyful. At last he had found relief, for that bygone business lay heavy on his heart, although he had not dared speak

215

of it. He kissed Louisette on both cheeks, and brought out another merry song after supper. And yet, when he went to bed, he had another qualm.

'You'll be staying with us, won't you?' he asked Pauline.

She hesitated for a moment and then, blushing at her own lie: 'Yes, of course,' she said.

The formalities took up a whole month. Thibaudier, Louise's father, gave immediate consent to Lazare's request; the young man was his godson. The only argument between them took place two days before the wedding, when Lazare refused pointblank to go to Paris to run an insurance company in which the banker was the principal shareholder. He intended to spend another year or two at Bonneville, writing a novel—a masterpiece—before setting out to conquer Paris. Thibaudier, moreover, merely shrugged his shoulders and good-naturedly called him a great fool.

The wedding was to take place at Caen. The last fortnight was taken up with comings and goings, an extraordinary frenzy of travelling. Pauline deadened her feelings by rushing about, coming back exhausted from trips with Louise. As Chanteau could not leave Bonneville, she had been obliged to promise to attend the ceremony, where she would be the only representative of her cousin's family. As the day drew near, she became terrified. On the eve, she contrived not to have to spend the night of the wedding at Caen, feeling she might suffer less if she went home to sleep in her own room, lulled by her beloved sea. She gave the excuse that she was anxious about her uncle's health and did not want to be away from him for so long. He himself urged her in vain to spend a few days at Caen; why, he was not ill! on the contrary, over-excited by the thought of the wedding, and of the feast of which he would not partake, he was slyly planning to extract from Véronique some forbidden delicacy, a partridge with truffles for instance, which he could never eat without inevitably suffering an attack. In spite of everything, the girl declared that she would come back that night; she hoped in this way to be able to pack her trunk and disappear next morning.

A fine rain was falling, and midnight had just struck, when Malivoire's old coach brought Pauline back on the night of the wedding. Wearing a blue silk dress and ill-protected by a little shawl, she was very pale and shivering all over, although her hands were hot. In the kitchen she found Véronique waiting for her, asleep at one corner of the table; and the candle-flame, burning high, dazzled her eyes, which were deeply black as though steeped in the darkness of the countryside at which she had been staring all the way from Arromanches. She could only extract from the drowsy maid a few incoherent words: Monsieur had not been good, he was asleep now, nobody had come. Then she took a candle and went upstairs; the emptiness of the house struck an icy chill into her heart, and the crushing weight of its gloom and silence plunged her into deathly despair.

On the second floor she was hurrying to take refuge in her own room when a strong, unaccountable impulse made her push open Lazare's door. She lifted the candle high to look, as if the room had been thick with smoke. Nothing had changed, each piece of furniture was in its accustomed place; and nevertheless she had a sensation of disaster and annihilation, a muffled terror, as if a corpse were lying there. Very slowly she went up to the table, looked at the ink-pot, a pen, a half-written sheet of paper lying on it. Then she went away. It was all over, and the door closed on the reverberating emptiness of the room.

In her own room the same feeling of strangeness awaited her. Was this really her room, with the blue roses on the wall-paper, the narrow iron bed with its muslin draperies? And yet she had lived here for so many years! All her usual courage deserted her and, without setting down the candle, she explored the place, drawing aside the curtains and peering under the bed and behind the furniture. She was so profoundly shaken and dazed that everything seemed to threaten her. She had never believed that such anguish could pour down from that ceiling, whose every spot she knew; and she now wished that she had stayed at Caen, feeling this house even more terrifying, so crowded with memories and yet so empty, in the chill gloom of this stormy night. The thought of going to bed was unbearable. She sat down without even taking off her hat and stayed for a few moments motionless, staring at the candlelight that blinded her. Suddenly she gave a start of surprise; what was she doing sitting there with her head full of a buzzing tumult that prevented her from thinking? It was one o'clock, she'd be better in bed. And she began to undress with hot, fumbling hands.

Although her life seemed shattered, her sense of method still prevailed. She carefully put away her hat and made sure that her boots had come to no harm. Her dress already hung folded on the back of a chair and she was wearing only a petticoat and chemise, when her glance fell on her own young bosom. Gradually a hot flush overspread her cheeks. In her troubled brain there rose up

217

a vivid picture of the other pair in their own room, over there, a room she knew, in which she had herself set flowers that very morning. The bride was lying in bed and he came up to her, laughing tenderly. With a violent gesture she let fall her petticoat, tore off her chemise; and, naked now, gazed at herself. Would she, then, never reap love's harvest? Was her own wedding never to be? Her eyes roamed over her breasts, firm as buds bursting with sap, to her broad hips, her belly within which lay dormant a promise of powerful motherhood. She became aware of her own ripeness, of the abundant life that filled her rounded limbs and made the black fleece grow in the secret folds of her body; she could breathe her own female odour, like a blossoming bough awaiting fertilisation. And it was not she but that other, in the distant room she pictured so vividly, who lay in ecstasy in the arms of that husband for whom she herself had waited so many years.

But she leaned further forward, surprised to see along her thigh the red trail of a drop of blood. Suddenly she understood; her chemise, lying on the ground, was splashed with blood as though from a knife-thrust. So that was why, ever since leaving Caen, she had felt such a faintness pervading her whole body? She had not expected it so soon; it was as though the loss of her love had wounded her there, at the very fount of life. And the sight of that life flowing uselessly away completed her despair. She remembered how she had shrieked with terror that morning when she had first found herself stained with blood. Later, before blowing out her candle that evening, she had yielded to a childish whim and examined herself with a furtive glance, proud, like a fool, of attaining physical and sexual maturity, relishing the delight of being a woman. Alas, to-day the red rain of her puberty was falling there, like the futile weeping of her virginity within her. Henceforward every month would bring back that stream as from a ripe grape pressed at the vine-harvest; and she would never be a wife, and she would grow old in barrenness!

Then jealousy stirred once more in the depths of her being, as her hectic imagination called up fresh pictures before her. She wanted to live, and live fully, and to give life, she who loved life! What was the good of existing, if you couldn't give yourself? She visualised the other two, and an urge to mutilate her own naked form made her look round for her scissors. Why not slash that bosom, break those thighs, rip open that belly and make that blood flow out to the last drop? She was more beautiful and stronger than that puny blonde, and yet he had chosen her. She would never know him, no part of her body could expect him henceforward—neither her arms, nor her thighs, nor her lips. It could all be cast away like a discarded rag. Was it possible that they should be together, while she was alone, shivering with fever, in this cold house?

Abruptly she flung herself face downwards on the bed. She had seized the pillow in her shaking arms and was biting it to choke her sobs; and she tried to subdue her rebellious flesh by crushing it against the mattress. Long shudders ran through her from head to heels. In vain she pressed her eyelids tight, so as not to see; she could still see those horrible visions rising up in the darkness. What must she do? Put out her own eyes, and then perhaps still see them, for ever maybe?

Minutes passed, but she was conscious only of the unendingness of her torture. A sudden alarm made her leap up. Somebody must be there, for she had heard a laugh. But it was only her candle which, burning low, had cracked the drip-glass. Yet supposing somebody had seen her? That imagined laugh still sent shivers over her skin, like some brutal caress. Was it really she, standing naked like this? Sudden shame overcame her, and she crossed her arms over her breasts in an attitude of confusion, so as not to see herself any more. At last she swiftly slipped on a nightgown and went back to bury herself under the covers, pulling them right up to her chin; she lay huddled there, shivering. When the candle went out she stayed motionless, prostrated by the shame of this experience.

Pauline packed her trunk next morning, but could not bring herself to tell Chanteau she was going. In the evening, however, she had to break it to him, for Dr. Cazenove was coming to fetch her the next day to take her himself to his relative's. When he understood, her uncle was horribly upset, and raised his poor crippled hands in a frantic gesture, as though to hold her back; and he stuttered out entreaties—she couldn't do such a thing, she couldn't leave him, it would be a murder, he'd die for certain. Then, when he saw her gently but firmly persisting, and guessed at her reasons, he decided to confess his misdeed of the previous night: he had eaten partridge. Already he felt a slight tingling in his joints. It was always the same story; when faced with the problem: should he eat? would he suffer? he always weakened, he always ate, certain of suffering, satisfied and terrified at once. But perhaps she would not have the courage to abandon him right in the middle of an attack.

219

And inevitably, about six in the morning, Véronique came up to inform Mademoiselle that she could hear Monsieur bawling in his room. She was in a shocking temper, she grumbled all over the house that if Mademoiselle went, she'd take her leave too, for she'd had enough of looking after such a tiresome old man. Pauline, once more, had to take up her position at her uncle's bedside. When the doctor appeared to fetch her away, she showed him the sick man who, triumphantly, was shrieking even louder, telling her to go away if she had the heart to. Everything was postponed.

Each day, the girl dreaded seeing Lazare and Louise come back; their new room—the old guest room, which had been rearranged for them—had been waiting for them since the day after the wedding. They had stayed on at Caen; Lazare wrote that he was taking notes on the world of finance before shutting himself up at Bonneville to start his great novel, in which he was going to speak the truth about business sharks. Then one morning he turned up without his wife, calmly announcing that he was going to settle in Paris with her; his father-in-law had persuaded him, and he was going to accept the position in the insurance company, on the pretext that he could thus take his notes from life; later on he'd see about returning to literature.

When Lazare had filled two cases with the things he was taking away, and Malivoire's coach had come to fetch him and his luggage, Pauline went indoors again in a state of bewilderment, finding in herself none of her old resolution. Chanteau, still in great pain, asked her: 'You're staying, I hope! Please wait till you've seen me into my grave!'

She would not answer straight away. Upstairs, her trunk had not been unpacked. She stared at it for hours. Since the others were going to Paris, it would be wrong for her to desert her uncle. True, she mistrusted her cousin's decisions; but if the couple came home, she would then be free to go away. And when Cazenove, furious, told her that she was throwing away a splendid situation in order to spoil her whole life among people who had been preying on her since her childhood, she suddenly made up her mind.

'Go off,' Chanteau kept telling her now. 'If you're going to earn so much money and to be so happy, I can't force you to hang around looking after a cripple like me ... Go off.'

One morning she answered: 'No, uncle, I'm staying.'

The doctor, who was present, went away raising his arms to heaven. 'She's impossible, that child! And what a hornet's nest the place is! She'll never escape from it.'

CHAPTER IX

THE days flowed by once more in the house at Bonneville. A very cold winter was followed by a wet spring; the sea, lashed by rain, looked like a muddy lake. Then the tardy summer lingered on into mid-autumn, with days of heavy sunshine when the vast expanse of blue seemed asleep in the oppressive heat; then winter came back, and another spring and another summer, passing away minute by minute, at the same regular pace, in the measured progress of the hours.

Pauline gradually regained her serenity, as though her heart were keeping pace with this clockwork rhythm. She came to feel her anguish less acutely, lulled by the regularity of her days and absorbed in constantly recurring occupations. She would come down in the morning and kiss her uncle; she would hold the same conversation with Véronique as on the day before; she would sit down at the table twice a day, sew in the afternoon, go to bed early at night; and next day the same sequence was repeated, its monotony never broken by any unexpected event. Chanteau, his limbs increasingly rigid with gout, his legs swollen and his hands deformed, sat mute when he was not howling, absorbed in the bliss of being free from pain. Véronique, who seemed to have lost her tongue, had lapsed into gloomy sullenness. The calm was broken only by the Saturday dinners. Cazenove and Abbé Horteur came punctually to dine; the sound of their voices could be heard till ten o'clock, then the priest's sabots clattered away over the paved yard, while the doctor's gig drove off, the old horse going at a ponderous trot. Even Pauline's gaiety had grown quieter, that valiant gaiety that she had retained through all her torments. Her ringing laugh no longer filled the staircase and the rooms, but her activity and goodness never failed, inspiring the household, day by day, with fresh courage to face life. At the end of a year, her heart seemed asleep; she felt as though the hours would henceforward lapse in the same way, in gentle uniformity, with nothing to revive the dormant pain.

At first, after Lazare had gone away, every letter from him had disturbed Pauline. She lived only for these letters, waited impatiently for them, re-read them, guessing at things unsaid between the written words. For three months they came regularly, every fortnight, long and full of details and overflowing with hope. Lazare had grown enthusiastic once again; he had thrown himself into the business and now dreamed of swiftly amassing enormous

221

wealth. According to him, the insurance company was going to yield huge profits; and he proposed to go even further and launch out into various other enterprises. He appeared delighted with the world of business and finance; the people he dealt with were all charming, and he reproached himself for his foolish poet's judgment on them. He seemed to have given up all literary ambitions. Then there were effusive descriptions of married bliss, full of lovers' nonsense about his wife, talk of kissings and teasings; he seemed to flaunt his happiness by way of thanks to his 'darling sister,' as he called Pauline. It was these details, these intimate passages that made Pauline's fingers tremble feverishly. The very paper gave off an amorous perfume that made her head reel—Louise's favourite heliotrope scent; this paper had lain close to their linen; if she shut her eyes she could still see the letters in lines of fire, could finish the sentences, felt as though she were sharing in the close intimacy of their honeymoon. But gradually the letters became rarer and briefer; her cousin ceased to speak of his business affairs and merely sent her his wife's love. Moreover he gave no explanation, he simply stopped telling her everything. Was he dissatisfied with his position, was he already disgusted with finance? Could any misunderstanding have occurred to impair the couple's happiness? The girl was reduced to guessing, and felt anxious about the boredom and despondency that she could feel underlying the brief messages sent, as it were, unwillingly. Towards the end of April she received a four-line note telling her that Louise was three months pregnant. And then silence fell once more, and she had no further news.

May and June went by. One of the jetties was broken by the tide, and this incident made a considerable stir; the whole of Bonneville chuckled ironically, and the shattered timbers were stolen by fishermen. There was another sensation: the Gonin child, aged barely thirteen and a half, gave birth to a daughter, and nobody could be sure if it was young Cuche's, for she had been seen about with an old man. Then quiet was restored. The village went on living at the foot of the cliff like some stubborn marine plant. In July the terrace wall and the whole of one gable of the house had to be repaired. At the first blow of the builders' pickaxes all the rest of the structure threatened to collapse. They spent a whole month working on it and the bill came to nearly ten thousand francs.

Pauline, as usual, paid. She had to dip into her hoard once more; her fortune had now dwindled to forty thousand francs.

Moreover she managed to keep the house going on their monthly income of three hundred francs; but she had had to sell some more securities in order not to disturb her uncle's investments. He kept telling her, just as his wife used to do, that they would settle their accounts some day. She would willingly have given everything; as her fortune was slowly frittered away, her avarice had vanished with it; now she only fought to save the pence for her charities. The thought that she might have to break off her Saturday almsgiving distressed her deeply, for this gave her the greatest joy of the whole week. Since the previous winter she had begun knitting socks, and now all the ragamuffins in the neighbourhood had warm feet.

One morning towards the end of July, as Véronique was sweeping up the debris of plaster left by the builders, Pauline received a letter that gave her a great shock. It had been sent from Caen, and contained only a few words. Lazare, without any explanation, announced that he would arrive at Bonneville the following evening. She hurried to tell her uncle the news. They gazed at one another. Chanteau's eyes held terrified apprehension lest she should leave him if the couple came to stay for any length of time. He dared not question her, reading on her face her firm determination to go away. That afternoon she went upstairs to see to her linen. However, she did not want to give the impression of running away.

It was a lovely evening when, about five o'clock, Lazare got out of his carriage at the courtyard gate. Pauline had gone out to meet him. But before even kissing him she stopped in astonishment.

'What, are you alone?'

He merely answered, 'Yes,' and kissed her heartily on both cheeks.

'Where's Louise?'

'At Clermont, at her sister-in-law's. The doctor advised mountain air for her . . . Her pregnancy is tiring her very much.'

As he spoke, he moved towards the porch, casting a long glance round the yard. He gazed at his cousin too, his lips quivering with repressed emotion. As a dog emerged from the kitchen and yapped at his legs, he showed surprise in his turn.

'What's that?' he asked.

'That's Loulou,' replied Pauline. 'He doesn't know you . . . Loulou, you're not to snap at the master!'

The dog went on growling.

'He's revolting, my dear. Where did you pick up such a horror?'

The dog was indeed a wretched mongrel, mangy and unprepossessing, and he had a dreadful temper and was always snarling, with the depressing melancholy of a pariah.

223

'I'm sorry, the people who gave him to me swore he'd grow into a fine strapping specimen, and you see he's stayed like this . . . He's the fifth we've tried to rear; all the others died, and only this one persists in staying alive.'

Sulkily, Loulou decided to lie down in the sun, turning his back on everyone. Flies were buzzing round him. Then Lazare thought of the days gone by, of the things that were no more and of the new, ugly things that had come into his life. He cast another look round the yard.

'My poor Mathieu!' he whispered very softly.

On the porch, Véronique greeted him with a nod of the head and went on scraping carrots. But he went straight to the dining-room, where his father was waiting, agitated by the sound of voices. Pauline called out from the door: 'You know, he's by himself, Louise is at Clermont.'

The anxiety lifted from Chanteau's eyes as he questioned his son, before even embracing him.

'Are you expecting her here? When is she coming to join you?'

'No, no,' Lazare replied. 'I shall go and pick her up at her sister-in-law's before going back to Paris . . . I'll spend a fortnight with you and then be off.'

Chanteau's gaze expressed deep, silent joy; and as Lazare embraced him at last, he gave him back two hearty kisses. He felt it incumbent on him nevertheless to express some regret.

'What a pity your wife couldn't come, we'd have been so happy to have her! You'll have to bring her another time, we insist on it.'

Pauline was silent, concealing under her laughing, affectionate welcome the inner shock that she had received. So everything was altered once again; she would not be leaving, and she could not have said whether she was glad or sorry, so completely was she at the service of others. Moreover, for all her gaiety, she was distressed at finding Lazare so much older-looking, with lack-lustre eyes and a bitter twist to his lips. She was familiar with the furrows on his brow and cheeks; but they had grown deeper, and betrayed an intensification of his boredom and anxiety. He, too, was looking at her; he was clearly struck by her development, by her increased beauty and strength, for he murmured with a smile: 'I say, you've not been pining away during my absence . . . You're all plump . . . Father looks younger, Pauline's superb . . . and it's odd, the house seems to be bigger.'

He cast his eyes round the dining-room, as he had scanned the courtyard, with surprise and emotion. His glance fell at last on

224

Minouche, lying on the table with paws neatly folded, so absorbed in feline bliss that she had not stirred..

'Even Minouche doesn't grow any older,' he went on. 'See here, you ungrateful creature, you might at least recognize me!' He went on stroking her, and she began to purr, but still did not move.

'Oh, Minouche cares for nobody but herself,' laughed Pauline. 'The day before yesterday she had five more kittens drowned; and you see, it doesn't worry her a bit.'

Dinner was put forward, because Lazare had had an early lunch. In spite of Pauline's efforts, the evening was not a happy one. Unspoken thoughts laid constraint on their talk; there were intervals of silence. Chanteau and Pauline avoided asking Lazare questions, seeing that it embarrassed him to answer; they did not try to find out how his affairs in Paris were going, nor why he had given them no warning until he was at Caen. He waved aside any direct question with a vague gesture, as though postponing the answer till later. Only, when tea was served, he gave vent to a great sigh of satisfaction. How comfortable it was here, and how much work he could have got through in this utter calm! He mentioned a verse drama at which he had been working for the last six months. His cousin was stupefied to hear him add that he expected to finish it off at Bonneville; he could do it in under a fortnight.

At ten o'clock Véronique came in to say that Monsieur Lazare's room was ready. But he expressed annoyance when she wanted to take him into the former guest-room on the first floor, which had been re-arranged for Louise and himself.

'If you think I'm going to sleep in there! I shall sleep upstairs in my own little iron bed.'

The maid grumbled. What fancy had taken him? Since the bed was made up, he didn't surely want to give her the trouble of making up another?

'All right,' he replied, 'I'll sleep in an armchair.'

And while Véronique furiously tore off the sheets and carried them up to the second floor, Pauline felt an unconscious joy, a sudden rush of gaiety that made her fling her arms round her cousin's neck to wish him goodnight, an impulsive return of their old childhood camaraderie. So he was living beside her once more in his big room, so near that she listened to him walking about for a long time, as though over-excited by the memories that kept her, too, awake.

It was not until the following day that Lazare began to confide in Pauline, and he did not reveal everything at once. At first she only discovered things through short phrases he let fall in the conversation. Then, emboldened by her affectionate concern, she began to question him. How were he and Louise getting on? Was their happiness still as perfect? He answered yes, but he complained of petty disagreements, he related insignificant facts that had provoked quarrels. The couple had not reached breaking-point, but, being both highly strung and hopelessly unbalanced in joy as in sorrow, they were continually wounding one another. There existed between them a sort of secret rancour, as if they had been surprised and angry at having made a mistake, at finding their love so shallow after the great passion of the early days. For a moment, Pauline got the impression that financial worries had embittered them; but she was wrong, their income of ten thousand francs was practically intact, it was merely that Lazare had tired of business as he had tired of music, medicine, and industry; and on that topic he broke into violent invective; he had never seen such stupidity, such decadence as in the world of finance. He'd rather endure anything—even the boredom of provincial life, in humble circumstances and with a reduced income—than be thus continually obsessed with money, in the wild whirl of figures that turned one's brain. In any case he had now left the insurance company; he had determined to try the theatre as soon as he went back to Paris next winter. His play was going to avenge him; he would show modern society devoured by the cancer of money.

Pauline did not worry overmuch about this new failure, which she had guessed at behind the embarrassment in Lazare's last letters. She was much more distressed by the disagreement that had gradually grown up between himself and his wife. She tried to find out the cause; how had they so quickly reached this painful situation, being young, in easy circumstances, with no concern other than their own happiness? A score of times she reverted to the subject, and only ceased questioning her cousin when she saw the disquiet he betrayed each time; he would falter and turn pale, averting his eyes. She had not failed to recognize that frightened, shamefaced look; it was that anguished apprehension of death which, in old days, he used to conceal as one conceals a secret vice; but could it be that the chill dread of Nevermore had come between them, in the warmth of their marriage bed? She was in doubt for several days, then, although he had admitted nothing more, she read the truth in his eyes one evening as he was coming from his room, without a light, looking as distraught as if he were flying from ghosts.

In Paris, amidst the feverish excitement of his love, Lazare had forgotten Death. He sought refuge, wildly, in Louise's arms, and afterwards, shattered with weariness, slept like a child. She, likewise, loved him like a mistress; with her voluptuous feline graces, she seemed to have been created solely to be thus adored by a man and felt unhappy and forlorn if he ceased to pay attention to her for a single hour. And they had continued thus in passionate satisfaction of their long desire, forgetting everything in one another's embrace, so long as they had thought sensual joys inexhaustible. But then satiety had come; and he had wondered why they could not surpass the intoxication of their earlier days; while she, craving nothing but caresses and having nothing else to give, could bring him no sort of support or encouragement in life. Were physical joys so short-lived, then? could one not explore them ever more deeply, discover in them endless new sensations powerful enough, in their unfamiliarity, to create an illusion of happiness? One night Lazare awoke with a start; he had felt the icy breath pass over his neck, making his hair stand on end; and he shivered, stammering out his cry of anguish: 'O God, O God! Death must come!' Louise was asleep by his side. Beyond their kisses he had found Death.

Other nights followed when once more he fell a prey to his old anguish. It would strike him unexpectedly as he lay sleepless; it was unpredictable and unpreventable. All of a sudden, in his calmest moments, he would feel that shudder run through him; while often, during a difficult day of fatigue and anger, he remained untouched by fear. And it no longer came merely as a sudden shock; his neurosis had grown worse, and every shock now seemed to reverberate through his whole being. He could not sleep without a nightlight; the darkness exacerbated his anxiety, in spite of his continual fear that his wife might discover his disorder. Indeed, this only increased his uneasiness, and thus aggravated his attacks, since formerly, when he slept alone, he could allow himself to be cowardly. It disturbed him to feel the warm presence of this living creature at his side. Whenever terror made him rear up on his pillow, dazed with sleep, he would look towards her, wildly imagining that he would see her eyes wide open, fixed on his. But she never stirred, and in the glow of the nightlight he could make out her motionless face, with its full lips and delicate bluish eyelids. And so he had begun to grow a little calmer, when one night he found her, as he had so long apprehended, with her eyes wide open. She was saying nothing, she was watching him shiver and grow pale. No doubt she too had felt the passing touch of death, for she seemed to understand, she clung to him desperately as though imploring help. Then, trying to keep up mutual deception, they pretended to have heard a noise of footsteps and got up to search under the furniture and behind the curtains.

Henceforward they were both haunted. No confession escaped their lips, this was a shameful secret that must not be spoken of; only when they lay in bed, stretched on their backs, with eyes wide open, they could clearly hear one another's thoughts. She was just as neurotic as he, they must have infected one another with anxiety, as two lovers fall victim to the same fever. If he woke and found her sleeping, he would take fright at her stillness: was she still breathing? he could not even hear her breath, perhaps she had suddenly died. For one instant he would examine her face and touch her hands. Then, even though reassured, he could not fall asleep again. The thought that she would die some day plunged him into a mournful reverie. Which of them would go first, he or she? He pursued each hypothesis in turn, imagining deathbed scenes in vivid detail, all the horrible distress of death-agonies, the wretchedness of the final preparations, the brutal fact of eternal separation. It was against this that his whole being rose in revolt: never to see one another again, never! When you had lived in such close physical contact; and he felt himself going mad, his brain would not accept the horror of it. Growing valiant in his terror, he would wish that he might be the first to go. Then he would feel sorry for her, imagining her as a widow, keeping up their familiar ways, doing this or the other thing that he would not be there to do. Sometimes, to drive away this obsession, he would take her gently in his arms, without waking her; but he could not hold her long, for the sensation of her aliveness in his embrace terrified him even more. If he laid his head on her breast he could not listen to her heartbeats without uneasiness, in constant apprehension of a sudden breakdown. Haunted by his nightmare of annihilation, he could no longer bear to touch those legs that had clung to his own, that waist that had yielded softly to his embrace, the whole of that supple beloved body, which now filled him with a sense of anxious foreboding. And even when she awoke, when desire threw them more closely together, mouth to mouth, and they sought the climax of their love in the hope of forgetting their misery so, they emerged from it still trembling as wildly, they would lie sleepless on their backs, sick of the joys of love. In the darkness of their bed, their wide stares were fixed again on death.

About this time Lazare grew weary of business. He became lazy again, and spent long days in idleness, pretexting a contempt for financiers. The truth was that this constant preoccupation with death detracted, every day, from his will and strength to go on living. He relapsed into his old apathetic attitude; what was the use of it? Since the last step into the dark was imminent—to-morrow, to-day, in an hour maybe—what was the use of bestirring oneself, getting excited, caring about one thing rather than another? All his efforts were abortive. His existence was nothing but a slow, daily death; as of old, he listened to the ticking of the clock within himself, and it seemed to him that it was slowing down, that his heart was beating less fast and all his other organs growing equally sluggish; soon the whole thing would stop, no doubt—and he shuddered as he observed this gradual diminution of life, the inevitable result of increasing age. Parts of himself seemed to drop away, as though his whole body were being continuously destroyed; his hair was falling out, he lost several teeth, he felt his muscles grow slack as though they were returning to earth. The prospect of middle age kept him in a state of black melancholy; old age would soon follow and finish him off. Already he imagined himself to be ailing in every part; something would certainly crack up, and his days were spent in feverish anticipation of some catastrophe. Then he saw others die around him, and the news of some contemporary's decease came as a personal shock. Was it possible that so-and-so was gone? He was three years younger, and had seemed tough enough to live to a hundred? And somebody else, how could that have happened? Such a prudent man, who measured out his very food! For two days afterwards he could think of nothing else, stupefied by the catastrophe, examining himself, cross-questioning his own illnesses, feeling resentful in the end towards the poor fellows who had died. Needing to reassure himself, he blamed them for their own deaths; the first had committed some unforgivable imprudence, and as for the second, he had succumbed to an extremely rare complaint to which doctors could not even give a name. But in vain did he strive to set aside the importunate spectre, he could always hear within himself the creaking of a machine about to break down, he was slipping without possible hope of a halt down the slope of years, at the end of which lay the great black abyss, the thought of which brought a cold sweat to his brow and made his hair stand on end.

When Lazare stopped going to his office, quarrels broke out between the couple. He went about in a state of restless irritability, which flared up at the least obstacle. The growing disorder which he so carefully concealed displayed itself outwardly by brusque behaviour, black moods, irrational actions. At one time he was ravaged by the fear of fire to such an extent that he moved down from a third-floor flat to a first-floor one so as to be able to escape more easily when the house caught fire. Continual anxiety about the future spoilt the present for him. He lived in constant expectation of disaster, starting at the sudden opening of a door and seized with palpitations on receiving a letter. Then he became mistrustful of everybody, hiding his money in small sums in different places and making a secret of his simplest plans; and he felt, moreover, a great bitterness against the world, convinced that he was misunderstood, that his successive failures were the result of a vast conspiracy of men and things. But, dominating and swamping everything, his boredom had become boundless; it was the boredom of an unbalanced man, driven by the ever-present thought of impending death to a distaste for action and leading a dreary, useless existence on the pretext of life's pointlessness. Why do anything? Science had its limits, one could prevent nothing and bring nothing about. His was the sceptical boredom of all his generation, no longer the romantic boredom of the Werthers and Renés, regretfully lamenting the passing of old beliefs, but the boredom of the new, doubting heroes, the young chemists who angrily declare the world an impossible place because they have not suddenly found life at the bottom of their retorts.

And in Lazare's case, by a quite logical inconsistency, the unconfessed dread of ceasing to be went with a constant display of bravado about annihilation. It was his neurosis itself, his unbalanced, hypochondriacal nature, that drove him to take up an attitude of pessimism and declaim furiously against life. He denounced it as a mere fraud, since it could not last for ever. Did not one spend the first half of one's days in dreams of happiness and the second half in regrets and terrors? And his pessimism outdid that of 'the old fellow', as he called Schopenhauer, the more violent passages of whose works he would recite from memory. He spoke of destroying all will to live, in order to bring to an end the barbarous and idiotic farce of existence with which the Power that ruled the world entertained itself for some unexplained egotistical end. He wanted to suppress life so as to suppress fear. Invariably he concluded that this was the only way out: to wish for nothing, for fear of something worse; to avoid all movement, which is pain, and then be entirely, swiftly overwhelmed by death. He brooded over the practical possibility of bringing about universal suicide, the sudden and total disappearance of all beings by their own consent. He referred to it continually in the middle of his casual conversation, in crude and savage tirades. The least vexation made him regret that he hadn't kicked the bucket yet; a mere headache set him grumbling furiously at his own carcase. Talk with a friend reverted immediately to the trials of existence, the confounded luck of those who were pushing up dandelions in the churchyard. Gloomy topics obsessed him; he was struck by an article by some whimsical astronomer announcing the arrival of a comet whose tail was going to sweep the earth away like a grain of sand: might not that be the cosmic catastrophe he was waiting for, the colossal petard that was going to blow up the world like an old rotten hulk? And this death-wish, this toying with theories of annihilation, merely represented his desperate conflict with his terrors, the vain rattle of words concealing his agonized anticipation of his own end.

His wife's pregnancy, at this juncture, gave him a further shock. He experienced an indefinable sensation, a mingling of great joy and intensified uneasiness. Contrary to the theories of 'the old fellow,' the idea of becoming a father, of having created life, filled him with pride. While he affected to say that fools misused the right of fatherhood, he reacted with self-satisfied surprise, as though such an event were his own exclusive prerogative. Then his joy faded, as he tortured himself with the presentiment that the confinement would go badly; he was soon convinced that the mother would die and the child perish unborn. It happened that during the first months of pregnancy Louise suffered some painful upsets, and the upheaval in the house, the disturbance of their habits, their frequent quarrels set the crown on his misery. This child, which ought to have brought the couple together, increased the misunderstanding between them, the friction of their intimate life. He was particularly exasperated by the way she complained from morning till night of vague discomfort. And so when the doctor suggested a spell of mountain air, it was with great relief that he took her to her sister-in-law's and escaped for a fortnight himself, under pretext of visiting his father at Bonneville. He was secretly ashamed of his flight, but he argued with his conscience that a short separation would do them both good by calming their nerves, and it would really be enough if he was there for her confinement.

On that evening when Pauline at last heard the whole story of the past eighteen months, she stayed speechless for a moment, appalled by the disaster. It was in the dining-room; she had put

231

Chanteau to bed, and Lazare had just finished his confession, while the teapot grew cold in front of them and the lamp smoked overhead.

After a silence she said at last: 'But, good heavens, you've stopped loving one another!'

He had risen to go up to his room. And he protested, with his worried laugh: 'We love one another as much as anyone can, my dear child . . . Are you really so ignorant, buried away here? Why should love last better than anything else?'

As soon as she was shut up in her own room, Pauline gave way to one of those fits of despair that had so often kept her in wakeful torment there, on that same chair, while all the house slept. Was their misery going to begin again? When she thought it was all over for others and for herself, when she had torn out her own heart to the point of giving Lazare to Louise, she suddenly learnt the futility of her sacrifice; they had already stopped loving one another, the tears and blood of her martyrdom had been shed in vain. This was the wretched result of all her efforts—fresh sufferings, impending conflicts, the presentiment of which increased her anguish. Was there never an end to pain?

And while she sat with her arms hanging loose, staring at her candle-flame, the thought that she alone was responsible for the whole business rose up from her conscience and oppressed her. She struggled in vain to deny the facts: she alone had concluded the marriage, without realising that Louise was not the right wife for her cousin; for now she saw Louise as she really was, too neurotic to stabilize him, ready to panic herself at the least breath, having nothing beyond her sexual attractiveness, of which he had quickly tired. Why had she only recognized these things to-day? Were they not the very reasons which had decided her to let Louise take her place? At one time she had thought Louise was more loving, and hoped that her kisses might save Lazare from his moods of depression. What wretchedness! To have done harm by trying to do good, to be so ignorant of life as to ruin those whom one wanted to help! True, she had meant to be kind, to put her charitable action on a firm basis, that day when she had bought their joy at the cost of so many tears. And she felt a deep contempt for her kindness, since kindness did not always bring happiness.

The house was asleep, and in the silence of her room she could hear nothing but the throbbing of her own pulse in her temples. A surging tide of revolt was gradually breaking out. Why had she not married Lazare? He belonged to her, she need never have given him up. Perhaps he might have felt desperate at first, but she would surely have been able to inspire him with courage afterwards and protect him against his absurd nightmares. She had always been foolishly distrustful of herself; therein lay the sole cause of their misfortune. And her consciousness of her own strength, her robust health, her boundless affection began at last to protest and assert themselves. Surely she was worth more than the other woman? Why had she been such a fool as to efface herself? Now she even denied the other's love, for she found in her own heart an ampler passion, the sort that can sacrifice itself to the loved one. She loved her cousin enough to have been willing to disappear, could the other woman have made him happy; but since the other did not know how to keep the great joy of having him, might she not act, break up this ill-assorted marriage? And her anger rose still higher, and she felt more conscious of her own beauty and courage, looking at her girl's body, her bosom, her belly, with sudden pride in the wife that she might have been. One shattering certainty stood out: it was she who should have married Lazare.

Then she was overcome with immense regret. The night hours passed one by one, and yet she never thought of dragging herself to bed. She sat absorbed in a dream, her eyes wide open, blinded by the tall flame of her candle, which she still stared at unseeing. Now she was no longer in her room, she imagined that she had married Lazare; and she pictured their life together, in a series of scenes of love and felicity. It might be at Bonneville, on the edge of the blue sea, or else in Paris, in a noisy street; the room was always the same, small and peaceful, with books lying about, roses blooming on the table, and the lamp shedding its golden light in the evening and casting still shadows on the ceiling. They sought one another's hands at every moment; he had recovered the careless gaiety of his youth, and she loved him so much that he had ended by believing that life would never end. Now they were sitting down at table; now they were going out together; to-morrow she would go through the week's accounts with him. And she lingered tenderly over these intimate domestic details, seeing in them the concrete tokens of their happiness, which was there at last, visible, from their morning laughter as they rose and dressed to their last goodnight kiss. In the summer they would travel. And then one morning she'd find herself pregnant . . . But a great shudder disturbed her dream and she went no further; she was back in her room in front of the candle, which was almost burnt out. Pregnant, great heavens! The other woman was pregnant, and never would these things happen to her, never would she know these joys! The shock was so cruel that tears gushed forth and she wept endlessly, her breast convulsed with great sobs. The candle went out, and she had to go to bed in the darkness.

That night's agitation left Pauline in a state of profound emotion, full of charitable pity for the estranged pair and for herself. Her grief had melted into a sort of tender hope. She could not have said what she looked forward to, she dared not analyse herself while such confused feelings disturbed her heart. Why torment oneself so? Had she not at least ten more days ahead of her? After that it would be time enough to take stock. What mattered was to give Lazare back his peace of mind and make his stay at Bonneville restful and beneficial. And she recovered her cheerfulness of spirit; together they took up again the happy way of life that they had known of old.

They were soon back on the old footing of camaraderie.

'Put away your play, you great silly! It'll only get hissed, that play of yours . . . Look, why don't you help me see whether Minouche has carried my reel of cotton on top of the cupboard.'

He held the chair while she stood on tiptoe to look. It had been pouring with rain for two days, and they were confined to the big room, which rang with their laughter at each new discovery that reminded them of bygone years.

'Oh, here's the doll you made with two of my old collars . . . And this, d'you remember this? A portrait I drew of you that day when you looked so hideous crying with rage because I wouldn't lend you my razor.'

She would bet him that she could still jump on to the table in one bound. He would jump too, glad to be disturbed in his work. His play already lay forgotten in a drawer. One morning when they discovered the great Symphony of Pain she played bits to him, accenting the rhythm comically; and he made fun of his own work, singing the notes to help out the piano, whose feeble sounds could scarcely be heard. One section, though, the famous March of Death, they took seriously; it really wasn't bad, it ought to be kept. Everything amused them and touched them; a collection of Floridaeae, pressed by her in the old days, which turned up under some books, a forgotten flask containing a sample of bromide produced in the factory, the tiny model of a jetty half-broken, as though shattered by the waves from a glass of water. Then they would roam all over the house, chasing one another like children let loose to play; they would run up and down stairs continually, crossing rooms and banging doors. Surely they were back in the past? She was ten and he was nineteen, and once more she began to feel for him the passionate friendship of her childhood. Nothing had changed; the dining-room still had its light walnut sideboard and its hanging lamp of polished brass, its View of Vesuvius and its lithographs of the Four Seasons, which still amused them. Under the glass case, the grandfather's masterpiece slumbered in the same place, having come to form part of the mantelpiece to such an extent that the maid would put down glasses and plates on top of it. One room alone they entered with silent emotion, Madame Chanteau's old room, which had been left untouched since her death. Nobody ever opened the writing-desk, but the bright sunlight which was occasionally let in had gradually faded the yellow chintz hangings with their green foliage. It happened that some anniversary occurred, and they filled the room with great bunches of flowers.

But soon, as a sharp wind had driven off the rain, they hurried outside, on to the terrace, into the kitchen garden, along the cliffs, and lived through the days of their youth again.

'Are you coming shrimping?' she would call to him in the morning through the wall, as soon as she was up. 'The tide's going out.'

They would set off in bathing suits, they would find the same old rocks on which the sea, after so many weeks and months, had barely left its mark. And it might have been only the day before that they had explored that corner of the coast. He had not forgotten.

'Take care! There's a hole there, with a lot of big stones at the bottom of it.'

She would quickly reassure him. 'Yes, I know, don't be afraid . . . Oh, just look at this huge crab I've caught!'

They stood waist-high in the cool surging swell, exhilarated by the salt freshness of the sea-breeze. And they resumed their old rambles, wandering far afield, stopping to rest on the sands, sheltering from a sudden shower in the depths of a cave, and coming home after nightfall, through dark paths. Nothing seemed to have changed, either, under the open sky; the sea was still there, infinite, ceaselessly repeating the same horizons in its continual inconstancy. Wasn't it only yesterday that they had seen it looking just that turquoise-blue colour, with those great shimmering patches where the widening currents ruffled it? And the leaden water under a livid sky, that squall of rain on the left coming in with the high tide, wouldn't they see it again to-morrow? They lost all track of the days. Little, forgotten facts came back to them with the vividness of immediate reality. He was twenty-six again and she was sixteen. When he thoughtlessly gave her a friendly jostle, she was overcome with a delicious uneasiness that took her breath away. She did not avoid him, though, for her thoughts were innocent. A sense of new life filled them, set them whispering to one another, laughing at nothing, and then left them trembling with emotion after long-drawn-out silences. The commonest things acquired extraordinary significance—a request for bread, a word about the weather, the goodnight said at their bedroom doors. The whole of the past was flooding back into their hearts, with the sweetness of old forgotten affections reawakened. Why should they have felt uneasy? They offered no resistance, lulled by the sea, soothed by the eternal monotony of its voice.

So the days passed smoothly by. The third week of Lazare's visit had already begun. He kept postponing his departure; he had received several letters from Louise, who was very bored, but whom her sister-in-law wanted to keep a little longer. Lazare wrote back urging her to stay, and forwarding advice from Dr. Cazenove, whom he had consulted about her. He was gradually getting used again to the peaceful, regular routine of the house, to the times for meals, for getting up and going to bed, which he had changed in Paris, to Véronique's grumpy ill-humours, to the unremitting sufferings of his father, who sat motionless, his face drawn with the same pain, while everything in the outside world altered so rapidly. At the Saturday night dinners he met again the old familiar faces of the doctor and the *abbé*, and heard the same unending conversation about the recent bad weather or the bathers at Arromanches. At dessert Minouche still leapt on to the table as lightly as a feather and came to butt his chin with her head, rubbing herself against him; and the light scratch of her cold teeth took him back a great many years. Amidst all these old-time things there was nothing new but Loulou, miserable ugly Loulou, who lay curled up in a ball under the table and growled when anyone went near him. Lazare tried in vain to feed him with sugar; the dog, after crunching it, bared his teeth and grew even sulkier. They had to give him up, and he lived alone like a stranger in the house, an unsociable being who asked nothing from men or gods but permission to lead his dreary life in peace.

Sometimes, though, when Pauline and Lazare went off on one of their long walks, they met with some adventure. Thus one day as they left the cliff-path so as not to pass in front of the Treasure Bay factory, they happened to meet Boutigny round a bend in a lane. Boutigny was now a prosperous gentleman, who had made a fortune by his manufacture of commercial soda; he had married the woman who had sacrificed herself to follow him into this god-forsaken region, and she had just borne him a third child. The whole family, accompanied by a servant and a nurse, were driving in a magnificent brake, drawn by a pair of big white horses. The two walkers had to stand aside and press close against the bank to avoid being caught up in the wheels. Boutigny, who was driving, slowed down the horses to walking pace. There was a moment's embarrassment; for so many years they had not been on speaking terms, while the presence of the woman and the children made the awkwardness more trying. At last their eyes met, they bowed to one another, slowly and in silence.

When the carriage had disappeared, Lazare, who had grown pale, said with an effort: 'So he lives like a prince nowadays?'

Pauline, who had merely been moved by the sight of the children, answered gently: 'Yes, apparently he's made enormous profits lately . . . You know he's been repeating your old experiments.'

That, indeed, was what wrung Lazare's heart. The fishermen of Bonneville, who took a cynical delight in being unpleasant to him, had informed him of it. For the last few months Boutigny, with the help of a young chemist, a paid assistant, had resumed the low-temperature treatment of seaweed ash; and thanks to his cautious persistence and practical sense, he was getting marvellous results.

'Of course!' muttered Lazare dully, 'every time science takes one step forward it's because some fool has given it a shove without meaning to.'

Their walk was quite spoiled; they went forward in silence, looking out into the distance where grey mists rose from the sea and veiled the sky. When they reached home at nightfall they were shivering. The cheerful lamplight on the white tablecloth soon restored their warmth.

Another day, as they were following a path through beet-fields in the direction of Verchemont, they stopped in surprise at seeing smoke rising from a thatched roof. The cottage was on fire, and the sunlight falling vertically had prevented them from noticing the flames; and it was blazing away, deserted, doors and windows closed, while the peasants were at work somewhere in the neigh-bourhood. They immediately left their path and started running and shouting; but they only startled some magpies that were chattering in the apple-orchard. At last, from a distant patch of carrots, a woman with a handkerchief over her head emerged, stared for a minute, then galloped wildly, frantically across the ploughed land. She was waving her arms, screaming and gasping out some unrecognizable word. She fell down, picked herself up, fell once more and then started off again with bleeding hands. Her kerchief had flown off and her hair was hanging loose in the sunshine.

'But what's she saying?' Pauline asked in sudden terror.

As the woman drew near they could hear her hoarse cry, like an animal's howl. 'The child! ... the child! ... the child!'

Since morning, the father and son had been working about three miles away, in a patch of oats they had inherited. She had only been gone a few minutes to pick a basketful of carrots; and she had left the child asleep and everything shut up, contrary to her custom. The fire had probably been smouldering for a long time, for she was quite amazed, swearing that she had put it out down to the last ember. Now the thatched roof was blazing like a furnace; the flames rose high, shaking the yellow sunlight with their red flicker.

'Did you lock the doors?' shouted Lazare.

The woman did not hear him. She was frantic; she ran round the house, for no reason, hoping perhaps to find some opening, some hole that she knew was non-existent. Then she fell down once more, for her legs could not carry her, and her grey old face was exposed now in an agony of despair and terror, while she kept up a wail of 'The child, the child!'

Great tears rose to Pauline's eyes. But Lazare was being driven crazy by that cry, which cut through him painfully every time. It was growing intolerable, and he suddenly said: 'I'm going to get that child out for her.'

His cousin stared at him in bewilderment. She tried to seize his hands and keep him back.

'You? You're not to ... the roof's going to collapse.'

'We'll see,' he replied simply.

And he shouted in the woman's face: 'Your key? Have you got your key?'

The woman stood gaping. Lazare hustled her, and at last managed to snatch the key from her. Then, while she lay screaming on the ground, he walked quite calmly towards the house. Pauline followed him with her eyes, but made no further attempt to stop him; she was rooted to the spot with fear and amazement, so naturally did he seem to perform his task. A rain of sparks was falling, and he had to press close to the door to open it, for handfuls of blazing straw were falling off the roof like streams of water during a storm; and there he met with an obstacle, for the rusty key refused to turn in the keyhole. But he never even uttered an oath; he took his time, managed to open the door, and stood for a moment on the threshold to let out the first cloud of smoke, which flew into his face. He had never before felt so self-possessed; he was acting as if in a dream, with a surety of movement, skill and prudence born of danger. He bent his head and disappeared.

'O God, O God!' faltered Pauline, choking with anguish.

With an involuntary gesture she had clasped her hands and was pressing them tightly enough to break them, raising them in a continuous swaying movement as sick men do under the stress of great pain. The roof was cracking and already giving way in places; her cousin would never have time to get out. She experienced a sensation of eternity; she felt as if he had been in there since the beginning of time. The woman, prone on the ground, was holding her breath; she looked quite dazed at having seen a gentleman go into the fire.

But a great cry arose; it was Pauline who had uttered it, involuntarily, from the very depths of her being, when she saw the thatch crum ..e between the smoking walls.

'Lazare!'

He was on the doorstep, with his hair barely singed and his hands lightly scorched; and when he had thrown the struggling, crying child into the woman's arms, he turned almost angrily to his cousin.

'Well, why are you so upset?'

She hung on his neck, sobbing, in such a state of nervous reaction that, for fear she should faint, he made her sit down on an old mossy stone, against the cottage wall. He began to feel weak himself now. There was a trough full of water there, and he dipped his hands in it with great relief. The sudden chill brought him back to his senses, and now he felt a great astonishment at his own action. What, had he really gone into the middle of those flames? As if his personality were split, he could clearly see himself amidst the smoke, showing incredible agility and presence of mind, and he watched this as though it were a prodigy accomplished by a stranger. A lingering exaltation of spirit uplifted him with a subtle joy that he had never before experienced.

Pauline had somewhat recovered, and she examined his hands, saying: 'No, it'll be nothing, the burns aren't deep. But we must go home. I'll attend to them. Good heavens, you did frighten me!'

She had dipped her handkerchief in the water to wrap round his right hand, which had suffered more than the other. They got up and tried to comfort the woman, who, after kissing the child frenziedly, had laid it down beside her and had stopped looking at it; and now she was lamenting about the house, screaming as loudly as ever, asking what her menfolk would say when they found everything in ruins. The walls, however, were still standing; black smoke issued from the furnace within, while showers of unseen sparks flew, crackling loudly.

'Come now, courage, poor woman,' Pauline kept telling her. 'Come and have a talk to me to-morrow.'

Some neighbours, attracted by the smoke, had run up. She was able to take Lazare away. They felt very happy on the journey home. He was not in great pain, but she insisted none the less on supporting him with her arm. Words still failed them, in their emotional agitation, and they looked at one another smiling. Pauline, in particular, was filled with a joyous pride. So he was brave, for all his terrors at the thought of death! As they made their way along the path, she was absorbed in amazement at the contradictions in the nature of the one man she knew well; for she had seen him spend whole nights at work, and then stay idle for months on end, behave with disconcerting frankness after telling a bare-faced lie, lay a friendly kiss on her forehead while she felt on her wrists the burning grasp of his masculine hands, feverish with desire; and now he had shown himself a hero! She had been right not to despair of life by judging everybody wholly good or wholly bad. When they reached Bonneville their tense silence broke in a flood of noisy words. The smallest details recurred to them, they related the adventure a score of times, constantly recalling forgotten incidents which they both suddenly remembered as a flash of lightning. They talked about it for a long time, and help was sent to the distressed peasants.

Lazare had been at Bonneville for nearly a month. A letter came from Louise, who was desperate with boredom. He replied that he would go and fetch her at the beginning of the following week. Terrible rains were falling again, those violent storms that so often swept the coast. as though a lifted flood-gate had carried away earth, sea and sky in one grey mist. Lazare had suggested making a serious effort to finish his play, and Pauline, whom he wanted to have beside him to encourage him, took up her knitting—the little stockings that she distributed among the village girls. But he did no work once she was sitting by the table. They carried on long conversations in low voices, saying the same things over unweariedly, gazing into one another's eyes. They risked no games now, avoiding the touch of each other's hands, with the instinctive prudence of children who have been scolded, conscious of the danger of letting their shoulders brush or their breaths mingle as they had done, in fun, only the day before. Moreover they asked for nothing sweeter than this weary peace, this drowsy state into which they drifted while the rain rattled ceaselessly against the slate roof. If a silence fell, they would blush; each word they spoke held an involuntary caress, under the impulsion of feelings which had gradually revived within them the past they had thought dead, and made it blossom.

One evening Pauline had been sitting till midnight in Lazare's room, knitting; he had let the pen drop from his fingers while he expounded to her, in slow phrases, his future works, dramas peopled by figures on a grand scale. The whole house was asleep; even Véronique had gone early to bed; and the great quivering peacefulness of night, disturbed only by the accustomed moan of the high tide, had gradually steeped them in a sort of sensual tenderness. He opened up his heart, and confessed that he had wasted his life; if literature, this time, let him down, he was determined to retire into some obscure corner and live a hermit's life.

'I tell you what,' he went on with a smile, 'I often think we ought to have left the country after my mother's death.'

'Left the country? What d'you mean?'

'Yes, run away very far off, to Oceania for instance, to one of those islands where life is so pleasant.'

'And your father, should we have taken him?'

'Oh, I tell you, it's only a dream . . . Surely one's allowed to imagine nice things when reality's so grim!'

He had left the table and come to sit on an arm of her chair. She let fall her knitting, and was laughing freely at his wild restless flights of imagination, fantastic as a child's; and she lifted her head towards him, leaning back in her chair, while he was so close beside her that he could feel the live warmth of her shoulder against his thigh.

'You're crazy, my poor dear! What should we have done out there?'

241

'Why, we should have lived! . . . Don't you remember that travel book we used to read together, twelve years ago? Out there, they live as though they were in Paradise. There's never any winter, the sky's eternally blue, you spend your time in the sun and under the stars . . . We'd have had a hut, we'd have eaten delicious fruit— and nothing to do, nothing to worry about!'

'Why not say at once two savages, with rings in our noses and feathers on our heads?'

'Well, why not? . . . We'd have loved one another from one year's end to the next, and never counted the days; that wouldn't have been so bad!'

She looked up at him; her eyelids fluttered and a slight shiver made her face pale. That thought of love sank right into her heart and filled her with delicious languor. He had taken her hand, unthinkingly, just from an urge to be nearer her and hold part of her; and he was playing with this warm hand, folding its slender fingers, still laughing, but with a laugh that was growing strained. She felt no anxiety, for they had played thus in their youth; and besides she was losing all her strength, and in her growing confusion seemed to belong to him already. Her very voice was failing.

'But a diet of fruit doesn't sound very satisfying. We'd have to go hunting and fishing, and cultivate a field . . . If it's really the women who do the work there, as they say, would you have made me dig the ground?'

'You, with those little hands? . . . What about monkeys? Don't they make good servants of them nowadays?'

She gave a faint laugh at this joke, while he went on: 'Besides, there'd be nothing left of your little hands . . . Yes, I'd have eaten them up, like this.'

He was kissing her hands, even nibbling at them, while the blood rushed to his face as a sudden storm of desire blinded him. And they said nothing more, seized by the same frenzy, plunging headlong together in the same dizzy rapture. She offered no resistance, she had slid down in the armchair with her face flushed and swollen and her eyes closed as though to shut out the sight of things. With rough hands, he had already unfastened her bodice and was breaking the hooks of her petticoat, when his lips met hers. He gave her a kiss that she returned frantically, clasping his neck with all the strength in her arms. But in this shock to her inexperienced senses she had opened her eyes, and she saw herself sprawling on the floor, she recognized the lamp, the cupboard, the ceiling whose slightest stains she knew; and she seemed to wake up, in

242

astonishment, like one emerging from a terrible dream into familiar surroundings. She struggled violently and got to her feet. Her petticoats were slipping off, her open bodice disclosed her naked breasts. In the breathless silence of the room a cry burst from her.

'Leave go of me, it's dreadful!'

Crazy with desire, he did not hear her. He took hold of her again and tore off the rest of her clothes. He set burning kisses at random on her naked skin, and each kiss set her quivering all over. Twice she nearly collapsed again, yielding to the invincible urge to give herself to him, suffering agonies from this struggle against herself. They had moved all round the table, panting, their limbs intertwined, when he succeeded in pushing her on to an old divan with creaking springs. With stiffened arms she held him off, repeating in a hoarse gasp: 'Oh, please, oh, let me go. You're trying to do something dreadful!'

Lazare, his teeth clenched, had not uttered a single word. He thought he had overpowered her at last, when she broke away once more with so sharp an effort that he was sent staggering against the table. Then, during her second's freedom, she succeeded in rushing out, crossed the passage at one leap and flung herself into her own room. He followed close on her heels, and she had not time to fasten her door. As he pushed it, she was obliged to lean against the wood with all her weight in order to slide the bolt and turn the key; and as she battled with him for this narrow opening, she felt she would be lost if he introduced so much as the tip of his slipper. The key creaked loudly, and a great silence fell, in which they could once more hear the sea battering the terrace wall.

Meanwhile Pauline stood there, without a candle, her eyes wide open in the darkness, leaning against the door. She was aware that on the other side of it Lazare had not stirred either. She could hear the sound of his breath; she still felt it, in imagination, hot against her neck. If she moved away he might perhaps break a panel with his shoulder. She felt safer standing thus; and, mechanically, she kept on pressing with all her strength, as if he were still pushing. Two more minutes passed, interminably, with each of them conscious of the other's stubborn resistance on the other side of the slender wooden barrier, and both afire and shaking with the fever of desire that they could not quell. Then Lazare's voice whispered very low, stifled with emotion: 'Pauline, open the door . . . You're there, I know.'

A shiver ran through her flesh; the voice stirred her from head to foot. But she did not answer. With her head bowed, she held her falling skirts with one hand, while the other clutched at the unfastened bodice to cover the nakedness of her bosom.

'You're as unhappy as I am, Pauline ... Open the door, I implore you. Why must we deny ourselves this happiness?'

He was afraid, now, of waking Véronique, whose room was next door. His entreaties were made in a low voice like a sick man's moan.

'Open the door, do ... Open, and we'll die afterwards if you like ... Haven't we loved one another since childhood? You ought to be my wife, you'll have to be some day ... I love you, I love you, Pauline ...'

She was trembling more violently, for every word wrung her heart. The kisses with which he had covered her shoulders were glowing on her skin like drops of fire. And she resisted more stiffly, afraid of opening and yielding through the overwhelming impulse of her half-naked body. He was right; why should they deny themselves this joy, which they could hide together from all the rest of the world? The house was asleep, the night was black. Oh, to sleep in the darkness in one another's arms, to have him for her own, if only for an hour! Oh, to live, to live at last!

'O God, you're cruel, Pauline! You won't even answer, and I'm standing here so miserable. Open the door, I'll hold you, I'll keep you, we'll forget everything ... Open, open, I implore you ...'

He was sobbing, and she too began to weep. She still spoke no word, in spite of the mutiny in her blood. For a whole hour he went on, entreating her, growing angry, letting fall cruel words and then relapsing into words of passionate endearment. Twice she thought he had gone away, and twice he came back from his room in a frenzy of exasperated love. Then, when she heard him shut his own door in a rage, she experienced a feeling of immense sadness. It was over this time, she had won, but such violent despair and shame accompanied her victory that she undressed and lay down without lighting a candle. The thought of seeing herself half-naked, with her clothes torn off, filled her with horrible confusion. However, the coolness of the sheets somewhat calmed her fevered shoulders, still tingling from his kisses; and she stayed a long time without stirring, as though crushed under the weight of misery and disgust.

Pauline lay sleepless till morning. She was obsessed by the dreadfulness of it all. The whole evening seemed to her a horrifying crime. Now she could no longer excuse herself, she had to admit the duplicity of her own affections. Her maternal fondness for

Lazare, her secret accusations against Louise, were nothing but the hypocritical awakening of her old passion. She had sunk to such lies, and now she probed deeper into the unconfessed feelings of her heart and discovered there a delight at the estrangement between the couple, a hope that she might benefit by it. Wasn't it she herself who had induced her cousin to resume their old way of life? Ought she not to have foreseen that it would inevitably lead to their fall? And now the terrible situation confronted them, it lay like a barrier across their lives; she had given him to another, and she adored him, and he wanted her. The thing whirled round inside her head, throbbing in her temples like a peal of bells. At first she determined to run away next day. Then such an escape seemed to her an act of cowardice. Since he was going away himself, why not wait? And in any case, her pride revived, and she resolved to conquer herself so as not to take away with her the shame of misconduct. She felt that she could never hold up her head again if she retained remorse for that evening.

Next morning Pauline came down at her usual time. Only her bruised eyelids could have betrayed the night's anguish. She was pale and very calm. When Lazare came down in his turn, he explained away his air of weariness by telling his father he had worked late. The day was spent at their usual occupations. Neither of them alluded to what had passed between them, even when they were alone together, far from eyes and ears. They did not avoid one another, seeming confident in their own courage. But that evening, as they said goodnight in the passage outside their bed-room doors, they fell wildly into each other's arms and exchanged a passionate kiss. And Pauline shut herself in her room in terror, while Lazare fled too, and went and flung himself on his bed in tears.

This, henceforward, was their life. Slowly the days rolled by, and they stayed side by side, in anxious anticipation of a possible lapse. They never spoke a word of these things, they never alluded to that terrible night, but their thoughts dwelt on it continually, and they were afraid of breaking down, of collapsing as though struck by lightning, somewhere, anywhere. Would it be in the morning, when they got up? Or at night, while they were exchanging a last word? Would it be in his room or in hers, or in some distant corner of the house? They could not tell. And they lost none of their clear-sightedness; each sudden impulse, each momentary madness, despairing embraces behind doors, burning kisses stolen in the dark, were followed by a revulsion of painful indignation. The ground was trembling under their feet, and they clung to the resolutions made in their calmer hours so as not to sink into the abyss. But neither he nor she had the strength to seek the only way of salvation, an immediate parting. Pauline, pretexting courage, dared danger obstinately. Lazare, entirely obsessed, carried away irresistibly by this new excitement, had even given up answering the urgent letters written by his wife. He had been at Bonneville for six weeks, and they felt as if this existence, with its cruel and delicious agitation, must go on for ever.

One Sunday at dinner Chanteau grew merry, having treated himself to a glass of Burgundy, an indulgence for which he invariably paid a high price. That day Pauline and Lazare had loitered for long, delightful hours by the sea-shore, under a wide blue sky; and they exchanged tender looks, which betrayed that uneasiness, that self-mistrust that gave their present companionship such a passionate intensity.

All three were laughing, when Véronique, just before bringing in dessert, appeared at the kitchen door, exclaiming: 'Here's Madame!'

'Madame who?' Asked Pauline in amazement.

'Why, Madame Louise of course!'

There were stifled exclamations. Chanteau, in alarm, looked at Pauline and Lazare, who had turned pale. But the latter rose abruptly, his voice faltering with rage.

'What, Louise? But she never wrote to me! I'd have forbidden her to come ... Is she mad?'

Twilight, clear and gentle, was falling. Throwing down his napkin, Lazare went out, and Pauline followed him, striving to regain her usual cheerful serenity. It was indeed Louise, climbing painfully out of Malivoire's coach.

'Are you mad?' called out her husband from the middle of the courtyard. 'You shouldn't do such crazy things without writing!'

She burst into tears. She'd been very unwell up there, and so bored! As he'd never answered her last two letters, she had been seized with an irresistible longing to go away, mingled with a keen desire to see Bonneville again. If she hadn't written to tell him, it was for fear he might prevent her from having her way.

'And I was so looking forward to surprising you all!'

'It's ridiculous! You must go back to-morrow!'

Louise, dreadfully upset at such a reception, collapsed into Pauline's arms. The latter had turned even paler on seeing her clumsy movements, her heavy figure under the dress; and now the contact of that swollen belly filled her with horror and pity. At last she succeeded in conquering her jealous revulsion, and silenced Lazare.

'Why do you speak so harshly to her? Kiss her . . . My dear, you were quite right to come, if you think you'll be happier at Bonneville. You know we're all fond of you, don't you?'

Loulou was howling, furious at the voices that disturbed the usual quiet of the courtyard. Minouche, having stuck her nose out on to the porch, had withdrawn, with a shake of the paws, as if she had just avoided getting mixed up in some disagreeable business. They all went in; Véronique set a place and began serving dinner again.

'So it's you, Louisette?' Chanteau said, laughing uneasily. 'So you wanted to give us a surprise? . . . I nearly swallowed my wine the wrong way!'

After all, the evening passed off well. They had all regained their self-possession; no plans were made for the following days. As they were about to go upstairs, there was another awkward moment when the maid asked whether Monsieur was going to sleep in Madame's room.

'Oh, no, Louise'll rest better without me,' muttered Lazare, whose eyes instinctively met Pauline's.

'That's right, you sleep upstairs,' said his wife. 'I'm horribly tired, and I'll have the whole bed to myself.'

Three days went by. Pauline made up her mind at last. She would leave the house on the following Monday. The couple were already talking of staying until the confinement, which was not due for a full month. But she had a strong suspicion that her cousin had had enough of Paris, and that he would end by living on his income at Bonneville, embittered by his perpetual failures. The best thing would be to clear out immediately, for she could not quite control her feelings, and she lacked strength, even more than before, to go on living with them in their married intimacy. Wasn't this also the best way to escape from the dangers of that renewed passion which had been causing herself and Lazare so much distress? Louise alone expressed surprise when she learned of her cousin's decision. Unanswerable reasons were put forward; Dr. Cazenove declared that the lady at St.-Lô had made Pauline a quite exceptional offer, which the latter could not refuse any longer; so that her relatives ought to force her to accept a post which promised her a secure future. Chanteau himself agreed, with tears in his eyes.

That Saturday there was a last dinner-party with the doctor and the *abbé*. Louise, who was feeling very ill, could hardly drag herself to the table. This completed the depression of the party, in spite of the efforts of Pauline, who shed smiles on everyone, anxious not to leave sadness in the house that for so many years had rung with her laughter. Her heart was overflowing with grief. Véronique waited with a tragic air. When dessert was served, Chanteau refused a drop of burgundy, having suddenly become exaggeratedly prudent at the thought that soon he would lose his nurse, who by her mere voice could allay his pain. Lazare, his nerves on edge, quarrelled the whole time with the doctor about some new scientific discovery.

At eleven o'clock the house had relapsed into utter silence. Louise and Chanteau were already asleep, while the maid was tidying up her kitchen. Then, upstairs, at the door of his old room, where he still lived as though he were single, Lazare stopped Pauline for a moment, as he had done each evening.

'Goodbye,' he murmured.

'No, not goodbye,' she said, trying to laugh. 'Just goodnight, for I'm not going till Monday.'

They looked at each other, their eyes grew troubled, they fell into each other's arms, and their lips met in a last passionate kiss.

CHAPTER X

NEXT morning at breakfast, as they were all sitting down to their bowls of coffee and milk, they were surprised not to see Louise. The maid was about to go and knock at her bedroom door when she appeared at last. She was very pale and walked with difficulty.

'What's the matter?' asked Lazare anxiously.

'I've been feeling ill since dawn,' she answered. 'I hardly slept a wink, and I think I heard every hour strike.'

Pauline protested. 'But you should have called us, we could at least have looked after you.'

Louise had sat down at the table with a sigh of relief. 'Oh,' she went on, 'there's nothing you can do. I know what it is, I've been having these pains almost constantly for eight months.'

Her pregnancy had been a very painful one, and she had grown used to continual nausea and abdominal pains so violent that she sometimes spent whole days bent double with agony. That morning her nausea had vanished, but she felt as if a tight belt were fastened round her, bruising her inside.

'One gets used to pain,' said Chanteau sententiously.

'Yes, but I have to keep moving,' the young woman concluded. 'That's why I came down . . . Upstairs, I can't bear to sit still.'

She swallowed nothing but a few mouthfuls of coffee. All morning she trailed about the house, leaving one chair to go and sit on another. Nobody dared speak to her, for she would fly into a temper and seemed to suffer more when people paid attention to her. Her pain gave her no respite. Shortly before noon, however, the attack appeared to decrease, and she was able to sit down at table once more and take a little soup. But between two and three o'clock she was seized with terrible gripes; and she wandered about without a pause, going from the dining-room into the kitchen, lumbering upstairs to her own room and then promptly coming down again.

On the top floor, Pauline was packing her trunk. She was to leave next day, and she had barely time to empty her drawers and tidy everything. Nevertheless she went out, every other minute, to lean over the banisters, distressed to hear those heavy steps, weary with suffering, that shook the floorboards. About four o'clock, as she heard Louise pacing about in great agitation, she made up her mind to knock on Lazare's door; he had shut himself up in a state of nervous exasperation against the misfortunes with which Fate, so he said, had overwhelmed him.

'We can't leave her like that,' she explained. 'We must talk to her. Come along with me.'

They found her standing in the middle of the first floor landing, bending over the banisters, without strength either to go up or down. 'My dear child,' Pauline said gently, 'we're worried about you . . . We're going to send for the midwife.'

Then Louise grew angry. 'Good heavens, how can you torment me like this when I only want to be left in peace? At eight months, what can you expect the midwife to do?'

'It would be more sensible, though, to see her.'

'No, I won't, I know what it is . . . For pity's sake don't talk to me, don't torment me!'

And Louise showed such stubbornness, such exaggerated anger that Lazare, in his turn, lost his temper. Pauline had to promise categorically that she would not send for the midwife. This midwife was one Madame Bouland from Verchemont, who had an extraordinary reputation throughout the region for her skill and energy. People declared that her equal was not to be found at Bayeux or even at Caen. For this reason Louise, who was very timorous of pain and who was obsessed by a foreboding that she would die in

249

labour, had decided to put herself into this woman's hands. But she was none the less terrified of Madame Bouland, with that irrational terror that makes one put off till the last moment a visit to the dentist who can cure one.

At six o'clock there was another sudden respite. Louise was triumphant; she'd told them so, it was just the usual pains, only more violent; a lot of good it would have done to disturb everybody for nothing. However, as she was quite worn out, she preferred to go straight to bed, after eating a cutlet. Everything would be all right, she assured them, if only she could sleep. And she obstinately rejected all offers of help; she wanted to be alone while they had their dinner, and she even forbade them to come up and see her for fear of being woken suddenly.

That evening, dinner consisted of broth and a piece of roast veal. The first part of the meal took place in silence, for Louise's attack added to the sadness caused by Pauline's imminent departure. They tried to avoid the clatter of spoons and forks as though it could reach the first floor and exasperate the sufferer even further. Chanteau, however, was just embarking on stories of extraordinary pregnancies when Véronique, as she brought in the dish of sliced veal, suddenly remarked: 'I don't know, but it seems as though she's groaning up there.'

Lazare got up and opened the door in the passage. They all stopped eating and listened attentively. At first they heard nothing; then long, muffled groans reached their ears.

'It's started again,' murmured Pauline. 'I'm going up.'

She threw down her napkin, without even touching the slice of veal the maid was putting on her plate. Luckily the key was in the door and she was able to go in. The young woman, sitting on the edge of her bed, barefoot, with a dressing-gown thrown around her, was swaying to and fro like a pendulum and uttering loud, rhythmical sighs, under the pressure of an unbearable, unremitting pain.

'Is it worse?' asked Pauline.

She did not answer.

'Will you let us fetch Madame Bouland now?'

Then she replied brokenly, with an air of harassed resignation: 'Yes, I don't care. Perhaps I'll have some peace after that . . . I can't stand it, I can't stand it . . . '

Lazare, who had followed Pauline and stood listening at the door, ventured to go in, saying that it might be wise to go on to Arromanches and bring back Dr. Cazenove, in case complications might develop. But Louise began to weep. Hadn't they any conception what state she was in? Why did they torture her like this? They knew quite well how much she had always loathed the idea of having a man to deliver her. Her feminine vanity took the form of a morbid modesty, an unwillingness to be seen in the dreadful disarray of pain, which made her, even before her husband and her cousin, pull her wrapper tightly round her poor tortured loins.

'If you go and fetch the doctor,' she gasped, 'I shall lie down, I shall turn my face to the wall and not speak a word to anyone.'

'Bring back the midwife in any case,' Pauline told Lazare. 'I can't believe myself that the time has already come. It's just a question of quietening her.'

They both went down again. Abbé Horteur had just come in to pay a brief goodnight visit to Chanteau, and he was standing silent in front of the frightened invalid. They tried to make Lazare eat a little meat at least, before setting off; but he was quite beside himself, and declaring that a single mouthful would choke him, he hurried off towards Verchemont.

'I think she called me,' said Pauline, running towards the staircase. 'If I need Véronique I'll knock . . . Finish your dinner without me, won't you, uncle.'

The priest, embarrassed at landing in the middle of a confinement, could not find his usual consolatory words. He finally withdrew, promising to come back after visiting the Gonins, where the old cripple was very ill. And Chanteau sat on alone, in front of the table covered with a confusion of dishes. The glasses were half-full, the veal was congealing in the plates, greasy forks and scraps of half-eaten bread were lying about where they had been thrown in the wave of anxiety that had swept over the table. The maid, while she set a kettle of water on the fire in case of need, grumbled at not knowing whether to clear up or leave everything in chaos.

Upstairs, Pauline had found Louise standing up, leaning against the back of a chair.

'It's agony when I sit down. Help me to walk about!'

Since that morning she had complained of a tingling sensation all over her skin as if insects had stung her sharply. Now she was suffering from internal cramps, as though her abdomen were held in in a vice, crushing her more tightly. As soon as she sat or lay down a mass of lead seemed to be crushing her inwards; and feeling she had to keep on the move, she took the arm of her cousin, who helped her to walk between the bed and the window.

'You're a bit feverish,' the girl said. 'Would you like a drink?'

251

Louise could not reply. A violent contraction bent her double, and she clung to Pauline's shoulders' with a great shudder that set them both trembling. She uttered involuntary cries of mingled impatience and terror.

'I'm dying of thirst,' she muttered when she was finally able to speak. 'My tongue's dry, and you see how flushed I am . . . Oh no, no, don't leave go of me, I might fall. Come on, let's keep moving, I'll drink later.'

And she started off again, dragging her feet, swaying her body, leaning ever more heavily on Pauline's supporting arm. For two hours she walked without a pause. It was nine o'clock. Why hadn't that midwife come? Now she was longing for her desperately, saying that they must want to see her die if they left her without help so long. Verchemont was only twenty-five minutes away, an hour should have been enough. Lazare must be amusing himself, or else there had been an accident, and it was too late, nobody would come back. A fit of nausea shook her and she vomited.

'Go away, I don't want you to stay here! Good Lord, what a state to have reached, to be an object of disgust to everybody!'

Throughout her appalling suffering, she was chiefly concerned about her feminine modesty and attractiveness. In spite of her delicate frame she had great nervous resistance, and she put all the strength that was left her into not letting herself go, worried because she had not been able to put on her stockings and ashamed of the least bit of naked flesh she might show. But an even greater embarrassment seized her; she was ceaselessly tormented by imaginary needs, and she insisted on her cousin turning her back while she wrapped herself in a corner of the curtain and tried to relieve herself. As the maid had come up to offer help, she stammered in a frantic voice, fancying she felt a sensation of heaviness coming on: 'Oh no, not in front of her . . . Please, take her into the passage for a minute.'

Pauline was beginning to grow desperate. Ten o'clock struck, and she could not account for Lazare's prolonged absence. Probably he had failed to find Madame Bouland; but however was she to manage, in her ignorance of what had to be done, with this poor creature who seemed to be getting worse all the time? She recalled some of the books she had once read, and she would have liked to examine Louise in the hope of reassuring herself and the patient too. Only she felt the latter so self-conscious that she hesitated to propose it.

'Listen, dear,' she said at last, ' suppose you let me look?'

'You? Oh no, no! You're not married.'

Pauline could not help laughing.

'That doesn't matter, I promise you! I'd be so glad if I could relieve you.'

'No, I'd die of shame, I'd never be able to look you in the face.'

When eleven struck they could bear to wait no longer. Véronique set off for Verchemont, armed with a lantern and instructions to search all the ditches. Twice, Louise had tried to go to bed, as her legs were aching with fatigue; but each time she had immediately got up again, and now she was standing with her elbows propped on the chest of drawers, making a ceaseless writhing motion with her hips. The pains, which had occurred spasmodically, now came closer together, and were merging into a single pain so violent that it took her breath away. She kept lifting her fumbling hands from the chest of drawers and sliding them along her flanks to clutch and grip her buttocks as though to relieve them of a crushing weight. And Pauline, who stood beside her, could do nothing for her, had to watch her suffering, had to turn away and pretend to be busy when she saw her draw the wrapper round her with a shamefaced air, still worrying meanwhile about the untidiness of her beautiful fair hair and the havoc wrought by pain on her delicate features.

It was almost midnight when the sound of wheels brought Pauline swiftly downstairs.

'What about Véronique?' she shouted from the porch, when she recognized Lazare and the midwife. 'Didn't you meet her?'

Lazare explained that they had come by way of Port-en-Bessin; he'd had every sort of misadventure, Madame Bouland had been visiting a woman in labour nine miles away, and having neither horse nor carriage to go and fetch her he'd had to run the nine miles; once there, there had been endless tiresome complications; fortunately, Madame Bouland had her own horse and trap.

'But the woman,' asked Pauline, 'was it all over there? Was Madame able to leave her?'

Lazare's voice quivered as he replied, in muffled tones: 'The woman died.'

They went into the hall, which was lit by a candle standing on one of the stairs. There was silence, while Madame Bouland hung up her cloak. She was a swarthy, lean little woman, sallow as a lemon, with a domineering beak of a nose; she had a loud voice and a despotic manner, which earned her the veneration of the peasants.

'Will you be good enough to follow me, Madame?' said Pauline. 'I didn't know what to do next, she's not stopped moaning since nightfall.'

In her bedroom, Louise was still standing in front of the chest of drawers, treading the ground restlessly. She began to cry again when she caught sight of the midwife. The latter asked her a few brief questions about dates, and about the location and character of her pains. Then she concluded curtly: 'Well, we'll see . . . I can't say anything until I've found out the position.'

'Is it going to be now?' whispered Louise in tears. 'Oh, my God! At eight months! And I thought I'd still got another month!'

Without replying, Madame Bouland was thumping the pillows and putting them up in the middle of the bed. Lazare, who had come upstairs, had the inevitably awkward air of a man in the middle of a scene of childbirth. However, he went up to his wife and laid a kiss on her sweating forehead, although she seemed unconscious of this gesture of affection and encouragement.

'Come on, come on,' said the midwife.

Louise, terrified, threw a glance of mute entreaty at Pauline, which the latter understood. She drew Lazare outside, and they both stood on the landing, unable to move further off. The candle, down below, lit up the staircase with a dim glow like a nightlight, intersected with strange shadows; and they stood there, one leaning against the wall and the other against the banisters, facing one another in motionless silence. They listened intently; vague moans kept issuing from the room, and there were a couple of heartrending cries. Then, after what seemed an endless lapse of time, the midwife opened the door again. They were about to go in, but she pushed them back and came out herself, shutting the door behind her.

'What's happening?' murmured Pauline.

She made a sign to them to go down; and it was not until they were at the foot of the stairs, in the passage, that she spoke.

'The case looks like being serious. It's my duty to warn the family.'

Lazare blanched. An icy shiver ran over his face. He faltered: 'What is it?'

'The child's presenting itself with the left shoulder forward, as far as I can make out, and I'm even afraid that the arms may come out first.'

'Well?' asked Pauline.

' In a case like this, the presence of a doctor is absolutely essential. I can't take the responsibility for the delivery, especially at eight months.'

254

There was a silence. Then Lazare protested desperately: Where was he to find a doctor at this hour of the night? His wife might die twenty times over before he'd been able to fetch the doctor from Arromanches.

'I don't think there's any immediate danger,' the midwife declared. 'Go off at once . . . I can't do anything by myself.'

And as Pauline, in her turn, implored her to do something, for pity's sake, to bring a little relief to the wretched woman whose loud moans still echoed through the house, she declared in her firm voice:

'No, I'm not allowed to . . . The other woman, over yonder, died . . . I'm not going to be responsible for this one.'

Just then they heard Chanteau calling from the dining-room, in a mournful whine: 'Are you there? Do come in! . . . Nobody tells me anything. I've been waiting for news for ages.'

They went in. Since dinner had been interrupted, Chanteau had sat there forgotten, in front of the table from which nothing had been cleared; he was twiddling his thumbs and waiting patiently, with the drowsy resignation of a cripple used to long periods of lonely immobility. This new disaster, which was upsetting the whole household, made him downcast; and he had not even the heart to finish eating, but sat staring down at his full plate.

'Isn't it going all right?' he murmured.

Lazare shrugged his shoulders, in a frenzy. Madame Bouland, who retained the utmost calm, advised him to waste no more time.

'Take my trap. The horse doesn't go very fast; but in two or two-and-a-half hours you can get there and back. I'll keep watch in the meanwhile.'

Then, abruptly making up his mind, he dashed outside, convinced that he would come back to find his wife dead. He could be heard cursing and hitting the horse, and the trap finally rattled off.

'What's happening?' repeated Chanteau, as nobody answered him.

The midwife was already on her way up, and Pauline followed her, after simply telling her uncle that poor Louise was having a difficult time. As she offered to put him to bed, he refused; he wanted to stay up, to know what happened. If he felt sleepy he could quite well doze off in his armchair, as he sometimes did for whole afternoons. Hardly had they left him alone when Véronique came in, with her lantern blown out. She was furious. Not for the past two years had she let out such a torrent of words.

'Why couldn't they tell me they were coming back by the other road? There was I looking in all the ditches and I even went as far as Verchemont, more fool I! . . . And there I waited a good half-hour stuck in the middle of the road.'

Chanteau was staring at her, round-eyed.

'Well, my lass, you couldn't possibly have met them.'

'Then on my way back who should I see but Monsieur Lazare driving along at a crazy gallop, in a wretched little cart . . . I shouted to him that he was wanted at home, and he only lashed out harder and nearly ran me down . . . No, I've had enough of these errands where you don't know what's happening. Besides, my lantern's gone out."

And she began to hustle her master, she tried to force him to finish eating, so that she could at least clear the table. He wasn't hungry, but he would just take a little cold veal for the sake of something to do. What worried him now was the fact that the *abbé* had let him down. Why promise to keep people company if you've decided to stay at home? Although really priests did seem rather out of place, when women were in labour! The notion tickled him, and he prepared quite cheerfully to have supper by himself.

'Now then, Monsieur, hurry up,' repeated Véronique. 'It's nearly one o'clock, and my dishes can't lie around like that till morning . . . What a house, where there's always something to upset you!'

She was beginning to take away the plates when Pauline called her from the stairs with an urgent ring in her voice. And Chanteau was left once more sitting forgotten at the table, and nobody came down to give him any news.

Madame Bouland had taken authoritative possession of the room; she gave orders, she hunted in drawers. First she had a fire lit, for the room seemed to her damp. Then she declared that the bed wouldn't do, it was too low and too soft; and when Pauline told her there was an old camp-bed in the attic, she sent Véronique up to fetch it. She fixed it up in front of the fireplace, laying a board on it and covering it with a single mattress. Then she needed a quantity of linen: a sheet which she folded in four to protect the mattress, more sheets, towels and cloths which she hung over chairs in front of the fire to warm. Soon the room, cluttered with linen and blocked up by the bed, began to look like a field-hospital hurriedly installed on the eve of a battle.

Meanwhile, moreover, she never stopped talking, exhorting Louise in soldierly tones, as though she were giving orders to pain. Pauline had begged her, in a whisper, not to mention the doctor.

'You're going to be all right, dear. I'd rather have you lying down, but if it worries you, just keep on walking, you can lean on

256

me . . . I've delivered some at eight months that had the biggest children of the lot. . . . No, no, it doesn't hurt you as much as you fancy. We're going to make you comfortable by and by, in next to no time.'

Louise could not calm down. Her cries took on a character of fearful distress. She clung to the furniture, uttering, at intervals, incoherent phrases suggestive of delirium. The midwife tried to reassure Pauline by explaining, in a low voice, that the pains caused by the dilatation of the mouth of the womb were sometimes more intolerable than the actual pangs of parturition. She had seen this preparatory process go on for two days, with a first child. She was chiefly afraid lest the waters should break before the doctor came; the operation that he was going to have to perform would, in that case, be dangerous.

'I can't stand it,' repeated Louise, gasping. 'I can't stand it . . . I'm going to die . . .'

Madame Bouland had decided to give her twenty drops of laudanum in half a glass of water. Then she tried massaging the lumbar regions. The wretched woman, whose strength was failing, lost all her self-control; she no longer demanded that her cousin and the maïd should leave the room, she merely tried to hide her nakedness by pulling down her wrapper, clutching the ends of it in her tense hands. But the brief respite induced by the massage did not last; and she began to suffer terrible dragging pains.

'We must wait,' said Madame Bouland stoically. 'There's absolutely nothing I can do. Nature must take its course.'

And she even launched into an argument about chloroform, against which she had the prejudices of the old school. According to her, women in childbirth died like flies when their doctors used the drug. Pain was essential, a sleeping woman could never have as good a labour as a wideawake one.

Pauline had read the opposite. She made no reply; her heart was brimming over with compassion at the sight of the ravages of pain, which were gradually destroying Louise and reducing all her grace, her charm, her delicate fairness into something appalling and pitiable. And she felt stirred by indignation against pain, by an urge to conquer it, which would have made her fight it like an enemy if she had known how.

The night was passing, it was nearly two. Louise had several times spoken of Lazare; and they lied to her, they told her he had stayed downstairs because he was so agitated himself that he was afraid of discouraging her. In any case, she had lost all sense of time;

hours passed, and minutes seemed eternal. The only feeling that persisted throughout her turmoil was that it would never end, that nobody was really trying to help her. She blamed the others for refusing to bring her relief; she abused the midwife, Pauline and Véronique, accusing them of knowing nothing of what ought to be done.

Madame Bouland said not a word. She kept casting furtive glances at the clock, although she did not expect the doctor for another hour, knowing the slowness of her broken-down old horse. The dilatation was almost complete now, and the waters would break any minute; and she persuaded the young woman to lie down. Then she warned her.

'Don't be alarmed if you suddenly feel wet . . . and stop moving about, for heaven's sake; I'd rather things didn't happen too quickly now.'

Louise stayed motionless for a few seconds. She needed an extreme effort of will to restrain the wild heaves to which her pain gave rise; it exacerbated her agony, and soon she could control herself no longer, but leapt from the bed with a frantic jerk of her whole body. At the very instant when her feet touched the carpet there came a dull sound like a water-skin bursting, and her legs were soaked, while two great wet patches appeared on her wrapper.

'There it goes!' said the midwife, cursing between her teeth.

Although she had been warned, Louise stood there trembling, watching the torrent stream out of herself, terrified of seeing the wrapper and the carpet soaked in her blood. But the patches stayed pale, and the flood stopped abruptly; and she felt reassured. They put her back to bed quickly, and she enjoyed a sudden sense of calm and unexpected well-being that made her say with an air of triumphant cheerfulness: "That was what was bothering me. Now my pain's quite gone, it's all over . . . I knew I couldn't have a baby at eight months; it'll be for next month . . . You none of you knew anything about it.'

Madame Bouland shook her head, not wanting to spoil her momentary respite by telling her that the major pangs of parturition were still to come. She merely warned Pauline, in an undertone, to stand on the other side of the bed to save Louise from falling in case she should struggle in her labour. But when the pangs started up again, Louise made no attempt to get up; she had neither the will nor the strength to do so now. At the first recrudescence of pain her face had become livid and resumed an expression of despair. She spoke no more, she withdrew inside that endless torture in

258

which she no longer counted on help from anybody, feeling so forlorn and so miserable by now that she wanted to die at once. Besides, it was no longer the involuntary contractions that had been tearing at her inwards for twenty hours; now it was an atrocious straining effort of her whole being, which she could not repress, which she even exaggerated, impelled by an irresistible need to seek relief. The downward thrust, starting just below her ribs, ran through her loins and reached the groin in a sort of ever-widening rent. All the muscles in her abdomen were in action, tightening over the hips, contracting and expanding like springs; even those of her buttocks and thighs were working too, and every now and then seemed to lift her off the mattress. She could not stop trembling; she was shaken from waist to knees by a succession of painful waves, visibly rippling downwards under her skin, while her flesh stiffened in ever more violent convulsions.

'Will it never stop? Great heavens, will it never stop?' whispered Pauline.

The sight had swept away her usual courage and serenity. And she found herself pushing too, in an imagined effort, at each of the moaning gasps with which the travailing woman accompanied her efforts. The cries, low at first, gradually swelled into wails of weary helplessness. It was like the maddened desperate groan of a wood-cutter who for hours has heaved his axe at the same knot of wood without even succeeding in breaking its bark.

Between each spasm, in the brief instant of rest, Louise complained of burning thirst. Her parched throat gulped painfully as if she were choking.

'I'm dying—give me a drink!'

She took sips of a light lime-tea that Véronique was keeping warm in front of the fire. But often, just as she was putting the cup to her lips, Pauline had to take it back, for another spasm drew on and her hands began to shake, while her upturned face flushed crimson and her neck broke out in sweat, as a fresh pressure tensed all her muscles.

Cramps overcame her too. She wanted constantly to get up and relieve herself; the midwife protested vigorously. 'Keep still, please! It's only an effect of your labour . . . If you do get up you won't be able to do anything, so what's the good?'

At three o'clock, Madame Bouland no longer concealed her anxiety from Pauline. Alarming symptoms were developing, especially a slow decrease of strength. It seemed as though the travailing woman were suffering less, for her cries and efforts had grown weaker; but the truth was that her labour was threatening to come to a stop through excessive weariness. She was giving way under this unremitting pain, and each minute's delay became dangerous. Once more she grew delirious; she even fainted. Madame Bouland took advantage of this to feel her again and ascertain the child's position.

'It's as I feared,' she muttered. 'Has that horse broken its legs, or why don't they come?'

And as Pauline begged her not to let the unfortunate woman die thus, she burst out: 'D'you think I'm enjoying myself? . . . If I try the operation and it goes badly, I shall get into all sorts of hot water . . . I tell you they don't have any mercy on us.'

When Louise regained consciousness she complained of a fresh discomfort.

'It's the little arm coming out,' whispered Madame Bouland. 'It's completely free . . . But the shoulder's stuck, it'll never come out."

At three o'clock, however, as the situation had grown even more critical, she might perhaps have taken on herself to act, when Véronique, who was coming up from the kitchen, called Mademoiselle into the passage and told her that the doctor was there. Leaving the maid in charge of the patient for a minute, Pauline and the midwife went downstairs. In the middle of the courtyard, Lazare was cursing brokenly at the horse; but when he heard that his wife was still alive his relief was so sharp that he suddenly calmed down. Dr. Cazenove was already running up the steps, questioning Madame Bouland hurriedly.

'It would frighten her if you suddenly appeared,' Pauline told him on the stairs. 'Now you're here she must be warned.'

'Be quick about it,' he answered shortly.

Pauline went in alone; the others stood in the doorway.

'Darling,' she explained, 'd'you know, when the doctor saw you yesterday he suspected something, and he's just come . . . You'd better let him see you, since it's going on such a long time.'

Louise seemed not to hear. She was desperately rolling her head about the pillow. At last she gasped out: 'Just as you like. Good Lord what do I care now? There's nothing left of me.'

The doctor had come forward. Then the midwife sent Pauline and Lazare downstairs; she would bring them news, or call them if help were needed. They withdrew in silence. Downstairs in the dining-room Chanteau had fallen asleep, sitting at the table, from which the things had been cleared. Sleep seemed to have overtaken him in the middle of his little supper, which he had prolonged for the sake of something to do, for the fork was still on the edge of the plate, on which lay the remains of some veal. Pauline, when she went in, had to turn up the lamp, which was smoking and going out.

'Don't let's wake him,' she whispered. 'There's no need for him to know.'

She sat down quietly on a chair, while Lazare remained standing, motionless. A terrible period of waiting began; neither of them spoke a word, and they could not even bear the anguish in one another's eyes, but averted their heads whenever their glances met. And no noises came from up above; the enfeebled cries could no longer be heard, and they listened attentively in vain, catching no sound but the throbbing of their own fevered pulses. It was this utter, tense silence, this silence of death, which, being prolonged, frightened them most. What could be happening? Why had they been sent away? They would rather have heard cries and struggles, some sign of life and resistance going on overhead. The minutes flowed by and the house sank ever deeper into this nothingness. At last the door opened and Dr. Cazenove came in.

'Well?' asked Lazare, who had finally sat down opposite Pauline.

The doctor did not answer immediately. In the dim, smoky lamplight—that uncertain glimmer that accompanies long vigils—they could not clearly distinguish his old tanned face, on which only the wrinkles turned pale even under the stress of strong emotion. But when he spoke, the broken tone of his words betrayed the conflict that was going on within.

'Well, I've done nothing yet,' he replied. 'I don't want to do anything without consulting you.'

And with a mechanical gesture, he passed his fingers over his brow as if to drive away an obstacle, a knot which he could not untie.

'But it's not for us to decide, doctor,' said Pauline. 'We're leaving her in your hands.'

He shook his head. An importunate memory haunted him, that of certain negresses whom he had delivered during his colonial days, one in particular, a big woman whose child, like this one, had been presented shoulder first, and who had died while he was delivering her of a parcel of bones and flesh. These were the only sorts of experience available to a naval surgeon, while doing his hospital service out there; occasionally he had had to rip the mother open. Since his retirement to Arromanches he had had more practice, and through habit had acquired skill; but the difficulty of the present case, and the fact that the family were his friends, had reduced him to his former lack of confidence. He was as nervous as any novice, and felt anxious about his old hands, which had lost the energy of youth.

'I've got to tell you everything,' he went on. 'It looks hopeless for both mother and child . . . Perhaps there's still time to save one or the other of them.'

Lazare and Pauline had started up, both smitten with the same chill horror. Chanteau, awakened by the sound of voices, had opened bleary eyes, and was listening in alarm to what was being said in front of him.

'Which am I to try and save?' repeated the doctor, trembling as much as the poor creatures to whom he was putting the question. ' The child or the mother?'

'Which? My God!' cried Lazare. 'I don't know, I can't say!'

Tears choked him again, while his cousin, very white, stood mute, confronted by this terrible alternative.

'If I attempt a version,' went on the doctor, discussing his own doubts aloud, ' the child will probably get smashed up on the way out. And I'm afraid of exhausting the mother, she's already been in pain too long . . . On the other hand, a Caesarean would guarantee the life of the child, but the poor woman's state isn't so desperate as to justify me in sacrificing her like that . . . It's a question of conscience, and I entreat you to give an opinion yourselves.'

Lazare could not speak for sobs. He had taken his handkerchief and was twisting it convulsively in a strenuous effort to collect his wits again. Chanteau still stared at them in stupefaction. And it was Pauline who managed to say:

'Why did you come down? . . . It's cruel to torture us, when you're the only one who can know and do anything.'

At that moment Madame Bouland came in to tell them that the situation was growing worse.

'Have you decided? She's getting weaker.'

Then, acting on one of his disconcertingly abrupt impulses, the doctor flung his arms round Lazare, addressing him affectionately:

'Listen, I'm going to try and save them both. And if the worst should happen, well, I'll be even sadder than you, because I shall think it was my fault.'

Briefly, with the alacrity of one who has made up his mind, he discussed the use of chloroform. He had brought the wherewithal, but certain symptoms made him fear a possible haemorrhage, which was an explicit counter-indication. The patient's fainting-fits and weak pulse worried him. He therefore resisted the entreaties of her relatives, who, deeply distressed by her pain which they had been sharing for nearly four-and-twenty hours, pleaded for chloroform; and he was encouraged in his refusal by the attitude of the midwife, who shrugged her shoulders with disgust and contempt.

'I deliver quite two hundred women a year,' she muttered. 'Do they need that stuff to pull through?... They put up with pain, well, everybody puts up with pain!'

'Come upstairs, my dears,' went on the doctor. 'I shall need you ... And besides I'd rather have you by me.'

They were all leaving the dining-room when Chanteau spoke at last. He called his son. 'Come and kiss me ... Oh, that poor little Louise! Isn't it terrible, the things that happen when you're not expecting them! If only it were daylight! Let me know when it's over.'

Once more, he was left alone in the room. The lamp was smoking, and he closed his eyes, dazzled by the uncertain light, and overcome with drowsiness again. Yet he struggled against it for some minutes, letting his eyes roam over the dishes lying on the table and the confusion of chairs, with napkins still hanging over them. But the atmosphere was too close, and the silence too oppressive. He yielded to sleep; his eyelids closed and a light regular breath stirred his lips, in the midst of the tragic disorder left by the interruption of last night's meal.

Upstairs, Dr. Cazenove advised them to light a big fire in the next room, Madame Chanteau's old room; it might be needed after the delivery. Véronique, who had been looking after Louise during the midwife's absence, went off to light it at once. Then everything was got ready; fresh fine linen was hung to air in front of the fireplace, a second basin was brought, and a kettle of hot water, a bottle of brandy and a plateful of lard were fetched up. The doctor thought it his duty to warn the patient.

'My dear child,' he said, 'don't be anxious, but it's absolutely necessary for me to help you ... Your life is precious to us all, and if the poor baby's in danger we can't leave you like this any longer ... You'll allow me to act, won't you?'

Louise seemed to hear nothing now. She lay tensely straining in unremitting involuntary efforts, with her head rolled over to the left on her pillow and her mouth open, uttering a low continuous moan like a death-rattle. When her eyelids lifted she gazed wildly at the ceiling as though she had woken up in a strange place.

'You'll let me?' repeated the doctor.

Then she faltered: 'Kill me, kill me at once.'

'Be quick, I implore you,' whispered Pauline to the doctor. 'We're here to take responsibility for everything.'

He persisted nevertheless, saying to Lazare: 'I can answer for her, provided there's no haemorrhage. But the child seems to me done for. Nine out of ten don't survive under these circumstances, for they always suffer lesions and fractures and sometimes get completely crushed.'

'Go on, go on, doctor,' answered the father, with a distracted gesture.

The camp bed was not considered solid enough. The young woman was transferred to the big bed, on which a board had been laid between the mattresses. She lay with her head turned towards the wall, propped up against a pile of pillows, and the small of her back on the very edge of the bed; her thighs were parted and her feet laid on the backs of two small armchairs.

'That's perfect,' said the doctor, as he contemplated these arrangements. 'We'll be all right, it's going to be quite convenient. Only you'd better hold her in case she struggles.'

Louise had lost consciousness. She lay inert and unresisting. Her feminine modesty, her unwillingness to be seen naked and in pain, had yielded at last, swept away by suffering. Too weak to lift so much as a finger, she was unaware of her nakedness and of the hands that were touching her. And she lay there uncovered up to the throat, her belly in the air and her legs wide apart, without even a quiver, exposing the bloodstained, gaping spectacle of parturition.

'Madame Bouland can hold one of the thighs,' the doctor went on, 'and you, Pauline, you'll have to help by holding the other. Don't be afraid, hold it firm and prevent any movement . . . Now if Lazare would be kind enough to hold up the light for me.'

They obeyed his orders, for they too had lost consciousness of her nudity. They saw nothing but the pitiful misery of it, the dramatic struggle for birth, which killed all sense of love. Thus brutally exposed to the light, all the disturbing mystery had gone from that delicate skin with its secret places, with its fair crispy fleece; nothing remained but suffering humanity, childbirth amidst blood and ordure, the mother's womb strained to bursting-point, the red slit stretched agonisingly, like the wound made by an axe in the trunk of some great tree, spilling its life-blood.

The doctor was still talking in an undertone, as he took off his coat and turned up his left shirt-sleeve above the elbow.

'We've waited too long, it's going to be difficult to get my hand in . . . You see, the shoulder's already engaged in the opening.'

Amidst the swollen, straining muscles, between pinkish folds of flesh, the child could be seen. But it had stopped there, unable to get past because of the narrowness of the organ. Meanwhile, however, the abdominal and lumbar muscles were still striving to expel it; even unconscious, the mother was still pushing violently, exhausting herself in labour, in the mechanical urge to be delivered; and the waves of pain still swept downwards, each accompanied by a cry in her stubborn battle against the impossible. The child's hand was hanging out of the vulva. It was a tiny black hand, its fingers opening and closing intermittently as though it were clutching at life.

'Let the leg give a little,' said Madame Bouland to Pauline. 'No need to wear her out.'

Dr. Cazenove was standing between the two knees, each held by one of the women. He turned round, puzzled at the way the light was flickering; Lazare, behind him, was trembling so violently that the candle shook in his hand as though in a great gust of wind.

'My dear fellow,' said the doctor, 'put the candlestick on the bedside table. I shall see better.'

Incapable of watching any longer, the husband retreated to the further end of the room and sank into a chair. But although he had stopped watching, he still kept on seeing the little creature's pathetic hand, clinging to life, seeming to grope for help in this world into which it had led the way.

Then the doctor knelt down. He had smeared his left hand with lard, and he began to introduce it slowly, laying the right hand on the abdomen. He had to push back the little arm, push it right inside again, to make room for his own fingers; and that was the dangerous part of the operation. After that stretching out his fingers like a wedge, he gradually worked them in with a light rotary movement, which enabled him to introduce his whole hand up to the wrist. The hand sank in deeper still, feeling for the child's knees, then for its feet; while the other hand pressed more firmly on the lower abdomen, helping the operation that was going on inside. But nothing could be seen of that operation; there was only an arm inside a body.

'Madame's very good,' observed Madame Bouland. 'It sometimes takes a couple of men to hold them down.'

Pauline could feel the wretched thigh shuddering with anguish, and she pressed it to her bosom with motherly tenderness.

'Be brave, darling,' she whispered.

There was silence. Louise could not have said what was happening to her, she only experienced a growing anxiety, a sensation of being torn apart. And Pauline could hardly recognize the slim girl with her delicate features and soft charm in this twisted creature lying across the bed, her face ravaged with suffering. Mucus slid between the operator's fingers and soiled the golden down that shadowed the white skin. A few drops of dark blood trickled through a fold of flesh and fell one by one on to the cloth that had been laid on the mattress.

Louise passed out once more; she seemed like dead, and her muscles practically stopped working.

'I'd rather have it like this,' said the doctor, when Madame Bouland warned him of it. 'She was crushing my hand, I was going to have to withdraw it, the pain was so unbearable! . . . Oh, I'm not as young as I was, or it'd have been finished by now.'

During the last few minutes, he had been holding the feet and was drawing them gently so as to turn the child over. There was a pause, and he had to compress the lower abdomen with his right hand. Then the left hand was smoothly withdrawn, first the wrist, then the fingers. And at last the child's feet appeared. Everyone felt a great relief; Cazenove heaved a sigh; his brow was bathed in sweat and he was panting as though after violent exercise.

'We're nearly home—I think it's all right, the little heart's still beating . . . But we haven't quite got the fellow yet !'

He had stood up again, with a show of laughter. He quickly asked Véronique for hot towels. Then, while he was washing his hand, which was soiled and bloodstained like a butcher's, he tried to cheer up the husband, who had collapsed in his chair.

'Nearly over, my lad. Take heart, for goodness' sake!'

Lazare did not stir. Madame Bouland, who had just roused Louise from her swoon by giving her a flask of ether to breathe, was chiefly worried by finding that the muscles were not working any more. She mentioned it to the doctor in an undertone; he replied out loud:

'I expected as much. I shall have to help her.' And he said to Louise, 'Don't hold yourself in, try and use your pains. If you help me a little, you'll see how easy it'll be.'

But she made a gesture to explain that she had no more strength left. They could hear her mutter faintly: 'I can't feel a single part of my body.'

'Poor darling!' said Pauline, kissing her. 'You're nearly at the end of your troubles now!'

The doctor had knelt down again. Once more the two women held the thighs, while Véronique handed him warm towels. He had wrapped them round the little feet, and drew these slowly down with a gentle, continuous pull; and as the child came out, he moved his fingers further up, grasping the ankles, the calves, the knees, seizing each new part as it emerged. When the child's hips appeared, he avoided putting any pressure on the mother's belly but passed his hands round her loins and pressed on the groin. The child was still sliding down, widening the folds of pinkish flesh, stretching them more tautly. But the mother, up till now submissive, suddenly resisted as she felt her pangs renewed. Now she was not merely straining; her whole body was shaking wildly, she felt as if it were being split in two with a heavy cleaver, like an ox's carcass in a butcher's shop. She fought against it so violently that she broke free from her cousin and the child slid out of the doctor's hands.

'Careful!' he cried. 'Try and stop her moving! ... We'll be lucky if the cord hasn't strangulated it.'

He had caught hold of the tiny body again, he hurriedly freed its shoulders and brought out the arms one after the other, to keep the volume of the head as small as possible. But the convulsive jerks of the mother made his task difficult, and he had constantly to stop for fear of breaking something. In vain the two women held her down with all their might on her bed of pain; she shook them off, arching her body, with an uncontrollable stiffening of the spine. As she struggled she seized hold of the frame of the bed, and could not be got to let go; she pressed against it, violently stretching out her legs, possessed by the need to shake off these people who were torturing her. She was in an utter frenzy, screaming horribly as she felt that she was being murdered, that her whole body was being ripped apart.

'There's only the head to come now,' said the doctor, his voice shaking. 'I daren't touch it, while she keeps leaping about so ... Since her pains have begun again she'll probably deliver herself. Let's wait a little.'

He had to sit down. Madame Bouland, without leaving go of the mother, watched over the child, which was lying between the bloodstained thighs, still held back by the neck and almost strangled. Its little limbs stirred feebly, then all movement ceased. They grew alarmed again, and the doctor thought of stimulating

267

muscular contractions to precipitate things. He got up, and brought sudden, repeated pressure to bear on the mother's abdomen. And there were a few appalling minutes, when the wretched woman shrieked louder still as the head came out, pushing back the flesh into a great whiteish ring. Below, between the two distended and gaping cavities, the delicate skin bulged horribly, worn so thin that a rupture seemed imminent. Then there was a spurt of excrement, and the child tumbled out in a final jerk, with a shower of blood and foul water.

'At last!' said Cazenove. 'Well, he can boast he didn't come into the world merrily!'

In the intense emotional excitement, nobody had bothered about the sex of the child.

'It's a boy, sir,' Madame Bouland informed the husband.

Lazare, his head turned to the wall, burst into sobs. He felt possessed by a boundless despair, by the thought that it would be better for them all to die than to go on living after such suffering. The birth of this new being made him deathly sad.

Pauline bent over Louise and kissed her brow once more.

'Come and kiss her,' she told her cousin.

He went up and bent over in his turn. But he was seized with a fresh shudder at the touch of that face, bathed in cold sweat. His wife lay there with closed eyes, not breathing. And he began to sob wildly again, leaning his head against the wall.

'I think it's dead,' said the doctor in a low voice. 'Fasten the cord quickly.'

The child, at its birth, had not uttered the usual mewing cry, accompanied by the low gurgling sound of the lungs filling with air. It was bluish-black in colour, livid in places, small for its eight months, with an excessively large head.

Madame Bouland neatly severed and tied the cord, after letting a slight discharge of blood flow out. The child was still not breathing and the heart-beats could not be felt.

'It's done for,' declared Cazenove. 'It might be possible to try rubbing it and breathing into it, but I think it'd be waste of time ... And besides the mother is badly in need of my attention.'

Pauline was listening.

'Give it to me,' she said. 'I'll see ... If it doesn't start breathing, it'll be because I've no more breath myself.'

And she carried the baby into the next room, after first taking in the bottle of brandy and some linen.

Fresh pangs, though much weaker ones, had roused Louise from her prostration. They were the last pains of delivery. When the doctor had helped her to expel the after-birth by pulling at the umbilical cord, the midwife lifted her up to take away the towels, which had just been stained by a thick rush of blood. Then the two of them stretched her out, with her thighs washed and separated by a napkin, and a broad linen binder fastened round her abdomen. The doctor was still harassed by fear of a haemorrhage, although he had made sure that there was no more blood left inside and that she had not lost more than the normal quantity. Moreover the afterbirth seemed practically entire; but the weakness of his patient, and above all the cold sweat that bathed her, were still very alarming. She lay quite motionless, with the sheet up to her chin, pale as wax, and cold despite the weight of her covers. The doctor was still feeling her pulse.

'Stay here,' he told the midwife, 'I'm not going to leave her till I'm quite reassured.'

On the other side of the passage, in Madame Chanteau's old room, Pauline was fighting against the increasing asphyxia of the wretched little creature she had brought there. She had hurriedly laid it down on an armchair in front of the big fire; and she knelt there, massaging it unceasingly with a piece of linen dipped in a saucerful of alcohol, with stubborn faith, unaware of the cramp that was gradually numbing her whole arm. The infant was so skinny and so pitifully frail that she was terrified of killing it right off by rubbing too hard. And so she used a to-and-fro movement that was as gentle as a caress, like the continuous brushing of a bird's wing. She turned it over carefully, trying to bring back life into each of the tiny limbs. But still it did not stir. The rubbing warmed it a little but its chest remained hollow, without any sign of breath. On the contrary, it seemed to take on an even bluer tinge.

Then, without shrinking from contact with that flabby, unwashed face, she pressed her mouth against the inert little mouth. She breathed out long slow breaths, adjusting them to the capacity of the narrow lungs into which the air had failed to enter. When she felt herself choking, she was forced to stop for a few seconds; then she began again. The blood rushed to her head and her ears buzzed; she felt dizzy. Yet she would not yield, she went on giving her breath for over half an hour, with never the least result to encourage her. When she breathed in, she could taste nothing but a faint, deathlike sickliness. She had tried in vain to get the child's sides into play by pressing them very gently with the tips of her fingers. Nothing succeeded, and anyone else would have given up this impossible resurrection. But she brought to her task the desperate stubbornness of a mother bringing into the world a puny child. She wanted it to live, and at last she felt a stirring of life in the poor little body, as the mouth quivered slightly under her own.

For almost an hour she had stayed in the room, oblivious of everything, frantic with the anguish of this struggle. That feeble sign of life, that brief sensation against her lips, gave her fresh courage. She began to rub the little limbs once more, she went on giving her breath, each in turn, without sparing herself, in her overflowing charity. She felt an ever-growing need to be victorious, to create life. For an instant she feared that she had been mistaken, for the lips to which hers were pressed still remained unmoving. Then she became aware once more of a rapid contraction. Little by little the air was going in; it was being taken from her and given back to her. Under her own bosom she thought she felt the heart begin to throb regularly. And her mouth clung to the little mouth, she shared the little creature's life, they had only one breath between them in this miraculous resurrection, a slow, prolonged breath that flowed between them like a shared soul. Slime and mucus soiled her lips, but her joy at having saved it banished all disgust; now she breathed in the sharp, warm air of life, and it made her dizzy with delight. When the child at last uttered a feeble, plaintive cry, she sank down in front of the chair, stirred to her very bowels.

The big fire was burning high, filling the room with a bright light. Pauline sat there on the ground in front of the child, at whom she had not looked. How puny he was! What a miserable half-formed creature! And she felt the stirrings of a last revolt within her, the protest of her own robust health against the wretched son that Louise had given to Lazare. She cast a despairing glance down over her own hips, over her virginal belly which had so lately thrilled with emotion. Her frame was broad enough to have held a strong sturdy child. An immense regret possessed her at the thought of her frustrated life, her womanhood doomed to wither in barrenness. The frenzy that had tormented her during that wedding-night began to flare up again at the sight of the newborn child. That morning, as it happened, she had woken to find herself bloodstained, with the useless discharge of her fecundity; and at this very moment, after the emotions of that terrible night, she felt it flowing away beneath her, like waste water. Never would she be a mother, and she could have wished that all the blood in her body might flow away like that, since she could not use it in the making of life. What was the good of that robust youth of hers, those organs and muscles swelling with sap, that flesh with its dark vigorous growth of down and its vital odour? She would be left like an unploughed field, to dry up neglected. Instead of the pitiful infant like a naked insect there on the chair, she imagined the sturdy boy that might have been born of her marriage, and she could not take comfort, and she wept for the child that she would not bear.

But the poor creature was still wailing. He began to struggle and she was afraid lest he should fall. Then at the sight of such wretchedness, such weakness, her charity was aroused. She could at least comfort him and help him to live, as she had, to her great joy, helped him to be born. And, forgetting herself, she took him on her knee, and attended to his essential needs, still weeping for her own unfulfilled maternity and with pity for the suffering of all living beings.

When Madame Bouland heard the news she came to help her wash the newborn infant. They wrapped it in a warm cloth at first, then they dressed it and laid it on the big bed until the cradle should be ready. The midwife, amazed to find the child still alive, had examined it carefully; she said it appeared to be quite well made, but so weakly that it would be difficult to rear. Then she hurried back beside Louise, who was still in considerable danger.

As Pauline was settling down by the child's side, Lazare, who had been told about the miracle, entered the room.

'Come and see him,' she said, deeply moved.

He was trembling as he drew near, and he could not help exclaiming: 'Good heavens! You've put him in that bed!'

A shiver ran through him on the threshold. This deserted room, so seldom entered and still overshadowed with mourning, had been transformed into a warm, luminous place, bright with flickering firelight. And yet the furniture was still in the same place, the clock still said thirty-seven minutes past seven, and nobody had lived here since his mother had died here. And it was in the very bed where she had drawn her last breath, that bed before which he had stood in awe and reverence, that he now saw his reborn son, so tiny in the middle of the broad sheets.

'Do you mind?' asked Pauline in surprise.

He shook his head. The strength of his emotion made him speechless. Then he stammered at last: 'I'm thinking of mother ... She's gone, and now here's this other who will go like her. Why did he come?'

Sobs interrupted his voice. Since Louise's terrible confinement, his fear and loathing for life had kept breaking out in spite of the effort he made to keep silent. When he had laid his lips on the child's wrinkled forehead he started back, feeling the softness of the skull yield beneath his lips. He felt desperate with remorse at the sight of this frail creature he had flung into existence.

'Don't worry,' went on Pauline, to reassure him. 'We'll make a sturdy fellow out of him . . . It makes no difference his being so small.'

He looked at her, so profoundly stirred that a whole confession broke from his heart.

'We owe his life to you—to you again. Am I always to be indebted to you?'

'Me?' she replied. 'I only did what the midwife would have done if she'd been by herself.'

He silenced her with a gesture. 'Do you think I'm so despicable that I don't understand that I owe you everything? . . . Since you first came into the house you've never stopped sacrificing yourself. I won't say any more about your money, but you still loved me when you gave me to Louise, I know that now . . . If you could only know how ashamed I feel when I look at you and remember! You'd have shed your own blood, and still stayed kind and cheerful even when I was breaking your heart! Oh, you were quite right, nothing counts but kindness and cheerfulness, all the rest is just a nightmare.'

She tried to interrupt him, but he went on, raising his voice: 'What a fool I've been, with my swaggering negativism, my wallowing in gloom out of sheer vanity and cowardice! It's my fault if our life has been spoilt—your life and my own and the whole family's . . . Yes, you've been the only wise one. Life becomes so easy when everybody's good-tempered, and people live for one another! . . . The world may be cracking up with misery, but let it crack up bravely and cheerfully, out of pity for itself!'

The violence of his expressions made her smile, and she seized him by the hands. 'Come now, calm yourself . . . Since you recognize that I'm right, you'll change your ways and everything'll go better.'

'Oh, yes indeed, change my ways! I'm saying this just now, because there are times when truth will out. But to-morrow I shall relapse into my old misery. Can people change? No, things won't get any better, on the contrary they'll get worse and worse. You know that as well as I . . . It's my own folly that infuriates me!'

Then she drew him gently to her and said, with her serious air: 'You're not foolish and you're not despicable, you're unhappy . . . Kiss me, Lazare.'

They exchanged a kiss, in front of the poor little creature that seemed to have dozed off; and it was the kiss of a brother and sister, where there was nothing left of the impulse of desire that only yesterday, had consumed them.

Dawn was breaking, a grey, infinitely gentle dawn. Cazenove came to look at the baby, and marvelled at finding it in such good condition. He suggested taking it back into the other room, for he now believed Louise to be out of danger. When the child was presented to its mother she gave a wan smile. Then she closed her eyes and sank into one of those deep, healing sleeps with which a mother regains her strength after childbirth. The window had been opened a little to let out the smell of blood; and a delicious coolness, a breath of life was wafted up with the high tide. They all stood motionless, weary and happy, by the bed where she slept. At last they withdrew with hushed steps, leaving only the midwife with her.

The doctor, however, did not leave till about eight o'clock. He was very hungry, and Lazare and Pauline themselves were starving; Véronique had to make them coffee and milk, and an omelette. Downstairs they had found Chanteau, forgotten by everybody, sound asleep in his armchair. Nothing had stirred, only the room was full of acrid fumes from the lamp, which was still smoking. Pauline observed with a laugh that the table seemed ready laid for them, as it was still covered with last night's dishes. She swept off the crumbs and tidied up a little. Then, as the coffee had not come, they attacked the cold veal, joking about the meal that had been interrupted by that terrible confinement. Now that the danger was past, they were as light-hearted as children.

'Believe me if you will,' Chanteau kept saying delightedly, 'but I wasn't really asleep . . . I was furious that nobody came down to give me any news, and yet I wasn't all that worried, for I dreamed that it was all going well.'

His happiness was increased by the appearance of Abbé Horteur, hurrying up after Mass. He made noisy fun of him. 'Well, how's this? So you deserted me? . . . Are you afraid of babies?'

The priest, to save his face, told how one evening he had delivered a woman by the wayside and then christened the child. After which he accepted a small glass of curaçao.

Bright sunlight was gilding the courtyard when Dr. Cazenove took his leave at last. As Lazare and Pauline walked down to see him off, he whispered to the girl: 'Aren't you leaving to-day?'

She stood for a minute in silence. Her great, thoughtful eyes seemed to search the distant horizon, looking into the future.

'No,' she answered. 'I must wait.'

CHAPTER XI

ALL May, the weather had been terrible; then June opened with fine, hot days. For the past three weeks the west wind had been blowing; storms had ravaged the coasts, smashed cliffs, sunk boats and killed people; and now the wide blue sky, the satin sea, the warm brilliant weather seemed infinitely sweet.

On this glorious afternoon, Pauline had decided to push Chanteau's armchair on to the terrace and to lay the baby beside him on a red woollen blanket. Little Paul was eighteen months old already; she was his godmother, and she spoilt the child as much as the old man.

'Shall you mind the sun, uncle?'

'No, indeed not! I haven't seen it for such an age! . . . And you're going to leave Paul asleep there?'

'Yes, yes, the air'll do him good.'

She was kneeling at the edge of the blanket, looking at the baby in his white frock, with his bare arms and legs. His eyes were closed and his little quiet, rosy face was upturned to the sky.

'It's quite true, he fell asleep at once,' she whispered. 'He was tired of rolling about . . . See that the animals don't worry him.'

She wagged a warning finger at Minouche, who was sitting on the dining-room window-sill, preening herself elaborately. In the sand, a little way off, Loulou lay stretched out, opening a mistrustful eye from time to time, ever ready to growl and snap.

As Pauline was getting up, Chanteau uttered a low cry.

'Is it starting up again?'

'Starting up again? Why, it never stops . . . Did I groan? Isn't it odd, I've got to the point when I groan unconsciously.'

He had become a dreadfully pitiable sight. Gradually his chronic gout had accumulated chalkstone in all his joints, and enormous tophs had formed, piercing through his skin in white growths. His feet, now concealed in slippers, were drawn up like the claws of a sick bird. But his hands displayed their deformity in all its horror;

each joint was swollen with red, glistening nodules, and the fingers were distorted by lumps that splayed them out and made them lopsided, particularly on the left hand, made hideous by a chalk-stone the size of a small egg. On the left elbow a heavier deposit had caused an ulcer. And his limbs were now completely anchylosed, he could use neither hands nor feet, and the few joints that still functioned a little creaked and rattled like a bag of marbles being shaken. His body had finally become petrified, as it were, in the posture he had adopted to make his pain more bearable, bent forward with a considerable twist to the right; so that he had grown into the shape of his armchair and stayed crooked even when he was put to bed. His pain never left him now, his inflammation reappeared at the slightest change in the weather, with the smallest glass of wine or mouthful of meat that he took beyond his rigid diet.

'Would you like a cup of milk?' asked Pauline. 'It might refresh you.'

'Oh, milk!' he answered between two groans. 'That was another invention, that milk cure! I think they finished me off with that . . . No, no, nothing at all, that's what suits me best.'

However, he asked her to shift the position of his left leg, for he could not move it by himself.

'The bitch is stinging to-day. Go on, shove it a bit further. Thanks, that's better . . . What a lovely day—oh Lord, oh Lord!'

With his eyes fixed on the boundless horizon, he went on moaning unconsciously. His cry of distress had become as natural as breathing. He was wearing a garment of thick blue flannel wide enough to conceal his gnarled limbs, but his deformed hands lay loose on his knees, looking pathetic in the broad sunlight. And he gazed absorbedly at the sea, that blue infinity over which white sails were drifting, that limitless road opening out before him, while he was no longer capable of setting one foot in front of the other.

Pauline, anxious about little Paul's bare legs, had knelt down again to cover him with a corner of the blanket. For three months, she had made up her mind each week to leave on the following Monday. But the child's frail hands held her back with invincible tenacity. During the first month, they had dreaded every morning that he would not live through the day. She alone had constantly renewed her life-saving miracle, for the mother was still in bed, and the wet-nurse they had had merely provided her milk, with the meek stupidity of a heifer. Pauline tended him unceasingly with the stubbornness of a broody hen, watching the temperature constantly, keeping him alive from hour to hour, to replace the month's gestation that he had missed. By the end of the first month he had fortunately become as strong as a full-term child, and had gradually developed. But he was still very puny, and she never left him for a minute, particularly since his weaning, which had been difficult.

'He won't take cold like this,' she said. 'Do look, uncle, how pretty he is on the red rug! It makes him look quite rosy.'

Chanteau painfully turned his head, the only part of his body which he could move. He whispered: 'If you kiss him you'll wake him up. Leave him alone, the little angel ... Did you see that steamer over there? It comes from Le Havre. It's going at a rate, isn't it?'

Pauline had to look at the steamer, to please him. It was a black dot against the immensity of water. A thin trail of smoke streaked the horizon. She stood motionless for a moment, under the wide limpid sky, watching the serene sea, rejoicing in this lovely day.

'Meanwhile my stew's burning,' she said, turning to go back to the kitchen. But as she was about to enter the house a voice called from the first floor: 'Pauline!'

It was Louise who, with her hair half done and wearing only a camisole, was leaning on the window-sill of Madame Chanteau's old room, which she and Lazare now occupied. She went on in a shrill tone: 'If Lazare's there, send him up.'

'No, he's not back yet.'

Louise lost her temper. 'I knew we shouldn't see him before this evening, if he even deigns to come back then! ... He stayed away last night again, although he'd promised faithfully! ... Oh, he's a nice one! When he goes to Caen he can't be got away from there.'

'He has so few distractions,' Pauline replied gently. 'And besides this fertiliser business must have taken a lot of time ... He'll probably get a lift home in the doctor's gig.'

Since they had been living at Bonneville, Lazare and Louise bickered constantly. They had no downright quarrels, only constantly recurring fits of ill-temper; theirs was the miserably spoilt life of two creatures who do not get on together. Her recovery after her confinement had been slow and painful, and now she led a wearisome, empty existence, for she had a horror of housework and would kill time reading or spend all day getting dressed. Lazare, once more a prey to boundless boredom, would not even open a book, but spent long hours in a daze, watching the sea; at rare intervals he would escape to Caen, whence he returned more weary still. And Pauline, who had to look after the house, had become indispensable to them, for she reconciled them three times a day.

'You'd better finish dressing,' she went on. 'The *curé*'ll be here soon, and you can stay with him and uncle. I'm so busy!'

But Louise clung to her resentment. 'How can he stop away so long? My father wrote to me about it yesterday; all our money's being squandered!'

The fact was that Lazare had already let himself be swindled in two unfortunate business ventures, so that Pauline, who was anxious for the sake of the child, her godson, had made over to him two-thirds of the money that was still left her by taking out an insurance which would provide him with a hundred thousand francs the day he came of age. Her income was now reduced to five hundred francs, but her only regret was that she had to restrict her usual charities.

'That's a pretty speculation, that fertiliser business!' went on Louise. 'My father's sure to have dissuaded him from it, so if he hasn't come back, he must be amusing himself . . . Oh, I don't care, let him go gadding about if he wants to!'

'Well then, why are you so angry?' retorted Pauline. 'Come now, the poor fellow doesn't mean any harm . . . You'll come down, won't you? What's possessed that Véronique to disappear on a Saturday and leave me with all the cooking on my hands?'

This was a mystery that had been puzzling them all for the last two hours. The maid had prepared the vegetables for the stew, plucked and trussed a duck, even laid the meat ready on a plate; then she had suddenly vanished as though the earth had swallowed her up; there was no further sign of her. Pauline, stupefied by this disappearance, had at last decided to cook the stew herself.

'Hasn't she come back?' asked Louise, forgetting her anger.

'Why, no,' Pauline replied. 'D'you know what my latest theory is? She paid forty sous for her duck from a woman that came to the door, and I remember mentioning to her I'd seen finer ones for thirty sous at Verchemont. Her expression changed immediately, and she gave me one of her dirty looks . . . Well, I bet she's gone off to Verchemont to see if I'd been lying.'

She was laughing, and there was a note of sadness in her laughter for she was much hurt by Véronique's renewed, unmotivated unkindness to her. The reversal of feeling which had been taking place in the woman's heart ever since the death of Madame Chanteau had gradually brought back all her old dislike of Pauline.

'For over a week now, we've not been able to get a word out of her,' said Louise. 'One can expect any kind of folly from her, with a temper like that.'

Pauline made a gesture of tolerance. 'Oh, let's allow her to satisfy her whims. She'll come back eventually, and we're not going to die of hunger this time!'

But the child had begun to stir on the rug. She hurried to bend over it.

'What is it, my darling?'

The mother, still at the window, watched for a moment, then disappeared into the room. Chanteau, preoccupied, only turned his head when Loulou began to growl; and it was he who warned his niece. 'Pauline, here's your gang.'

Two ragged urchins were arriving, the first of the band that came to visit her every Saturday. As little Paul had dropped asleep again immediately, she got up, saying: 'Well, they've chosen their time well! I've not got a minute to spare . . . Stay here though, sit down on this bench . . . And you, uncle, if any more come, will you make them sit down by these? I simply must have a look at my stew.'

When she came back after a quarter of an hour, there were already two boys and two girls on the bench; they were poor children, her former protégés, grown taller now but still inveterate beggars.

Bonneville, indeed, had lately endured unprecedented misery. During the great storms in May, its three last houses had been crushed against the cliff. That was the end of it ; the spring tides had completed the destruction of the village, after centuries of attack in which the sea had continuously encroached on it, every year swallowing up another bit of the land. Now only the conquering waves remained on the shingle, wiping out the very traces of the ruins. The fishermen, driven from the corner where generations of their forebears had obstinately stayed under the eternal threat, had been forced to go higher up, into the ravine, where they were encamped, huddled together, the richer ones building homes and the others sheltering under rocks; together they were founding a new Bonneville, which would endure till after further centuries of battle the water should again drive them out. To complete its work of destruction the sea had had to sweep away, first of all, the jetties and breakwaters. That day the wind was blowing from the north, and monstrous masses of water came crashing down so thunderously that the church shook. Lazare knew, but would not go down. He stayed on the terrace, watching the sea come in; while the fishermen ran to look, excited by this furious onslaught. They were brimming over with terror and pride: what a hell of a din, and wouldn't it sweep all that rubbish away! And indeed, in less than twenty minutes everything was gone; the breakwaters had been ripped apart, the jetties shattered and smashed into smithereens. And the men roared with the roaring sea, they gesticulated and danced like savages, drunk with wind and water, surrendering to the horror of the holocaust. Then, while Lazare shook his fist at them, they ran away, pursued by the madly galloping waves which nothing, now, held in check. To-day, they were destitute; they moaned with hunger in their new Bonneville, blaming that devil, the sea, for their ruin and turning for alms to the kind young lady.

'What are you doing here?' cried Pauline, when she caught sight of young Houtelard. 'I'd forbidden you to come back.'

He was a hulking lad of nearly nineteen now. His former doleful, timid look, the look of a beaten child, had given way to slyness. He answered, dropping his eyes: 'You got to take pity on us, miss. We're so wretched now that father's dead.'

Houtelard had gone to sea one stormy night and had never come back; his body had never been found, nor had that of his mate, or even a single bit of the boat. But Pauline, who had to be careful of her almsgiving nowadays, had sworn to give nothing to the son nor to the widow as long as they lived together openly. After the father's death the step-mother, that former maidservant who used to belabour the boy, had taken him for a husband now that he was too old to be beaten. The whole village thought the new arrangement a great joke.

'You know why I don't want you to set foot here any more,' went on Pauline. 'When you've mended your ways, then we'll see!'

Then with a pleading voice he pleaded his case. 'She made me do it. She'd have beaten me again. And then she's not my mother, what does it matter if it's with me or somebody else . . . Give me something, miss! We've lost everything. I could manage for myself, but it's for her, she's ill, that's the truth, I swear!'

The girl, moved to pity, finally sent him off with a loaf and a bowl of broth. She even promised to go and see the sick woman and take her remedies.

'Oh, remedies indeed!' Chanteau muttered. 'Try and get her to swallow one of them! She'll not be satisfied with anything but meat.'

Pauline had already turned her attention to the Prouane girl, whose cheek was badly hurt.

'However did you do that?'

'I fell against a tree, miss.'

'Against a tree?... It looks rather as if you'd knocked it against a bit of furniture.'

She was a big girl now, with prominent cheekbones and still the same wild, visionary look in her staring eyes; she was making a vain attempt to stand up politely. Her legs were giving way, and her thickened speech made her words unintelligible. Pauline, gazing at her, exclaimed: 'But you've been drinking, wretched child!'

'Oh miss, how can you say such a thing?'

'You're drunk, and you fell down at home, didn't you? I don't know what's possessing you all ... Sit down, I'll fetch some arnica and some linen.'

She dressed the wound, trying meanwhile to make the child feel ashamed of herself. Wasn't it shocking for a girl of her age to get tipsy like that with her father and mother, a couple of drunk ·ds who would be found dead one of these days, knocked out by *calvados*? The child listened, hazy-eyed and half asleep. When the dressing was finished she stuttered: 'Dad complains of his aches, I could rub him if you'd give me a little spirits of camphor.'

Pauline and Chanteau could not help laughing. 'No, I know what would happen to that! I'm willing to give you a loaf of bread, although I'm sure your folk'll sell it and drink the cash ... Sit here, Cuche'll take you home.'

It was young Cuche's turn to get up. His feet were bare and his only garments were an old pair of trousers and a ragged piece of shirt that revealed his skin, tanned almost black and scratched with brambles. His mother had now sunk into such loathsome decrepitude that men would have nothing to do with her; and the lad had to scour the countryside to fetch her customers. He was to be seen running along the roads, jumping hedges with wolf-like agility, living like a hungry animal that seizes on any prey. This was the very bottom of abject misery, such a degradation of humanity that Pauline felt remorseful as she looked at him, as though she herself were guilty for leaving any creature in such a cesspool. But whenever she attempted to rescue him from it, he always tried to run away, such was his aversion to work and bondage.

'Since you've come back,' she said gently, 'I suppose you've thought over what I told you last Saturday. I take it that you've got some decent feeling left, if you still come to see me . . . You can't go on living such a horrible life, and I'm no longer rich enough to keep you in idleness . . . Have you made up your mind to accept my proposal?'

Since losing her fortune, she had endeavoured to make up for her own lack of funds by interesting other charitable people in her protégés. Dr. Cazenove had at last arranged for Cuche's mother to be accepted in the Home for Incurables at Bayeux, and Pauline had kept back a hundred francs herself to buy clothes for the son, for whom she had found a place in the crew of a Cherbourg steamer. While she spoke, he hung his head and listened with a mistrustful air.

'That's settled then?' she went on. 'You'll take your mother along, and then you'll go and join your boat.'

But as she moved towards him, he leapt back. He still glowered up at her, thinking she meant to seize him by the wrists.

'What's the matter?' she asked in surprise.

Then he muttered, shyly suspicious as a wild animal: 'You're going to take me and shut me up. I won't go.'

Nothing was any good after that. He let her go on speaking, and seemed convinced by her arguments; but as soon as she stirred he made a dash for the gate; and he shook his head obstinately, repudiating help for his mother or himself, preferring to go hungry and live in liberty.

'Get out, you lazy rascal!' cried Chanteau at last, indignantly. 'Pauline, you shouldn't take all that trouble about such a good-for-nothing.'

Pauline's hands were shaking at the uselessness of her charity, the frustration of her love for others by this self-sought destitution. She made a gesture of hopeless tolerance.

'For all that, uncle, they're in trouble, they've got to eat.'

And she called back Cuche, to give him a loaf and a forty-sou piece, as on other Saturdays. But he shrank back again, saying at last: 'Put that on the ground and go away . . . I'll pick it up.'

She had to obey him. He advanced cautiously, keeping a watchful eye on her. Then, when he had picked up the forty sous and the bread, he tore away on his bare feet.

'Young savage!' exlaimed Chanteau. 'He'll come and strangle us all one of these nights . . . As for that jailbird's brat there, I'll swear she's the one that stole my neckerchief the other day.'

He was referring to the Tourmal child, whose grandfather, as well as her father, was now in prison. She was left alone on the

281

bench now, beside the Prouane girl in her drunken stupor. She jumped up without seeming to have heard the charge of theft, and began whining. 'Take pity on us, kind lady . . . There's only ma and me left at home, and the cops come in and beat us every night, I'm all black and blue and mother's dying . . . Oh, kind lady, we need money, and nourishing broth and good wine . . .'

Chanteau writhed in his chair, exasperated by these lies. But Pauline would have given away the shirt off her back.

'Hush,' she murmured, 'you'd get more if you talked less . . . Stay there, I'll make you up a basket.'

When she came back with an old fish-hamper into which she had put a loaf, two bottles of wine and some meat, she found another of her clients on the terrace—the Gonin girl, who had brought her daughter, a baby already twenty months old. The young mother, who was only sixteen, looked so fragile and undeveloped that she might have been the baby's elder sister. She could hardly carry it, but she dragged it along with her because she knew that Mademoiselle adored children and could refuse them nothing.

'Good heavens, how big she is!' exclaimed Pauline, taking the little girl in her arms. 'And to think that she's not six months older than our Paul!'

Involuntarily her gaze reverted sadly to the baby boy, who was still asleep in the middle of the rug. This child-mother was fortunate in having so sturdy an infant. And yet she grumbled: 'If you knew how much she eats, miss! And I've got no linen, I don't know what to dress her with . . . And then since dad died, mother and her chap are always on to me. They treat me like dirt, they say girls who go out on the spree ought to bring in money instead of costing money.'

The old cripple had been found one morning dead in his coal-bunker; and his body was so blackened with blows that, at one point, the police seemed likely to take up the matter. And now the wife and her lover talked of strangling the useless brat who devoured her share of the soup.

'Poor darling!' murmured Pauline. 'I've laid some things aside for her, and I'm knitting her some socks . . . You ought to bring her here oftener, we've always got milk, and she could have some gruel . . . I'll go and see your mother and give her a talking-to, since she still threatens you '

The Gonin girl had picked up her baby again, while Pauline got ready a parcel for her too. She had sat down and was holding the child on her knees as awkwardly as a schoolgirl playing with a doll.

Her clear eyes expressed perpetual surprise at having produced it, and although she had suckled it, she often nearly let it fall when she rocked it against her flat bosom. Pauline had scolded her severely one day when, in order to throw stones at the Prouane child, she had laid the baby down by the side of the road, on a heap of pebbles.

Then Abbé Horteur appeared on the terrace. 'Here come Monsieur Lazare and the doctor,' he announced.

At the same instant the sound of the gig was heard; and while Martin, the old sailor with the wooden leg, was taking the horse into the stable, Cazenove came up from the courtyard, calling out: 'I've brought you back a truant, so it seems. Aren't you going to chop off his head?'

Lazare came up next, with a wan smile. He was ageing rapidly; his shoulders were bowed, his face was ashy, as though he were consumed by an inward anguish that was destroying him. He was apparently just about to give the reason for his delay when the window on the first floor, which had been ajar, was slammed furiously.

'Louise isn't ready,' explained Pauline. She'll be down in a minute.'

They all exchanged embarrassed glances; that angry noise preluded a quarrel.

Lazare took one step towards the staircase, then changed his mind and waited. He kissed his father and little Paul; then, to conceal his uneasiness, he turned on his cousin, muttering crossly: 'Get rid of all this trash quickly. You know I don't like finding them in my way.'

He was referring to the three girls who still sat on the bench. Pauline hurriedly fastened up the parcel for the Gonin girl. 'Off you go now,' she said. 'You must take care of your friend and see that she doesn't tumble down again . . . And look after your baby, you! Try and not leave her by the way.'

As they were going off at last, Lazare thought of searching the Tourmal child's basket; she had already hidden in it an old coffee pot which she had found in a corner and stolen. The three of them were sent packing, the tipsy one staggering along between the other two.

'What a set!' cried the *curé*, sitting down beside Chanteau. 'God certainly seems to have given them up. They've barely taken their first communion when the little wretches start having babies and drinking and stealing like their fathers and mothers . . . Oh, I'd foretold all the misfortunes that have afflicted them.'

'By the way, my dear fellow,' the doctor ironically asked Lazare, 'are you going to rebuild your famous jetties?'

Lazare made an angry gesture; any reference to his lost battle against the sea exasperated him. He cried: 'Am I? . . . I'd let the tide come right up here without putting so much as a broomstick across the way to stop it . . . Oh, no, certainly not! I made a fool of myself, and one doesn't commit that sort of folly twice! When I think how I saw those wretches dancing, the day of the disaster! And d'you know what I suspect? They must have sawed through my beams the day before the high tide, for the timbers couldn't possibly have given way on their own.'

Thus he safeguarded his engineer's self-respect. Then, pointing towards Bonneville, he added: 'Let them all rot! It'll be my turn to dance.'

'Don't be so unkind,' said Pauline quietly. 'Only the poor have the right to be spiteful . . . You'll rebuild your jetties for all that.'

He had calmed down already, as though this last burst of passion had exhausted him. 'Oh, no,' he muttered, 'it'd be too boring . . . But you're right, nothing's worth getting angry about. Whether they drown or whether they don't, what do I care?'

Silence reigned once more. Chanteau, after raising his head to receive his son's kiss, had relapsed into his former painful immobility. The *curé* was twiddling his thumbs, and the doctor pacing up and down with his hands behind his back. All of them were now looking at the sleeping child, whom Pauline protected even against his father's caresses, for she did not want him woken up. She had been begging them, ever since they arrived, to lower their voices, to tread more lightly round the baby's rug; and now she even waved a threatening whip at Loulou, who was still growling because he had heard the horse being led to the stable.

'If you think that'll quieten him!' went on Lazare. 'He'll go on deafening us for another hour . . . I never saw a more disagreeable dog. The slightest movement disturbs him, and he's so wrapped up in himself that you can't even say you've got a dog of your own. He's an odious character, and he only serves to make one miss poor old Mathieu.'

'How old can Minouche be?' asked Cazenove. 'I've always seen her here.'

'She's over sixteen,' Pauline replied, ' and none the worse for that.'

The cat, who was still performing her toilet on the dining-room windowsill, raised her head when the doctor uttered her name. She stayed for an instant with one paw lifted, sunning her belly; then she began to lick her fur again daintily.

'Oh, she's not deaf,' went on the girl. 'I think she's losing her sight a little, though that doesn't stop her behaving like a hussy . . . Would you believe it, less than a week ago we had to drown seven kittens of hers. She keeps on having them in such quantities that one's really appalled. If they'd all been allowed to live, over the past sixteen years, they'd have devoured the whole countryside . . . Well, she went off again on Tuesday, and now look at her preening herself! she only came back this morning, after three nights and three days of debauchery.'

Gaily, without any sort of shame or embarrassment, she told about the cat's amours. Such a cleanly beast, so dainty that she would not go out in wet weather, and yet four times a year she wallowed in every muddy stream! The night before, Pauline had seen her on top of a wall with a big tom, both of them sweeping the air with their raised tails; and after a brief scuffle they had rolled into the middle of a puddle, with a horrible caterwauling. And this time Minouche had come back with a split ear and her coat black with dirt. She was still the worst of mothers, moreover; whenever one of her litters was destroyed, she just went on licking herself as in the days of her youth, with no apparent doubts as to her inexhaustible fecundity; and off she'd go again to collect a fresh bellyful.

'There's this to be said for her, at least she's clean,' concluded Abbé Horteur, watching Minouche wear out her tongue cleaning herself. 'So many sluts don't even wash!'

Chanteau, whose eyes were also turned towards the cat, heaved a louder sigh; nowadays he was hardly conscious of his own moans, which had become continuous and automatic.

'Are you in worse pain?' asked the doctor.

'What's that? Why?' he said, coming to with a start. 'Oh, because I took a deep breath? . . . Yes, I'm in great pain this evening. I thought the sun would do me good, but it's unbearable all the same, I've not got a joint that's not burning.'

Cazenove examined his hands. And they all shuddered at the sight of those poor misshapen stumps. The priest uttered another sensible observation.

'Fingers like that aren't much use for playing draughts . . . You must miss your game these days.'

'Be careful what you eat,' advised the doctor. 'Your elbow's badly inflamed, the ulceration is spreading wider.'

'How can I be more careful?' groaned Chanteau in despair. 'My wine's measured, my meat's weighed, must I stop eating altogether? Really, life's not worth living ... If I could feed myself! But how can I, with objects like these at the end of my arms? Pauline, who feeds me, can tell you that I don't take too much of anything.'

The girl smiled. 'Yes, yes, you ate too much yesterday ... It's my fault, I don't know how to refuse you when I see how unhappy your greed makes you.'

They all pretended to laugh and teased him about his self-indulgence. But their voices quivered with compassion as they looked at him—an inert mass, all that was left of a man, only alive enough to go on suffering. He had relapsed into his old position, his body twisted to the right and his hands on his knees.

'For instance,' went on Pauline, 'we're having a roast duck ...' Breaking off, she asked: 'By the way, you didn't happen to meet Véronique when you came through Verchemont?' And she told them of the maid's disappearance. Neither Lazare nor the doctor had seen her. They discussed these whims of hers with surprise and finally with amusement; the joke would be to watch her face when she came home and found them all at table ready.

'I'm leaving you, for I'm on duty in the kitchen,' went on Pauline merrily. 'If I let the stew burn, or serve the duck underdone, I'll get a week's notice from my uncle!'

Abbé Horteur gave a great guffaw, and even Dr. Cazenove was smiling at her comment, when the first-floor window opened again sharply, with a furious click of the handle. Louise did not show herself, but merely called out in a curt voice through the half-open window: 'Come upstairs, Lazare!'

Her husband, with an indignant gesture, refused to obey a summons made in such a tone. But Pauline gazed at him in mute entreaty, anxious to avoid a public scene; and he went up, while she lingered for a moment on the terrace, to try and counteract the unpleasant impression. Silent and embarrassed, they all stared at the sea. In the slanting sunlight it glittered like a sheet of gold, with tiny flames flickering on all its wavelets. The distant horizon was turning a soft lilac colour. The lovely day was ending in supreme serenity; the infinite sky and the infinite sea stretched out without a cloud, without a sail.

'Oh, well,' Pauline ventured with a smile, 'since he's been spending the night out, he's got to be scolded a little.'

The doctor was looking at her, and he too gave a smile, in which she recognized the shrewdness with which he once warned her that she wasn't making them much of a present by giving them to one another. And so she went off towards the kitchen.

'Well, I must leave you, try and amuse yourselves . . . And uncle, please call me if Paul should wake up.'

In the kitchen, when she had stirred the stew and got ready the spit, she clattered the saucepans impatiently. The voices of Louise and Lazare reached her from the room above, growing louder and louder, and she was in despair, thinking that they could surely be heard from the terrace. Really, it was unreasonable of them to shout at each other as though they were deaf, letting everybody know about their disagreements. And yet she did not want to go up; for one thing she had the dinner to cook, for another she disliked the idea of intruding between them thus, in their very bedroom. Usually she effected her reconciliations downstairs, when they were all living together. She went into the dining-room for a moment, and laid the table noisily. But the voices still went on, and she could not bear the thought that they were making each other miserable; she went upstairs, under the impulsion of that active charity which had made her whole life dependent on the happiness of others.

'My dears,' she said, abruptly entering the room, 'you may say it's none of my business, but you're really shouting too loud . . . There's no sense in distressing yourselves like that and upsetting the whole house.'

She crossed the room and hurriedly closed the window, which Louise had left ajar. Fortunately neither the doctor nor the *curé* had stayed on the terrace. The rapid glance which she threw out showed her only Chanteau sitting there brooding, by the side of the sleeping baby.

'You could be heard from down below, as if you'd been in the room,' she went on. 'Now, what's the matter this time?'

But they were launched by now, and went on quarrelling without even seeming to have noticed her entry. She was standing motionless now, feeling ill at ease once more in this bedroom of theirs. The yellow chintz with its green flowers, the red rug, the old mahogany furniture had been replaced by heavy woollen hangings and furniture in fastidious feminine taste; nothing was left of the dead mother, a scent of heliotrope hung about the dressing-table, on which damp towels lay strewn; and the scent oppressed her, and her eyes roamed involuntarily round the room, where every object spoke of their private lives. She had finally consented to live with them, allowing her resistance to be worn down daily, so that she could now sleep at nights even though she knew that they were close at hand, in one another's arms maybe; but this was the first time she had gone into their room, into this scene of conjugal intimacy, where clothes lay scattered untidily about and the bed was already prepared for the night. A shiver ran through her again, her old jealous shiver.

'How can you torture one another like that?' she said softly, after a silence. 'Will you not be reasonable?'

'Why, no,' cried Louise, 'I've had enough of it by now!... Do you suppose he's going to admit he's done wrong? No indeed! I merely told him how worried we'd been at his not coming home yesterday and he promptly fell on me like a savage and accused me of spoiling his life, so that he's threatening to run away to America!'

Lazare interrupted her in a terrible voice. 'You're lying!... If you'd merely reproached me as gently as that, I'd have kissed you and it'd all have been over. But it was you who accused me of making your life a misery. Yes, you threatened to throw yourself into the sea if I went on ruining your existence.'

And they both started off again, freely voicing the rancour accumulated by their constant friction. On the least provocation they would begin to bicker, gradually reaching a state of acute mutual antipathy which cast a cloud over the whole day. Louise, for all her apparent gentleness, was becoming spiteful since he interfered with her pleasures, as spiteful as a cat that rubs itself caressingly against you and then shows its claws. Lazare, for all his indifference, found that the stimulus of quarrelling roused him from the numbness of his ennui, and often persisted in it merely for excitement's sake.

Pauline listened to them meanwhile. She was suffering more than they were, unable to understand their kind of love. Why couldn't they spare one another, out of mutual pity? Why not make allowances, when they had to live together? It seemed to her so easy to find happiness in habit and compassion. And she was heartbroken, for she still looked on their marriage as her own work, and she would have liked her work to be good and enduring, so that the certainty of having acted wisely might have been some compensation for her sacrifice.

'I'm not reproaching you for squandering my fortune,' went on Louise.

'That would be the last straw!' cried Lazare. 'It wasn't my fault if I was swindled.'

'Oh, you only get swindled if you're fool enough to be taken in ...
None the less, we're reduced to a wretched income of four or five

thousand francs, barely enough to live on in this hole. If it weren't for Pauline our child would be stripped naked one of these days, for I quite expect you to run through all the rest with those extraordinary notions of yours, those schemes that come to nothing, one after the other.'

'Carry on, your father paid me all those pretty compliments yesterday. I'd guessed that you'd written to him. And so I dropped the fertiliser deal, although it was a dead cert and would have brought in a hundred per cent. But I'm like you, I've had enough of it, to hell with any more efforts. We'll live here."

'A nice life, indeed, for a woman of my age. A real prison; not a single chance even to go out and see people; only that idiotic sea in front of one, making life even more tedious . . . Oh, if only I'd known, if only I'd known . . .'

'And d'you think I'm enjoying life? . . . If I weren't married I could cut loose and go somewhere far away in search of adventure. I've felt like doing so twenty times. But it's all over now, I'm pent up in this godforsaken place, where there's nothing left for me but to go to sleep. You've finished me, I'm well aware of that.'

'*I* finished you? . . . Did I force you to marry me? Couldn't you have seen that we weren't meant for one another? . . . It's your fault, if our life's a failure.'

'Oh, yes, our life's a failure, and you do all you can to make it more unbearable every day.'

At that moment, although she had vowed to herself to keep out of it, Pauline broke in, quivering. 'Be quiet, you wretches! It's quite true that you're doing your best to spoil your life, and it might be so happy. Why d'you provoke each other to say irreparable things that will make you suffer afterwards? . . . No, no, be quiet, I won't have any more of it.'

Louise had collapsed weeping on a chair, while Lazare, in a state of violent agitation, was striding about the room.

'It's no good crying, my dear,' the girl went on. 'Really you should be more tolerant, you've got plenty of faults yourself . . . And you, Lazare, how can you treat her so roughly? It's horrid, I did at least think you were kindhearted . . . Yes, you're a couple of silly children, you're both equally to blame, and you're doing everything you can think of to torture yourselves. But I won't have it, d'you hear? I won't have miserable people around me . . . Please kiss and make friends right away.'

She was trying to laugh, she had lost all trace of that disturbing jealous shudder. She was left only with a fervent charitable longing

289

to see them in one another's arms, to make sure that the quarrel was ended.

'Kiss him? No, certainly not!' said Louise. 'He's been too rude to me.'

'Never!' cried Lazare.

Then she burst out laughing. 'Come on, don't sulk. You know what a pigheaded creature I am ... My dinner's burning, everybody's waiting ... I shall push you, Lazare, if you don't obey me. Go down on your knees in front of her, put your arms round her nicely ... Come on, now, better than that.'

And she thrust them into a lover-like embrace, she watched them kiss one another's faces, with an air of joyful triumph, her clear eyes untroubled by distress. Joy glowed in her like a subtle fire; she seemed uplifted far above them. Meanwhile her cousin clasped his wife with frantic remorse; while she, still half dressed, with her arms and neck bare, returned his caresses with a renewed flood of tears.

'You see, isn't that better than fighting?' said Pauline. 'Now I must run, you don't need me any more to make your peace.'

She was at the door as she spoke, and she closed it quickly, shutting out this room with its atmosphere of love, its uncovered bed, its scattered garments, and that scent of heliotrope that touched her heart now, as though she felt it was in collusion with her and would complete her task of reconciliation.

Downstairs in the kitchen Pauline began to sing as she stirred her stew once more. She set a log of wood alight, fixed up the turnspit for the duck and supervised its roasting with an expert eye. She enjoyed this servant's task; she had put on a big white apron and delighted in being of service to everybody, undertaking the lowest and humblest duties so as to be able to tell herself that to-day they would owe their merriment and their well-being to her. Now that she had set them laughing, her dream was to provide them with a real feast, with delicious food of which they would eat plentifully, all cheerfully relaxing round the table.

She remembered her uncle and the little boy, and hurriedly ran out on the terrace, where to her great surprise she found her cousin sitting beside the child.

'What,' she cried, 'so you've come down already?'

He answered with a mere nod, overcome once more by his weary apathy, his back bowed and his hands hanging idle. She asked in some anxiety: 'I hope you didn't begin again behind my back?'

'No, no,' he finally brought himself to reply. 'She's coming down when she's put on her dress ... We've forgiven each other. But as for its lasting! To-morrow it'll be another story, and every day, and every hour! Can a person change? Can one prevent anything?'

Pauline had grown grave, and dropped her eyes sadly. He was right; she had a clear vision of days like this unfolding ahead, when she would have to go on ceaselessly appeasing the same quarrel between them. And she herself was not sure of being cured, of never giving way to jealous violence. Oh, what an everlasting repetition of these everyday miseries! But presently she raised her eyes again; she had conquered herself so often! And then, surely they would tire of quarrelling before she tired of reconciling them. This notion amused her, and she repeated it merrily to Lazare. What would there be left for her to do if the whole household was too happy? She'd get bored; they must leave her a few trifling wounds to heal!

'Where have the *abbé* and the doctor got to?' she asked, surprised at no longer seeing them.

'They must be in the kitchen garden,' Chanteau answered. 'The *abbé* wanted to show the doctor our pears.'

Pauline was going to the corner of the terrace to have a look, when she stopped short in front of little Paul.

'Hey, he's woken up,' she cried. 'D'you see how he's beginning to gad about already?'

Paul, in the middle of the red rug, had pulled himself up on to his little knees, and was trying to crawl away furtively. But before he got as far as the gravel he tripped up on a fold in the rug, and tumbled over sprawling on his back, with his frock tucked up and his arms and legs waving in the air. He lay there kicking, pink and naked against the peony-red of the rug.

'Good! he's showing us all he's got,' she went on merrily. 'Wait, you shall see how he's learnt to walk since yesterday.'

She knelt down beside him and tried to put him on his feet. He had grown so reluctantly that he was very backward for his age; they had even feared, at one time, that his legs might be permanently weak. And so it had been a great delight for the family to see him take his first steps, groping in the air with his hands and tumbling on to his bottom at the least bit of gravel that got in his way.

'Stop playing now!' Pauline told him. 'No, this is serious, show them that you're a man . . . There, keep steady, go and kiss daddy, and then you shall go and kiss granddad.'

Chanteau, his face drawn by twinges of pain, turned his head to watch the scene. Lazare, in spite of his dejection, consented to join in the game.

'Come on,' he said to the child.

'Oh, you've got to hold out your arms to him,' explained the girl. 'He won't venture without; he wants to have something to fall into. Come on, my treasure, be a brave boy . . .'

There were three steps to be taken. And shouts of excitement and enthusiasm arose when Paul made up his mind to cross the narrow space, swaying like an uncertain tight-rope walker. He flopped into the waiting arms of his father, who gave him a kiss on his scanty hair, and he laughed with a baby's vague, delighted laugh, opening wide his moist, rose-pink mouth. Then his godmother even tried to get him to speak; but his tongue was more backward than his legs, and he merely uttered guttural cries, in which only the parents recognized the words 'daddy' and 'mummy.'

'It's not over yet,' said Pauline, 'he's promised to go and kiss granddad . . . Eh, what a journey this time!'

There were at least eight steps between Lazare's chair and Chanteau's armchair. Paul had never yet ventured so far out into the world; it proved quite an undertaking. Pauline stood on the route to avert disasters, and it took two whole minutes to get the child started. At last he set off, staggering wildly and waving his arms. At one point she thought he was going to fall into her arms; but he charged boldly forward and it was against Chanteau's knees that he finally collapsed.

'Did you see how he dashed off? Oh, he looked absolutely fearless; he's going to be a plucky one, for sure!'

After that he was made to repeat the journey a dozen times. He was no longer scared, but started off as soon as they called him, going from his grandfather to his father and then back to his grandfather, laughing loudly, entranced with the game, and always on the point of tumbling, as though the ground were shaking under his feet.

'Once more to daddy!' cried Pauline.

Lazare was beginning to weary of it; children, even his own, soon bored him. As he watched the baby, safe and sound now and so merry, the thought that this little creature was carrying on his own life and would doubtless watch over his deathbed, sent the old shudder of anguish running through him. Since he had made up his mind to vegetate at Bonneville, he was obsessed by one remaining thought—that he would die in the room where his mother had died; and he could not go up the stair without telling himself that one day, inevitably, his coffin would pass down it. There was a bottleneck at the entry to the passage, a difficult corner about which he worried continually, anxiously wondering how the men would manage to get him out without jostling him. As time wore away a little of his life each day, this thought of death hastened the disintegration of his being and undermined him to the point of destroying the last traces of his manhood. He was finished, as he said himself, useless henceforward, seeing no point in bestirring himself, growing emptier day by day in the futility of his bored existence.

'Once more to granddad!' cried Pauline.

Chanteau could not even hold out his hands to catch and clasp little Paul; he parted his knees in vain; those fragile fingers clinging to his trousers drew from him prolonged sighs. From living in the old man's company, the child was already used to his endless moaning, and with his barely-awakened intelligence imagined, probably, that all grandfathers suffered thus. And yet to-day, in the bright sunlight, as he came tumbling against the old man, he lifted up his little face and stopped laughing, watching him with his unsteady gaze. The two distorted hands looked like monstrous blocks of flesh and chalk; the face, ploughed over with red wrinkles, ravaged with suffering, was violently twisted over on the right shoulder; while the whole body was as cracked and knobbly as some old broken stone saint, badly stuck together. And Paul seemed surprised to see him in the sunshine, so ill and so old.

'Once again! Once again!' Pauline was calling. Vibrant with health and gaiety, she kept urging him from one to the other, from the grandfather, sunk obstinately in his pain, to the father, consumed already by dread of the morrow.

'Perhaps he'll belong to a less foolish generation,' she said suddenly. 'He won't accuse chemistry of spoiling his life, and he'll believe that it's possible to live even if you know you're going to die some day.'

Lazare gave a shamefaced laugh. 'Pooh! he muttered. 'He'll have gout like father and his nerves'll be worse than mine . . . Look how weak he is? It's the law of degeneration.'

'Will you be quiet!' exclaimed Pauline. 'I shall bring him up, and you'll see if I don't make a man of him.'

There was a silence, while she gathered up the child in a maternal embrace.

'Why don't you get married, if you're so fond of children?' asked Lazare.

She stared at him in amazement. 'But I've got a child! haven't you given me one? . . . Get married? Certainly not, indeed!'

She was cradling Paul in her arms, laughing more gaily as she declared humorously that her cousin had converted her to great

Saint Schopenhauer, and that she wanted to remain single so as to work for the deliverance of all mankind; and indeed she embodied renunciation, love of others, goodness extended to the whole of sinful humanity. The sun was setting in the immense sea, the fading sky seemed to shed an atmosphere of serenity, the infiniteness of the water and the infiniteness of the sea assumed the touching gentleness of a lovely day at its close. Only a small white sail, very far off, gleamed like a last spark which died out when the sun had sunk under the long unbroken skyline. Then there was nothing but the slow falling of dusk over the still waters. And she still stood there rocking the child, laughing valiantly, among the blue shadows on the twilit terrace, between her cousin, sunk in gloom, and her uncle, moaning with pain. She had despoiled herself of everything, yet her ringing laughter told of happiness.

'Aren't we having any dinner to-night?' asked Louise, appearing in an elegant grey silk dress.

'Well, I'm ready,' replied Pauline. 'I can't think what they're up to in the garden,'

At that moment Abbé Horteur came back, with a look of consternation on his face. As they questioned him anxiously, he finally announced with brutal bluntness, after hunting for some phrase to deaden the blow: 'We've just found your poor Véronique hanging from one of your pear-trees.'

All uttered a cry of surprise and horror, blanching as they felt Death pass by like a cold gust of wind.

'But why?' cried Pauline. 'She had no motive, she'd even started cooking dinner . . . Oh, good heavens, it couldn't be because I told her she'd paid ten sous too much for her duck?'

Dr. Cazenove came up now. For the last quarter of an hour he had been vainly trying to revive her in the coachhouse, where with Martin's help, they had carried her. How could one tell what went on in some crazy old servants' heads? She had never got over her mistress's death.

'It can't have taken long,' he said. 'She simply hanged herself on one of her own apron strings.'

Lazare and Louise, frozen with fear, said nothing. Then Chanteau, after listening in silence, suddenly rebelled at the thought of his ruined dinner-party. And the wretched creature, lacking hands and feet, who had to be put to bed and fed like a child, this deplorable remnant of humanity whose diminished life was nothing but one long howl of pain, exclaimed with furious indignation: ' How can one be so stupid as to kill oneself!'